WYOMING
WINTER

For a complete list of titles available by Diana Palmer, please visit www.dianapalmer.com.

DIANA PALMER

WYOMING WINTER

HQN™

HQN™

ISBN-13: 978-0-373-80372-9

Wyoming Winter

Copyright © 2017 by Diana Palmer

The publisher acknowledges the copyright holder
of the individual work as follows:

Christmas Cowboy

Copyright © 1997 by Diana Palmer

Recycling programs
for this product may
not exist in your area.

This edition published by arrangement with Harlequin Books S.A.

For questions and comments about the quality of this book,
please contact us at CustomerService@Harlequin.com.

® and TM are trademarks of Harlequin Enterprises Limited or its
corporate affiliates. Trademarks indicated with ® are registered in the
United States Patent and Trademark Office, the Canadian Intellectual
Property Office and in other countries.

www.HQNBooks.com

Printed in U.S.A.

CONTENTS

Dear Reader,

Some books start in awkward ways. This was one. I had a snow scene in my mind. A man and a little girl. She was hiding and crying. Her jacket had blood on it.

From that scene came a whole book. This one is very character-driven. I did get caught up in the lives of the hero and heroine, and I felt equally sorry for both of them by the middle of the story. But it was fun to write, if something of a challenge.

It's dedicated to my niece, Betty, who died recently. She was an avid reader of my books, like her daughter, Amanda. My first sight of her was when our late nephew, Bobby, brought her by the house early one morning to meet us. They'd been swimming in the river, and her long, black hair was wet. She looked so young and so beautiful. I have kept that image of her all these years. She never looked older than that, to me, ever. She was kind and sweet and forgiving, and the whole family loved her. We will miss her very much.

Diana Palmer

WYOMING WINTER

In loving memory of Betty Patton Hansen, 1956–2017, our niece. She leaves behind a daughter, Amanda; a son, Johnny; a sister, Gail Davis; and six grandchildren. She had a sweet and kind nature, and we all loved her. She will be missed.

CHAPTER ONE

COLIE THOMPSON WAS in a mild panic. Her brother, Rodney, was bringing over his friend J.C. Calhoun. J.C. was thirty-two, pretty much at the end of his Army Reserve service—the cutoff age was thirty-two. He and Rodney had met in Iraq, almost four years ago. Both men were with the same Army unit. Rodney was serving his first tour of duty. J.C.'s Army Reserve unit had been called up for limited duty, and he was assigned to the same area as Rodney. In one of those wild coincidences, they started talking and discovered that they lived in the same Wyoming town, J.C. having taken a job with another Catelow resident, Ren Colter, whom he'd met during his first tour of duty. Rodney looked up to J.C., who was a little older. The older man had been a police officer before he went into the Army the first time, almost twelve years earlier.

Rodney left the Army before his tour of duty was officially up, never saying why. He'd been home for several months. After J.C. finished his overseas duty, he came home with him sometimes, although they'd grown apart since Rodney started a new job. They still went around together, but not often. One memorable visit to the Thompson home was on Colie's birthday, when J.C. had unexpectedly given her a cat. It was the high point of her recent life. She named the huge Siamese cat Big Tom and it slept on her bed every night.

Even though he didn't come home with Rodney much, Colie often saw J.C. around Catelow, which was a small and very clannish town. There were only a couple of restaurants, and Colie, whose real name was Colleen, worked as a receptionist and typist for a law firm downtown. Inevitably, she saw J.C. from time to time, occasionally with her brother. And since he was single, and handsome, and mostly avoided women, he was the subject of much gossip.

He always made time to talk to Colie if he saw her. He was polite, teasing, friendly. He made her glow inside. Once, when he brought Rod home after his car had quit, J.C. had helped her into her jacket when she was going outside to get the mail. Just the touch of his hands was like an explosion of pleasure. The more she saw of him, the more she wanted him.

Rodney had invited J.C. to come to supper before this, but he'd always had an excuse. This time, he accepted. It had been just after Colie had started walking back to the office, in the snow, and J.C. had stopped and given her a ride the rest of the way. Sitting with him, in the cozy warmth of the big black SUV he drove, she'd been hesitant to get out again. They'd talked about the upcoming presidential election, the state of the country, the beauty of Catelow in the snow. He'd teased her about wearing high heels to work instead of sensible boots, with snow already piling up, and she'd retorted that boots would hardly complement the pretty pantsuit she was wearing. He'd pursed his lips and looked at her, long and hard, and said Colie would look good in anything. She'd gone inside the law office, reluctantly, flushed and beaming after the unexpected pleasure of his company.

J.C. worked full-time locally, but he went back over-

seas periodically to train troops in Iraq in police procedure. He was supposed to go back in a few months
to do it all over again with a new group. J.C. worked
as security chief for Ren Colter, who had a huge cattle
ranch, Skyhorn, outside Catelow, Wyoming. Ren was
ex-military as well, and he had somebody fill in for J.C.
while he accommodated a former commander by drill-
ing new recruits.

Giving orders was something J.C. was very good at.
He was also gorgeous. He had jet-black hair, cut short,
and eyes so pale a gray that they glittered like silver. He
was tall and muscular, but not like a bodybuilder. He
had the physique of a rodeo cowboy, lithe and powerful. Colie liked to just sit and look at him when she had
the opportunity. She'd never known anybody quite like
him. He had a unique background, about which he rarely
spoke. Rodney had told her that J.C.'s father was a member of the Blackfoot nation up in Canada. His mother had
been a little redheaded Irish woman. Quite an uncom-
mon pairing, but it had produced a handsome child. J.C.
never spoke of his father, Rodney added.

Colie wanted a family of her own, badly. She and Rodney had lost their mother two years previously to bone
cancer. It had taken her a long time to die, but even then,
she'd been cheerful and upbeat around her children and
her husband. Colie's father was a Methodist minister, a
pillar of the community. Everybody loved him, not just
his own congregation. They'd loved Colie's mother, too.
The little woman, named Beth Louise but called Ludie,
had always been the first to arrive if there was a sick person who needed caring for, or a child who needed a temporary home. She'd even fostered dogs that were picked

up by the local no-kill animal shelter while they waited for an adoptive family.

All that had passed, along with her. The house was suddenly empty. Jared Thompson, Colie's father, had been almost suicidally depressed after his wife's death, but his faith had pulled him through. It was, he told Colie, not right to mourn someone who had lived such a full life and had gone on to a happier, more wonderful place. Death was not the end for people of faith. They simply had to accept that people died for reasons that were, perhaps, not quite clear to those left behind.

Colie and Rodney had grieved, too. Rodney had been overseas for almost four years, with only brief visits. He couldn't come home for his mother's funeral, although he Skyped with his father and sister after the services. He was a sweet, biddable boy until he went into the service. When he came home, he was…different. Colie couldn't figure out why. He became fixated on fancy cars and designer clothes, neither of which fit in his small budget. He'd obtained a job at the local hardware store when he came home, because it was owned by a friend of the reverend Thompson. Rodney seemed to be a natural salesman. But he complained all the time about getting minimum wage. He wanted more. He was never satisfied with anything for long.

The one thing that bothered Colie most was that her brother wasn't quite lucid much of the time. He had red-rimmed eyes and sometimes he staggered. She worried that he might have been hurt overseas and wasn't telling them. She knew it wasn't from alcohol, because Rodney almost never took a drink. It was puzzling.

During Rodney's tour of duty in the Middle East, J.C. and Rodney hung out together when Rodney was off duty.

Rod didn't write often, but when he did, he mentioned things he and J.C. had done overseas during the time J.C. was there. They went out on the town when Rodney was on liberty. Odd thing about J.C., Rodney had commented. He never drank hard liquor. He'd have the occasional beer, but he didn't touch the heavy stuff. Like Rodney. But the brother who used to tease her and bring her wildflowers and watch television with her seemed to have gone away. The man who came back from overseas was someone else. Someone with a darkness inside him, a lust for things, for material things.

He'd been vocal about the old things in the house where he lived with his sister and father. It was primitive, he scoffed.

Colie didn't find it so. It looked lived-in. The small house was immaculate, Colie thought as she looked at her surroundings. The sofa had a new cover, a pretty burgundy floral pattern, and her father's puffy armchair had a solid burgundy cover. The spotless wood floors had area rugs, which were beaten clean by Colie on a regular basis. There were no cobwebs anywhere. The marble-topped coffee table that her father had found at an antiques shop graced the living room, where an open fireplace crackled with orange flames and the smell of burning oak.

Colie didn't look too bad herself, she reflected, glancing in the hall mirror at her wavy collar-length dark brown hair. It never needed curling. It was naturally wavy. She had an oval face, sweet and pleasant, but not beautiful. Her eyes were large and dark green under thick lashes. Her mouth was a perfect bow. She had an hourglass figure, with long legs always clad in denim jeans. She had only a few dresses and a couple of nice pantsuits, which she wore to church and to work at the local attorney's office where she was a receptionist and typist. Around the house, she wore jeans and boots and pullover sweaters. This one was a nice medium green, long-sleeved and V-necked. It showed off Colie's small, firm breasts in a nice but flattering way. She never wore low-cut things or suggestive dresses. After all, her father was a minister. She didn't want to do anything that would embarrass him in front of his congregation. She didn't even curse.

Rodney did. She was constantly chastising him about it.

Just as she thought it, he walked in the door, stomping snow off his big boots on the front porch as he stood in the open doorway, letting in a flurry. He closed it quickly behind him.

"Damn, it's cold out!" he swore. "Snowing like a son of a…"

She interrupted him. "Will you stop that? Daddy's a minister," she groaned. "Rodney, you're such a pain!"

He had her dark green eyes, but his hair was straight and thick and a shade lighter than hers. He was tall, with perfect teeth and a rakish smile. No choirboy, Rodney, he was always in trouble throughout high school. Presumably, he'd been better behaved in the military, since he was discharged early.

"Daddy can curse," he retorted. "Haven't you heard him?"

"Yes, Rodney, he says 'chicken feathers!' That's how he curses." She glowered at him. "That's not what you're saying when you lose your temper." He lost it a lot lately, too.

He shrugged her off. "I have issues," he said easily.

"I'm working on it. You have to remember that I've been around soldiers for several years, and in combat."

"I try to take that into account," she said. "But couldn't you tone it down, just a little bit? For Daddy's sake?"

He made a face at her. "God, you're hard to live up to, do you know that?" He sighed, exasperated. "You've never put a foot out of line. Never had a parking ticket, never had a speeding ticket, never even jaywalked! What a paragon to try to live up to!"

She grimaced. "I just behave the way Mama taught me." The thought made her sad. "Don't you miss her?"

He nodded. "She was the kindest woman I've ever known. Well, besides you." He chuckled and hugged her, and just for a minute, he was the big brother she'd adored. "You're just the best, sis."

She hugged him back. "I love you, too." She sniffed and her nose wrinkled as she drew back. "Rodney, what's that smell?" she asked, frowning as she sniffed him again. "It's like tobacco, but not."

He let her go and averted his eyes. "Just cigarette smoke. Some of that imported stuff. I have a friend who gets them."

"Not J.C. He doesn't smoke," she said, curious.

"Not J.C.," he agreed. "This is a guy I know from Jackson Hole. He and I pal around sometimes."

"Oh." She smiled. "Sorry. I thought it was marijuana."

He raised both eyebrows. "If I smoked marijuana in this house, Daddy would call Sheriff Cody Banks and have him lock me up in the county detention center in a heartbeat! You know that!"

"Well, yes, I do." She didn't add that plenty of men did smoke that awful stuff, and managed to keep their parents from suspecting. She'd had a girlfriend in high school who even bragged about it.

Colie had never used drugs of any sort, especially not any kind that had to be smoked. She had weak lungs. She didn't smoke, period.

"Didn't you say J.C. was coming to supper?" she asked after a minute, trying not to sound as excited as she felt.

"He is," Rodney said, pursing his lips as he saw the excitement she was trying so hard to hide. She was an open book, especially about his best friend. "He'll be here in a few minutes. He had to run an errand for Ren."

"Oh. Okay. I've still got leftover turkey from Thanksgiving that we have to eat, and mashed potatoes and a green salad, with apple pie for dessert. He does like turkey, doesn't he?" she added worriedly.

"He's not fussy about food," he said, smiling down at her. "Actually, he said snake wasn't bad if you had enough pepper..."

"Yuck!" she burst out.

"He was spec ops, back when he was in the Army," he laughed. "Those guys can eat anything, and have, when they're out on a mission. Bugs, snakes, whatever they can catch. There was this guy attached to his and Ren's unit overseas, years ago, who cooked an old cat for them when they couldn't find anything else."

"Oh, that's heartless," she said, wincing.

"It was a very old cat," he replied. "They were starving." He hesitated. "He said it tasted awful, and they got sick."

"Good!" she returned enthusiastically.

He laughed and hugged her again. "You softy," he mused. "You're just like Mama. She loved her cats." He frowned, looking around. "Where's Big Tom?"

"Out back, chasing rabbits," she said. The big seal point Siamese cat loved the outdoors. He slept inside at night, because there were predators all around, including bears and foxes and wolves. The Thompsons' home was outside Catelow, nestled in a forest of lodgepole pines, with no really close neighbors except Ren Colter. Ren's ranch ran right up to the Thompson property line, but he didn't run cattle close enough to worry any of the residents.

"Funny," Rodney mused, thinking about Big Tom.

"What is?"

"J.C. giving you a cat," he remarked.

It had touched Colie, that unusual gift from J.C. It had been a birthday present, the cat he'd found wandering around near his cabin. He'd had the vet clean him up and give him his shots, and he'd brought him over to Colie, who was a sucker for stray animals. Big Tom turned out to be housebroken and he never used his claws on the furniture. He was a lot of company for Colie while her father was visiting his congregation, which he did often. Rodney had been away in the military, so there was just Colie in the small house. Well, Colie and Big Tom.

"He's a very nice cat," she remarked.

Rodney laughed. "J.C.'s not big on animals, although he likes them. He's good with cattle. Even Willis's wolf will let him pet him. That's an accomplishment, believe me," he added with a huff. "Damned thing nearly took my hand off when I tried it…"

"Rodney!"

He ground his teeth. "Oh, hell."

"Rodney!"

He let out a breath. "Set up a jar," he said with resignation, "and I'll put a nickel in it every time I forget."

"If I do that, we can have a Tahiti vacation in a month," she accused.

He laughed. "Not nice."

"I'll find a big jar," she returned. "And you'll put a quarter in. Every time."

He drew in a long breath and just smiled. "Okay, Joan of Arc."

She chuckled and walked back to the kitchen to check on her apple pie in the oven.

J.C. LOOKED INCREDIBLY handsome in a shepherd's coat, jeans and boots, with snow dusting his thick, black, uncovered hair.

"You never wear a hat," Colie mused, trying not to let her hands tremble as she took the coat to hang up for him. He was so tall that she had to stand on her tiptoes to pull it back off his shoulders.

"I hate hats," he remarked. He glanced at her as she put the coat on the rack in the hall, his pale gray eyes narrow and appraising on her slender, sexy body. She dressed like a lady, but he knew all about women who put on their best behavior around company. She was just out of school; college, he was certain, because she had to be at least twenty-two or twenty-three. Catelow had several thousand people, and J.C. didn't mix with them. He only knew what Rodney told him about his sister. And that wasn't much.

"I noticed," Colie said as she turned, smiling.

His eyes flickered down to her pert breasts and he fought down a raging hunger that he hadn't felt in a long time. He had women, but this one stirred him in a different way. He couldn't explain how, exactly. It irritated him and he scowled.

"It wasn't a complaint," Colie added quickly, not understanding the scowl.

He shrugged. "No problem. What are we eating?"

"Leftover turkey with cranberry sauce, mashed potatoes, salad and apple pie." She hesitated, insecure. "Is that okay?"

He smiled, his perfect white teeth visible under chiseled, sensuous lips. "It's great. I love turkey." He chuckled. "I like chicken, too, although I usually get mine in a bucket."

Her eyes widened. "You put it in a pail, like you milk cows with?" she asked, shocked.

He glowered at her. "There's this chicken place. They sell you chicken and biscuits and sides…"

She went red as fire. "Oh, gosh, sorry, wasn't thinking," she stammered. "Let's go in! Daddy's already at the table."

Rodney went ahead, but J.C. slid a long finger inside the back of Colie's sweater and gently stopped her. He moved forward, so that she could feel the heat and power of him at her back in a way that made her heart run wild, her knees shiver. "I was teasing," he whispered right next to her ear. His lips brushed it.

Her intake of breath was visible. Her whole body felt shaky.

His big hands caught her shoulders and held her there while his lips traveled down the side of her throat in a lazy, whispery caress that caused her to melt inside.

"Do you like movies?" he whispered.

"Well, yes…"

"There's a new comedy at the theater Saturday. Go with me. We'll have supper at the fish place on the way."

She turned, shocked. "You…you want to go out with me?" she asked, her green eyes wide and full of delight.

He smiled slowly. "Yes. I want to go out with you."

"Saturday?"

He nodded.

"What time?"

"We'll leave about five."

"That would be lovely," she said, drowning in his eyes, on fire with the joy he'd just kindled in her with the unexpected invitation.

"Lovely," he murmured, but he was looking at her mouth.

"Colie? Supper?" her father's amused voice floated out from the dining room.

"Supper." She was dazed. "Oh. Supper! Yes! Coming!"

J.C. followed close behind her, his smile as smug and arrogant as the look on his face. Colie wanted him. He knew it without a word being spoken.

He seated Colie, to her amazement, and then pulled out a chair for himself.

"Good to have you with us, J.C.," the reverend said gently. "Say grace, Colie, if you please," he added.

J.C. felt stunned as the others bowed their heads and Colie mumbled a prayer. He wasn't much on religion, but he did bow his head. When in Rome…

It was a pleasant meal. Reverend Thompson seemed shocked at J.C.'s knowledge of biblical history as he mentioned a recent dig in Israel that had turned up some new relics of antiquity, and J.C. remarked on it with some authority.

"My mother was from southern Ireland. Catholic," he

added quietly. "She was forever asking the local priest to loan her books on archaeology. It was a passion of his."

"She couldn't get them off the internet?" Rodney queried.

J.C. laughed. "We lived in the Yukon, Rod," he told him with some amusement. "We didn't have television or the internet."

"No TV?" Rodney exclaimed. "What did you do for fun?"

"Hunted, fished, helped chop firewood, learned foreign languages from my neighbors. Read," he added. "I still don't watch television. I don't own one."

"Do you hear that?" Reverend Thompson interjected, pointing to J.C. "That's how people become intelligent, not from watching people take off their clothing and use foul language on television!"

"It's his soapbox," Rodney said complacently. "He only lets me have satellite because I help pay for it."

"The world is wicked," the reverend said heavily. "So much immorality. It's like fighting a tsunami."

"There, there, Daddy, you do your part to stop it," Colie said gently, and smiled.

He smiled back. "You're my legacy, sweetheart," he said. "You're so like your mother. She was a gentle woman. She never went with the crowd."

"I hate crowds," Colie said.

"Me, too," Rodney added.

J.C. just stared into space. "I hate people. The best of them will turn on you, given the opportunity."

"Son, that's a very harsh attitude," the reverend said gently.

J.C. finished his turkey and sipped black coffee. "Sorry. We're the products of our environment, as much as our genetics." He glanced at the older man with dead eyes. "I've been sold out by the people I loved most. It doesn't encourage trust."

"You have to consider that we all have a purpose," the reverend said solemnly. "I've heard it said that people come into our lives when they do, for a reason. Some bring out good qualities in us, some bring out bad. Life is a test."

"If it is, I've sure failed it already." Rodney sighed. He nodded toward Colie. "She's got a big jar. Every time I swear, I have to put in a nickel. I'll be bankrupt in days!" he moaned.

Reverend Thompson laughed wholeheartedly. "Now, that's creative thinking, my girl!"

"I'd take a bow, but the pie would get cold," she teased, as she served it up.

She noticed that J.C. seemed to love his. He glanced at her, saw her watching him and grinned. She flushed and fumbled with her fork.

The reverend watched the byplay with amusement and concern. Colie was an innocent. He knew things about J.C., who was vocal about his distaste for family life and children. Colie would want marriage and kids. J.C. wouldn't. It was a mismatch that could lead to tragedy for his daughter. He saw the danger ahead and wished he could stop it.

They had relatives in Comanche Wells, Texas, a small town in Jacobs County. He could send Colie there. She'd be away from J.C...

Even as he thought it, he realized how impractical it was. Colie had a good job. She loved Catelow. And if her continual sighing over J.C. Calhoun was any indication, she was already halfway in love. She'd never dated much, except for an occasional double date with an older girlfriend who'd later married and moved to Billings. She didn't go out these days. She worked and cooked and cleaned and read books. Even the reverend realized it wasn't much of a life for a young woman, who should be out learning about life.

It was just that she was going to learn things that he disapproved of. He looked at J.C., saw the way the man was watching Colie, and something inside him tightened like a rope around his throat. He averted his eyes. He didn't know what to do. He only knew that Colie was headed for disaster.

COLIE WALKED J.C. out onto the porch, where a small light burned overhead. Snow was falling softly.

"They say we're looking at six inches of snow," she remarked with a long sigh.

He smiled. "I can drive in six feet of snow," he mused. "If the theater is open, we'll get there. If it isn't, you can come home with me and I'll teach you how to play chess."

Her lips parted on a rush of excitement. He really wanted to be with her. He wasn't teasing. She looked up into narrow, pale silver eyes and wanted nothing more in the world than to be in his arms.

He saw the look. It amused him. She had her act down pat. Playing innocent, showing all the right sort of excitement for a woman headed for her first love affair. He didn't believe what he was seeing. He'd had too many experienced women tease him with displays of innocence, only to become wildcats once he had them in bed. It was a trust issue, he supposed. He didn't trust women. He had good reason not to.

But he was willing to play along. In fact, he knew

tricks that Colie might not know. He moved closer, taking her gently by the waist and holding her away from him just a little.

"You'll get cold," he whispered, bending his head so that his mouth was just above hers, not touching, but taunting.

"It's not that cold," she whispered back, her voice unsteady as she looked up at his mouth, focused on it with all the pent-up hunger she'd been saving for the right man, the right time, the right place.

"Isn't it?" His voice was deep, dark velvet. He brushed his nose against hers, while his big hands smoothed up and down her rib cage, almost brushing her taut breasts—but not touching.

Her lips parted. They felt swollen. She felt swollen all over. She didn't know enough about men to understand what he was doing to her. It was a game. A very old game. Tease and retreat, to make a woman hungry for more.

"I have to go," he whispered, his breath mingling with hers, he was so close.

"Do you?" She was standing on her tiptoes now, almost begging for the hard, chiseled mouth so close to hers. She could almost taste the coffee on it.

"I do." He brushed his nose against hers again, teased her mouth without touching it, and suddenly put her away from him. "Don't stay out here. You'll catch cold."

"O…kay," she said. She was disappointed, frustrated.

He saw that. It delighted him. He smiled at her. "I'll see you Saturday. Five sharp."

She nodded. "Five sharp."

"Good night, Colie."

He went down the steps before she could reply and

back to his black SUV. He got in, started the engine, backed out and drove away. He didn't look back. Not once.

COLIE WENT BACK INSIDE, frustrated and cold. Why hadn't he kissed her? She knew he wanted to. His eyes had been hungry as they stared at her parted lips. But he'd pushed her away. Why?

She wished she had a really close girlfriend, somebody she could trust, to talk to about men and their reactions. Well, there was Lucy, at work, the closest thing she had to a friend. But she'd be too embarrassed to ask Lucy, who was married, questions about men and sensual techniques. Lucy would know why she wanted to know, and she'd tease Colie, who was too shy to invite the attention. Still, she wondered why J.C. had been so hesitant to kiss her, when she knew he wanted to. Muffled gossip, movies and explicit television shows hadn't really educated her about how men felt and why they behaved in odd ways.

She started clearing the dining room table.

"J.C. get off all right?" her father asked.

She nodded and smiled. "It's snowing again."

"I noticed." He was still sitting at the table, with his second cup of black coffee. He took a breath. "Colie, I know how you feel about J.C.," he said unexpectedly. "But you have to remember that he's not a marrying man."

She stopped what she was doing and looked at him. Her expression made him wince.

"You've never really been exposed to anybody like him," her father continued quietly. "Most of the boys you dated were like you, innocent and out of touch with the modern world. J.C. has seen the elephant, as the old-time cowboys used to say. He's well-traveled and he's lived among violent men…"

"I know all that, Daddy," she said softly. "It's just that…" She bit her lower lip. "I've never felt like this."

"You're nineteen," he replied. "Such feelings are natural. But you should also remember that despite what you see in social media, people of faith live by certain rules. Ours teaches that we get married, then we have children. We don't encourage intimacy outside marriage."

"I remember."

"It's natural to feel such things. We're human, after all. But just because a lot of people do something immoral, that doesn't make it right. Any man who truly loves you will want to marry you, Colie, have kids with you, go to church with you. If you interact with a man who has no faith, you risk falling into the same trap that many young women do. I've seen the result of broken relationships where illegitimate children were involved. It is not something I want my daughter to experience."

She wanted to mention that there was such a thing as birth control, but she bit her lip. Her father, like many of his congregation, saw things in a different light than the rest of the world. He was out of touch with what was natural for young women today.

She wanted J.C. Why was it so wrong to sleep with someone you loved? It was as natural as breathing. At least, she imagined it was. She'd never been intimate with anyone. One date had fumbled under her blouse, but his efforts to undress her had been interrupted and Colie hadn't been sorry. She was curious, but the boy hadn't stirred her with his kisses.

J.C., on the other hand, made her wild for something she'd never had. She wanted him. Her body burned, for the first time. He felt the same thing for her, she was sure of it. Except she didn't understand why he'd drawn back so suddenly, why he hadn't kissed her. It was disturbing.

"Think of your mother," the reverend added, when he saw that his arguments were having no effect.

She lifted her eyes. "Mama?"

"She was the most moral human being I ever knew," he said. "She waited for marriage. So did I, Colie," he added surprisingly. "I loved her almost beyond bearing." He lowered his eyes. "Life without her would be empty, except for my faith and my work. I carry on, because that's what she'd want me to do." He looked up. "She'd expect you to live a moral life."

Yes, she would, Colie agreed silently. But perhaps her mother hadn't been as hungry as Colie was, as much in love. Her parents had been together in a different time, when things were less permissive in small towns. Goodness, half the young people in town were in relationships. Few of them actually married.

"If you live with someone, you get to know them and you find out if you're suited enough to get married," she ventured without looking at him.

He drew in a slow breath and sipped his coffee. "It's your life, Colie," he said gently. "You're a grown woman. I can't tell you how to live. I can only tell you that many people who live in an open relationship don't eventually marry. There's no real commitment. Not like there is in marriage, where you bring children into the world and raise them. J.C. doesn't want children."

"He could change his mind," she said.

"He could. But I doubt he will. He's how old, thirty-two? If he still feels that way, at his age, he's unlikely to change. There's something else," he added quietly. "You can't involve yourself with someone with the idea that you can change things about them that you don't like. People don't change. Bad habits only grow worse."

"Not liking children," she began, moving silverware around on an empty plate. "That might change, if he had a child."

He closed his eyes and winced.

Colie saw that. It wounded her. "Daddy, I can't help how I feel," she ground out. "I'm crazy about him!"

He drew in a long breath. "I know." He looked up at her and saw her stubborn resolve. He finished his coffee and got to his feet. He brushed a kiss against her cheek. "I'll always be here for you. Always. No matter what you do. I'm your father. I will always love you."

Tears sprang to her eyes. She put down the plates and hugged him, tears bleeding from her eyes.

He patted her on the back and kissed her hair, as he had when she was very small, and hurt, and she ran to him for comfort. It had always been like that. She loved her mother very much, but she was Daddy's girl.

"It will all work out," he said, trying to reassure both of them.

"Of course it will," she replied, fighting more tears.

CHAPTER TWO

COLIE WAS DRESSED and ready to go by three o'clock on Saturday, and so nervous that she could hardly settle anywhere. J.C. had said they'd eat at the fish place, but she didn't know if he'd want her to wear a nice dress or jeans or what. She'd never seen him in a suit or even a conventional jacket, so she assumed he'd wear jeans, as he always did.

She wore jeans, nicely laundered, with lace inserts on the side from the hem up to the knee, with a pretty white blouse, also with lace inserts. Against her dark hair and light olive skin, she looked exotic. The excitement made her green eyes sparkle. She looked almost pretty, even without gobs of makeup, which she detested. She had a naturally smooth complexion, which she touched up with just a little face powder and a glossy lipstick. She couldn't abide mascara. In fact, she was allergic to most of it. But she had thick, black lashes that looked as if she used it.

Her hair had a natural wave. All she did was wash it and comb it. She grinned at herself in the mirror. She didn't look half-bad, she thought. Maybe J.C. would kiss her. She caught her breath at the anticipated pleasure. J.C. had been around. He'd know how to kiss. Hopefully, he'd teach her, because she hadn't a clue.

"Primping?" Rodney teased as he joined her in the hall. "You look fine, sis."

She laughed. "Thanks."

"You know, J.C. isn't big on family," he said unexpectedly. "He doesn't have any left. His mother is dead, and he and his father don't speak. I'm not sure he even knows where his old man is."

She turned and looked up at him. "Why?"

"He doesn't talk about it," he said. "He let something drop, just once, about a family that adopted him when he was ten. A man and wife, up in the Yukon. She was a teacher. So was his mother, so maybe they knew each other or something. Anyway, he lived with them for a while. Tragic thing, there was a fire. Both of them died. J.C.'s been alone for a long time."

"He has you," she said.

"We're not that close," he replied. "You can't get close to him. He doesn't trust people. He doesn't share anything." He frowned. "I know how you feel. Maybe that could change," he added when he saw her pained expression. "Just don't let him hurt you, okay?"

"What do you mean?"

"He had this really bad experience with a woman. He didn't tell me. I heard it from one of the guys he taught with overseas, who was in basic training with him. She was a call girl. He didn't know. At that time, he'd had very little to do with women and he was naive. He fell head over heels for her. Then he heard her talking about him to another man, laughing at how he'd bought her so many fancy things and he thought she was innocent. She said she'd worked at that pose for years, because so many of her paying customers liked it. J.C. went wild. They said he wrecked a bar and put another man in the hospital afterward. When he left the military, the guy said, he was so different that he hardly knew him anymore," he added quietly. "He's had some knocks."

"Poor guy," she said softly.

"So forewarned is forearmed," he added. "J.C.'s attitude toward women changed after that. He's no playboy, but he does have women."

She ground her teeth together. She'd suspected it, but she was learning things about J.C. that were very disturbing. "A lot of men are that way. Aren't they? They still get married and have families…"

"Don't count on it," he returned. "J.C. does a job that invites violence, haven't you noticed? He heads up security for Ren's ranch, and he goes overseas all the time to help train policemen, in areas where insurgency is high. He likes risk. That doesn't mesh with grammar schools and birthday parties, sweet girl."

She was feeling sicker by the minute.

Rodney saw that and winced. "I know how you feel about him," he said in a gentler tone. "That's why I'm saying these things. You already know that Daddy doesn't move with the times. He lives in a fantasy world of happy-ever-after, because he and Mama had that. It doesn't work that way for most people. We take what we can get and move on."

"You mean, we enjoy what we can and don't look ahead," she said in a hollow tone.

"Something like that." He drew in a breath. "Colie, I'm not trying to hurt you. I just want you to know what you're up against. J.C.'s my friend. But you're my sister. He doesn't respect women. Not anymore."

She moved her shoulder restlessly. "You think I shouldn't go out with him."

He hesitated. There were reasons why he wanted to

keep her away from his best friend that had nothing to do with her well-being. J.C. was a stickler for law and order. Rodney was into some very bad things. J.C. knew that he used drugs, and it was why they didn't spend as much time together as they had overseas. He knew other things about Rodney that he didn't want his father finding out, too. J.C. wouldn't rat him out because he didn't know what was really going on. But his baby sister would, if she had any inkling. He needed to prevent her from becoming close to his friend.

On the other hand, he cared about her, in his way. "Honey, you do what you think is right," he said after a minute. "I'm on your side. Whatever you decide to do. Okay?"

She hugged him impulsively, her cheek resting on his chest so that she missed the agonized look on his face.

"Thanks, Rod." She drew back. "Daddy said he'd always be here for me, whatever happened." She looked up. "He thinks I can't resist J.C."

"No woman can resist him, if he wants her," he said. He caught himself and clenched his teeth.

"It's okay," she said, forcing a smile. "He likes variety, they say."

"He does, now," he replied. "Before, that guy told me, he was Mr. Conventional. That changed after the call girl took him for the ride of his life."

"Somebody should give her a taste of her own medicine."

"Women like that don't feel anything, honey," Rodney told her. "They're cold as ice inside. A woman who prostitutes herself usually does it because it's easy money. Maybe there are control issues, as well. It gives a woman power over a man, when she sells a service."

She just nodded. It was a world she'd never seen.

"Maybe you'll change J.C. back to the way he was," he said gently. "Who knows?"

She smiled. "Right. Who knows?" She sniffed him. "Honestly, Rod, you reek of smoke…!"

"My buddy from Jackson Hole came up to visit. He's staying at a local motel. I have to go see him tonight, so I'll be late. Very late. We're talking to another man he knows, from the West Coast."

She frowned. It sounded odd.

"Hardware store business," he said quickly. "It's samples of tools."

"Oh! I see." She laughed and turned away. She missed Rodney's quickly erased look of guilt.

J.C., AS SHE'D SUSPECTED, was wearing jeans with hand-tooled boots and a long-sleeved blue plaid shirt and a shepherd's coat. He smiled when he saw her pretty but casual clothing.

"I hoped you'd realize it isn't a formal date," he chuckled. "I should have said so."

"Oh, it's okay," she assured him. "I read minds."

His dark eyebrows arched.

"Really," she said, green eyes sparkling.

"If you say so," he returned. "Ready to go?"

"Oh, yes."

Her father came out into the hall, glanced at J.C. and smiled. He had a book in his hands. "Have fun. Don't be too late, Colie, please?"

"I won't, Daddy." She kissed him. Even though he smiled, there was concern in his whole look as he turned back to his study. He hadn't said a word to J.C.

"Daddy's not comfortable with people," Colie defended him when they were settled in J.C.'s big black SUV headed for town. "It's funny, for a minister, because he has to be available to his congregation when they need counseling or comfort."

"I noticed."

"It isn't that he doesn't like you." She was trying valiantly to explain something that wasn't really explainable.

He glanced at her and smiled. "It's okay," he said softly. "Don't sweat it."

She smiled. "Okay."

"Do you like fish?"

"Oh, yes. Fried, poached, grilled, any way at all. Do you?"

He chuckled. "I grew up in the Yukon. There are lakes and rivers everywhere. My grandfather taught me to fish when I was about four years old."

She noticed that he didn't speak of his father, and she recalled what Rodney had told her. "My grandfathers were both dead when I was born," she said. "I only had one grandmother living, and she died when I was in grammar school."

"That's sad. I had my grandfather until my mother died. He was a grand old fellow. Blackfoot," he added with a smile. "His family came from Calgary." He noticed her puzzlement. "It's in Alberta. Western Canada. Have you ever heard of the Calgary Stampede? It's a rodeo they hold every year. My granddad rode in it."

"Gosh! Yes, I've heard of that."

"My father didn't care much for rodeo, but he was bulldogging with grandad when he saw a pretty little redheaded Irish woman in the stands, cheering him on. He found her after the event and started talking to her. He was fascinated with her coloring. She was an anthropology student, and she was fascinated with First Nation people, like my father. They dated for a week and got married."

"It fascinates me that you had a redheaded mother," she said, staring at him. His hair was coal black, his eyes that odd, beautiful shade of pale silver.

He chuckled. "It doesn't show, does it?"

"Not really."

"I get my eyes from her. They were pale gray, like mine."

"You loved her."

He stared ahead at the snow-lined road. "Very much. She was always there for me. She took terrible chances to keep me safe." He drew in a long breath. He'd never spoken of these things, even to Rodney. There was something about Colie that drew his confidence. "I lost her when I was ten. I went to live with an adoptive family." He forced a smile. "They were good, kind people. They had no kids of their own, so I was pretty much spoiled rotten." His face hardened. "They died in a fire. I was just getting home from school. I got there just before the ambulances and fire trucks did." He averted his eyes. The memory still hurt. "I couldn't get them out. The whole structure was involved by then."

"I'm so sorry," she said gently.

The sympathy twisted something inside him, something he'd hidden for years. "I couldn't get past the flames at the front door," he gritted. "I tried. A neighbor pulled me back and sat on me until the fire trucks got the hoses going. They were good people."

Her face contorted. She could only imagine standing helplessly by while people she loved died.

He glanced at her, saw the sympathy that wasn't

feigned. "You don't push, do you?" he asked after a few seconds, his attention turning back to the road. "You just let people talk when they want to."

She smiled sadly. "I'm not interesting," she said. "I listen more than I talk."

"I noticed that about you, when I first met you, that you listen more than most people do. Rod used to talk about his kid sister who sat and daydreamed and played guitar. You still play?"

"Not often. I don't practice as much as I used to. I have a full-time job and I'm taking night courses in business two days a week."

"You work for Wentworth and Tartaglia, don't you?" he asked, naming a well-known law firm in Catelow.

"I do. I went to work for them just out of high school."

"That was a while back, I guess," he chuckled.

It was six months, but he didn't know her real age, apparently. Rod must not have mentioned it. She wasn't going to, either. If he knew she was barely nineteen, he might not want to take her out. He was thirty-two; Rod had told her. Just as well to let him think she was more mature than she was. She couldn't bear the thought that he might not want to keep dating her.

"I guess," she replied with a smile.

He settled down. He'd never asked Rod how old his baby sister was. He knew there were a few years between them, but not how many. It didn't matter. He wasn't about to get serious. He just wanted someone cute and responsive to spend time with. She didn't seem the sort of woman who'd cling, and that suited him very well.

THE FISH PLACE was crowded, but J.C. found them a table that was just being vacated and captured it before another young couple. They laughed as he grinned at them.

"Wow," Colie mused, letting him seat her. "That was a nice takeover."

"Thanks. I can do it with enemy positions, too," he chuckled.

She cocked her head and laughed. "You really do have a flair for it."

"I'm hungry and the place is crowded. What do you see that you like?"

She wanted to say "you" but she was far too shy to flirt overtly. She settled down with the menu and made her choices.

THEY ATE IN a comfortable silence.

"Do you fish?" he asked.

She paused with her fork in midair. "Well, yes," she said. "I used to go with Daddy. We'd sit on the dock for hours waiting for something to bite. Not much ever did."

"Come spring, I'll take you fishing."

Her heart jumped. That was a long-term invitation. She was touched. "I'd love that," she said, with her heart in the eyes that slid over his face like exploring hands.

"Me, too," he said softly.

He held her gaze for so long that her heart ran wild and her fingers trembled. She dropped the fork into her plate with a clatter that stunned her. She dived for it, flushing.

He chuckled. Her headlong reaction to him was delicious. He couldn't remember a time when a woman had appealed to him so much in ways beyond the purely physical. He hated the memory of the call girl who'd shattered his pride and his ego. But that was in the days before he became experienced and sophisticated. That was before he learned to turn the tables, to make women beg for him and then walk away from them.

His pale gray eyes narrowed on Colie's face. Could he do that to her? Make her beg, make her do anything he liked, and then just walk away? The thought of giving her up was troubling, even at this very early stage in their relationship. Better not to dwell on it. Live for the moment.

He smiled at her. "How's the fish?" he asked, to relax the tension.

"It's great," she said. "I love the French fries, too. They make them fresh. No frozen stuff here."

"I noticed. I'm partial to a good French fry."

"I make them for Daddy sometimes. He likes fish and chips."

"Your father doesn't like me."

"It's not that." She struggled for words. "He's protective of me. He always has been. I go to Sunday school and church, I sing in the choir, I teach primary classes in Sunday school." She gnawed her lower lip. "I guess that sounds painfully conservative to someone like you, who's traveled and is sophisticated. But around here, it's pretty much the normal thing. Not everyone is conservative," she confided. "We have people in our congregation who live together and aren't married, we have people who do drugs, we have people who have babies out of wedlock, stuff like that. Daddy never judges, he just tries to help."

His eyes fell to his plate. He wasn't in the market for a wife. Did she know?

"I know you're not the settling-down kind, J.C.," she said out of the blue. "But I like going around with you."

His eyes lifted. He laughed shortly. "You really do read minds, don't you?"

She grinned, green eyes twinkling. "I tell fortunes, too, but not where Daddy can hear me," she whispered. "He thinks it's witchcraft!"

He grinned back. "My father's mother could see far," he said. "She had visions. I suppose a doctor might say she had aura from migraines and was hallucinating, but her visions were pretty accurate. She saw the future."

"Did she ever tell yours?"

He nodded. He scowled as he finished his meal and lifted the coffee cup with cooling black coffee to chiseled, sensuous lips. "Yes, but it made no real sense."

"What did she say?"

He put the cup down. "She said that one day I'd want something out of my reach, that I'd make bad decisions and cause a tragedy that would hurt me as much as it hurt the other person. She said that a third person would suffer the most for it." He paused and then laughed at her puzzled expression. "Sometimes she was vague. I was very young at the time, too. She said that I was too young to understand what she was telling me." His face hardened. "I lost her at the same time I lost my mother. I lost touch with my grandfather. By the time I was old enough to search for him, he was long dead."

"I'm really sorry," she said quietly. "I know how it feels to lose people you love. At least, I still have Daddy and Rod."

He understood what she wasn't saying. She was saying that J.C. had nobody. She was right.

His big hand reached for hers and closed over it. "You have a knack for pulling painful memories out of me," he said quietly. "I'm not sure I like it."

She felt her heart soaring at the touch of his hand on hers. It was like tiny electric shocks running through her. She loved the way it felt to hold hands. "You don't let people get close. I'm that way," she confessed hesitantly. "But we're different, because I trust people and you don't. I'm shy, so I keep to myself."

His thumb smoothed over her soft, damp palm. He studied her quietly. "I enjoy my own company."

She nodded. "So do I."

"But I enjoy yours, as well."

She smiled. She beamed. "Really?"

"Really." His fingers tightened. "We'll have to do this again."

"That would be nice."

"Dessert?"

"I don't really like sweets," she confessed.

He chuckled. "Something else in common. Okay. Movie next." He picked up the check, pulled out her chair and they left.

THE MOVIE WAS FUNNY. Colie thought she'd probably have enjoyed it, but her whole body was involved with the feel of J.C.'s arm around her in the back of the theater, in one of the couple seats. His fingers brushed lazily over her throat, her shoulder, down to her rib cage, in light, undemanding brushes that made her heart race, made her body feel swollen and hungry.

His cheek rested on her dark hair while they watched the screen. The theater wasn't crowded, despite the great reviews the movie had gotten. There was an usher. He went up and down the aisles and left.

"Alone at last," J.C. teased at her ear, and his lips traveled down her neck to where it joined her shoulder, under the lacy blouse.

She felt just the tip of his tongue there and she shivered. She'd never had such a headlong physical reaction to any man she'd ever known. The boys in her circle of friends were just that: boys. This was an experienced man, and she knew that if he ever turned up the heat, there would be no resisting him.

J.C. knew that, too. It should have pleased him. It didn't. She wasn't the sort of woman he was used to these days. She was like his grandmother. His mother. They were conservative, too. Neither of them had ever been unfaithful to their mates. His mother once spoke of being so naive that she hardly knew how to kiss when she married his father. They were women of faith, although his mother had been Catholic and his grandmother a practitioner of her native religion. They were the sort of women who loved their men and had families with them. J.C. didn't want any part of that.

But he loved the feel of Colie's soft body beside him. He wanted her, desperately. There were so many reasons why he should just walk away, cut this off now, while there was still time.

Her cheek moved against his hair. He could almost feel her heart beating. Her breath was shallow and quick. She was trembling.

He had to fight the surging need to push her down on the floor and have her right there. It was the first time in his life he'd ever wanted anyone that badly.

Because it shocked him, he drew away a little. He had to slow things down. He needed time to think.

She looked lost when he moved away. He caught her hand in his and held it tight, tight.

She relaxed. It was as if he was comforting her, cooling things down. She appreciated it, because she'd sensed his need. Perhaps he'd been alone too long, she thought, and he was hungry. That disturbed her. She couldn't do what he wanted, not without some sort of commitment.

She couldn't shame her father in a town so small that gossip ran rampant.

She forced a smile and tried to concentrate on the movie.

J.C. DROVE HER HOME, still holding her hand. He liked her a lot, but he was getting cold feet. This was going to be a mistake if he let it continue. He should have left her alone. She was getting emotionally involved and he couldn't afford to. He liked his freedom too much.

He walked her to her door. "It was a pretty good movie."

"Yes, it was," she agreed, thinking privately that she couldn't remember a single scene.

He turned her to him and he was solemn in the porch light. "It's unwise to start things you can't finish," he said after a minute.

Her heart sank, but she understood. He didn't want involvement. She'd known that. It still hurt.

She forced a smile. "Still, it was nice. Fish and a movie."

He nodded. He looked troubled. His big hand touched her cheek, felt its warmth, its smooth contours.

"You live in a conservative household," he began. "You work at a conventional job. I don't. I like risk…"

She reached up and put her fingers over his mouth. "You don't have to say it, J.C.," she said softly. "I understand."

He caught the fingers and kissed them hungrily. Then he put them away. "You're a nice woman," he said after a minute.

"Thanks."

"It wasn't a compliment," he said sardonically.

She laughed.

He drew in a breath and shook his head. She was a puzzle.

He stuck his hands in his coat pockets, to keep from doing what he wanted to do with them. He cocked his head and studied her through narrowed eyes. "What am I thinking?"

"That you'd love to kiss me good-night, but you think I might become addictive, so you're going to rush out to your truck and go home," she said simply.

His eyebrows arched. It was so close to the truth that it made him uncomfortable.

She laughed. "Now you're thinking that I'm a witch," she mused.

His breath rushed out in a torrent.

"And now you're shocked," she continued. "It's okay. I'm used to it. One of the Kirk boys married a psychic. I'm not nearly in her class, but she said people wouldn't even come into an office where she worked because they were afraid of her."

"I'm not afraid of seers," he replied.

"You're just uneasy, because it's one of those spooky things people keep hidden," she said.

He burst out laughing and shook his head. "My God."

"I don't usually talk about it around people. I wouldn't want my bosses to fire me because clients ran for the hills."

"It's a rare gift," he said after a minute.

"It can be," she said, but her face clouded.

His eyes narrowed. "You see things you don't want to see."

She nodded. "I know when bad things are going to

happen to people I love," she said sadly. "I knew when my grandmother was going to die. She had the gift, too."

"What did she tell you?"

She shifted her purse in her hands. "She said that my life was going to be a hard one," she replied. "That I'd make a very bad decision and I'd pay a high price for it. She said that I'd marry, but not for love, and that tragedy would stalk me like a tiger for several years. But that I'd have a happy, full life afterward."

He was surprised at the commonality in the predictions his grandmother and hers had given for both of them.

"It is odd, isn't it?" she asked, as if she'd read the thought in his mind. "I mean, that your grandmother would have told you almost what mine told me."

"Odd," he agreed.

"On the other hand, maybe they were both just rambling," she said, and smiled. "Predictions are just that. Predictions. I don't read the future at all. I just get cold, hollow feelings when something bad's going to happen. Mostly when it concerns Daddy."

"I've never had that."

"Lucky you," she said. She searched his lean face. "You've had a hard life, J.C. I don't even have to know about you. It shows. So much pain…"

"Stop right there," he interrupted, his jaw taut.

"Overstepped the boundaries, did I?" she asked, and smiled. "Sorry. I just open my mouth and stuff my foot in, all the time."

That amused him and he laughed.

"It was a nice night out. Thanks," she said.

He shrugged. "It was nice," he agreed. "But we're not doing it again."

"Of course not," she agreed, hiding the pain.

"I'm not in the market for a picket fence, no matter how attractive the accessories."

It took her a minute, but she got it. She laughed. "Okay."

"You're quick."

"Not so much." She sighed. "It was fun."

"It was fun. Good night."

"Good night."

"Tell Rod I'm still on for the poker game, if he is. He'll understand," he added as he turned to leave.

"I'll tell him."

He forced himself to walk to the SUV, open the door, get in and crank it. He didn't look at her. If he had, he knew he wouldn't be able to leave.

COLIE WATCHED HIM drive away. He didn't wave. He didn't look back. She felt a sense of terrible loss. But he was right. They had no future. Their outlooks were far too different. Still, he needed somebody. He was so alone, so tormented.

She opened the door and went inside. Her father was just coming out of his study. His quick glance showed him that it had been a conventional date, and that nothing had happened. He tried to hide his sense of relief.

"Have fun?" he asked.

"Oh, yes," she said, grinning. "It was a great movie. We had dinner at the fish place. I love their fries."

"They're good," he said, nodding. He cocked his head. "Going out again?"

She shook her head. "He's very nice, but he hates picket fences," she said.

He moved closer. She was putting on a show, and he

knew it. She was in pain. "Daughter," he said gently, "there's a reason for everything, a plan behind whatever happens to us. You have to let life happen. You can't force it to be what you'd like it to be."

She smiled and hugged him. "And we can't get involved with people who aren't like us. I know all that. It's what he said, too." She closed her eyes. "It still hurts."

"Of course it does. But pain passes. Everything does, in time."

"Yes. In time," she agreed.

BUT IT DIDN'T PASS. Every time Rod mentioned J.C., Colie felt it like a stab in her heart. She knew that J.C. was totally wrong for her. It didn't help. She wanted him. Loved him. Hungered for him.

She went to work, came home, cooked and cleaned, read books, went to bed. She got up the next day and did the very same things. But she felt as empty inside as a tennis ball.

SHE DIDN'T KNOW IT, but J.C. was having the same problem. Every day, he went to work and was haunted by the soft twinkle in a pair of loving green eyes. He was used to women who wanted him. But one who loved him… that was new. It was frightening.

Could he take her and walk away afterward? Could he not take her and live? He agonized over it.

His boss, Ren Colter, noticed his preoccupation while they were inspecting a downed fence on the edge of the property.

"That tree needs to come down," Ren remarked.

"I'll tell Willis," J.C. replied. Willis was the foreman.

"What's eating you?" Ren asked suddenly, and from

the standpoint of the friend he'd been for years. "You're not yourself."

"Just a few sleepless nights, that's all," J.C. lied.

"Umhmmm. And it wouldn't have something to do with Colie Thompson…?"

J.C.'s pale gray eyes flashed. "Listen, just because I took her to a movie…!"

"Oh, can it," Ren said shortly. "You've been mooning around here for a week, like a ghost trying to find a place to haunt. I hear she's doing the same thing."

"She is?" J.C. asked.

The other man's expression was like a statement. Ren chuckled. "You have to take the path to see where it leads. Ask yourself, are you happier now?"

"No."

"Then why don't you do something about it?"

J.C. clenched his jaw. "Her father's a minister and I don't want to get married."

"You don't have to propose just because you take her out on dates," was the reasonable reply. "Do you?"

J.C. sighed. "It will complicate things."

"Life is too short to avoid complications."

J.C. studied him. After a minute he laughed shortly. "I guess it is, at that."

COLIE WAS JUST getting into her old beat-up pickup truck in the parking lot of the law firm where she worked when a big black SUV pulled into the spot beside her.

She turned and J.C. was getting out of it.

He stopped just in front of her. He looked angry, conflicted, worried. He drew in a breath. "The hell with it," he said curtly.

"What?" she began.

He pulled her into his arms and bent his head. "We'll take it one day at a time," he whispered as his mouth burrowed softly, slowly into hers.

She would have questioned him, but a shock of pleasure ran the length of her body and left her trembling. She reached up and held him, hung on for dear life, while he made a five-course meal of her soft, eager mouth.

CHAPTER THREE

IT WAS A long time before J.C. lifted his head. The kiss had filled a hollow place inside himself that he hadn't even known about. Colie's face was flushed, her pretty bow mouth swollen, her green eyes soft and drowsy with feeling. It puzzled him that she didn't kiss him back so much as she allowed herself to be kissed. Perhaps, he thought, her other boyfriends hadn't cared about foreplay. He was used to experienced women who didn't care much for it, either. They were usually so hungry, so eager, that they just went at it.

He gave one last thought to his suspicions about her, but Rod was a rounder and he was a minister's son. J.C. figured that Colie was probably as sexually active as her brother, but she put on a good show for her father. She certainly wasn't protesting.

J.C. had her so close that she could feel how aroused he was. She'd never felt a man like that, but she was a great reader. She knew from her romance novels how men's bodies changed when they wanted a woman. It thrilled her that J.C. wanted her so much.

She didn't want to discourage him, but she wasn't sure how she was going to live with what he was certainly going to want from her. She'd lived a moral life, she'd never put a foot wrong. And yet here was temptation and sin, wearing blue jeans and dying for her.

She sighed. "That was nice."

"Nice." He chuckled, looking around as he moved a step back. "Lucky thing that there isn't much traffic on this side street at this time of the day." He leaned close. "I was starving."

"I noticed," she whispered, and flushed.

He ruffled her hair. "I'll come get you in an hour. Long enough for you to serve something up for your father and Rod?"

"Oh, yes," she lied. She'd manage something. There were leftovers that she could reheat. "Where are we going?"

"To Jackson Hole," he said with a grin. "I'm going to take you to a nightclub. Got a flashy dress?"

Her face fell.

Damn! He'd forgotten. Her father wouldn't be encouraging that sort of thing. She probably didn't own an evening gown.

"Change of plan," he said abruptly. "Wear jeans and we'll hit a casino over near Lander. I'll teach you how to play the machines." He grinned.

She laughed. "I don't own an evening gown. I guess it showed, huh?"

"We'll have to do something about that," he began.

"No, we won't," she replied curtly. "I pay my own way. Just in case you were thinking you'd buy me one."

His eyebrows really arched now. "It's just a dress…"

"I pay my own way," she repeated. She had a stubborn look on her face.

He recognized it, because he had one just like it. He chuckled. "Okay, Miss Independence. We'll do things your way."

She smiled. "Fair enough. I'll be ready and waiting."

She was still flushed. He loved her reaction to him. No coy withdrawal, no teasing; she just went in headfirst when he touched her. It boded well for the future. He had one slight twinge of conscience, but it passed quickly. She was old enough to know the score, and he was certain he wouldn't be her first man. Why did that disturb him? It was stupid. He'd never been the first man.

"I'll see you in an hour," he told her.

"Okay."

She watched him leave. She got into her old, beat-up truck that guzzled gas and looked at herself in the rearview mirror. She looked…loved. Her breath caught as she relived the hungry, passionate kiss, the first of its kind she'd ever had. She was in love with J.C. And he must feel something for her, because he'd come back when he said he wouldn't.

She smiled all the way home. She only stopped when she had to tell her father she was going out with J.C. and saw the disappointment and sorrow on his face.

ROD WAS STILL away when she got ready for her date. She'd fixed a meager supper for her father. She wasn't hungry. Excitement robbed her of any appetite.

"Where are you going?" her father asked gently as he finished the impromptu meal.

She ground her teeth together. "To Lander," she said with a forced smile. "It's over near Jackson Hole…"

"Casinos," her father said with a deep sigh. He studied her guilty face quietly. "It's your life, Colie. I won't interfere. But you're headed down a path I wouldn't wish for you. I think you already know that J.C. isn't a person of faith."

"I know that. People can change," she said stubbornly.

"They can. But most don't," he said, uncharacteristically negative. He locked his hands around his coffee cup. "Try not to let him influence you in bad ways. You were raised to have principles. Don't discard them for a man who'll never marry you."

"He's not a bad man," she began.

"I didn't say that he was. I'm only saying that he's used to a very different lifestyle than you are." His eyes were old and wise as they met hers. "People of faith are very challenged in the modern world. It's hard to hold on to ideals when so many people live without them."

"I know that, Daddy. But I'll still be myself, whatever decisions I make."

He knew that further argument would be futile. He could see in her eyes that she was already too much in love with J.C. to deny him anything.

He managed a smile. "You'll always be my daughter, whatever choices you make, and I'll always love you. I'll be here when you need me."

"I know that." She felt her regrets deeply. She was disappointing him, but she couldn't help it. She wanted J.C. more than she wanted to go on living. "I love him, Daddy," she said simply.

"I know that, too."

"It will be all right," she said. She only wished that she could believe that.

She fed Big Tom, who rolled around her ankles with such fervor that she laughed, picked him up and kissed him before she left.

THE CASINO WAS big and noisy. The place was run by the Eastern Shoshone tribe, and it was a huge boon to the economy of the Native people. Located near Lander, and the Wind River Range, the view must have been spectacular. It was dark by the time J.C. and Colie arrived, but the beautiful, colorful glitter of lights out front lessened her disappointment in not getting to see the view.

"It's so…glittery," she enthused, holding tight to J.C.'s hand as they walked around the huge room.

"I can see the wheels turning in your head," he teased. "Sinful gaming! I expect your father had a lot to say about this trip."

"Enough," she confided. "But it's my life. I have to make my own choices."

He glanced down at her. He did feel a pang of regret. She was so sheltered, in so many ways. She didn't live in the real world, in his world.

She looked up in time to catch that expression. She wrinkled her nose. "Don't look so guilty. You're not leading me astray."

"Feels that way," he said softly. He searched her soft green eyes and felt a shock of pleasure all the way down to his toes. He smiled reluctantly. "On the other hand, maybe you're leading me astray," he mused. "I don't like attachments."

"I'll never send you an email that has any," she promised.

He chuckled and pressed her hand tight. "Torment."

"I brought five dollars," she said, glancing around. "Let's see how long it lasts!"

He was privately of the opinion that she'd lose it in the first three minutes, but he only nodded.

AN HOUR LATER, she was still playing.

"This has to be some sort of record," he said when the fruits lined up on the screen for her.

"I'm lucky," she said, distracted. She glanced up at him. "Otherwise, I'd never be here with you."

"What do you mean?"

"You're gorgeous, J.C.," she said softly, and her eyes echoed it. "You could have any woman you wanted, but you're going around with me."

"What's wrong with you?"

"Everything," she said miserably. "I'm not pretty."

He scowled. "Of course you're pretty," he said curtly. "You have wonderful qualities. You're kind and sweet and you never complain, even when you should."

She flushed.

"I mean that," he added, sketching her face. "You remind me of my mother, in a way. She had that incurable optimism." His face hardened. "She was almost too kind and forgiving."

She wanted so badly to ask what had happened to his mother, but the machine sang out and she laughed and threw up her hands. "Look! I won again!"

He glanced at his watch. "And I hate to break this up, but it's a long drive home. Your father won't appreciate it if I get you home in the wee hours of the morning. I've probably gotten you in enough trouble, just bringing you here."

She stood up. "It was my choice, too," she told him. "Daddy doesn't interfere. He counsels, which is a different thing."

He drew in a long breath. "We come from very different backgrounds," he said after a minute.

"It doesn't matter."

"It might, one day," he replied. His eyes narrowed. "I don't want to get mixed up with you."

"Gee, thanks, I like you, too," she mused.

"I wish I could just walk away," he said huskily. He touched her face with long, gentle fingers. "I can't."

Her heart jumped up into her throat. It was the most encouraging thing he'd said to her so far.

"You may wish that I had, Colie," he said quietly. "I meant what I said. I'm not interested in white picket fences and babies."

"You said that before. I'm not trying to change you, J.C. You really can't change people," she added.

"That's my point."

She just stared at him, so much in love that she wondered if her feet were really touching the floor as she met his searching gaze and felt her breath suspended as her heart ran wild.

He ground his teeth together. "We should go. Let's collect your winnings and call it a night."

She was delighted with her small win. It was only about a month's salary, but it would help catch up on some bills and let her add a few minutes a month to her phone messaging.

She said so.

J.C., who had money stashed away in offshore accounts as well as his local bank, frowned.

She saw the look. "I make a nice salary, but it doesn't go very far," she told him. "I help with the bills and I pay for my cell phone. It's not top of the line, but it has a few features. I pay for gas for my old truck that has mechanical issues every other week. I pay for the internet because I'm the one who uses it, mostly. Rod helps, because he games. He does love his console life."

"He always liked gaming," he replied. He didn't tell her that Rodney had changed a lot with his overseas duty. That happened to men who were raised with solid beliefs.

It was challenging to retain them when you saw so much death and torture in the military.

"What are you thinking about so hard?" she wondered as they drove back home down snow-lined roads toward Catelow.

"I was remembering my service overseas, with Rod," he said. "It isn't something I talk about. I don't imagine Rod shared any of it with you, either."

"Not really. He had nightmares when he first came home. He didn't say why. He and Daddy talked about it, but not in front of me." She glanced at him. "Daddy fought in the first Gulf War," she added. "He was a chaplain, but he was on the front lines."

"That must have been hard on him," he said.

"Very hard. He said it challenged his faith, seeing the misery of the people he encountered."

"Life challenged mine," he said shortly. "I lost what little I had when I was ten."

She was curious. Very curious. But she didn't speak.

He drew in a breath. "My father worked in mining, after he and my mother married," he began. "It was hard work. Not what he'd planned for himself. He wanted to own a ranch. He thought if he worked hard and saved his money, he'd be able to buy land, build a house, start a herd of cattle. But it didn't happen." His eyes stared straight ahead as the windshield wipers slid rhythmically over the windshield, wiping away flurries of snow. "He was trapped. Mom got pregnant with me, and suddenly there were doctor bills and all the debt that comes with a baby. There was nothing left over every week. Mom couldn't work, because there was nobody who could take care of me, and they couldn't afford help."

"There are government agencies," she began.

He laughed shortly. "My father was a proud man," he returned. "He refused to even speak of it. He tried to get my mother to contact her people and ask for a loan. She wouldn't do it." He glanced at her. "They disowned her when she married my father. They had deep prejudices."

What he'd said, about the differences between his parents, suddenly made sense. "That was sad."

"Prejudice doesn't have a home," he said simply. "So they soldiered on. Mom said he started drinking soon after I was born. Dreams die hard. He couldn't bear the loss of his." His big hand gripped the steering wheel hard. His free hand found hers and linked her fingers with his. It helped the pain. "She wanted to go to a meeting at the local school that I attended, for parents. I was ten and I was watching a movie on television. I didn't want to go. She said I could stay home, it didn't matter. My father complained because he didn't want to go, but she pleaded. She got in the car with him. He'd been drinking all day."

She tightened her fingers in his.

"He took a curve too fast and went off into the river. She drowned while he swam to shore."

"Oh, gosh," she ground out.

"I didn't know until the local police came to the door. My father ran for his life. He'd have gone to jail without a doubt, under the circumstances. My mother was dead. Something inside me died with her. I haven't seen my father or spoken to him since," he added curtly. "I was placed in state custody until I was adopted by a kind older couple who didn't have any kids of their own. They were well-to-do. I was spoiled. But it didn't quite make up for what I'd lost. And I didn't live with them long, just until the fire that took their lives."

"What about your mother's people?" she wondered.

"Dead," he said icily. "I wouldn't have known, but I turned out to be the only legal heir they had. I inherited their estate." Which amounted to a few million dollars, but he didn't say so.

"I'm really sorry," she said softly. "I can only imagine how hard that would have been for you. But at least you had somebody who loved you, J.C. A lot of people don't even have that."

"I know."

Her fingers tightened on his. "You're still living in the past," she said, her voice tender. "You can't do that. Life doesn't have a reset button."

He laughed shortly. "Tell me about it." He took a breath. "I lived in the Yukon Territory in Canada, but I was born in Montana. My folks were visiting a cousin who lived near Billings when Mom went into labor. So I have dual citizenship. When I was old enough, I joined the American Army," he added, skipping over much that had happened to him in between. "I served overseas, in Special Forces, which is where I met Ren and your brother."

"Were you in the Army a long time?" she asked.

"Somewhat."

So there were still secrets. He didn't trust her enough to tell her. But he'd told her things she was certain he hadn't shared with any other woman. It was flattering.

"Then there was her," he added coldly, and his fingers became bruising.

"Her?"

"Cecelia," he said through his teeth. "I was just out of basic training. I'd never been to a town larger than White-horse, up in the Yukon. Just a few thousand people, an isolated community," he added. "I wound up in New Jersey on liberty. I didn't smoke or drink, so I always had pocket money, even before I inherited my grandparents' estate. Cecelia knew one of the boys in my unit, and he said I was loaded. So she came looking for me."

"Oh, dear," she said, because she could guess where this was going.

"I didn't know that, of course. I thought it was an accidental meeting, when one of my friends in basic introduced me to her. I didn't know she'd arranged it." He stared straight ahead. "She was beautiful. The most beautiful human creature I'd ever seen. She was poised, sophisticated, talented." He grimaced. "I thought she was perfect. I fell head over heels in love the first night. She could turn me inside out. She was like a drug, an addiction. I'd never known so much pleasure."

She was jealous, but she didn't let on. She just listened.

He was lost in the past, drowning in misery. "We went around together for weeks. I took her to the opera, the theater, to symphony concerts. Even to a rock concert. I bought her designer clothing and diamonds. She really seemed to love me. I certainly loved her."

His fingers were hurting, but she didn't move, didn't speak.

"It was her birthday. I'd bought her a sapphire necklace she'd admired at a high-end jewelry store and I went to her apartment to give it to her. The door was open. She was talking to a male friend who was with her. She was talking about me, about how stupid and gullible I was, about how she'd scammed me into buying her all sorts of expensive presents. She thought it was hilarious. I didn't even have enough sophistication to realize that she was a call girl, that she sold her body for money."

"What a miserable human being," she said quietly.

He laughed. It had a hollow sound. "She was right. I was naive. But I grew up very suddenly. I opened the door and walked in. She was wearing a negligee, almost transparent, and her companion had on nothing except his underwear. I'll never forget the look on her face when she saw me and realized what I'd overheard. I didn't say a word. I turned around and walked out."

"Did she try to call you?" she wondered.

"She asked one of my friends to tell me she was sorry and that she'd like to start over. I told him where she could go, and how fast. I never saw her again."

"I really do live a sheltered life," she remarked after a minute. "I didn't know there were people like that in the world. I don't really understand greed. I've never felt it."

"I noticed that about you."

She smiled. "I like simple things. Flower gardens. Kittens. Just walking in the woods. Stuff like that. I've never liked diamonds or fancy jewelry, or fancy clothes. It's not me."

He loosened the tight grip of his fingers. They became caressing. "You're nothing like her."

"Thanks." She hesitated. "I think."

He laughed. "It was a compliment."

"Okay."

He glanced at her curiously. "I've never talked about her. Or about my parents."

"I never repeat anything I'm told. I work as a legal administrative assistant," she added. "Even though I just basically answer the phone and take dictation, I've been trained to keep my mouth shut. I guess it carries over to my private life."

"I guess." He smiled. "You're a good listener."

"Sometimes people just need to talk. That's what

Daddy says. He went to see a man who was suicidal. The man put down the gun he was holding and walked out of the room with Daddy. The place was surrounded with police, even a SWAT team. They all just gawked. They asked Daddy how he talked the man out of it, and he said he didn't say a word. He just listened. That was all the poor soul needed, somebody to just listen. He'd lost his wife and child in a wreck and he didn't think he could go on. He had nobody to talk to. So Daddy just listened."

"You listen, too, Colie. It's a bigger help than you realize." His mouth pulled to one side. "I don't have anyone of my own," he added quietly.

"Yes, you do," she said boldly, and curled her fingers around his, without looking at him.

He couldn't have imagined anyone getting a hold on his heart this quickly, but she'd managed it. She'd become the color in his life, in a space of only weeks. For her own sake, he should let her go. But he couldn't.

HE WALKED HER to her door. The porch light was on. There was still a light burning in her father's study. He'd be working on Sunday's sermon, she knew. He spent days putting just the right words together.

"Your dad's waiting up for you," he mused.

She laughed. "Not really. He works on his Sunday sermon a little every night, until he has it the way he wants it."

"He looks out for you, too, though." He touched her short, wavy hair. "I'll bet he's never taken a drink in his life," he said, with more bitterness than he realized.

"No," she agreed. "He doesn't drink or smoke. He says addictions are much too dangerous. It's better not to acquire them."

"He has a point." He bent and rested his forehead against hers. "I don't drink or smoke, either. Well, I have a beer occasionally. Never any hard liquor."

"I don't think I've ever tasted liquor," she confessed.

"Just as well." He bent and brushed his mouth gently over hers. "I enjoyed tonight."

"I did, too."

He drew back all too soon. He put his hands on her shoulders and just looked at her. "I'm going to be out of town for several days." His mouth pulled to one side. "Ren signed me up for a gadget convention—new toys for ranch security. I have to go."

"Where?"

"Just Denver," he said. "Not too far away. Stay out of trouble until I get back."

She laughed. Her eyes lit up when she did that. "Okay."

"Not that you ever get in trouble in the first place," he mused.

"I wouldn't dare," she said in a stage whisper, indicating the house behind her.

He smiled. "We might see a movie when I come back."

"There's that new science fiction one opening next week," she pointed out. They'd discussed it on the way to Lander.

"We'll go, then. See you."

"See you."

He walked away. She noticed that he never looked back. She wondered why. It seemed to be a long-standing habit.

She went inside and put up her coat and purse. She tapped on the door of her father's study and opened it.

He looked up from his notes. He smiled. "Did you have a good time?"

"I did. I won enough to catch up the bills." She grinned at his expression. "I know, it's sinful money. But it will be very useful for the electric bill." She struck a pose. "If it wasn't meant to happen, I'd have lost every penny."

He laughed. "All right. I won't say anything." He was looking at her intently. After a minute he turned his attention back to his notes. "Sleep good."

"You, too. Night."

She closed the door.

Her father was wise enough to notice that she hadn't indulged in any heavy petting with J.C. Such signs were quite visible. It gave him a little hope. J.C. might not turn out to be as bad an influence as he'd feared.

THE WEEK DRAGGED BY. Colie typed up briefs, printed them out, took dictation, scheduled clients, helped open mail and generally buried herself in work to keep J.C. out of her mind.

"You're daydreaming, girl," Lucy, her coworker teased. "It's that handsome man from the Yukon, isn't it?"

She didn't deny it. "Small towns," she laughed, shaking her head.

"Well, my cousin runs the filling station where J.C. buys gas and he mentioned he was going to Lander with a friend. Since he doesn't have any friends…" Lucy trailed off.

"He does so. He has me."

Lucy grinned at Colie's mischievous expression. "Anyway, we figured he was taking you over to the casino. Win much?"

"I won enough to pay the light bill," Colie said. "And get a few extra minutes a month on my phone. It was nice."

"I know what you mean. I had to give up bowling for two nights because I blew a tire and had to replace it," the other woman sighed. "Ben's so understanding. I ran over a piece of metal in the road. I wasn't paying attention. He didn't even blink. He just kissed me and said he was grateful that I didn't get hurt. That's what I call a nice husband."

"You two really are great together," Colie said. "You're the same kind of people. You come from similar backgrounds."

"And we've known each other since kindergarten," was the droll reply.

"Did you ever think of just living together?" Colie asked, trying not to sound as curious as she was. She was thinking ahead, in case J.C. ever brought it up.

"Not really," Lucy confided. "My dad's a pharmacist. Good luck trying to get birth control in Catelow without him finding out. Besides that, he's a deacon in your father's church. People around here are clannish, and they don't move with the times. Maybe we have couples who sneak around at night to motels over near Jackson Hole, but we really don't have many who just live together. They get married and raise kids."

"I'd love to have kids," Colie said softly. "I can't think of anything in the world I want more."

"So do Ben and I," Lucy said. "But we're just starting out. We figure we'll have a couple of years to grow together better before we start on a family."

"That's wise."

"We think so." She cocked her head. "What about you and J.C.?" she asked. "I'm not prying."

"I know." She hesitated. "I don't know, Lucy," she said honestly. "He's already said he's not the pipe-and-slippers type, and he doesn't really want children." She bit her lower lip. "You can't change people. You have to just accept them the way they are." Her face was drawn with pain. "I keep thinking, if I'd refused to go out with him…"

"It wouldn't have changed anything," Lucy said wisely. "People fall in love. I don't think they get a choice about who they fall in love with."

Colie laughed. "No. It's like your family. You don't get to choose them, either."

Lucy grimaced. "Your father would give you a real hard time if you tried to move in with J.C. To say nothing of the rest of the community. There's barely a thousand people who live in and around Catelow. You couldn't hide it."

"I've worried about that. I'd like to think I'd say no. But…"

"He might turn out to be conventional," Lucy ventured. "He knows how your father feels."

"It wouldn't matter. I don't think J.C. had much of a home life," she confided. "He was more or less orphaned in grammar school."

"That's tough."

"You mustn't repeat that," Colie said.

"You know me. I work for lawyers," she whispered, pointing down the hall. "They'd barbecue me on the front steps if I ever talked about what I know!"

"Same here," Colie said, laughing. The smile faded as she shuffled papers on her desk, across from Lucy's. "He doesn't know what it's like to have a settled, happy home. That might explain the way he is. He doesn't like attachments."

"He's obviously attached to you," her friend said.

"So far," Colie sighed. "I don't know how long it will last. We're very different."

"May I make a suggestion? Stop trying to control your life and just live it."

Colie drew in a long breath. "That's what I keep telling myself. Then I remember how Daddy looked when I said I was going out with J.C. and I feel guilty all over again. He reminded me that J.C. isn't a person of faith. In some circumstances, that can be a huge drawback."

"People compromise," Lucy said. "Ben and I have. You and J.C. will find a way to be together that works for both of you."

"I hope so." She lowered her eyes. "I can't give him up, Lucy," she whispered. "I love him too much, already."

"If you ever need to talk, I'm here. And I'm not judgmental," Lucy reminded her.

Colie smiled. "Thanks."

CHAPTER FOUR

COLIE HAD NOTICED that Rodney was acting oddly. He stayed out until all hours. Once, she was up getting a drink of water when he came in. His face was flushed and his eyes looked strange.

"Are you okay?" she asked worriedly.

"What? Okay? Sure, I'm okay," he replied. But he seemed foggy. "I've just had a long drive, all the way from Jackson Hole. I'm tired."

"You spend a lot of time over there lately," she pointed out.

He blinked. "Well, yes. There are some presentations on new gadgets and appliances and tools. I go to get familiar with them, for work."

He worked at the local hardware store as a clerk. She did wonder why a clerk would need to know about appliances, but perhaps that had become part of his duties. So she just smiled and took him at his word.

But the next day, he had company. Colie's father had gone to visit a member of his congregation who was at the hospital. It was Saturday, and Colie was working in the kitchen when the front door opened.

"Can you make us some coffee, sis?" Rod called from the doorway. "We've had a long drive. This is my friend, Barry Todd," he added, introducing a taciturn man in a gray suit. The man was impeccably groomed, but there was something disturbing about him. Colie, who often got vivid impressions about people, distrusted him on sight.

"Of course," she told her brother.

He and his friend went into the living room. She heard muffled conversation. It sounded like arguing. Rod raised his voice once, and the other man replied in a sharp, condescending tone.

Colie filled two mugs with coffee and started to take them in, but Rod met her at the door, thanked her and nudged the door closed behind him.

She went back to the kitchen, puzzled and uneasy.

LATER, WHEN THE visitor left, Colie asked about him, trying not to sound as suspicious as she felt.

"Barry's a salesman for a tool company," Rod told her, but he averted his eyes. "We do business together. He's opening up sales in this territory and I'm going to be his representative."

"Oh, I see," she said. "Like moonlighting."

He hesitated. "That's it," he agreed quickly. "Moonlighting."

"Your boss at the hardware store won't mind, will he?" She worried.

"Of course not," he huffed. "He doesn't tell me what to do on my own time."

"Your friend dresses nicely."

"Yes. He's loaded. Did you see the car he drives? It's a Mercedes!" He made a face. "All I've got is that old Ford. It looks shabby by comparison."

"Hey, it runs," she pointed out. "And it's worlds nicer than my truck!"

"Your truck belongs in a junkyard," he scoffed. "I'm amazed that they had the gall to actually sell it to you."

"Now, now, I can't walk to work," she teased.

He didn't smile. In the past, Rod had been happy and joking and fun to be around. More and more, he was short-tempered, impatient and morose.

"Are you okay?" she asked worriedly.

"I'm fine." He tugged at the neck of his polo shirt. "I'm just hot."

"It's cold in here," she began.

"You're always cold," he shot back. He turned away. He stopped and looked back at her. "You still going around with J.C.?"

"Sort of," she said, surprised. "We went over to the casino at Lander last week."

He laughed hollowly. "I'll bet Daddy loved that."

"He doesn't interfere."

His eyes narrowed. "J.C. won't settle down, you know."

"I know that, Rod." She studied him. "You and J.C. were close before you got out of the service. You don't spend much time with him now."

"We have different interests, that's all." His face hardened. "He's such a straight arrow," he muttered. "I guess it's his background."

"His background?" she probed, always interested in any tidbit of information about J.C. that she didn't already know.

"He was a policeman before he went into the armed services," he said. "Worked in Billings for a couple of years as a beat cop. They said he was hell on wife beaters. Almost put a man in the hospital. The guy had beaten his pregnant wife bloody and threw his toddler down the steps. Killed the little boy. J.C. did a number on him.

There weren't any charges. The guy attacked J.C. the minute he walked in the door with his partner. Bad move. He's a lot stronger than he looks."

"I can't imagine anyone bad enough to hurt a child," Colie said solemnly.

"The guy used," he said. "Idiot. You never take more than you need for a buzz. That's just stupid."

He was using terms she'd heard at work when her bosses dictated letters about drug cases they were defending.

"I don't know anything about drugs," she commented.

"Just as well," he told her. "What's for supper?" he added, changing the subject.

"Meat loaf and mashed potatoes. And I made a cherry pie."

He managed a smile. "Sounds good."

"I'll get busy."

He watched her walk away. He was uneasy. He didn't dare let anything slip that she might pick up on. If she found out what he was doing and told J.C., his friend would go to the authorities in a heartbeat, despite their years of friendship. J.C. had serious prejudices about people who used drugs. He was even worse about dealers.

COLIE WISHED SHE'D thought to give J.C. her cell phone number, or that she'd asked for his. She could have sent him text messages.

Then she caught herself. He didn't seem the type of person who did a lot of chatting. She'd had only one phone conversation with him, if you could call that. He'd called that time when he was invited to dinner, that first time that he'd asked her out. He'd said he was going to be a few minutes late. He'd said barely two words to her and hung up. That was the extent of their phone conversations.

She wished he'd called her, though. She'd have loved to hear the sound of his voice, even if it was only two or three words' worth. But he didn't call. And his two or three days turned into a week.

She knew he was still in Denver because her friend Lucy had a cousin who worked in retail, and he was also attending the gadget convention. He mentioned to Lucy that J.C. was chatting up a gorgeous platinum blonde and said maybe that was the reason he hadn't come home sooner.

Lucy told Colie when she persisted, but she hated doing it. Colie's face fell. It was what she'd expected to happen. She wasn't pretty or sophisticated. J.C. had even mentioned that the girl he fell in love with was like a supermodel in looks.

She was so depressed. She'd had all sorts of stupid dreams, about being with J.C. for the rest of her life, of changing his mind about having a home of his own and a family. Now those dreams were being changed into nightmares with platinum blonde hair.

IF SHE COULD have seen J.C., the depression would have lifted. As most gossip was, the bit about him and the blonde was blown all out of proportion. He'd been overseas with another man who trained local law enforcement in the Middle East during his vacations, an Apache man named Phillip Hunter who worked private security in Houston. Hunter's wife, Jennifer, was a geologist. She was so beautiful, even in her thirties and with two children, that she turned heads everywhere. It was Jennifer that J.C. had been talking to while Hunter went to talk to one of the vendors about an updated closed circuit camera system for Ritter Oil Corporation, where Hunter was head of security.

Jennifer was as conservative as her husband, and it would never have occurred to her to cheat on him. She was simply enjoying talking about her work to J.C., who knew something about the mining industry. Geology was an interest of his. When he was very young, his father was always bringing home unusual rocks from work. J.C. hated the memory of his father, but he'd always loved geology.

He missed Colie. He didn't want to. He knew that he could never give her the things she wanted. It was sad, because she was the kind of woman any man would be proud to call his own. But a family, kids…that wasn't him. He'd been on his own too long.

Maybe he was overthinking it. He should just take it one day at a time and not take life so seriously.

Phillip Hunter rejoined them, smiling. He was older than Jennifer, probably in his forties by now. He had silver at his temples and threads of silver in his thick, straight jet-black hair. But he was still as fit a man as any J.C. had ever seen. He kept in fighting trim. He and Jennifer had two children, a daughter, Nikki, and a son, Jason. They seemed perfectly happy together, for an old married couple. J.C., who had rarely seen a good marriage, was impressed. His foster parents had been like these two. Their deaths had been worse than a tragedy to him. He was only eleven when he lost them in the fire. That placed him in other foster homes, ones not as nice or welcoming or secure as the one he'd had. He had painful memories of those days, after the fire, memories he'd shared with no one. Not even with Colie.

"Are you going back over month after next?" Phillip asked J.C., meaning Iraq, where they both were involved in training courses. But while J.C. taught police procedure, Phillip taught private security.

"I am," J.C. replied. "I like the challenge."

"You like the risk," Jennifer chided, glancing at her husband with a grin. "Like someone else I know."

Phillip pulled her against him and kissed her hair. "I can't live without a little risk. You knew that when you married me, cover girl," he teased.

She pressed close with a sigh and closed her eyes. "Yes, I did. Warts and all, I can't imagine any other way of life. It's been wonderful."

"It has," her taciturn husband replied gently. The look they shared made J.C. uncomfortable. It spoke of a closeness he'd never known.

"I guess you're going to be a bachelor forever," Jennifer mused as she studied J.C.'s hard face.

"Looks like it." He sighed. He smiled. "I'm not domesticated."

Phillip chuckled. "Let's get something to eat. All these electronic gadgets remind me of stoves, and stoves remind me of wonderful meals," he added, winking at Jennifer.

"Lucky you, that I finally learned to boil water!" She laughed.

It was a private joke. She'd always been a great cook.

J.C. was impressed by the way they got along. He'd had lovers; never a woman he could tease or joke with, or just enjoy talking to. Then he thought of Colie, and how easy it was to talk to her. She made him feel warm inside, safe. These were new feelings, for a man who didn't court domestication.

He put it out of his mind. He didn't have to worry about Colie right now. And he was confident that she was his, if he wanted her. She wouldn't be looking at other men, any more than Jennifer Hunter was. If there was one thing he was certain of, it was that Colie belonged to him.

AT THAT VERY MOMENT, Colie was accepting a date with a visiting accountant who'd come to audit the books at the savings and loan company down the street from the law office where she worked.

His name was Ted Johnson, and he was from New Jersey. He was a pleasant man, just a few years older than Colie, and he'd been around the world. They met at the local hamburger place and struck up a conversation after he'd mistakenly been given part of her order. They laughed about it, sat down together and found a lot in common.

"I don't know the area very well," Ted told her, "but they say there's a fairly good theater here. Want to take in a movie with me? I'm only here for a couple of days, so I won't be proposing marriage tonight or anything," he joked. "Besides that, I'm doing my best to coax a woman at my office to go out with me. So this would be just friends."

"I have my own coaxing challenge, with a man who doesn't want to be domesticated." She sighed.

"Life is hard," he said. He grinned. "So we take in a movie and drown our sorrows in sodas and popcorn."

"Suits me!"

IT WAS A fun date. No pressure, no physical attraction, just two people having a good time together. When they got back home, Ted went inside with her and challenged her father to a game of chess, having seen the chessboard on the side table.

Her father was delighted to see Colie out with an acceptable, conventional man. Who knew where it might lead, he thought privately.

Ted trounced him. It only took a smattering of moves to checkmate the reverend.

"Sorry about that," Ted chuckled. "But I was chess champion of my fraternity in college. Probably should have mentioned that earlier," he added with a grin.

"Probably should have, young man," Reverend Thompson agreed with a smile. "You're very good. I enjoyed the challenge."

"If I'm ever back this way, I'll give you a rematch. I really enjoyed it, Colie," he added as he started for the door. "If I wasn't committed, I'd come back and go the whole deal—roses and chocolates and serenading."

"Thanks for the thought," she said, laughing.

He shrugged. "I'm disgustingly conventional."

"Convention is what keeps the world turning," Colie's father said quietly. "Fads and fancies don't last."

"True words. Well, see you!"

"See you." Colie shut the door and turned back to her father, who looked disappointed.

"He's got a girlfriend?" he asked her.

She nodded. "He's hoping she'll notice him. He's a very nice man."

"Yes, he is." He sighed. "Well, I should get back to work on my sermon."

"I'll clean up the kitchen and go to bed, I think," she said. "We're going to have a busy day tomorrow at work. Clients out the front door."

"Good for business," he remarked.

"Yes, very good," she agreed with a smile. "If they're busy, I have job security."

He smiled and went back to his study.

J.C. SLID HIS bag into his cabin and went up to the main house to tell Ren about the convention.

Merrie, Ren's wife, was carrying their son around in her arms, crooning to him. She grinned as J.C. walked in.

"Delsey and I made a pound cake. There's coffee, too, if you want some. I have to go sing Toby to sleep."

"He's grown, just since I've been away," J.C. remarked with a quiet smile.

"In no time, he'll be learning to drive and wrecking my car." Ren chuckled as he joined them. He kissed his son on the forehead and brushed his mouth over his wife's cheek.

She wrinkled her nose at him. "I won't be long."

Ren settled down at the kitchen table with J.C. Outside, snow was coming down in buckets.

"I've got the nighthawks working overtime with this weather," Ren remarked. "We're having to truck feed out to the northern pastures."

"No news there."

"What did you find that you liked at the gadget show?"

J.C. pulled out some brochures and went over them with his boss.

"I like this new facial recognition software," J.C. told him, indicating the statistics provided on the brochure. "If ours had been a little more sophisticated, we might have been saved a lot of trouble when that assassin was after Merrie," he added, alluding to a time when Merrie and her sister had been the targets of a determined contract killer, revenge for a life their criminal father had taken before his death.

"It would have helped. But he disabled some of our communications, as well," Ren remarked.

"I've put in redundant systems since then," the younger man replied. "It won't happen again."

Ren nodded. His black eyes narrowed. "What's the cost?"

J.C. told him. "It's expensive, but it can be updated and the vendor guarantees it for ten years."

"Cost-effective," Ren agreed. "Okay. Order it."

"I'll get right on it."

"Anything else look good?"

"Lots of stuff, but mostly robotics. I'm not a fan," he added quietly. "My phone is my best gadget, and I don't want to replace it."

"I like mine, too." Ren stared at his security chief. "What's this we hear about you and some blonde woman over in Denver?" he asked. "We thought you were going around with Colie."

J.C.'s eyes widened. "A blonde…? Oh!" He laughed. "I was talking to Phillip Hunter's wife. He's head of security for the Ritter Oil Corporation in Houston. She's a knockout. She has a master's degree in geology. It's an interest of mine."

"I see."

"Damn," J.C. muttered. "If the gossip got to you, it probably got to Colie, too," he added quietly.

"I wouldn't know about that." Ren sipped coffee. "But she's dating an accountant from New Jersey."

The cup jumped in J.C.'s hand and spilled coffee. He mopped it up with a gruff apology. Clumsiness in that steady hand was a dead giveaway.

Ren, amused, averted his eyes. Apparently J.C. was surprised that his girl would go out with someone else. "I guess she heard about the blonde, then," Ren said drily.

J.C. finished his coffee. "I'd better get to work."

"Willis has something he wants to talk to you about," Ren added. "He thinks we need some security cameras at the line cabins. We had a break-in while you were gone. Willis thinks it was just a trapper who got caught out in the storm. Nothing stolen, that we could tell. But there are televisions in those cabins."

"I'll check it out," J.C. said.

He was preoccupied as he went out the front door. Colie, dating another man. Did she think he wasn't serious about her, when she heard about the blonde? Because he knew Colie was crazy about him. She wouldn't have gone out with another man unless she thought there was no hope where J.C. was concerned. It must have hurt, even though he'd told her they had no future and he wasn't starting anything he couldn't finish. The blonde woman was truly ravishing, and that would have gotten around, too. Colie, with her low self-esteem, would think J.C. had dropped her because she wasn't pretty enough for him.

He hesitated when he was inside his SUV, watching snow pile up on the windshield before he cranked the engine and turned on the windshield wipers. It was a chance to draw back, to let her think he didn't care. It was an opportunity that might not come again. He could ignore her. He could let her believe he was seeing other women.

But it was a lie. There was only Colie in his life. There had never been a woman he could talk to, pour his heart out to. Not before Colie came along. Brief liaisons didn't encourage closeness. He took what was offered and moved on to the next woman. But Colie wouldn't be as disposable as the women who came and went in his life. She'd want commitment. He wasn't sure he could give her that, even briefly.

On the other hand, he hadn't looked at another woman since he'd been going around with Colie. He couldn't imagine one of his brassy dates taking her place. She was gentle and kind and giving. She roused him like no one else ever had.

He should stop it now, while he could. He'd be cheating her if he let things progress. Inevitably, he was going to end up in bed with her. Once that happened, he might not be able to let go. That frightened him. His poor mother had been trapped by her feelings, tied to a man who abused her, hurt her. He'd seen the dark side of love. He'd watched his mother die of it. Love was an illusion that led to tragedy. He wanted no part of it.

If he could take her and enjoy her without his emotions becoming involved, perhaps they could stay together for a while. It would cause friction with her father, but Colie was a grown woman. She didn't answer to anyone. He could enjoy what they had while it lasted and then move on, as he always did. He'd make sure Colie knew it wasn't forever that he was offering.

It didn't occur to him then that he was eaten alive with jealousy when he thought of his Colie with another man, or that someone who wasn't emotionally involved wouldn't be jealous in the first place.

COLIE WAS HAVING a quick meal at the local café when a tall, irritated man pulled out a chair and sat down beside her.

She caught her breath audibly.

"What's this about an accountant?" J.C. asked with a bite in his voice. His pale eyes were glittering like metal in sunlight.

She gaped at him with her coffee halfway to her mouth. She put it down and glared at him. "Oh, yeah? What's this about a glittery, beautiful blonde woman in Denver?" she countered right back.

He waited while a waitress took his order for a hamburger and fries and coffee. Then the laughter seeped out, drowning the anger.

"Jennifer Hunter," he told her. "She's married to Phillip Hunter, who's head of security for Ritter Oil Corporation in Houston. He teaches with me in Iraq, although in different areas," he said, watching her cheeks flush. "They have two kids."

The flush got worse. She averted her eyes to her plate.

"The accountant?" he prompted.

She moved one shoulder restlessly. "He's trying to impress a woman he works with. He just wanted company for a movie. He was very nice. Daddy liked him."

He nodded. His big hand slid over Colie's free one and linked into it. "I was jealous," he said, surprising himself, because he didn't want to admit that. It was like showing weakness.

"I was jealous, too, when I heard about the blonde," she confessed.

"Two idiots with insecurity issues," he murmured drily.

She looked up into his eyes and the whole planet shifted ten degrees. Her heart ran away with her.

"I missed you," he whispered huskily, his own heart racing as much as he tried to hide it.

"I missed you, too."

Around them, curious and amused faces were trying not to stare. Colie was loved by the community for her good works. J.C. was an object of curiosity, not really a local but accepted as one. The curiosity was benevolent, at least.

THEY FINISHED THE MEAL. J.C. caught up both tickets and paid them, then he led Colie out the door and over to his SUV.

"But I have to get back to work," she protested weakly when he drove out of town. "It's so close that I walked down to the café…"

"How much longer is your lunch hour?"

"Ten minutes," she said, staring at him.

"So, we'll have dessert and go back."

"Dessert?"

He pulled into a deserted parking lot next to the river that ran through Catelow, cut the engine and reached for Colie as if he was starving to death.

"Dessert," he whispered huskily as his mouth covered hers and burrowed hungrily into it.

Colie linked her arms around his neck and held on for dear life, making up with enthusiasm for what she lacked in experience.

J.C. wrapped her up tight and kissed her until her mouth felt bruised.

"I hate being away from you," he said against her swollen lips.

"I hate it, too," she managed, burying her face in his warm throat, in the opening of his shepherd's coat. She hit his chest. "You didn't even call me!"

"What could I have said? I'm lonely, I miss you, I wish

you were here? What good would that have done?" he asked against her ear.

"A lot," she said. "For one thing, I wouldn't have believed local gossip about the blonde!"

He chuckled. "I haven't looked at another woman since you've been haunting me," he told her. "You're everywhere I go, all the time. Even when I'm away."

Her arms tightened.

"I don't guess you could plead a sick headache and go home with me right now?" he asked in a tone that was joking, but also serious.

"I'd love to," she said. "But there's only me and Lucy and the office is full of people today."

"You and your sense of responsibility," he scoffed.

"You and yours," she shot back.

He lifted his head. His eyes were soft and tender as they searched her face. "I don't like talking on the phone," he said. "It's a long-standing prejudice."

"Rod said you were a policeman in Billings before you went into the service," she said.

He nodded. "Maybe that's why I don't like phones," he said. "There was usually tragedy on the other end of the line."

She smoothed over the hard line of his cheek with her fingers. "You're still doing it."

He caught the hand and kissed the palm. "Doing what?"

"Taking care of people," she said simply. "Except that now you're taking care of people on a ranch instead of people in a city."

He smiled. "I hadn't thought of it like that."

She smiled back. "I have to go."

"I know."

He kissed her again, but differently than he ever had. His lips barely touched hers, brushing, lifting…cherishing. When he lifted his head, there was a light in his eyes that she didn't remember seeing.

"Dinner tonight?" he asked when he let her out in front of the office.

"What time?"

"Six. That will give you time to fix something for Rod and your dad."

"Okay. Where are we going?"

He drew in a long breath. "Wherever you want to, honey," he said softly.

She blushed again. Her eyes twinkled. "Okay." She shut the door and ran into the office.

He watched her until she was out of sight before he pulled away. He was getting in way over his head, and it felt like walking into an abyss. He couldn't stop. He was going to hit bottom one day with her. It would damage both of them. But he still couldn't stop.

He drove back to the ranch, his mind anywhere but on his work.

COLIE PUT UP her coat and went to her desk. Her eyes were twinkling, full of joy.

"He came back," Lucy guessed.

She laughed. "The blonde is married to a friend of his. They have two kids."

"Oh, thank goodness," Lucy said. "I hated telling you what my cousin said. That's gossip. I'm ashamed of myself for passing it on."

"Don't be. Making up is so much fun," she confessed.

Lucy laughed. "Don't I know it!" She sat down at her desk. "I'm glad it worked out, Colie."

Colie picked up notes she was supposed to type for her boss. She grimaced. "I'm not sure it has, really. I mean, he was jealous, but that doesn't mean he's going to rush me to the first minister he can find." She glanced at Lucy with eyes gone sad. "I guess, in life, we take what happiness we can find. And then we pay for it."

Lucy frowned. "Stop sounding ominous," she chided.

Colie sighed. "My grandmother had these feelings. She could tell when someone was going to be hurt, when bad things were going to happen. I don't have the gift the way she did, but I really do feel the weight of sorrow in my life." She looked up. "J.C. and I are very different. I don't know if there's going to be any sort of happy ending."

"If you don't try, you'll never find out," came the reply.

"I suppose that's true." She glanced up as the door opened and four people walked in. She grimaced. "And we'd better get to work or we'll be out looking for a job!" she laughed under her breath as she got up to take the names of the newcomers and announce them to her boss.

CHAPTER FIVE

RODNEY SAT AT the kitchen table while Colie rushed around to fix a meal for him and her father. He was quiet and somber.

"You shouldn't get mixed up with J.C.," Rodney said out of the blue.

She glanced at him. "Why?"

"He's a loner."

"So am I," she pointed out.

His jaw set. "He's judgmental. You ever step out of line, do anything he doesn't like, and he'll walk right out of your life and never look back."

She paused as she mashed potatoes. "Is that what happened to you?" she asked.

He didn't answer.

"Rod?"

"I just mentioned that a friend of mine liked to smoke weed and I didn't see anything wrong with it," he said. "So, J.C. doesn't go around with me anymore."

Her heart jumped. "Rod, I do see something wrong with drugs," she told him. "I see the result of drug use every single day in my job. Families are destroyed by it. People die. It always starts with a gateway drug. Marijuana is the gateway."

"They should legalize it, then it wouldn't cause so much trouble."

"Didn't you hear a word I said?" she asked him. "Anything that distracts when you're driving, even an aspirin tablet, can cause a wreck! Imagine if drugs were legal and people could use them anytime they pleased. What a world that would be. A nightmare world."

"You've seen worst case scenarios," he scoffed. "A little mild drug use never hurt anybody."

She glared at him.

He glared back.

Their father walked into the kitchen. He'd been visiting members of the congregation. He sat down beside Rod. "Something smells good," he remarked.

"Steak and mashed potatoes. I'm feeding you two early because I'm going out with J.C." She glanced at her father as she said it, and her rigid expression added an emphasis to the statement. She wasn't going to argue, she was just going to do it.

The reverend just smiled sadly. "Okay," he said. "It's nice of you to cook for us. We could have had cold cuts. I wouldn't have minded."

"Me, neither," Rod said belatedly, and managed a smile for his sister. "You take such good care of us, sis. I don't know what we'd do without you."

"You'd manage," she said simply.

"We'd starve," Rod said, glancing at his father. "I can't boil water, and I remember painfully the one time you tried to make breakfast," he added.

The reverend grimaced. "Well, I trained at seminary, not cooking school," he said mildly. "I can at least make toast."

"If you scrape off the burned parts," Rod said behind a feigned cough.

Reverend Thompson chuckled. "I guess so."

"And there it is," Colie said, putting platters of food on the table, which was already set. "I have to get ready. J.C.'s picking me up at six. We're going to eat something I don't have to cook," she teased.

"Cook's night out," the reverend said, nodding as he picked up a fork. "You've certainly earned it. This is delicious, Colie."

"Thanks, Daddy." She dropped a kiss on his head and winked at Rod as she went to feed Big Tom before she went to her room to dress.

J.C. WAS PROMPT. Colie met him outside, sliding into her coat just before she climbed up into the SUV with his help.

"Running from trouble, are we?" he teased as he got in behind the wheel.

"Avoiding it," she replied. She laughed. "Rod and I had a little tiff before Daddy came home. Honestly, I don't know what's gotten into my brother lately. He's…weird."

He didn't reply. He pulled out into the main road and drove out toward the general direction of Ren's ranch.

"You've noticed it, too, but you don't want to say anything bad about your best friend," she said with sudden insight.

He glanced at her with raised eyebrows.

She shrugged. "I know, I'm weird. My grandmother had visions."

"So did mine," he replied.

"Did they come true?"

"Most have. One hasn't, at least, not yet." He glanced at her with a smile. "I told you about it, at the casino."

She nodded. "I told you about mine, too." She laughed

and made a mock shiver. "We come from strange people, I guess."

He reached for her hand and held it. "We come from gifted people," he corrected with a smile. "And I don't think you're strange."

"Thanks." She stared at him. "I just love to hear you talk," she confessed. "You have a voice like deep velvet, J.C. It's…well, sexy."

He chuckled. "That's a first."

"Oh, I see, women are too busy telling you how gorgeous you are, so they don't notice your voice."

"There's not that much talking."

She went quiet.

His hand contracted. "And that could have been better put. I didn't mean to hurt you."

"I knew you had women."

"Not anymore," he said suddenly. "Not since you came along. I told you that, and I meant it. I never lie."

She drew in a slow breath. The feel of his fingers curling into hers made her tingle all over. "I try not to lie. Well, I didn't tell Mrs. Joiner that the dress she was wearing was too tight and too short for a woman in her forties, or that you could see everything she had when she stood in the light. I guess that was lying by omission…"

He chuckled. "She goes to your church, I guess."

"She's the pianist," she replied, shaking her head. "She's not the sort of person to be brassy, but her cousin bought her a dress and she didn't want to hurt her feelings, so she wore it to church." She grimaced. "It was really sad. I didn't say anything, but the choir director did. Mrs. Joiner went home in tears. Daddy had to go smooth things over. He's good at that."

"He has a kind heart," J.C. said. "I respect him."

Colie wished her father felt like that about J.C. But she knew he didn't. He'd never approved of the relationship.

"Your father doesn't like me," he said, as if he'd read the thoughts so plain on her face.

"It isn't you. He knows you aren't a person of faith, and I am. He thinks, well, he thinks you're corrupting me."

"God knows, I'm trying to," J.C. shot back, and grinned at her.

She laughed. "At least you're honest." She looked around at the snowy, deserted countryside. "Can I ask where we're having dinner? In Denver, maybe?"

"I'm taking you home for venison stew."

Her heart jumped. "Home? Your home?"

He nodded. "It's a nice cabin. Two bedrooms, lots of space. I bought the land from Ren. I run a few head of purebred cattle. It's isolated and cozy. I've never had a home of my own until now. I'm rather proud of it."

"And venison stew?"

He nodded again. "I went hunting and got a seven-point buck. I keep the meat in a freezer locker in town at the deer processing place." He smiled. "My grandmother used to make venison stew, when I was small. She stayed with us in Whitehorse during the last winter my family was together. She taught me how to cook."

"I imagine she thought it would be a useful skill. Was she the one who had visions?"

"Yes."

"Are any of your grandparents still alive?"

"No. Most of them died relatively young."

"Mine, too. I'm sorry. I wish I'd had time to get to know them. My grandmother, the one who had feelings about things, was an herbalist. She could name every medicinal plant known to man and she knew how to process the plants. She kept us healthy. I was in grammar school when she died."

"My grandfather was an herbalist, too. Most of those old home remedies made their ways into pharmacies under different names."

"Yes, they did. Oh, J.C., this is beautiful!" she exclaimed when he pulled into a long driveway between lodgepole pines. The house sat in a backdrop of distant mountains, nestled in a thick forest. Lights burned in the windows and smoke came out of the chimney. With snow lying on the ground all around, it reminded her of a Christmas card she'd received one year. She kept the card for the cover.

"I think so, too," J.C. said, smiling. "I reinforced the walls and added insulation, so it's warm even when the temperature drops far below freezing."

It looked like an oversize log cabin. It had a long, wide front porch and there were two rocking chairs on it. There were empty planters. She wondered if he put flowers in them, in the spring.

Inside, the furniture was overstuffed and cozy, in earth colors. The curtains were a deep tan. Scattered around were blankets with patterns in them. There was a dream catcher against one wall, a bow and arrows in a buckskin quiver on another wall. Over the open fireplace, over the mantel, was a painting of a tall man standing surrounded by wolves in the snow. When she got closer, she saw that it was J.C. The portrait was masterful. It looked just like him, except that it radiated loneliness and sorrow, especially in the pale silver eyes.

"Wow." It was the only thing she could manage. The portrait literally turned the inner man outside.

"Revealing, isn't it?" he mused, hands in his pockets. "Merrie, Ren's wife, paints. She has a rare talent for capturing the real person. I had to be talked into it, too." He chuckled. "I wasn't sure I was ready to have my life spread out in public."

"It's not public," she pointed out. She studied him. "I imagine not many people ever get invited in here."

"Ren and Merrie came for venison stew, before their son was born," he remarked. "Willis and I play poker occasionally. He brings the wolf, who sits in the corner and growls every time I move," he added on a laugh.

"Willis? The foreman?" she asked, and he nodded. "He has a wolf?!"

"He has a wolf," he replied. "It has three legs. He's a licensed rehabilitator. The wolf couldn't be released back in the wild with a handicap like that, so Willis got to keep it. The damned thing sleeps with him," he added. "No wonder he's alone."

She grinned. "I like wolves. I've never seen one up close, but I've seen them in the distance. They're so big!"

"Very big. Dangerous in packs, when they're hunting."

"The wolf doesn't like you?"

"It's jealous of Willis. Man, woman, anybody. Well, anybody except Merrie," he amended, leading the way into the kitchen.

"Ren's wife," she recalled. "The one who paints."

"Yes. The wolf went right to her when she and Ren were visiting Willis's cabin, before they married. The wolf came up to her and laid its head in her lap. She has a way with animals."

"I wish I could have more pets," she said with a sigh. "Mama, when she was alive, fostered animals for the local shelter. I loved the variety. But Daddy says one big cat is enough."

He smiled slowly. "One the size of Big Tom really is enough."

She smiled back. "I was so shocked when you showed up at our house with Big Tom," she confessed. "It was unexpected."

"I know." He grinned. "I hadn't planned it. The cat just hung around all the time. I don't mind cats, but... Anyway, Rod said you had a birthday and you loved cats. It seemed the solution to two problems."

"He's a wonderful pet." She pursed her lips. "Daddy likes him even more since he caught a mouse in the kitchen," she added, laughing.

He laughed, too. "Does your father get along with the cat?"

"More or less. He's not really keen on animals, although he's never cruel to them. He loves people. I guess it's a trade-off."

"Rod isn't an animal lover, either," he said.

"No, he isn't. How do you know?"

"Something that happened when we were overseas when your brother was finishing up his tour of duty." He clammed up.

She wondered if it was something bad. Rod had a mean temper all of a sudden, and he was often out of control. He'd never been that way when he was younger. She felt cold inside suddenly.

He glanced at her as he brought the stew out of the refrigerator. "I spoke out of turn. I shouldn't have said that. Now you'll worry yourself to death."

"No, I won't. I know Rod has an awful temper," she added. "Mama got really angry at him once for doing something mean to one of the dogs she was keeping for the animal shelter. I never knew what, because neither of them would tell me what happened. But she died not too long afterward, and we had no more animals at home. Until you gave me Big Tom, at least."

"Some people are better kept away from animals," he said noncommittally. "I can make corn bread, if you'd like some to go with the stew."

"Oh, not for me," she said. "Stew's fine. I don't like to fill up at supper. It keeps me awake."

He laughed. "Everything keeps me awake. I'm good if I can manage five hours a night. Usually, it's a lot less. Hand me that saucepan, would you?" He nodded toward it with his head.

She handed it to him. It was a nonstick one, red in color. Very clean. "You keep an immaculate house," she noted.

"I try to. First thing you learn in the military is to keep your bunk clean," he chuckled. "Nobody wants to fail inspection."

"I'll bet terrible things happen if they do."

"Yes. Kitchen patrol," he added. "Peeling potatoes." He made a mock shiver.

"I love potatoes."

"I can do without them most of the time. I'll eat French fries, but I'm not keen on any other method of preparation."

She watched him heat up the stew. It smelled like heaven. When he put it on the table, she couldn't wait to dig in.

THEY ATE IN a comfortable silence.

"This is really good," she said in between bites. "I can make beef stew, but I'm afraid of venison."

"Why?" he asked curiously.

"Because it's hard to cook it right. It's a dry meat."

"It can be. My grandmother taught me how to get around that. But I also have a cookbook that belonged to my mother's mother," he added. "It has recipes from the turn of the twentieth century. God knows how far back in the family it went before it landed with my mother. It has recipes for all sorts of wild game."

"I'd love to see it."

"I'll show it to you. Not tonight," he added with a grin. "It's wrestling night."

Her eyebrows arched. "Wrestling?"

He nodded as he finished his stew. "WWE."

She just stared at him.

"Don't have a clue, do you?" he mused. "Ever heard of Dwayne Johnson?"

"Oh! He was the voice of Maui in that cartoon movie, *Moana*! I love him!"

"He started out as The Rock on WWE."

"He was a wrestler?" she exclaimed.

"Yes. So was his father. I miss seeing him in the ring, but I enjoy the movies just as much. He did one called *Race to Witch Mountain* that I watch over and over."

"I liked him in *Central Intelligence*." She beamed. "But I never knew he'd been a wrestler. I'll have to turn it on occasionally."

"It's a rough sport. People say it's all put on. But men get seriously damaged in the ring from time to time. So do women wrestlers."

"Now I'm really fascinated."

"Bring your coffee to the living room. It's almost time."

She watched him put the dishes in the sink and pick up his own coffee before she followed him to the sprawling, comfortable sofa with its soft upholstery and equally soft throw cushions.

"You said you didn't own a television," she reminded him as she sat down and put her coffee on the big wooden coffee table.

He chuckled. "I always tell people I don't. That way, I don't have to listen to people rave about talent competitions and reality shows."

"I know what you mean. We watch movies and this one television show on BBC. It's got the actor who played in *The Hobbit*. Well, the other actor was in *The Hobbit*, too, he was the voice of the dragon."

He glanced at her after he turned on the television and put it on the wrestling channel. "You don't mean *Sherlock*, do you?"

"Yes!"

He burst out laughing as he sat down beside her. "It's my favorite show. One of the very few I watch."

"Small world," she commented.

"Very small. Here. Curl up against me." He drew her across his lap and held her close, kissing her hair.

She sighed. It was like coming home, after being separated from him for almost a week. She laid her cheek on his broad chest and listened to his heart beat. He smelled of some spicy cologne that suited him.

He smoothed over her dark hair. "This is nice," he commented.

"Very nice," she sighed. "Much better than sitting at a restaurant listening to people argue."

"What?" he asked.

"I went out to eat with Rod and Daddy two weeks ago at the fish place. There was a couple having a vicious argument. It was so bad that the manager actually went to their table and told them to leave or he was calling the police. They argued all the way out the door, too."

"Pitiful lack of manners," he mused. "To say nothing of pride. Most people don't air their dirty linen in public."

"Tell that to the people on social media," she said, tongue in cheek. "Honestly, they talk about things I wouldn't even discuss with my mother, God rest her soul, if she was still alive."

"I don't do social media."

"Why am I not surprised?" she asked, looking up at him with a wide grin.

He searched her eyes slowly. She felt soft and warm against him. She smelled of roses. He traced around her mouth with his fingertip and listened to her breathing change.

"You're winding yourself around me like ivy," he whispered. "You're always with me, even when you aren't."

"I know," she said on a shaky breath. "It's like that with me, too." She reached up and traced his hard mouth. "I feel so cold and empty when you're not somewhere close by."

He bent and drew his nose against hers, nuzzling it. "I won't make promises, Colie," he said huskily. "No matter what happens."

"I know."

He bent his head and drew his mouth slowly over her parting lips, loving their softness, the instant response that she gave him. She went in headfirst. He didn't, usually. But he had less control with her than he'd had with a woman since the call girl turned his life and his pride inside out. He wanted her the second he touched her.

He turned her so that her hips were pressed intimately

against his. Even through two layers of denim, his arousal was stark and noticeable. She should have protested. But all she could think about was how wonderful it felt to be close to him, to be wanted by him. She'd never known what desire was, before. Now it tormented her night and day. She stayed awake at night imagining all sorts of erotic things that she wanted to do with him.

She arched when she felt his hand sliding under the hem of her pullover blouse. Her lips parted on a shock of breath that he felt going into his mouth. But she wasn't protesting. If anything, the jerky twisting of her body told him that she wanted much more than just his hands on her back.

He deepened the kiss as his fingers unfastened the simple cotton bra she wore. He felt her hesitate. But seconds later, when he traced around her bare breast and teased the nipple until it went hard, she shivered and just lay against him, letting him do whatever he wanted.

His hands went to the snaps that held his shirt in place. He unfastened it to his belt and pulled it out of his jeans, inviting her hands into the thick wedge of hair that covered warm, hard muscle.

She'd never touched a man so intimately. It was intoxicating, like the feel of his big hands on her breasts. She'd never imagined that she could be this uninhibited with anyone.

And J.C., who seemed so self-contained and controlled, was quickly running out of self-control. She felt his breathing go quick, his heartbeat rough in the silence that was broken by the murmur of voices on the television and the heightened breathing that accompanied growing passion between the two people on the sofa.

He turned her under him, his mouth going suddenly to cover one soft, pert little breast.

He was shocked when she caught his head in her hands and pushed it away. Her eyes were wide and full of fear.

"What is it?" he asked, looking down to appreciate the soft pink flesh with its hard mauve peaks.

"S-sorry, it just sort of surprised me," she whispered.

"I won't bite you," he teased huskily. "I only want to draw you into my mouth and taste you," he added as he bent again. "God, this is sweet!"

She stopped protesting. She hadn't known quite what to expect, but this was far different from her expectations of intimacy. His mouth was warm and slow and hungry. He suckled her and she came off the sofa, desire washing over her in a hot tide of oblivion.

"Oh...gosh!" she bit off, arching up and shuddering.

"Baby," he whispered unsteadily as he eased down over her. "Baby, I want you so much! Feel me...!"

He was between her jean-clad legs, and all she could manage was a faint hesitation. She wanted him. Her body burned. She ached all over.

There was just an instant when she could have drawn away, stopped him. But his fingers unfastened the zipper down the front of her jeans and slid inside, under her cotton briefs, to a place no man had ever touched.

She shuddered as he teased her body, incited her to recklessness. In her passion, she bit him on the shoulder, hard, as the need exploded in her like fireworks.

"Oh, God...!"

He picked her up and carried her to the bed. He kissed all the way down her body, carrying her clothing away bit by bit, piece by piece, until she was totally nude. She didn't care. The air felt good on her body. She was so hot. So hungry. She needed...more.

He managed to undress himself in between intimate touches. She'd been reluctant until tonight. He wasn't going to give her a chance to refuse him. He'd die if he had to let her go. His body was throbbing with its anguished need. It had been a long time since he'd had a woman. He'd never wanted anyone the way he wanted Colie right now.

It was a miracle that he was able to fumble something to use out of the bedside table. He didn't usually keep the necessary item there. He got it in place between kisses that grew hotter and deeper by the second.

He felt her hesitate, but he imagined he was going too fast. He tried to slow down, to his credit. He kissed the inside of her thighs, feeling her arch and cry out at the intensity of erotic ardor he was showing her.

He touched her intimately, feeling her response. She was ready for him. Odd, how tight she felt. But he was too far gone to worry about that. He knew he was rushing her. But it would be all right.

He went into her quickly, containing her faint cry of shock, one big hand under her hips, lifting her to the thrust of his body.

"Oh, baby, it's so sweet," he ground out against her mouth. "Never this sweet, never with anyone!"

She heard the words, but through layers of pain. Was it supposed to hurt this much? She'd read books, but they weren't explicit enough. She tried not to fight him. Surely it would stop hurting. She did want him. It was her first time. Did he know?

She wanted to tell him, but she was afraid. She knew he expected her to be experienced. He'd said as much in

one of their earlier conversations. He'd be livid if he knew
the truth. He'd probably throw her right out of his life.

So she took a deep breath and let him have her. He
cried out with the pleasure. She was happy that her body
was giving him so much joy, she only wished she could
share it. But she felt torn and uncomfortable.

At least it didn't take a long time, she wasn't sure she
could have managed not to start crying.

He drew away from her and fell onto his back, letting
out a rough, shuddering sigh. "I thought I was going to
die, it was so good," he whispered roughly. He dragged
her against him, wrapped her up in his arms. He kissed
her eyelids, closing them. "Thank you," he added huskily. "I know you weren't ready for me. I'm sorry. I'll
make it up to you."

"It's all right," she said, hiding her discomfort. It was
heaven to have him hold her like this, to be tender with
her. It was like a narcotic. She closed her eyes and curled
closer. "I love being with you like this," she whispered
huskily.

His arm contracted around her. He didn't say it, but
he felt it. There was a connection between them that he'd
never experienced. His women were sophisticated. They
demanded, instructed. This one loved anything he did to
her. It made him feel a foot taller.

But it worried him that he'd lost control with her. She
needed more time, and now he was wasted. She probably realized that. Some men could go all night, but he
couldn't.

"Next time," he whispered, "we'll go slow. I promise."

Her heart jumped. So he wasn't disappointed with her
lack of response. She felt relief and guilt, and disappointment, all at once. Guilty, because good girls didn't do

what she'd just done. Relief that he still wanted her. Disappointment because there wasn't any pleasure, beyond foreplay. Was that what sex was really like? A buildup to a big letdown? She was far too shy to talk to him about it. And there was nobody else she could talk to. Maybe there were books...

"You're very quiet," he remarked, kissing the top of her head.

"I'm happy," she said softly.

So was he. In fact, he'd never felt more at peace. He rolled over and brushed his mouth over her face, her eyelids, her nose, her soft, swollen mouth.

"I should take you home," he whispered. "You can have the bathroom first."

"Thanks."

She was grateful that the room was dark. Apparently he wasn't one of those people who liked the lights on. She wasn't, either. It was embarrassing now that the hot passion was gone, to be nude with him.

She dashed into the bathroom and closed the door. There was blood. Not a lot, but enough that she knew why it had been uncomfortable. Wasn't there a barrier to be gotten through the first time? That was probably why it had hurt. Maybe next time it wouldn't.

She cleaned herself up and dressed. When she got back in the bedroom, he was dressed. The lights were on. He looked uncomfortable.

"I'll drive you home before I shower," he said. He hesitated, took her by both shoulders and grimaced. "You should have told me, Colie."

Her heart raced. So he did know that she was innocent...!

"If I'd known your period was starting, I would have waited," he added. "I'm sorry."

She felt relief and something else, something worrying. Maybe he didn't care about being the first. It would be better not to tell him. Not now.

She forced a smile. "I'll tell you next time," she promised.

He bent and kissed her tenderly. "Sweet girl," he whispered. "I've never enjoyed anything as much as tonight."

"Me, too," she lied, pressing close. Well, she had enjoyed the tenderness. It was just the other part that was uncomfortable. Maybe she could get used to it.

"Let's go."

He helped her down from the SUV and stood with her for a minute before he spoke.

"There's a new cartoon movie playing downtown," he remarked. "Since we're going to be best friends for a few days, we might as well pig out on the cinema," he added with a grin.

She laughed. "I'd like that very much."

"Me, too. I'll call you." He dropped a light kiss on her lips and went back to the SUV. He left without a wave or a backward look. Same as always.

Colie hesitated before she opened the door. She hoped that what she'd done didn't show. She felt such guilt. Her father would be disappointed in her. It would prove what he'd already said, that J.C. was corrupting her.

On the other hand, she could keep it from showing. And J.C.'s assumption gave her a defense.

She went inside, bending over slightly and groaning as she hung her purse beside the door.

"Colie?" her father asked gently, approaching from the kitchen with a cup of black coffee. "Are you all right?"

She grimaced. "Cramps," she said huskily. "I need to lie down."

"You poor kid," he sympathized. "Got something to take for it?"

She nodded. "My usual over-the-counter stuff. It works. But I'm going to bed."

"How was the meal?"

She didn't turn. She laughed. "He can cook," she said. "He took me home for venison stew. It was wonderful. He said his grandmother taught him to make it."

"Venison stew," her father sighed. "I remember the taste of it myself."

"Good night, Daddy."

"Good night, sweetheart."

She made it to her room without him noticing that her life had taken a new route. She got clean pajamas and underwear out of her drawer and went straight to the shower. She could still smell J.C.'s cologne on her. At least she'd managed to keep her distance so that her father wouldn't notice. But, then, he'd just assume that she'd kissed her boyfriend, not that she'd been intimate with him.

It was the first of many white lies she was going to have to invent if she kept seeing J.C., and she couldn't stop. She was more in love than ever. Whatever happened, she couldn't give him up. Not even if her conscience flayed her nightly.

CHAPTER SIX

COLIE FELT DIFFERENT, more mature, more in step with the world. Now, when she watched movies on television or entertainment news and she heard about couples living together, it didn't shock her. In fact, she envied them. She wanted to be near J.C. all the time.

Since they'd been intimate, it was almost an obsession, to be with him. Even if she just heard him on the phone and he said only one or two words. Apparently he felt the same way, because he met her for lunch just about every day and they went to movies all the time.

Then, a week after they'd been intimate, J.C. grew insistent when he took her home with him for steak and potatoes, the only other dish he could cook well.

Colie was nervous about it, because it had been so uncomfortable the first time. But she knew that if she started drawing back, J.C. would leave. She was certain of it. He liked her, of course, but more than that, he was hungry for a woman. She didn't have any illusions that he wouldn't stray if she refused him.

So she didn't refuse him.

As he'd promised, he took longer with her. But her body, still recovering from the shock and pain of the first time, was uncooperative. She loved the foreplay. He was very skilled, and she enjoyed the feel of his mouth on her bare skin, the touch of his hands intimate on her.

She gave every indication that she was enjoying it as much as he was.

That was, until he penetrated her. She ground her teeth together and tried to relax, but it was almost as uncomfortable as it had been the first time.

J.C. didn't notice. He was starving for her. It had been a week of agony, while he tried to occupy his mind and keep it off the delicious hour he'd spent in bed with Colie. Now, here she was, soft and warm and eager, and he went over the edge almost at once. He tried to slow down. He couldn't. It had been a long time between women. His body was totally out of control.

He shuddered and cried out, the pleasure biting into him so hard that he thought he might pass out. She was still tight. He wondered why. She didn't respond, or demand, as his other women had. She did whatever he wanted her to do. But he felt guilty, because he knew she wasn't feeling the same pleasure he felt when he took her.

He lay beside her, calming slowly, his big hand tender in her hair as he held her beside him.

She didn't like sex. She was certain of it now. But she loved J.C. Being close to him like this, having him be tender with her, was so wonderful that she accepted whatever he wanted to do to her, for the closeness.

An old adage came to her as she lay against him. Men gave love to get sex, and women gave sex to get love. It had never seemed as appropriate as it did right now.

"I hate being away from you," he said out of the blue. "Even at night. Especially at night. I want you here, all the time."

She caught her breath. "You do?"

His arm contracted in the soft darkness of the room. "Don't you want to be with me all the time?" he asked.

"Of course I do."

He drew in a long breath. "Your father isn't going to like it," he said curtly.

"It's my life," she began.

"Yes, it is. But choices have consequences." He hesitated. "Colie, I'm not proposing marriage. You understand that, don't you? I'm asking you to live with me. That's all. And I'm not promising anything."

She felt sadness all the way to her bones, but it was no use protesting. She loved him so much that she was willing to give up everything just to be with him. She knew that if their situations were reversed, he wouldn't give up anything for her. He didn't love her.

But if she lived with him, if she took the gamble, it might pay off. Look at how she'd won on the slot machines at the casino. If life was like that, she might get lucky. It was a pipe dream, but she wanted J.C. too much to refuse.

"I'd like that," she said simply.

He let out the breath he'd been holding. "We'll take turns cooking," he promised. "And in case you wondered, there won't be other women. I'll never cheat on you."

She laughed. "I believe you, about the blonde geologist."

He chuckled. "I know. I'm just making the statement."

"Thanks."

He kissed her damp hair. "I'm going too fast with you, in bed," he confessed. "I'm sorry. It's been a long time since I've been with anyone. It will get better," he added. "I promise it will. I'll learn to slow down, to wait for you. I want you to feel as much pleasure as I do. You give me the moon, Colie. I've never known such satisfaction."

She smiled. "I'm glad." She nuzzled closer. "You don't have to worry about me. I love the closeness. I love lying with you like this. It would be more than enough for me, even without the other."

That statement really worried him. She was as much as admitting that he didn't satisfy her. He was going to work at his self-control. He hated cheating her.

"It will be get better," he said again.

She just sighed and closed her eyes. "Okay."

He smoothed over her bare back with his fingertips. He was frowning, although she couldn't see it, in the darkness. He'd never known a woman who was so giving, so forgiving, so sweet and gentle. She was tender with him. His whole experience of women was with wildcats who didn't want foreplay, didn't want tenderness, they just wanted raw, carnal sex.

Colie was so different from them. Even the call girl, when she was fooling him, trying to play the innocent, had been demanding and hungry in bed. He was certain that Colie wasn't totally naive, but she did give the impression of a woman who didn't like sex. He hoped he could change her mind, make her feel what he did. It would just take time, he told himself. He could learn to slow down.

Unaware of his worrying thoughts, Colie nuzzled closer and enjoyed the feeling of oneness she got with him. She was going to live with him, be with him all the time.

Her heart fell. Her father wouldn't rage and yell, nothing like that. But he'd be so disappointed in her. That was going to be the hardest thing of all. She'd toed the line her whole life. He'd blame J.C. for her downfall, when it was going to be her decision as much as his.

IN FACT, HER father said nothing. He'd known for some time how things were going.

"I said it before, but I'll repeat it," he said softly when her bags were packed and she was waiting for J.C. on the front porch. "I'll always love you. Whatever happens, I'll be right here if you need me."

She hugged him. "I'm sorry," she whispered, fighting tears. "I can't help it. I love him so much. Maybe he'll change."

The reverend, who'd heard too many sad tales that began like this and ended in misery, just sighed. "You can never tell," he added.

He went back inside when he heard J.C. drive up.

J.C. helped Colie into the SUV and put her luggage in the back. He got in beside her, noting the traces of tears. He felt guilt all the way to his soul.

"Maybe this isn't such a good idea," he began.

She looked up at him. "I love you," she said simply. And the pain and sweetness of it was in the sad, resigned smile she gave him.

He pulled her close for a minute. He was sure he'd never had a woman say those words to him, in his whole life. Only his mother ever had. His sweet, kind little mother who'd gone through hell with an alcoholic husband who resented her and her child for taking away his dreams of being a rancher.

"I'll take care of you," he said quietly.

"I'll take care of you, too, J.C.," she said, and felt joy like a living thing, flowing through her veins.

That, too, was new. He laughed as he started the truck. "I don't really need taking care of," he confided. "I never will!"

A WEEK LATER, burning with fever and so sick that he couldn't hold his head up, he had cause to remember that brash statement.

Colie sat with him, bathed the sweat away, ladled the antibiotic and cough syrup the doctor had given him into him and ignored his weak protests that he didn't need nursing.

She knew he was lying. He looked at her as if she was Florence Nightingale, adoring her with those pale, glittery silver eyes as she fussed over him, fed him hot soup, made sure he had anything he needed to make him comfortable.

He'd rarely ever been sick in his life. He only remembered having a virus once, and his mother and father had left him at home, because the household depended on both paychecks just to keep going.

To be fair, his mother sat up with him at night, even so, feeding him chips of ice so that he didn't get dehydrated. But it was nothing like this, with Colie caring for him so tenderly that he didn't want to rush to get well again.

That was a weakness. He was ashamed of himself. Not too ashamed, though. It felt very good to have someone love him. No woman ever had, until Colie came along. He'd never thought of himself as a lovable person. She made him feel different inside, of worth. She built him up.

"I should be taking care of myself," he protested, just once, while she fed him soup.

She smiled. "You're so self-sufficient, J.C. It makes me feel good to do things for you. Even if it's just rarely."

He managed a laugh. "Ivy," he accused. "You're wrapping around me like ivy."

"Be careful," she said with a mock taunt. "Ivy can even bring down big trees if it wraps around too tight."

He sighed. "Not a worry. Not right now, anyway." He studied her. "Have you gone to the health clinic yet?"

She flushed. They'd had this discussion about birth control. He said that what he used was risky. He wasn't confident about the shot they gave women to prevent children; a fellow worker on Ren's ranch had seen it cause terrible weight gain in his own wife. But the pill had been around for years and years.

"I'll go when you're better," she promised.

"We've had one slip already," he reminded her. His protection had torn. It had worried him, although she wasn't showing any symptoms of pregnancy. He knew what they were, because Merrie had given birth a few months ago. He and Ren were friends, so he was around her a lot while she was carrying their son.

"I know. But it wasn't a good time to get pregnant," she lied. She was very regular and it was dead center between periods; the very best time to get pregnant. She understood he didn't want children. She wanted his child so much. She had this stupid, persistent hope that if she did get pregnant, he might change his mind about a lot of things.

He read that thought in her face. "Colie, I won't change my mind," he said forcefully; at least, as forcefully as a sick man could sound. "I don't want to settle down. I like training cops overseas. I might get a yen to go back in the military or join a merc group. I'll only stay with you as long as I'm free to go where I please. I won't settle down. And there's no way in hell you're getting pregnant. Give it up."

She drew in a wistful breath. "Hope springs eternal?" she ventured.

"It will get strangled, here," he promised.

"Okay," she said. "I'll go to the health department next week. It won't matter," she added. "You're too sick to do anything right now, anyway."

He was. He didn't like admitting it.

He studied her quietly while she fed him. She still wasn't getting anything out of intimacy. She tried to fake it, but he knew. She was uncomfortable, tight, strung out, every single time. He wanted her to go on birth control because he had a feeling what he used for protection was the problem. She'd complained of a rash, and he knew it wasn't a disease he'd given her—unless another lover before him had given her something. But he didn't think it was disease. She might have an allergy.

"Colie, have you ever been tested for a latex allergy?" he asked out loud.

The spoon jumped in her hand. Fortunately, it was empty at the time. "A latex allergy? You mean, like rubber gloves?"

"I mean like the rubber things I use to keep you from getting pregnant," he said starkly.

She just stared at him. That had never occurred to her. She had a rash every time he made love to her.

"I, well, I never was tested for any sort of allergy. I do break out every time…" She flushed.

"It would explain a few things," he remarked. "Next week. For sure."

"Okay."

"Don't you have a family physician?"

The flush got worse. "J.C., he goes to my dad's church. In fact, he sings in the choir. I…couldn't."

He really hadn't considered how living with him was damaging her, and her father, in the small community. He'd lived in big cities for a long time, so long that modern attitudes had become commonplace to him. It was different in Catelow. And her father was a minister. He preached against what he considered immorality—like two people living together without the sanctity of marriage. He hated the sudden guilt he felt.

"The health department is fine. Really," he said.

She nodded and fed him more soup.

SHE GOT A prescription for the pill, which she was to start at the beginning of her next period. She had J.C. drive her to Jackson Hole to get it filled, where there would be a pharmacist who didn't know her.

"I'm sorry," she said when they were on the way back home.

"I understand." He caught her hand tight in his. "I really do, Colie."

"I guess I don't understand things as well as I would, if I were older."

"Older," he scoffed. "What are you? Twenty-two, twenty-three? Rod mentioned that you'd graduated from school last year. I assumed he meant college…"

"I'm nineteen," she said starkly.

He stood on the brakes and stopped in the middle of the road. "What?"

"I'm nineteen," she repeated, wondering why he looked so devastated. "I graduated from high school last year. The graduation was in the papers, I thought Rod would have mentioned it to you?"

"He said you graduated." He was trying to catch his breath. No wonder her father had been so protective of her, so distant with J.C. She was barely out of high school. A teenager! Why hadn't he realized…?

"Now you're going to torture yourself because you

think you're robbing the cradle. Listen, I'll be twenty in a month," she pointed out. "Lots of girls get married at eighteen." She flushed. "I mean, live with people. Other people."

"Dear God."

"J.C.," she began, worried because of the look on his face.

He started the SUV moving again. He felt such guilt that it was choking him. Why hadn't he known? Well, he lived on the ranch and he didn't go into town much. He didn't read the local paper or listen to the news, he didn't go to church. He knew Rod, but they'd grown distant in the past few months since Rod mustered out of the military. He hadn't known much about Rod's little sister until he went to supper at their house. She worked at a law office and she'd mentioned taking courses in business.

"You took business courses," he mentioned, thinking out loud.

"Sure. Just after I got the job with the law firm. I went at night. I only needed a couple of courses, just enough to help me learn the software they used and how to cope with dictation and stuff."

"Nineteen."

"Twenty next month," she repeated. "I don't understand why you're so conflicted, J.C. I'm not a child."

"Colie, I'm thirty-two."

"Oh, yes, and you've got gray hair and you have to walk with a cane..."

"I'm serious!" he shot back, more forcefully than he meant to. He grimaced when he saw her hurt expression. He caught her hand again and held it tight. "Almost thirteen years between us. At your age, that's a lot. I wish I'd known how old you were, before..."

"But you didn't. You don't. I love you, you silly man," she chided. "What has that got to do with age?"

The words went through him like sugary sweet joy. He loved hearing her say it. But it didn't assuage the guilt he felt. "No wonder your father didn't like me."

"Daddy wouldn't have liked you if I'd been thirty," she pointed out. "You're not a person of faith. I can accept that. He can't. He has a different view of life than I do. Daddy lives in the past, J.C. It's a new world."

"New." He drew in a long breath. He glanced at her hungrily and knew that he'd die before he'd give her up, no matter her age. "Twenty next month, huh?"

She grinned. "Twenty next month. I'll try to get at least four or five gray hairs started, if that will help your conscience."

He laughed at the blunt statement. "Okay. We'll muddle through somehow."

"That's the spirit!"

THEY WERE STILL using the same thing for birth control that they'd started out with. They had to, because she couldn't start the pill until her period. She told J.C.

"You're not enjoying this," he pointed out when they were lying together. He was sated. She wasn't.

"I love being with you, any way at all," she said. "You're the most perfect man who ever lived, and I love you madly."

"But you don't enjoy having sex with me," he persisted worriedly.

"When I start on the pill, it will change," she promised, hoping it wasn't going to be a lie. She was uncomfortable when he went into her. She wasn't sure the lack of latex was going to solve the problem.

His fingers tangled in her hair. "Maybe I need to read a few books."

She burst out laughing. "Maybe I do, too."

SHE WAS JUST leaving the café after lunch. J.C. had gone to Jackson Hole to get some new equipment he'd ordered, so she was eating alone. She came face-to-face with old Mrs. Meyer, one of the elders of her father's church.

"Hi, Mrs. Meyer," Colie said with a smile.

The woman didn't return the smile. She looked at Colie as if she was dirty. "Have you no pride?" she asked quietly. "Have you no shame? Your father is a minister. He stands in the pulpit and preaches morality while his own daughter lives openly with a man in this small community."

Colie flushed. "I love him…"

"I married at twenty," Mrs. Meyer went on. "He was a good, kind man. He said that any man who truly loved a woman would want to give her his name, give her children, become a part of the community." Her dark eyes narrowed. "Your lover gives nothing to the community. He never goes to church. He's an outsider who doesn't want to fit in. You used to be a person of faith. What's become of you, Colie? Your mother, God rest her soul, would be ashamed of you!"

Before Colie could even think of a lukewarm comeback, the old woman turned and toddled away, leaning heavily on her cane.

Colie went back to work and went through the motions, but she was eaten up with guilt. She'd felt it often enough, but to have one of her father's congregation speak to her like that brought home just how much she was shaming Reverend Thompson with her behavior.

"What's wrong?" Lucy asked gently as they were getting ready to leave. "You've been unsettled all afternoon."

"My father is a minister and I'm living with a man," she said quietly. "I didn't realize how much I was shaming him." She looked up. "We make decisions and never consider how our actions will affect the people we love."

Lucy drew in a breath. "Everything we do affects everybody who loves us, I guess," she said. "I'm sorry. I can only imagine how conflicted you are."

"Conflicted," she replied, "is a very good word."

LATER, J.C. SAW the emotional upset and questioned her about it.

"It was Mrs. Meyer. She's an elder in our church…" she hesitated. She hadn't been to church since she moved in with J.C., another strike against her. "In Daddy's church," she amended. "She said that my behavior was shameful, that my father was having to live down what I was doing. He's a minister, preaching against immorality, and his only daughter is living openly in sin." She laughed hollowly, trying to make a joke of it.

J.C. winced. She was so young. He gave a thought to her father, who'd never yelled at him or cursed him when he certainly must have felt like it. He was a forgiving man; something J.C. never had been. He held grudges. A few, he held for life.

He took her into his arms and rocked her. "I'm sorry. I've never had to consider public opinion. But Catelow is a very small town. I'm sure it's hard for your father to understand that not everybody follows a narrow path."

"I guess so."

He held her tighter. He knew he was going to regret

this, but he valued Colie. He didn't want her hurt. "You can tell people we're engaged," he said after a minute.

She drew back and looked up at him with soft, worshipping green eyes. "What did you say?"

"I said, you can tell people we're engaged. It will keep gossip down, maybe," he added. His face hardened. "I'm still not interested in marriage, Colie. But if you spread it around that I'm serious about you, it will make things easier for your father. He's a good man," he added heavily. "I don't like hurting him any more than you do. But I am what I am. I've never seen a good marriage," he added shortly. "I grew up more or less an orphan from the age of eleven. A settled, happy home is an illusion to me. It's not real."

She searched his pale eyes and saw such pain there that she grimaced. "I had a happy one," she said softly. "A mother who loved us, who took care of us, who loved my father deeply. He loved her. We had little tiffs now and again. Everyone does. But we loved each other. It was a happy childhood."

His face hardened even more. "We come from different worlds, different backgrounds," he said. "Part of my ancestry is First Nations—Blackfoot. My father practiced his native religion until my mother died. She was buried under Catholic rites, because she was Roman Catholic. I've never been a person of faith. She took me to Mass every Sunday, but most of the foster homes where I lived were anything but religious."

There was something dark and cold in his eyes as he said that. She wondered if there had been an even worse experience than his mother dying because his father was drinking and got behind the wheel of a car.

He held up a hand when she opened her mouth to ask. "I don't talk about my childhood. That's private."

Private. When they were living together, sleeping together. He was shutting her out. She realized belatedly that he almost never talked about his past, about any of his likes or dislikes. She knew so little about him.

"My life is an open book," she mused. "Yours is a mystery novel."

He laughed shortly. "Not bad."

She hugged him. "It doesn't matter. Nothing matters, except that I love you more than anyone in the world."

It made him glow inside when she said that. He ate it up like honey. He held her close and kissed her hungrily.

"I have to go to Iraq next week," he said at her ear.

"So soon?" she wailed.

"I'm sorry. I made a commitment months ago. I can't cancel at this late date." He smoothed back her hair. "When I come home, you'll be on the pill and I'll make sure you feel what I feel when we're intimate. Missing each other will make the homecoming explosively passionate."

She laughed. "I like that. Explosively passionate."

He kissed her again. "I think the latex is the problem."

"We could not use it…?"

"No." He let her go. "I'm not taking any chances with you, Colie. You know that already."

She sighed. "I know it."

"You need to stay with your father and Rod while I'm gone," he added quietly. His thick eyebrows met. "I'd worry myself sick if you stayed out here alone. It's too deserted. We get all sorts of people on the ranch, part-timers and visitors alike. We do vet them, but there's always that one who slips between the cracks." He framed her face in his hands and studied her hungrily. "I couldn't bear it if something happened to you. All the color would go out of the world."

It was as close to a declaration of love as he'd ever come and she realized it. She reached up and kissed him so tenderly that he felt his heart run wild. He drew her close and deepened the kiss to intimacy.

"I'll stay at home while you're gone," she promised.

He swung her up in his arms. "Meanwhile," he whispered, "we can make some more memories…"

Latex and all, she was thinking, but she gave in, as she always did, dreading the discomfort but loving the exquisite closeness. In bed was the only place she was ever allowed that close. J.C. was standoffish, aloof, quiet when they were around other people. In private, he was passionate and tender and almost loving.

She enjoyed the intimacy, even if she didn't enjoy the sex. Maybe he was right, she pondered. Maybe the pill would make all the difference, even though he'd be overseas when she started it. Nevertheless, he'd come home again.

SHE WORRIED. SHE COULDN'T hide it. He packed and she watched, her heart in her eyes.

"It's dangerous, where you're going," she pointed out.

He chuckled. "It's dangerous where I am," he countered. He glanced at her. "Ever try to hold down a bull in a field while you're treating an injury?"

"Well, I know that," she said. "But bulls don't have guns."

He stopped what he was doing, pulled her up and kissed her softly. "I've been at this for a long time. I don't take chances, and I know the people I'm working with.

Yes, there are risks. But there are risks when you drive a car, walk up a hill. Life doesn't come with guarantees. I live every single day as if it were my last day on earth. That's how I get through it. Yesterday is a memory and tomorrow is a hope. All we really have is today."

She thought about that. "I guess that's so. And on my today, you're leaving."

He kissed her nose. "Only for a few weeks. When I come back, we'll have a long, slow, sweet celebration. How about that?"

She grinned. "Okay."

"I'm going to miss Christmas," he said suddenly, scowling.

"You can bring me back a cactus or something," she said.

He chuckled. "I'll manage something better than that, I promise."

"Just bring yourself back," she said solemnly. "Because there's nothing I want for Christmas more than you. Okay?"

He hugged her close, feeling as if he was empty inside as he contemplated weeks without her. "Okay," he whispered. "I'll miss you, sweet girl."

"Not nearly as much as I'll miss you," she whispered back.

He kissed her with what felt like desperation. She kissed him back the same way. She had a horrible, cold feeling that everything was about to change. And not for the better.

CHAPTER SEVEN

GOSSIP HAD DIED down in Catelow since Colie made it known that she and J.C. were engaged. Even if it was a lie, it gave her a little relief from the censure.

Her father knew better. He accepted what she told him, but his eyes said that he didn't believe a word of it.

He was so happy to have her back home that he didn't question anything.

"It's been lonely without you, Colie," he said when she'd unpacked her few things and was puttering around the kitchen. "Rod's gone so much lately that it's like I live alone."

"And I haven't visited, either," she replied. "I'm sorry. We get so wrapped up in our own lives that we just don't think." She turned to him. "I'm sorry that I've made things hard for you in Catelow, Daddy," she added. "I didn't even realize how bad it was until Mrs. Meyer spoke to me."

"I didn't put her up to it," he said.

"I know that. But she was right. I didn't consider how it would be for you."

"Life is hard," he pointed out. "We make choices and then we have to live with them. Some have more consequences than others."

She nodded slowly and went back to her chores.

"How long will he be gone?" her father asked.

"A few weeks, he said." She gnawed her lip. "It's dangerous work. He makes a lot of money, but he earns it."

"I know two men in our congregation who have done the same thing, in the past. It's a fairly secure area," he said to comfort her. "I'm sure he'll be fine."

She managed a weak smile. "Sure he will."

"Is he going to marry you, Colie?" he asked quietly.

She drew in a long, slow breath and studied the sponge in her hand. She was wiping the stove top with it. "I'd like to think so," she said after a minute. "But I don't really know. J.C.'s deep. He doesn't share much."

"Maybe you'll influence him."

She laughed. "That's a pipe dream, Daddy. He is what he is." She turned. "But I love him. So I…deal with it. It's not the way I want things. It's the way they are."

He nodded. He still hoped that one day she might see the light and leave J.C. He knew it was a long shot. Years ago he'd loved like that. He'd loved Colie's mother. But he'd married her, had children with her. He'd never lived a less than moral life. He sorrowed for his child, because he knew better than she did what was likely going to be the result of her liaison with J.C. He wasn't a man who wanted ties, and he wasn't going to settle down. Colie would likely learn that the hard way. But her father would be there for her, when it happened. And he'd do all he could to help her. That was what life was all about. Not being judgmental, even in his position, and trying to ease the pain of loss and love for those to whom he ministered. It was his job. He took it very seriously.

MISSING J.C. SUDDENLY became the least of Colie's problems. She got up as usual and made breakfast before she dressed and went to work. But soon after she cleared the table and went to her room to dress, she had to make a mad dash for the bathroom.

She lost her breakfast and what felt like supper last night, as well. It was a virus. It had to be a virus. J.C. would go crazy if she got pregnant. She'd never see him again. He'd walk right out of her life. He'd insinuated as much many times.

It couldn't be a baby. Not when they'd only messed up one time. Just one time. She took deep breaths before she cleaned up and brushed her teeth. Surely it was just a virus. There was one going around. She'd heard her father mention it. Everything would be all right. She just had to keep her head and not panic.

She went back down the hall, dressed, her hair brushed, her purse over her shoulder. She reached for her coat and popped her head into her father's study. "I'm on my way out. Need anything else?"

"No, thanks. Breakfast was great," he added on a chuckle. "I am really very tired of black toast."

"I'll make biscuits tomorrow morning. See you tonight."

"Drive carefully. Lots of snow out this morning."

"I'll go slow," she promised. She might have added that J.C. had given her lessons on how to drive in snow. She didn't. Things were going nicely without that.

SHE'D HOPED SHE might hear from J.C. She knew he had a phone with overseas capability. But he hated to talk on the phone. Still, he might miss her enough to call.

He didn't call. Days went by without a word from him. Colie missed him so much that it was like having a limb removed. She ate without tasting anything. The nausea, thankfully, had passed. There were some odd symptoms.

She was tired a lot. She went to bed earlier than ever. Her breasts were tender. But her period was due, and some of those symptoms went with the monthly curse. She had to think positively.

She put up a Christmas tree and decorated it. She didn't have much money to buy presents, but she did the best she could. There was a sweater for her father, a new wallet for Rod and part of a keychain for J.C. It was in the shape of a heart, but two halves. The inscription was in French. It said *Plus que hier, moins que demain.* More than yesterday, less than tomorrow. A promise of love. The keychain was in two parts, one for each lover. Colie's parents had carried such a keychain when Colie and Rod were small. Perhaps she thought it might work some magic on J.C.

SHE RAN INTO Merrie Colter in town. Merrie had left the baby with Ren long enough to go Christmas shopping. Catelow was dressed in colored lights and tinsel for the holiday. Merrie was just getting into her car when she saw Colie on the sidewalk.

"Hi," she called.

"Hi!" Colie grinned from ear to ear. "You're without the baby? My gosh! It's the end of the world!"

Merrie laughed good-naturedly. "Ren's babysitting while I get some shopping done and buy something special to cook for supper. It's Delsey's night off. How are you?" she added.

Colie grimaced. "Missing J.C.," she said honestly. "It's lonely."

"I know how that feels," Merrie said. "Ren and I had a rocky courtship. He was a horror when I first met him."

"That's what people said," she replied.

Merrie cocked her head. "You're wondering if we've heard from J.C."

Colie caught her breath.

"Sorry," Merrie said. "I get these strange insights from time to time. But it's common sense. I'd miss Ren, if he'd gone overseas."

"It wouldn't be so bad if he'd write or call," Colie confessed. "I guess it's hard for him to find time to do those things."

Merrie didn't dare admit that J.C. had called the house twice already to talk to Ren about things he'd had the men start setting up at the ranch.

"I imagine it is," was all Merrie would say. "Anyway, he won't be gone that long. Honest, the ranch would fall apart without him."

Colie laughed. "So would my life," she confessed.

"Men. You can't live with them sometimes and you can't live without them. I guess we just take the good with the bad and go on."

"Sometimes that's all you can do," Colie agreed. "I have to run. I'll be late back from lunch."

"See you."

"See you."

COLIE WAS DEPRESSED after she'd seen Merrie. She knew, somehow, that J.C. had talked to Ren since he left. It made her feel sick to her stomach. If J.C. had really cared about her, he'd have called. He'd have written. He'd be as desperate to talk to Colie as she was to talk to him.

But he was self-contained. Aloof. He didn't get involved with people. He didn't trust them. She knew that if she ever gave him a reason, she'd never see him again. He held grudges and never made a secret of it. He wouldn't talk about his father, who was presumably still alive somewhere. He didn't forgive, even after twenty-two years. It was disturbing.

He did want her. She knew that for certain. But wanting wasn't enough to hold a couple together for years and years. Desire was a fleeting thing, easily satisfied and then lost. She was afraid that J.C. would tire of her. She could tell he wasn't happy with the way she was in bed. He knew she didn't get much out of sleeping with him. Maybe he was right about the latex thing. But it was uncomfortable beyond that.

Perhaps if she'd leveled with him at the beginning, told him her age and that she was innocent, things might have gone in a different direction. He might not have taken her out at all. She'd had a major crush on him, but once they started dating, she fell in love, fell hard and deep.

Life had been uncomplicated. She'd gone to work, to business classes at the local community college at night, she'd cooked and cleaned for her father and Rod. Her life had been vaguely satisfying, if stale and boring.

J.C. had changed all that. He'd made every day an adventure. She looked forward to getting up in the morning because she knew she'd see him most days.

Not that he'd been around a lot. He'd gone on that trip to Denver that had almost caused them to break up. Now he was gone to Iraq to train policemen. It seemed sometimes that they'd been apart more than they'd been together.

She sensed that J.C. had been trying to draw back from her before things got too serious. He worried about her. He couldn't hide it. He was surprised and pleased at the way she'd taken care of him when he was sick. He didn't like being dependent on anyone, especially a woman.

Was that what made him get cold feet? Or was it just that he was determined to stay single, and he resented Colie for wanting things he couldn't give her?

SHE WAS NO closer to an answer on Christmas Eve, when the nausea returned. Her period was almost a month overdue. She was regular. She never missed it by even a day. The fatigue was growing, as well.

She'd hoped that J.C. would call her on Christmas Eve. He knew how special Christmas was to her. But, as her father often said, J.C. was a man who avoided religion. Merrie Colter phoned her to say that Ren pulled strings to get a call through to J.C. There had been a communications blackout, so J.C. hadn't been able to call out. Ren, with his military connections, managed to get through. J.C. had asked him to have Merrie call and wish Colie a Merry Christmas from him, and to tell Colie that he missed her and would be home soon.

It made her day. She beamed all through making the special meal for her and her father. Rod had phoned and made a jerky apology about not being able to make it home because of car trouble. Even that didn't spoil her mood. She was glowing. J.C. missed her. It would be all right. All her worries had been for nothing.

She drove to a nearby town and bought a pregnancy test. She went to a local shopping mall and used the test in a stall in the ladies' restroom.

When the little paper changed color, she felt her heart freeze in her chest. It could be a false positive, of course. But with her other symptoms, she was certain that it wasn't. She was pregnant.

Her first reaction was overwhelming joy. She'd never felt so happy in her entire life. Her second reaction was stark terror. She couldn't have a child out of wedlock in Catelow, Wyoming. It would destroy her father's ministry. Well, maybe not destroy, but it would shame and humiliate him. He was such a good man. It would hurt him even more than she'd already hurt him.

There was a slight chance that J.C. might actually change his mind, despite what he'd said about not wanting to settle down. Surely, if he knew there was going to be a child, his sense of responsibility would kick in. Surely, he'd do the right thing!

She convinced herself that it was just a matter of putting it to J.C. the right way. She'd make him a wonderful supper when he got back from overseas. She'd make him comfortable, curl up in his arms. And then she'd tell him, gently. He was a good man. He wouldn't throw her away because of an unplanned pregnancy.

She put the pregnancy test in the trash can and went home.

KEEPING IT SECRET was going to be the hard thing. Her father knew how pregnant women behaved. He'd been through two pregnancies with Colie's mother. She was careful to eat just enough of Christmas dinner not to arouse suspicion, and she made sure she had the water running in the sink when she threw up, so he wouldn't hear.

He took her word that cramps were making her so sick that she went to bed early. He didn't question her. He was proud of his new sweater. He'd given Colie a bathrobe, a nice white chenille one that was very soft. Rod hadn't come home for Christmas. He'd called to wish them a happy day, but hung up almost immediately.

She was grateful that Rod was hardly ever home. But

he wouldn't have noticed that she was pregnant, anyway. He was acting more and more erratically. She was beginning to think he was mixed up in something very dangerous. He hardly spoke a word to his father and sister at the supper table on the rare times when he ate with them, and he was always going to Jackson Hole on the weekends.

Colie and her father celebrated the new year together with glasses of eggnog. Her father was sad that his son hadn't even called this time. He went to bed with his steps dragging. Colie was sorry, but there was nothing she could do about her brother. She only wondered why he was acting so strangely.

COLIE HAD STARTED going back to church with her father. It helped her fit back into the community that had started to shun her. People of faith were big on forgiveness, and Colie was loved.

But one Sunday morning in January, she was too sick to go. She pleaded an overnight stomach virus and apologized, but her father just patted her on the back and smiled. He'd had three members of his congregation out with it already. She'd be over it in no time.

She saw him off and then went back to bed.

SHE WAS DOZING when she heard cars drive up outside. The front door opened and closed. She heard voices.

Curious, she got up and pulled on a thick robe before she went into the living room. What she saw shocked her so badly that she couldn't even speak.

Rodney was taking possession of a suitcase absolutely packed with drugs. There were bottles and bottles of prescription drugs and several packets of what looked like white powder.

"You know how to distribute it," his friend in the smart suit told him. "Make sure your contacts hand it out free at the local schools, that gets them hooked... What the hell?!"

He'd glanced toward the doorway and saw Colie standing there, white-faced and shocked. Rod's mouth fell open.

"You take care of that," he told Rod. "Do it right now! One word of this gets out, you're a dead man, you hear me?!"

He went out the door and slammed it behind him.

Rod glared at Colie. "What the hell are you doing home?" he demanded. "You're never here on Sunday!"

"I got a virus," she said. "Oh, Rod, what are you doing?" she wailed. "Dealing drugs?"

He looked guilty and sick for a minute, then he glared harder. "You're one to talk," he shot back. "Living with a man, and Daddy a minister!"

"I love J.C.," she said defensively.

"He'll never marry you," he returned icily. He laughed coldly. "Daddy doesn't suspect, but I'd bet money that's no virus that's keeping you home. You're pregnant."

She gasped and went pale.

He'd been guessing. Apparently he was right. He lifted his chin. "You keep what you saw to yourself, or I'll make you sorry. I'm making a lot of money. I'm sick of working for chicken feed when I can have nice things like my buddy does. I'm going to have whatever I want..."

"You're poisoning children!"

"If they get hooked, it's their own business, not yours," he said. "They're not kids, they're teenagers."

"People die from drug use," she persisted.

"It's not your business," he repeated.

He closed up the suitcase. "You keep your mouth shut, or I'll make you pay for it. Don't even think of going to the sheriff!"

"I don't have to go to the sheriff," she said coldly. "All I have to do is tell J.C."

As threats went, it was masterful. He knew J.C. better than Colie did. He had no desire to end up in federal prison for dealing hard narcotics.

"You'd better not, Colie. I mean it."

"Will you stop right now? Give that—" she indicated the suitcase "—back to that son of the devil you're going around with!"

"Not on your life," he retorted.

She lifted her chin. She didn't say another word.

She didn't have to. Rodney knew what it meant. He turned away. He was going to have to stop her. He wasn't going to prison or the mortuary because his baby sister suddenly developed morals again. He knew exactly what he was going to do.

J.C. SENT COLIE a message by Ren, who had Merrie call her.

"He said to tell you he's coming back Sunday," Merrie said, laughing at the delight in Colie's voice. "No, he doesn't want you to meet him, he's got his SUV at the airport in Jackson Hole. He said if you wanted to come over and fix supper for both of you, he'd be delighted. It's going to be a long flight and he'll be hungry."

"I'll make something wonderful," Colie said dreamily.

Merrie smiled to herself. "I think what he really wants is to see you. Food would be nice, but Ren said J.C. talked about you every time he called. He wanted to make sure you were staying at your father's place, and that you were okay."

"I wish he'd called me," Colie sighed.

"He hates talking on the phone," Merrie said. "He told Ren he never knew what to say and he hated trying to put his thoughts into words over a long-distance line. He said he'd say them in person when he saw you. He missed you," she added. "Ren thought it was hilarious, although he didn't tell J.C. Neither of us ever imagined we'd see J.C. Calhoun go crazy over a woman."

"Is he? Crazy over me, I mean?" Colie asked huskily.

"From what we see, yes, he certainly is. He's just been sold out too many times to trust people easily, Colie. That's all it is. He'll learn to trust you, in time."

"I'll never let him down," she promised. "Oh, gosh, I have to get busy! It's Saturday. He'll be home tomorrow! I'll go crazy waiting!"

"Anticipation is nice," Merrie said demurely. "It leads to amazing memories."

Colie laughed. "I'm anticipating that," she confessed. "Thanks so much for calling me!"

"You're more than welcome. We'll be waiting to hear how things work out. I'm sure we'll have exciting news in the near future," she added drily.

"I hope so!"

HER FATHER WAS sitting at the kitchen table, finishing supper. Rod was there, glowering at Colie.

"Well, what lit a fire in you?" her father asked amusedly.

"J.C. will be home tomorrow!" she said excitedly. "He's flying into Jackson Hole tomorrow afternoon. I have to go make supper for him. I'm so happy!"

Her father hid his misgivings quickly. "I'm happy for

you. Just put out cold cuts for us tomorrow night," he added. "Save you a little time."

She kissed his cheek. "Thanks, Daddy."

Rod didn't say anything. He kept his eyes down. He was having an epiphany. He knew exactly what he was going to do now.

After supper, he even smiled at Colie as he went into his room, took out his cell phone and made a call.

COLIE HAD MADE roast beef and a potato casserole and English peas, with a cherry pie for dessert. She'd shopped for the ingredients and taken them to J.C.'s place, using the key he'd given her when they first moved in together.

She was so excited that she almost burned the potatoes. She couldn't wait to see J.C. again. It had been almost two months, two long and lonely months without him. She put a hand on her flat stomach. It was far too soon to even feel a rising there, but she knew there was a baby. Her symptoms were such that she couldn't have mistaken them, even without the positive pregnancy test she'd used. Pretty soon she'd have to see a doctor. If J.C. didn't want to marry her, she could see a doctor at the health department and swear him to secrecy. What she'd do about hiding her condition was a puzzle, but she'd work something out. Surely, there would be a way.

But she might be worrying for nothing. Once J.C. knew, if he'd missed her as much as Merrie said he had, there might not be any need to worry at all.

SHE WAS ON pins and needles as darkness fell. The snow had melted somewhat, but it was still in the shady areas of the property, shining, glowing, in the moonlight. It gave the cabin's surroundings a fairy-tale look. She hoped her personal fairy tale would have a happy ending.

She punched up cushions and watched the news, but still J.C. didn't come. It was almost nine o'clock, and she'd just reheated the meal again when she finally heard his SUV drive up outside.

Odd how he slammed the door of the vehicle. He didn't usually. She heard his footsteps on the porch. The door opened abruptly. And there he was, shepherd's coat, boots, jeans and all.

She started to run to him until she saw his face close enough to recognize the furious temper he was in.

"H-hi, J.C.," she began uneasily.

His jaw was clenched so hard that it looked as if his teeth were in danger of breaking. His pale gray eyes were glittering like hot sun on a gun barrel.

"What's wrong?" she said, moving a step closer.

"You tell me," he replied icily. His eyes went homing to her stomach.

He knew! How did he know? She hadn't told anyone!

Her hands went protectively to her belly. She felt sick all over. "I haven't said anything…!"

"When were you going to tell me?" he asked, lifting his face to sniff the air. "After a home-cooked meal and some passionate sex?" he added. He laughed coldly. "Not that you'd know passion if it sat on you, you little icicle."

The joy drained out of her all at once. "Who told you?" she asked sadly.

"Your brother."

"Rod?" She was trying to think. He'd made threats. He knew about the baby… "When did you hear from him?" she asked.

"He met me at the airport, with the father of that child you're carrying," he said in a voice as cold as the grave.

Her lips parted on a shocked breath. "What?"

"He brought your boyfriend Barry with him. Rod said he was absolutely disgusted with the way you'd behaved. It hurt him that you'd two-time his best friend with another man. It hurt even more that you were willing to pass the child off as mine, because your boyfriend didn't have as much money as I did."

"What…boyfriend?" she exclaimed. "I don't have a boyfriend!"

"Give it up," he shot back. "You're busted, Colie," he added. "I was sick of you, anyway," he said as he headed toward the bedroom. "You never did anything in bed except lie there like a plastic doll. You never wanted me. You couldn't even pretend that you did. I guess your boyfriend was better in bed, even if he was poor. Rod said you couldn't keep your hands off him, even in front of your father."

She started after him, shocked, sickened, absolutely bereft of words.

He pulled her things out of drawers and stuffed them into the big duffel bag she'd left there. He shoved her trinkets and the photo of her mother and father and Rod into the bag with them.

"What are you doing?" she asked.

"What does it look like?"

He finished, very efficiently, and zipped up the bag. He carried it out through the living room to the front porch and slid it toward the steps.

"Do you have your cell phone?" he asked with icy politeness.

"Yes. In my pocket…"

"Good. You can call your father to come get you. Goodbye, Colie. I'm sorry I wasn't quite gullible enough to make it work out for you."

"He lied," she managed through tight lips and tears.

"Sure he did." He looked her up and down with eyes that hated her. "I almost fell for it. Sweet, gentle Colie who loved me more than anyone in the world and just wanted to live with me and take care of me. What a line!"

"I meant it."

He wasn't moved by her white face or the hot tears rolling silently down her cheeks. "Just for the books, I wouldn't have married you, even if that child had been mine," he added. "I told you. I love my freedom."

She just looked at him, so wounded that she couldn't even manage a defense.

He was still glaring at her. "Maybe you'll have better luck with your new lover."

It was cold. She had on a thin jacket. She hadn't expected to need anything warmer. Her truck wouldn't start, so she'd called a cab to bring her here. It had been warm inside the cab and she'd imagined she'd stay with J.C. once he was home. She hadn't counted on being put outside like this. It was freezing.

"Women," he finished with pure venom. "Two-timing prostitutes, the lot of you! I thought you were different. I really did. But you were just out for what you could get, like all the others."

Her gaze fell to the porch. *Please, God, don't let me faint at his feet*, she pleaded silently.

Her silence made him even angrier. "How long did you wait to crawl into his bed?" he demanded. "Did you even wait until I was out of the country? Or was it going on before, when I was in Denver? You said you'd dated another man, was it really him and not some out-of-town accountant?"

"I told you the truth," was all she said.

"What would you know about the truth, Colie?" he asked. "Did you have to grit your teeth every time you slept with me? You never gave anything back. I had to do it all. And you made me feel inadequate, every time. It got to the point that I hated even touching you!"

She swallowed, hard. She could have told him why, but he wasn't listening.

"I hope it goes without saying that I never want to see you again," he said finally. "If I see you in town, I'll look right through you. I won't speak. From this day forward, you don't exist for me."

She drew in a breath. She was so sick that she hardly even felt the cold.

"Go home," he said coldly. He went back inside and slammed the door, enraged that he couldn't make her apologize.

She opened her cell phone a minute later and called her father.

"Can you drive over to J.C.'s house and get me, Daddy?" she asked in a haunted whisper.

He knew immediately what was wrong. "I'll be right there, honey." He hung up.

She started crying. The wind cut through her like a knife. She didn't care. Her life was over.

THE REVEREND DROVE her home and made hot chocolate for her. Then he just sat and let her talk. She told him that Rodney had gone to J.C. with a lie that broke them up, but not what it was.

He caught his breath. "Rodney did this to you? But, why?" he asked, aghast.

"You can ask him," she said. "I won't carry tales."

"I don't understand why he'd lie to his best friend about something so important," Reverend Thompson persisted. "This isn't right, Colie. I'll call J.C. myself…"

"No!"

He hesitated.

She laid her hand over his on the table. "He was looking for an excuse to get rid of me, Daddy," she said sadly. "He said so. He was tired of me."

He grimaced.

"There's something more," she continued, shamed and sick at heart. "I'm…pregnant, Daddy."

He groaned out loud.

Tears rained down her face in a silent torrent. "I'm so sorry!" she sobbed. "I've ruined my life and your life, because I was in love. I thought he loved me. I thought…" She swallowed down nausea. "I've been such a fool. I'm so sorry!" she repeated.

He got up and pulled her into his arms, rocking her as he had when she was little and someone had hurt her.

"We'll manage," he said. "Don't you give it a thought. We'll manage!"

"It's so shameful," she wept.

"It's a baby," he said softly. "Babies aren't shameful."

"It doesn't have a father," she reminded him.

"It has a mother," he retorted. "You'll be a wonderful mother. The very best!"

That made her feel worse. She'd expected censure, anger. But he was kind and caring and loving. Just as he'd always been. She realized that she didn't really know her father at all. What she'd taken for disapproval was his knowledge of how things were going to turn out, his sorrow for her. He'd known, as she hadn't, how it was going to end. But he loved her just the same. She wailed.

"You get a good night's sleep," he told her when the crying stopped. "In the morning, we'll talk and make decisions. Meanwhile, I'm going to have a very long talk with my son!"

"It won't do any good," she said quietly. "He's mixed up with bad people, Daddy. It would be better if you didn't say anything about this to him."

"Colie…"

"Promise me," she said. She knew what her brother was doing. If her father pushed him too hard, found out what was going on, he'd put himself in danger. She didn't want that. Rodney wasn't the son her father remembered. He was a stranger now.

"What do you know, Colie?" he asked.

"Things I'll never say. Not now." It was true. She'd have told J.C., and he'd have handled it. But J.C. would never believe her now. He'd taken Rodney's word over hers, knowing that Rod couldn't tell the truth if his life depended on it. There was no going back now.

"All right, then," the reverend replied. "I'll let it drop. Things usually work out."

"Usually." She didn't believe it, but it was easier to agree. "Thanks for not being mad at me."

"You're my daughter. I love you. I may not approve of what you've done, but that doesn't mean I'll turn away from you, ever."

She smiled and hugged him again. "Thanks, Daddy. Good night."

"Good night. Try to get some rest." He hesitated.

"Colie, it might be as well if you called in sick tomorrow. We're going to need to discuss a few things."

She nodded. "I'll do that."

CHAPTER EIGHT

A NEW SECURITY hire was supposed to meet with J.C. to discuss his duties. But J.C. never showed up at the line cabin where the man was assigned. Ren was concerned enough to go looking for him. J.C. was punctual, always.

He knocked on the door of the cabin. Merrie said that Colie had gone last night to cook supper for J.C., so possibly they'd had a very long and passionate reunion and J.C. had slept late.

He was disabused of that suspicion when the other man finally struggled to answer the front door.

It was a J.C. that Ren had never seen before. His clothes were rumpled, as if he'd slept in them. He had a day's growth of beard. His eyes were red and bloodshot, and he absolutely reeked of whiskey. That alone was alarming. J.C. never drank hard liquor.

Ren was at a loss for words. He just gaped at his security chief.

"She's pregnant and it isn't mine," J.C. said, slurring his words a little. "And that's the only thing I'll ever say about it. She's history. I never want to hear her name mentioned again or I'll walk out."

Ren ground his teeth together. He knew, as Merrie did, that Colie had never looked at another man since she'd been with J.C. She'd dated the accountant, just once, and everybody knew he'd taken her home early and played chess with her dad. And that had only been because gossip put J.C. in the arms of some gorgeous blonde in Denver.

God knew where J.C. had heard that Colie was two-timing him. The pregnancy was news, though. He knew that his security chief didn't want kids, or marriage. Either J.C. had gotten careless or there really was another man in Colie's life. Hard to believe that, though, considering how crazy she was for J.C.

"I can't work today," J.C. said apologetically. "Sorry. I had...a lot to drink."

"It's okay," Ren said. "I'll put him to work updating software until tomorrow."

"I'll be fine tomorrow."

"Sure you will."

"Damn women!" J.C. said icily. "Damn them all!"

It was like looking in a mirror. Not too many years ago, that's what Ren was saying. He'd had his own bad experience with a woman and it had soured him so much that he'd almost lost Merrie. Here was J.C., walking in his footsteps.

But Ren couldn't reach him. He didn't want to lose J.C. He shrugged. "Life goes on," he said philosophically. He smiled. "See you tomorrow."

"Yeah."

J.C. closed the door and Ren went home.

Merrie looked up when he came into the living room. "Well?"

"He was so hungover, he could barely talk."

"What happened?" she exclaimed.

"It all boils down to the fact that Colie's pregnant and J.C. thinks it's some other man's."

"Oh, dear. That's not true. Colie's so much in love with him, she couldn't have slept with anyone else."

"We know that. J.C. doesn't. Or doesn't want to."

"Poor Colie," she groaned. "And her poor father!"

"They'll get through it," he said. "We all have hard times. We survive them." He pulled her close and kissed her warmly. "My treasure," he whispered against her mouth.

She smiled and kissed him back.

COLIE AND HER father sipped coffee. His was strong and black. Hers was decaf.

"I want to go to Jacobsville," she said. "Cousin Annie Mosby and her brother Ty live there. She said I was always welcome."

"Honey, Jacobsville is bigger than Catelow, but it's still small enough that people gossip..."

"I've got that figured out," she said. "A little white lie. Just a little one. I was married and my husband died, and I'm pregnant." She drew in a breath. "I don't want people stigmatizing my child. I deserve it, but..."

"Stop that. God forgives everything."

She smiled sadly. "I'm very glad, but a lot of people don't forgive. It will be easier if I'm in a place where everybody doesn't know how I got this way. It will be easier on you, too, Daddy," she added when he started to protest. "I've caused enough harm. I can get a job in Jacobsville. There are several law offices."

"You're sure?"

She nodded. "I'm sure. We can keep in touch through Skype. We can talk anytime you want to," she added with a warm smile. "It won't be like I'm gone at all."

"Except for the burned toast," he said, tongue in cheek.

"I'll teach you to make it before I leave," she promised.

SHE CALLED HER cousin Annie and told her what was going on.

"You come right down here to us," Annie replied quickly. "We'll take care of you. And there's a job going at Blake Kemp's old law office, with Darby Howland. Poor old thing, he's got cancer and he doesn't have a long time left, but he's determined to keep the law firm going just the same. You'd love him. He's forty, but he looks much younger and he's a ball of fire. He's looking for an assistant who can type and take dictation and work reception."

"He might not want me…"

"I'll phone him when I hang up and talk to him," Annie said.

"I'm going to invent a dead husband," Colie added quietly. "It's a long, sad story. I did a stupid thing. Several stupid things. But I want my baby very much."

"Of course you do. You can't help it if the father is an idiot. Now get packed. I'll send you an e-ticket. Your dad can drive you to the airport in Jackson Hole. There's a nonstop to San Antonio, and we'll have a car pick you up and bring you to us. Don't fuss," she added when she heard the protest. "You know we're filthy rich. Just hush and come live with us. Ty will be happy to have the company, he says I drive him batty. He'd never say a word unless I forced him to. Honestly, it's no wonder he won't marry somebody. He never speaks!"

Colie laughed. She remembered Ty, who was something of a hell-raiser. He owned one of the biggest ranches in Texas and raised purebred German shepherds as a hobby. He didn't like people very much, but he loved animals. He loved Colie, too. She was as much like his sister as his first cousin.

"All right. I'll come. And thank you. Thank you so much. I've really made things hard for Daddy in the community, although he never said a word. I want to spare him this. An unwed mother, and it's his own daughter, when he preaches morality…it's more than I want to put on him."

"He loves you," Annie reminded her. "He wouldn't care."

"Yes, but I would. I'll see you in a couple of days. My bosses here are letting me go without working a two-week notice. They've been so kind!"

"Mr. Howland says they're a great bunch to work for."

"They are. And I'll miss my friend Lucy. But I can Skype her as well as Dad," she added.

"Lovely electronic media," Annie chuckled. "It does help us keep in touch. I'll arrange it all and email you the details. Okay?"

"Okay!"

COLIE HAD HER things packed and ready. Rod hadn't come home since Colie had been thrown out by J.C. She hoped it was because he was ashamed, but it was probably that he was too busy selling drugs. She really wished J.C. had listened to her. It might have been Rod's salvation.

As it was, she was too afraid for her father to turn her brother in to the law. She'd seen something dark and cold in that friend of his, and she didn't want her father to end up floating in a river because she'd opened her mouth. She hoped Rod would realize that she was leaving town to keep his secret.

Well, she was leaving it for a lot of reasons. One tiny part of her had hoped against hope that J.C. would finally cool down and call her, ask for her side of the story. But he didn't. There was no contact at all.

She'd seen him at a distance in town the last day she worked. He hadn't even turned his head in her direction. It was just as he'd said. She no longer existed for him. She wished with all her heart that she could feel that way about him. It would make her life so much easier.

Her father hugged her goodbye and fought tears as she walked away from him down the concourse, tugging her wheeled luggage behind her. It was a long way to Texas. But she really had no choice. She had to think of it as starting fresh, beginning a new life, leaving the old one full of pain behind.

It would be all right. She'd have her baby and everybody would think he had a father. His real father didn't want him, but Colie would never tell him that. She'd invent a father who adored him, wanted him desperately, but tragedy had befallen him. It wouldn't do for a child to think his own father didn't care about him.

THE TRIP WAS long and Colie was sick most of the way there. A driver was holding up a placard at baggage claim with her name on it. He helped her retrieve her luggage from the carousel and carried it out to the limousine for her.

"I brought the super stretch, just for you, miss," the driver chuckled when she gaped at the waiting vehicle. "Your cousin said you'd never ridden in one, and you needed something to cheer you up."

"Gosh, this is a great way to cheer someone up," she laughed. "I feel like a rock star!"

"Hop in. It's not far to Jacobsville. Just about twenty minutes. You can even watch television if you like," he added.

"Oh, no, I'll look out the window," she said. "I've never seen Texas before!" She noticed his curious look. "My cousins always came up to Wyoming for family reunions, when my mother was alive. This is the first time I've been out of Wyoming at all."

"You'll enjoy it here. It's beautiful country. Lots of ranches. Like your cousin's," he added drily.

She laughed. "I'm looking forward to that, too."

ANNIE WAS WAITING on the porch. She had blond hair and brown eyes. She was tall and willowy, very elegant with her hair drawn up into a bun, wearing a beige pantsuit with high heels. Beside her was her brother, Ty.

He wasn't dressed up, unless you included the Stetson perched on jet-black hair, slanted over black eyes in a hard, tanned face. He was built like a rodeo rider, lanky but muscular, with long, powerful legs and big hands and feet. He almost never smiled. Unlike Annie, who ran to meet Colie and hugged her half to death.

"I'm so glad you came!" she told Colie. "It's so lonely here," she added with a glare at her imperturbable brother.

"I told you I'd let one of the dogs sleep with you, if you're lonely," her brother drawled in his deep voice.

"I don't want a dog. I don't like dogs. I like cats!"

He made a face. "Nasty, furry things that pick holes in cloth," he muttered. "Damned Siamese terror clawed my curtains so bad we had to replace them."

"They were old, and Santa is just a kitten."

"Santa?" Colie asked.

"Santa Claws," Annie laughed. "He's a baby. I lost my

sixteen-year-old Ragdoll a month ago. I needed something to help my heart heal, so we have Santa."

Mention of the kitten reminded Colie of her cat that J.C. had given her, Big Tom, left behind with her father. She missed him already.

"All we need is locusts to go with that kitten," Ty muttered. "Nice to have you here, cousin," he added. "Maybe she'll stop talking my ears off if she has you to worry."

She laughed and smiled at him. He wasn't the sort of man you hugged. "I'll try not to get in the way."

"You're pregnant, she said," he noted.

She flushed and gritted her teeth.

"I love kids," he said softly, and he smiled. It changed his face entirely. His black eyes gleamed with warmth. "We'll take care of you."

She bit her lower lip and fought tears. "Thanks. Thanks so much."

He shrugged. "We live in a damned hotel," he muttered, indicating the huge mansion. "Two stories, eight bedrooms, five bathrooms…for two people! Our father was out of his mind to build something like that." He waved his hand at it. "Could have had a nice big log cabin with an open fireplace…"

"Ignore him, dear," Annie said, taking her arm. "Phil will bring your bags in for us, won't you, sweetie?" she asked the driver, who beamed and nodded. "He always drives for us. I don't trust anybody else at the wheel. Especially not him," she added on a loud whisper toward her brother's back.

"I'm a great driver," he retorted.

"You're a demolition derby in a cowboy hat!" she shot back. "You've wrecked two Jags and a Lincoln in the past two years…!"

"Not my fault," he said doggedly. "I was hit, all three times."

"Because you pulled right out into the road without looking!"

"Their fault for not knowing I'd do that," he said, unruffled. "Show Cousin Colie to her room and then do you think Cook could scare up something to eat? I'm starving!"

"I offered to cook you lunch," she returned.

"Real men don't eat quiche," he scoffed, glaring back at her with black eyes. "That's all you can cook."

"Well!" Annie burst out.

"I like steak and potatoes. You ever learn to cook something that doesn't start with eggs, I'll eat it. Hasn't happened in fifteen years, but you never know," he added, mumbling to himself as he wandered back toward the kitchen.

Annie laughed all the way upstairs. "Isn't he the living end? I keep hoping somebody will finally notice what a great catch he is and marry him. But he doesn't like most women. He says they're too brassy and career-minded. He loves kids."

"I'm so glad. I thought he was going to say something entirely different," Colie confessed when they were in the guest bedroom, done in soft blues and grays.

"He's not judgmental," Annie said easily. "Neither am I." Her eyes flashed. "Besides that, we're a founding family here. Nobody, but nobody, gossips about us or our relatives. You'll find that out when you've been here long enough."

Colie let out a long sigh. "I'm so happy to be here. You don't know how happy. It's been pretty rough, even if I did bring it on myself."

Annie put her arms around her. "You got mixed up with a man who doesn't know what forgiveness is. That's his problem, not yours. You just heal and thrive and show him what he missed." She grinned. "We'll love having a baby in the house! It's like Christmas all over again!"

As if on cue, the pretty white Siamese kitten walked in the door, meowing.

"And speak of the devil, there's Santa," Annie said, waving a hand at the cat.

Colie laughed.

J.C. HAD TOLD Ren he'd be back at work the next morning. He wasn't. With resignation, Ren went back to the cabin again and knocked on the door. While he sympathized with the man, there was work that needed doing and only J.C. knew how.

The man who answered the door was a stranger. J.C. Calhoun was immaculate. He was always well dressed, even in jeans and shirts, his nails were manicured, his hair perfectly combed.

But this man was a total mess. He was wearing the same clothes he'd had on the previous morning. His hair stood up in all directions. And he still absolutely stank of whiskey. Since J.C. never drank hard liquor, it was totally out of character. Especially two days in a row.

"What the hell?" Ren asked, aghast.

Bloodshot pale gray eyes looked into Ren's. "What day is it?" he asked slowly.

"It's Tuesday."

"Tuesday," he said icily. He groaned. "I can't even get properly drunk, damn it!" he muttered. "That witch! She got pregnant by another man, and she was going to tell me it was mine, because I had more money than he did."

Ren just stared at him. It was a well-known fact that Colie was passionately in love with J.C. If there was going to be a child, it was a fair bet that it belonged to the man denying any part in its creation.

"Colie loves you," Ren said.

"Sure she does," he said, slurring his words. "That's why she shacked up with another guy while I was overseas. What a sweetheart! Just like that call girl I mistook for love eternal when I was younger. I can sure pick 'em, can't I?" he ground out.

Ren took a breath. "J.C., she hasn't even dated anybody else, the whole time…"

"Her own brother told me what she did!" he burst out. "Rod. My best friend!" He blinked. "My former best friend, anyway," he added. "He met me at the airport, with the…the father of Colie's child," he hiccuped in the middle of the sentence. He blinked drunkenly. "She sold me out, Ren."

The other man didn't know what to say. He just stared at his security chief.

"I can't work today," J.C. groaned, holding his head. "I'm sorry. Really sorry. I know I promised I'd be back on the job today, but I…I just need a little more time. Okay?"

"Okay." Ren put a hand on his shoulder. "Take all the time you need."

"Thanks."

Ren wanted to say something else, but he didn't know what to say. He was overwhelmed by J.C.'s condition. In the end, he just smiled and walked away.

J.C. CAME BACK to himself slowly. He went back to work, went through the motions of living. But it hurt him, remembering what Rod had told him about Colie.

It hurt more when his sanity returned, and he started

thinking rationally again. Rod, his best friend, had lied often when they were overseas together. He did it to get out of duties he didn't like, pleading illness. He did it to make money. He laughed at J.C.'s outrage. A little lie didn't hurt anything, he'd said defensively. J.C. and his sterling character. Once a cop, always a cop, he'd said, and not in a nice way.

So Rod was used to bending the truth. Colie, not so much. In fact, J.C. couldn't remember a single time she'd lied to him. She'd even told him about her one other date, when she got even with him for dating, as she thought at the time, that glamorous blonde in Denver who turned out to be a married mother of two.

There was something else. Colie loved him. She nurtured him, took care of him. She cared enough to defy her father and all the ideals she'd been raised with, to move in with him.

As for her wanting someone richer, Colie had even refused to let J.C. buy her a dress to wear on a fancy date. She'd never let him buy her a single thing, except lunch once or twice. And she'd paid for lunch as much as he had. It was sobering.

There was going to be a child. At first, it was easy to think it was the other man's. But he'd never heard of the other man, Barry, the one Rod had brought with him to the airport. There was something suspicious about the whole thing. The man was wearing designer clothes and handmade shoes; not someone local, because J.C. would have recognized him.

Rodney was wearing designer stuff, too. Funny how he'd missed that, until now. Gossip said that Rod was driving a new Mercedes, as well. No way he could afford that kind of high-end car, or clothing, on what he made as a clerk at the local hardware store.

The more he thought about it, the more it worried him. Colie hated intimacy. She even hated it with J.C., whom she loved. So why would she go to another man's bed? He remembered how nervous she'd been the first time, that she'd bled. She'd kissed him back, held him tight, enjoyed the closeness even if she hadn't enjoyed the actual act of sex.

A sharp breath escaped from his throat. Colie had been nineteen, raised by religious parents. She went to church every week, except when she'd lived with J.C. Would a woman raised that way actually be permissive? He'd never heard a whisper of gossip about her until she'd moved in with him. Rod had complained for years about his straitlaced, overly moral sister.

Dear God, what if she'd been a virgin? The pieces of the puzzle all seemed to fit. It would explain a lot. And J.C. had treated her like an experienced woman, making no allowances for her lack of skill in bed. If she was innocent, no wonder she hadn't liked the first time, or the times that followed. He'd always been in a hurry. The women in his life had liked it rough and quick. But if Colie had been a virgin…

He picked up the phone and called her home. It had been almost three weeks since he'd put her on the porch like an unwanted package, in the freezing cold. She hadn't even been wearing a good coat. He winced inwardly as he recalled her sad, tear-drenched eyes. He hadn't given her a chance to defend herself at all, even to explain his accusations. He'd insulted her, railed at her, called her names, ridiculed her behavior in bed.

She probably wouldn't even speak to him, but he had to try.

The phone rang four times before Reverend Thompson picked it up. "Hello?" he asked softly.

"Reverend, it's J.C. May I speak to Colie, please?"

There was a brief silence, then the sound of the receiver being replaced. He recalled that the reverend used the hard-wired phone at home. He tried again, but the answering machine had been turned on.

He drew in a long breath. Well, he might have more luck with Rod. He wanted to question him about his airport performance, anyway.

HE STOPPED BY the hardware store, where one of his coworkers told him that Rod had taken a day off. Something about needing to go to Jackson Hole on urgent business. Just as well, the man remarked sourly. Rod didn't do much when he was there, except to chat up women when he should have been helping customers.

J.C. STOOD OUTSIDE in blowing snow, grinding his teeth. Now what? He could go to the reverend's house and demand to see Colie, but that would be unwise. He'd caused the poor man enough trouble already, by living openly with his only daughter. He wasn't religious himself, but he knew how religious people looked at immoral conduct. It couldn't have been easy for the pastor to get in the pulpit and talk against sex outside marriage when his daughter was living with a man and everybody knew.

He couldn't track Rod down in Jackson Hole. He'd have to wait until the man came home and catch him.

He was frustrated. He needed to find Colie. Where the hell was she? Then he remembered. He checked his watch. She'd be on her lunch hour. He hadn't gone near the cafeteria since they broke up, but he got into his SUV and drove there.

He looked around inside the crowded place, but there was no Colie. However, her coworker, Lucy, was having a salad and coffee alone at a table.

He pulled up a chair and straddled it. "Where's Colie?" he asked abruptly.

Lucy paused with her fork in midair and just stared at him.

"Her father won't let me speak to her. I can't find her brother." He was frustrated and irritated, and his voice reflected it. "Where is she?"

She put the fork down. "I don't know, J.C.," she said, but she averted her eyes.

"Yes, you do," he returned. "You can't lie to me, Lucy. I was a police officer for two years. I know a lie when I see one."

She looked up and drew in a breath. "She made me promise I wouldn't tell you," she said after a minute.

"Is she in Catelow?"

She didn't answer.

"I need to talk to her," he said shortly. "I never even gave her a chance to defend herself..."

"Yes, I know," she said, her tone icy. "You put her on the porch of your cabin with her belongings and closed the door. You put her outside like a dog that had misbehaved."

He had the grace not to protest the accusation. He couldn't. She was telling the truth.

He traced a pattern on the back of the chair he was straddling, his heart heavy, his mind busy.

"I did," he confessed after a minute. "I lost my temper. Rod came to meet me at the airport and told me…" He hesitated. He looked up. "Is she really pregnant?"

Lucy's face closed up. "That's no longer any of your business. Colie's gone, J.C. You might as well get used to it."

"Gone where?"

"I told you…"

"For God's sake, is it mine?" he ground out, his pale gray eyes lancing into hers. "Is she carrying my child?"

Her face grew hard. "What do you care?" she asked. "You told her you never wanted a child. So you won't be having one."

He looked confused. His regrets were plain on his face. "I made some mistakes."

"You made a lot."

He nodded. "I want to make things right, if I can," he said quietly. "I've messed up pretty badly." He managed a faint smile. "But Colie doesn't hold grudges. She'll forgive me."

She lowered her eyes. She didn't say anything.

The silence was revealing. He felt something cold touch him, inside. "Is she in Wyoming?" he asked quietly.

She shook her head.

He drew in a long breath. "Will you ask her if you can tell me where she is?" he tried another tack. "Just that."

She looked up. Her expression was no longer hostile. It was sad. "It's too late, J.C.," she said after a minute.

"What do you mean, it's too late?" he returned.

"You can't say anything, do anything, that will make it up to her. Not now. It won't matter if I ask her. She'd just say no, anyway."

"Why are you so certain of that?" he demanded.

"Well, it's like this," she began, hesitating.

He felt cold inside. Empty. He felt a sense of premonition that was stronger than anything he'd ever experienced.

"Just tell me," he said.

"Okay." She took a deep breath. "She won't talk to you because she's married, J.C."

He just sat there. His face paled under its olive tan. His pale, silver eyes looked blank. "She's what?"

"She's married," Lucy replied. She got up with her tray. "I'm sorry. That's what I meant, when I said it was too late. You can't go back, J.C. Life doesn't come with a reset button."

She turned and walked away.

MARRIED. COLIE WAS MARRIED. She was pregnant and her child wouldn't have a name. Her father would be even more humiliated in the pulpit with an unwed mother, who was his own child, sitting in a pew in his church.

Colie knew that. She was already guilty that she'd caused him so much pain. J.C. knew it, even if she'd never put it into words.

So she'd found someone and gotten married, to give her child a name. She'd put herself beyond J.C.'s reach, and she'd done it deliberately.

He got up like a sleepwalker and went outside to the SUV. He stood in the ice-cold wind, with snow blowing around him, and never felt a thing. Colie was gone forever. He'd thrown her away, like a used shoe. He would never have her in his life again. Never have that tenderness, that nurturing, that he'd craved even when he'd resented it.

Colie was gone, and it was his fault. Gone, with a child that might be his own child; a child who would grow up thinking another man was its father. A child he'd never know.

He knew what it was to be without a father. He'd left his behind at the age of ten. He'd blamed him for all the misery of the years in between. Now he was doing the same thing to a child that might be his.

Not quite. Colie had a husband. Hopefully, he'd treat her better than J.C. had. Did the man know she was pregnant? He dismissed that thought at once. Of course he knew. Colie wouldn't lie, even about that.

He'd never misjudged anyone so badly in his whole life. He was ashamed, eaten up with guilt. His hot temper had cost him the one person in his adult life who genuinely loved him. Perhaps he'd done it deliberately, if subconsciously. He expected people to betray him. He didn't trust anyone.

He should have trusted Colie. He should have gone after her, while there was still time to fix things.

Now, he was going to be alone for the rest of his life. As he got into the SUV and drove away, he thought that probably he deserved what he'd gotten. He probably deserved all of it.

CHAPTER NINE

J.C. DROVE BACK to the ranch without seeing anything along the way. He knocked at the front door. Delsey let him in.

"Hi, J.C.," she began.

"Ren in?" he interrupted her. He looked like a man who'd tried to swallow a watermelon whole.

"Yes, in the study…"

"Thanks." He cut her off and strode off toward the den.

Ren looked up when his security chief walked in and closed the door behind him.

"Did you know that she was married?" he asked shortly.

Ren's thick, dark eyebrows arched toward his hairline. "Excuse me?"

"Colie. Did you know she was married?"

Ren's lips fell open. "Colie's married?" he exclaimed. "When? To whom…?"

J.C. sank into a chair. "I don't know. Lucy told me. I was trying to find Colie. Her father just put the phone down without answering. Rod's out of town. There wasn't anybody else to ask…" He swallowed, hard. "Married!" he exclaimed. His olive complexion had actually gone pale.

Ren knew what the other man was going through. He'd

also misjudged a woman, but fortunately he came to his senses in time not to lose Merrie. "I'm sorry," he said.

J.C.'s pale gray eyes were tormented. "I don't know why she'd do that!"

Ren hesitated for a few seconds. Then he leaned forward, both hands on the desk locked together. "J.C., she was pregnant," he said gently. "Probably she felt her father had endured enough gossip already, without having to get up in the pulpit with a pregnant but unmarried daughter in the congregation."

J.C. closed his eyes on a wave of sickness. It was what he'd thought himself. The reverend had endured some painful gossip already, he knew, and he'd helped cause it. He'd done a lot of damage to a man who'd only ever tried to help people.

Colie was pregnant. Was it his child? Now he'd never know. She was gone. Out of reach forever. Married! Why hadn't he realized it was what she was most likely to do, out of guilt and shame.

But who had she married? Nobody locally had mentioned anything about a wedding. No, he thought. She'd never stay in Catelow, or anywhere nearby. She'd have gone away somewhere, someplace that people didn't know her, didn't know that she'd lived with J.C. and he'd thrown her out of his life. Someplace where she'd found someone who married her, to give her child a name.

What if it was his own child? He'd never see it, never know it. And it was his own fault. He felt the pain all the way to his soul. He'd never been so wrong about a human being in his whole life. He'd thrown Colie away, called her names, accused her of lying, ridiculed the way she was in bed.

"Sometimes, we dig our own graves long before we die," he said out of the blue.

Ren, who didn't know what the other man had been thinking, only nodded.

COLIE WAS NERVOUS her first couple of weeks on the job in Darby Howland's law office. Her cousin Annie had assured her that he wanted her there, and was sure she was going to be an asset. Colie was less than confident.

She was all too aware of her condition, although the pregnancy was in such early stages that it didn't really show yet. She owed Mr. Howland a great debt for being so kind to a total stranger. But she wasn't sure how he would react when she told him her true circumstances. She'd made sure Annie hadn't spoken of it to anyone. She didn't want to start out in Jacobsville, Texas, with everybody knowing what she'd done.

But it wasn't like that at all. Mr. Howland was tall and lanky, with thick silver-sprinkled black hair. He had dark eyes, an olive complexion and a deep, carrying voice. He never seemed to stop smiling.

She answered the phone, took dictation, fielded appointments, did everything that was asked of her without a complaint. The office ran smoothly. It was very much like the office she'd left behind in Catelow.

She was especially fond of the big boss, who headed the three-attorney firm. Mr. Howland was the kindest man she'd ever worked for. But the longer she put off telling him the truth about her circumstances, the harder it got. She knew she looked guilty. He seemed to sense that something was wrong. So at the end of her second week in Jacobsville, he called her into his office, closed the door and turned off his cell phone.

"Let's get the unpleasant things out of the way first, shall we?" he asked, motioning her to a seat in front of his huge oak desk after he'd closed the door. "You look like a fugitive anticipating an arrest warrant," he added with faint humor. "Want to just tell me about it?"

Colie sighed. "Mr. Howland, I should have let Annie tell you…"

He just smiled. "Go on, Colie."

She hesitated.

"Oh, I see." He smiled as he sat down, wincing with the action. He drew in a long breath. "All right, we'll put your unpleasant things off a bit. The main unpleasant thing doesn't concern you. It concerns me." He locked his hands together on the desk. "I'm dying."

She caught her breath. Even though Annie had told her he had cancer, she hadn't registered that it was a death sentence. So many kinds of cancer could be successfully treated these days.

"Sorry. That was rather stark," he added, smiling sadly. "You see, I have a very rare cancer. It's multiple myeloma. I had a backache that wouldn't go away, but I thought it was arthritis. I was diagnosed with that in my twenties. So I didn't go to my doctor. Eventually, it showed up in tests, but by then, it was too late for much to be done."

"I'm so sorry," she said helplessly.

He smiled. "I was married. She was the only woman in my life from sixth grade onward. We couldn't have children, but we had each other. It was such an idyllic marriage that, after I lost her, I never wanted anyone else. When I die, I'll see her again. That's why it's not so bad." He grimaced. "Well, the pain gets pretty bad.

But in this case, it isn't the journey, it's the destination, if you know what I mean."

"I see." She thought about losing J.C. That had been like a death. She mourned him. If he'd really died, and she was facing life without him, death wouldn't be such a terrifying thing. Even though he'd hurt her, love couldn't be killed, apparently.

He cocked his head. His dark eyes narrowed. "You were thinking about another sort of unpleasant thing. May I know what it is?"

She drew in a long breath. "I got involved with a man back home. I loved him…more than anything in the world. So when he asked me to move in with him, I did. My father is a minister and it's a small town. It was scandalous," she said with a sad smile. "But the worst was yet to come. He didn't want children and we had an accident. So I'm pregnant and he doesn't think it's his. He tossed me out on my ear. I couldn't shame my father even more by becoming an unwed mother in his congregation. My cousins Annie and Ty said I could come live with them and they knew about a job here, at your office." She looked down at her feet. "So I guess I should spare us both any more unpleasantness and just leave. I was going to invent a dead husband…"

"Why don't you just marry me instead?"

Her lips fell open. She stared at him numbly. "What?"

He shrugged. "I don't want a real marriage. I don't think you do, either. But you're going to have a child and you need a husband." He smiled from ear to ear. "God, I love kids! I never could have one with Mary, but I can help you with yours, for whatever time I've got left."

Tears ran down her cheeks like rain down a window. "But…you don't know me…"

"Annie told me everything," he confided. "Don't be mad at her. Her father and I were best friends for years. We don't have secrets. Besides, I'm a lawyer. We're trained not to tell what we know."

She managed a smile as she dashed at tears. "I was trained that way, too. I worked for a wonderful firm of lawyers back in Catelow."

"I know. I phoned them. They said everyone in the office was crying in their beer. You were much appreciated."

She flushed. "Wow."

"You'll be appreciated here, as well. We'll get a license tomorrow and get a minister to do the honors."

"Everyone will think you've lost your mind," she pointed out. "We just met week before last."

"What the hell," he chuckled. "They'll feed on the gossip for months. It will be nice gossip. Jacobsville is a kind town, and I don't say that lightly. We have people who live here who've committed all sorts of crimes and came back into society. Nobody chastises them for it. They've paid their debts. We also have one of the most famous counterterrorism schools on earth in Jacobs County, run by a former mercenary named Eb Scott. See? All sorts of interesting people live here. I forgot to mention that our police chief is a former government assassin and our sheriff is married to the daughter of one of the most notorious drug lords on the continent."

She just sat, gaping.

"It's a very colorful town," he added with a big grin. "So a quick marriage between two strangers isn't even going to raise eyebrows. Not much, at least."

"What a fascinating place to live!"

"That's what I've always thought." He scowled. "One

thing, though. Are you certain that the father of your child won't change his mind and come after you?"

She smiled. It was a sad and wistful smile. "He said he never wanted to see me again. He said the child I'm carrying isn't his. He said…" She hesitated. "He said a lot of things that I can't forget. He's basically a loner. He doesn't want a family. So, no. There's no chance he'd come after me." She looked up. "I'm even glad. I'd go crawling back to him on my knees through broken glass." She laughed, but her voice broke. "I loved him so much. I had no pride at all."

"I loved Mary like that," the man said quietly. "I love her still. She echoes through my life every day, every hour, every minute. I lost her three years ago, but it seems like yesterday. They say time helps. The hell it does."

She nodded. "A wound that deep doesn't heal, I think."

He leaned forward. "So. Going to marry me? I snore, but you won't mind, because you'll have a nice bedroom all to yourself. I have to have chemo and radiation periodically, so I'm sick a lot. You'd have to live with that, too."

"Oh, I don't mind," she said gently. "J.C. got really sick with flu and I nursed him, even when he threw up."

His expression softened. "You looked like that kind of woman," he said softly. "I'll bet total strangers sit down and tell you their most horrible secrets."

She laughed out loud. "Well, yes, they do. Some of them are really embarrassing. I just listen and don't say anything."

"I imagine your father's good at that, too. You'd better call him and tell him about this incredibly impetuous thing you're about to do."

She nodded. "I'll call him tonight." She grimaced.

"I don't own a lot of dresses. Does it have to be a wedding gown?"

"Of course not. Get married in blue jeans for all I care," he chuckled. "I'll wear a suit, but only because I always wear one to work."

"This is so sudden," she blurted out.

"Not on my part." He cocked his head. "The minute Annie said her pregnant, unmarried cousin was going to come and live here and needed a job, I started thinking about it. I've never been around babies. I wanted one of my own, so much. For me, it will be the greatest adventure of my life, next to living with Mary and passing the state bar exam," he added drily.

"It's so kind of you," she said, fighting tears.

"It's kind of you," he replied. "It won't be easy, Colie. I said I was sick a lot, and I meant it. I don't sleep well, either, so I roam the house and watch television when I can't sleep."

"I won't mind," she replied. "I just want my baby to have the best start I can give him, or her. I don't want my baby to be called a bad name because of what I did."

"We'll make sure of that."

"Then, if you really mean it, I'll marry you, Mr. Howland. And I'll take care of you as long as you need me to."

He smiled. "Darby."

"Oh. Darby," she tried it out.

He laughed. "I was named for my great-great-grandfather. He was a deputy sheriff in Jacobs County."

"I'd love to hear about his history. Maybe on one of those nights when you can't sleep," she added.

He nodded. "It will be nice to have company. I've missed that."

"I'll have to call my dad."

"Why don't we do that right now? I have Skype on my office computer." He turned it on, pulled up the app and looked at Colie. "What's his phone number? I'll have to send a contact request…"

She got up. "No, you won't. Can I use the computer? I'll sign in on my account."

He grinned. "Nice thinking." He got up and perched on the edge of the desk while Colie fed her information into the computer and called her father. It was early in the day, and he was usually at home.

The phone rang. He answered it and when he recognized Colie's name, he turned on the camera. There he was, beaming at her.

"Hi, sweetheart," he said. "How are you?"

Darby moved into the picture beside Colie and smiled. "Hello, Reverend. I'm Darby Howland and I'm marrying your daughter tomorrow."

Reverend Thompson was speechless. He just gaped at them.

"The baby needs a name," Darby continued gently. "And I'm dying of cancer. The baby will make what time I have left worth living. I lost my wife three years ago. I don't have anything to give, as far as a real marriage goes, but I can give Colie my name and the baby will have everything he needs."

Reverend Thompson found his voice. "Mr.…?"

"Howland. Darby Howland. I own the law firm here in Jacobsville where Colie's working now."

"Mr. Howland, both of us will be forever in your debt," the reverend managed. He fought tears. "I've been so worried about my daughter…!"

"I'll take care of her," Darby promised. "She'll never want for a thing. The baby won't, either." He smiled.

"Mary and I wanted kids more than anything in the world, but she couldn't conceive. I'll look forward to being a dad, even if it's just on paper."

"It's a noble thing you're doing," Colie's father said quietly. "I'll mention you in my prayers every night."

Darby smiled sadly. "I'll take all the prayers I can get. I believe in it. I'm an usher at our church. I'm Methodist…"

"So are we!" Reverend Thompson burst out laughing. "What a coincidence!"

"A nice one," Darby said. He grinned. "We have a fine minister here in our church. He's a little eccentric—drives a Shelby Cobra Mustang. But he's great in the pulpit or when someone's in trouble."

"Daddy is, too," Colie said, smiling at her father.

"Do you want to fly down for the ceremony?" Darby asked. "I can send a car for you at the airport."

"I really wish I could," Reverend Thompson said. He sighed. "I have a member of my congregation going in for major heart surgery in the morning. I gave her my word that I'd be there with her."

"If he gives his word, he always keeps it," Colie told Darby. She looked back at her father, whose expression was tormented. "It's okay," she said. "We'll take photos and send you some. How about that?"

He relaxed a little. "That would be very nice, Colie." He glanced at Darby. "You've landed well, my girl. You take care of yourself. Call me often."

"I'll do that," she promised. "Love you, Daddy."

"Love you back. Thanks, Darby," he added, to the other man. "Thanks very much, from both of us."

Darby grinned. "No thanks necessary. I'll get to be a father!"

Colie just laughed.

SHE AND DARBY were married in the local Methodist church, with just her cousins for witnesses. It wasn't formal, although Darby had bought her a beautiful bouquet to carry, of poinsettias and white roses and baby's breath. He'd bought her rings, as well. She'd protested the expense, but he said it was pocket change.

A two-carat diamond engagement ring in a eighteen-karat setting with a matching band of diamonds. Two years' salary as far as Colie was concerned. Pocket change? she'd exclaimed.

"Forgot to tell you," he said as they walked out of the church with Annie and Ty. "I'm rich."

"Oh, dear, and I didn't know beforehand, so I could tell everyone I was marrying you for your money," she quipped with a mischievous smile.

He hesitated and then burst out laughing. "What have I let myself in for?" he exclaimed.

Reverend Jake Blair joined them outside the church. "Marriage is a serious business. No laughing."

He looked so somber that everyone stared at him.

Then he grinned. "Fell for it, didn't you?" he teased. He chuckled. "You two are a great match. I can already tell." He shook Darby's hand. "I'm glad to see you take an interest in life again."

"I don't have much of it left," Darby said wistfully.

"Life is measured in happy days, not in anticipation of the loss of it," Jake told him. "Honestly, yesterday is a memory and tomorrow is a hope. All we really have is today, right now. Nobody is guaranteed one more day. Not even the youngest people."

Darby studied him. "You really are a philosopher, Jake."

"Not quite, but I'm working on it." He smiled at Colie.

"I have a daughter your age. She and her husband have a little boy. He's the light of my life."

"I'll look forward to meeting her," Colie said. "I'm so new here. It's going to take time before I know people."

"Darby knows everyone. He'll make sure you're introduced," Jake assured her. "It's a small town, but not clannish or full of prejudiced people. It's one of the kindest places on earth. You're going to love it here."

"I know that," she agreed.

"I hear that your father is a minister, too," Jake said. "I'd love to meet him, when he comes to visit you."

She'd explained earlier why her father wasn't at the ceremony. "He takes his job very seriously."

"So do I," Jake replied. "Congratulations again."

"Thanks, Reverend Blair," Colie said, and Darby added his own.

"Now," Darby said. "Let's go home!"

HE LIVED ON a sprawling property with a stream running through it, surrounded by mesquite and oak and pecan trees.

"It's so different from Wyoming," Colie remarked. "Beautiful. Just…different."

"No lodgepole pines, no aspen trees, no cottonwoods," he chuckled. "I know. The vegetation is different, but the people are just the same, wherever you go. I love living here. It's like one big family."

"I've noticed that," she agreed. She gasped as the house came into view. It was enormous; a Victorian dream of perfection, with gingerbread woodwork and white paint, two stories high and surrounded by trees of all sorts.

"Incredible," she remarked breathlessly. "It's so beautiful!"

He smiled sadly. "I built it for Mary," he said. "It's the only place we ever lived together."

"Except you probably got married first," she said wistfully. "I'd hoped my life would be like that. Conventional." She shook her head. "When I slip, I slip badly."

"You're very young, Colie. Time enough for regrets when you get to my age," he counseled.

She sighed. "I guess so." She glanced at him. "Do you have a housekeeper?"

"A part-time one, Mrs. Lopez. She works for one of our three florists the rest of the week. You'll like her."

"Is she here today?"

"No. She works for me on Wednesday and Thursday. She leaves me frozen meals that I just heat up in the microwave."

"I'll make sure you have homemade ones every day," she promised. "I can cook."

He grinned. "I can see now that I've made a very good decision." He chuckled.

"I'm more grateful than I can tell you…"

He held up a hand. "It's a partnership. We both get benefits." He stopped the car at the front steps. "Home," he said, indicating the wide front porch, which boasted a porch swing and padded furniture. There was even a hammock in a stand at one end, near a towering tree.

"That's a pecan tree," he told her, indicating the tree as they walked up onto the porch. "But I still have to buy pecans. Doggoned squirrels." He sighed. "They strip the trees when the nuts are still green. I've lived here for thirty years and I've yet to get a pecan off my own tree."

She laughed. "Well, it's not like the squirrels can go to

the store and buy nuts," she pointed out. "I see bird feeders and birdhouses, too," she exclaimed. "I love them! I only had a few back home, but I loved to fill them every morning."

"I like birds myself," he said. "It's too early for them to start nesting, but we'll have a front row seat for baby birds when spring comes."

She nodded. "When spring comes."

She gave a thought to J.C., who was gone from her life forever now. He would never come near her when he heard that she was married. She pretended that it didn't matter. It did. She would never stop loving him. But she couldn't let her child grow up outside marriage, in a small town. She'd done what she had to do.

Besides that, Darby was a good man. She'd take care of him, as long as he needed her to.

PREGNANCY WAS AN ADVENTURE. She went from tender breasts to morning sickness, to heartburn as the baby grew.

"This is terrible," she groaned to Darby when they were having lunch one day. She was six months along, and it showed. Most people assumed with delight that it was Darby's child, so the community was delighted for him. They already loved Colie. She'd never felt so much at home.

"What's terrible?" he teased.

"Heartburn! I crave sour pickles and I have heartburn! It's the most awful combination," she said, laughing.

"It won't be for much longer."

She drew in a breath and touched her stomach. She smiled gently. "I probably should have let them tell us if it was a boy or a girl. Mr. Kemp's wife is giving me a baby shower and everybody will bring yellow stuff."

"I like yellow. Don't you?"

She smiled. "I like it a lot." She studied his hard face. There were new lines in it. His pain grew steadily worse. He went every week for chemo and radiation. She went with him. The course of treatment had been stepped up as his condition worsened. She hoped that he was going to make it long enough to see the baby. He'd looked forward to it with so much joy.

"I'm not going anywhere just yet. In case you wondered," he added on a soft chuckle.

"Sorry. I worry."

He cocked his head and smiled at her. "I'm tough as old nails. No way I'm kicking off before that baby's born. I've put too much time into anticipating him."

Her father was the same. They all talked on Skype almost every day.

"Daddy says he's coming down when the baby's born, no matter what."

"He doesn't like to travel, does he?"

She shook her head as she finished her sandwich. "No, he hates it. He's afraid of airplanes, but he hates riding in cars for long distances, too. I don't think he's even been out of Catelow, except when he was in the Army. But that was before I was born, when he and my mom were first married."

"Your mother must have been a sweet woman."

"She was like Daddy," she replied. "Kind and loving and gentle." She looked up at him. "I made things so hard for him. Love is really blind. I mean, you get in so deep that you don't care about anything except being with the person you love."

"That's true," he agreed. He smiled. "And sometimes, it leads to horrible crimes."

"I noticed."

They were referring to a case where a man in love with a woman who didn't want him actually kidnapped her and tried to force her to marry him. They were defending him, pleading extenuating circumstances. But the police had turned the case over to the feds, because kidnapping was a federal crime. It was going to take some fancy legal work to get the man a reasonable sentence.

"Poor guy," Colie said. "And his poor mother." She grimaced. The man's mother was in the office or on the phone with the attorneys every week, crying and upset.

"IF YOU WANT a job that doesn't depress you, avoid the law," he said with a grin. "We only see the sad parts, don't we, honey?"

"Yes. But sometimes people get lucky."

"Not where the federal government is involved," he said on a sigh. "The US Attorney prosecuting the case has said he won't rest until our client is behind bars for life."

"I guess he's never been in love," she mused.

"That guy?" He just shook his head. "I doubt he's ever allowed himself time to get involved with anyone. He's strictly by the book. Damned good attorney, though," he conceded. "Does his homework, has an elegant voice and does his best for the victims."

"I've heard that."

He studied her with warm, caring eyes. "You stay tired a lot these days. I know I don't help. Every time I come home from chemo, I'm sick as a dog."

"I don't mind." She placed a hand over his. "We're sort of taking care of each other. Right?"

He laughed. "I hadn't thought of it that way." He searched her eyes. "Three more months."

She grinned. "Three more months."

REVEREND THOMPSON GOT the call at midnight on a hot Thursday in August. He'd been expecting it, but he almost panicked when he thought about that long airplane ride.

Incredibly, Darby had friends who owned a private jet, and they sent it to Catelow to bring him to Jacobsville. The Mosbys would have offered, if Colie had asked them. So would Sari Fiore. But this was better. Darby's friend had no connections to Catelow, or to J.C. Colie didn't want J.C. to know about the baby, although she had no logical reason why.

The pilot ushered the reverend inside, seated him and proceeded with his walkaround to make sure the plane was airworthy. One of the mechanics at the Jacobsville airport was in the reverend's congregation. He watched the jet take off and couldn't wait to share the news. It was a big deal for the minister to even get on a plane. But apparently he had acquaintances who owned a baby jet!

He told his wife, who told the florist, who told the attorneys in the firm where Lucy still worked. She told a friend at the restaurant during lunch, vaguely aware that J.C. Calhoun was waiting at the counter behind her to pick up an order for himself and his men.

"It's so exciting!" Lucy told her friend. "She wouldn't let them tell her if it was a boy or a girl. They say her husband's got cancer," she added sadly. "She said she just wanted him to live long enough to see the baby. He's been as joyful as she has about it. And he's very well-to-do! Colie wouldn't even need to work. Not that she's stopped," she added on a laugh. "Can you see Colie staying at home and hosting teas? She's never cared about money."

J.C. felt his heart stop. The baby was on its way. He ground his teeth together. It had been a long few months since he'd lost Colie. Since he'd thrown her out of his life, he amended bitterly. She was married. Another man would hold her hand while she gave birth, see the baby in her arms, help raise it. While the man who likely fathered it would never see it.

He shut off the stream of painful thoughts. Rod had said baldly that it wasn't even J.C.'s baby. He'd brought Colie's boyfriend to meet him, when J.C. came back from overseas, at the airport. Rod had cried about his sister's deceit.

But Colie had never deceived anybody in her young life. She was as honest as the day was long. Rod, on the other hand, wouldn't know the truth if it came up and bit him on his rear end.

Only now, months removed from the sudden knowledge of Colie's pregnancy, and the loneliness of life without her, was he even able to think straight. All the joy had gone from him, leaving him cold, like the winter snows that had been so persistent all the way to May. It was August now. Everything was in glorious bloom in Catelow. In Jacobsville, Texas, too, he thought. Colie's child would come into the world surrounded by people who loved her, including her husband. He wondered if she ever gave him a thought, even to hate him. It was nothing more than he deserved.

He'd been alone most of his life, abused in childhood

in ways that he'd never shared with a soul, not even with Colie. He'd hated the idea of children. Now, when he thought of Colie's baby, it made him sad and depressed. If it was really his, he'd done both of them a terrible injustice. Yes, she'd landed well. She had a husband who apparently took good care of her and gave her anything she wanted.

Colie had never wanted anything, though, he recalled. She wouldn't even let him buy her a meal. He winced at the memory. He'd accused her of being mercenary, the last thing she was.

The waitress brought his order to the counter. While he was paying for it, Lucy's phone rang.

"It's Colie's husband!" Lucy exclaimed. "Yes," she spoke into the phone. "Yes, Reverend Thompson's on his way…What? It's a girl! Colie has a little girl!"

There was pandemonium at Lucy's table. J.C. lost his concentration and had to dig in his pocket for another five to add to the bill. He accepted his change, gathered his order and walked out the door in a fog.

A little girl. Maybe she'd look like Colie, with the same wavy dark hair and green eyes. A little girl who'd grow up to be like her mother, sweet and gentle and kind. He bit down on the pain. Very likely it was his child. His daughter. He paused by his SUV and closed his eyes on a wave of pain that hit him in the gut like a body blow.

He could have been at the hospital with Colie, welcoming the child, comforting her, reassuring her. But she was married. He was alone and apart, as he'd always been. Nobody would know that the little girl she'd just delivered wasn't the child of her husband.

But he would know. He would blame himself as long as he lived for denying her, for not believing Colie. For ruining her life, and his. And the pain would never stop.

CHAPTER TEN

COLIE WAS BARELY aware when they put the baby in her arms. It had been a long and painful labor. She hadn't dilated enough at the end of several hours of agony, so the obstetrician made the decision to do a c-section.

"It's a little girl, sweetheart," Darby whispered in her ear. "She's so beautiful!"

"A girl." She managed a smile. She felt the pain all the way through her heart. Things should have been so different. She should be married to J.C. He should be here, looking at his daughter, holding her for the first time, loving her. Loving Colie.

Instead, this kind man who'd given her his name was being a father for the first time. He was having all the experiences that belonged to an unforgiving man who'd thrown away a woman who loved him, and his child, all at once.

Tears ran down her cheeks. She hadn't meant to cry. "Hurts," she managed, letting poor Darby think it was physical pain, not emotional pain, that prompted the hot tears.

"I'll tell them," he whispered. "Everything's all right now. Everything's fine."

It wasn't. It never would be.

SHE SLEPT. WHEN SHE opened her eyes, foggy from the pain meds, her father was bending over her. There were tears in his eyes.

"She's beautiful," he whispered. "Colie, she looks just like you did when you were born," he said, choking up.

She managed a smile. "We were going to do Lamaze," she whispered. "Natural childbirth. Darby and I went to classes."

"You can never tell what's going to happen," her father replied. "Just trust that God knows what He's doing, even when we don't," he chuckled. "Your minister's here, too."

"Reverend Blair?"

He nodded. "He's coming in to see you, but we all agreed that I should go first," he added with a wisp of humor. "We've all been worried."

"I'll be fine," she promised. "So sleepy. I want to see her."

"Soon," he promised.

Her eyes closed again.

"SHE REALLY IS BEAUTIFUL." Colie choked up when they placed the tiny child in her arms. "She's perfect!" She was touching little fingers and toes, a sweet little nose, the shock of reddish-blond hair on the child's head. "Daddy, I think she's going to be a redhead," she laughed.

He looked troubled. She knew why. There were no redheads in the whole family, anywhere.

"Maybe far back in our line," she said.

"Recessive genes," Reverend Blair, the local Jacobsville Methodist pastor, commented easily, smiling. "That's where red hair and light eyes come from. Brown hair and eyes are dominant."

"Smart man," Reverend Thompson commented with a grin.

Jake Blair shrugged. "I did a course in biology when I was in the military, years before I went to seminary. I remember genetics."

"Recessive genes." Colie's father relaxed a little. They were both remembering that J.C. had once told him that his mother had red hair and gray eyes. Neither she nor her father was comfortable thinking that the child might be her image.

"I live in Jacobsville, now, Daddy," Colie reminded her father when they were alone just briefly. "Even if J.C. saw her, he'd never think she was his. Rod told him that another man was her father. He met him at the airport with the news." She was still bitter about her brother's betrayal.

Reverend Thompson's face was sad. "I still don't understand why he'd do such a thing."

"I'm sure he had his reasons," she replied. She couldn't tell her father what Rod was really doing with his life. She didn't want to put him in danger. Supposedly, Rod was even more involved with the drug trade than he'd been before she left town. Her departure had reassured her brother that she wouldn't sell him out. She hoped it did. She couldn't bear the thought of her child being in danger.

The reverend looked at the child in her arms. She'd named the baby Beth Louise, for her mother. She'd be called Ludie, the same nickname her late mother had. Colie was feeding Ludie with a bottle, because she was recovering very slowly from the C-section and she couldn't nurse her.

"I never told you, but J.C. called."

Her heart jumped. She hated the pleasure the knowledge gave her, but she clamped down on it, hard. "Did he?" she asked, trying to sound nonchalant.

"Yes. About three weeks after you left town." He sighed and slid his hands into his pockets. "I didn't speak to him. I just put the receiver down." He grimaced. "Perhaps I should haven't have done that, Colie. I understand he went to see Lucy, too, trying to find you."

Had he believed her, at last? Had he regretted what he'd said to her? Had he wanted to patch things up?

She felt hard as rock inside. "I told Lucy not to tell him where I was going," she said quietly. "I made her promise." Lucy had never mentioned that J.C. had spoken to her; probably to spare Colie any more hurt. She looked up. "I've hurt you enough already."

He looked guilty. "I never tried to see things from your point of view. I don't really move with the times. I live in a world where people were moral, where being honorable and upright actually meant something. I can't change…"

"I would never ask you to," she cut him off. "J.C. refused to believe that I hadn't lied to him. What sort of relationship would that have been, Daddy? If you love someone, if you truly love someone, you believe what they tell you. J.C. never trusted me. He doesn't trust anyone, and he doesn't forgive." She looked back down at the baby. "I don't think he wanted to make up with me," she said sadly. "Maybe he just wanted to make sure that I was okay." Her chest rose and fell and she grimaced, because any movement hurt. "I don't believe he thought Ludie was his, or that he'd want her. He isn't the fatherly type, and he said often enough that he never wanted kids."

"I suppose so."

"Darby did," she added, and she smiled. "He was with me every minute of childbirth classes, obstetrician appointments, everything." She laughed. "Even when he was so sick from chemo, he never missed a class. He's as excited about Ludie as I am. It's been wonderful, having someone care so much." She looked up. "He loved his wife. He still mourns her. But the baby has given him so much happiness. I'm lucky that I have him in my life, for whatever time he has left."

"He's a fine man. I pray for him every night. And for you and Ludie," he added with a smile.

"Isn't she a little doll?" she asked breathlessly.

"I remember when you were just born," he recalled. "Your mother and I were so excited. We loved Rod, but we wanted a little girl, too. I wanted a baby who looked like Louise." He took a long breath. "You do, my dear. You're so much like her."

She looked up. "I miss her, too, Daddy."

"It's just a little separation," he said philosophically. "If we believe in an afterlife, we have to believe that we'll see our loved ones again. It's what makes religion so comforting."

"I guess it is." She smoothed back the baby's curly hair. She wondered if J.C.'s mother's hair had been curly like Ludie's, but she bit down hard on the thought. "I have to get some photos to send Lucy…"

"I can do that right now." The reverend pulled out his iPhone and started snapping, grinning the whole time.

LUCY WAS SHOWING the photographs to her friends at the restaurant. J.C. had just finished his steak and salad and was on his way out when he heard the woman talking about Colie's baby.

He paused by her chair, hesitant, when he was never hesitant.

"May I?" he asked solemnly.

Lucy, surprised, held up the phone with the photo of Colie holding little Ludie. He clenched his jaw. The child was the image of his mother, even at that tender age. He'd never felt such emotional pain in his whole life, not even during his childhood. He knew—*knew*—that the baby was his now. Rod had lied. Why had Rod lied?

"She's very pretty," he said half under his breath. "What did Colie name her?"

"Beth Louise," Lucy replied. "But she and Darby are going to call her Ludie. It was her mother's nickname."

He just nodded. He took one long last look at the photo and handed the phone back with a smile that was just a jerk of his chiseled lips. He turned and walked out of the restaurant. People would gossip about that. He shouldn't care. Colie had married someone else…

The child was beautiful. Red-gold curls and light eyes. There was something of Colie in the shape of her little mouth. She had long fingers. His mother had them, too; she'd played classical piano.

HE GOT INTO the SUV, hurting. If he'd needed confirmation that the child was his, he had it now. But it was months too late. Months too late.

COLIE WENT HOME from the hospital the following week. The baby was such a joy that she largely ignored the pain of the stitches and the incision, but Darby insisted on a nurse staying with them.

It was for his benefit, too, he argued, because he was back in chemo again, and losing ground. He had to go for platelet transfusions every other day, to keep the cancer at bay. His condition worsened. He was thin and pale and although he tried to hide it, he wasn't really well enough to go to the office.

One morning, he went missing. The hospital phoned to ask where he was. He'd missed his appointment for the transfusion. Colie didn't know. She worried until he came home.

He was quiet and somber. He went into the room with her, taking time to look at the sleeping baby in the bed next to hers before he paused by her bedside.

"I've made a decision," he said softly. "You won't like it."

She looked up at him, waiting, sad.

"I'm going to stop taking the transfusions." He held up a hand. "Colie, there's quality of life and quantity of life. They are not compatible. I'm sick all the time, I hurt all the time. I can't work anymore. You and the baby make what life I have bearable, but the cancer is growing. You must be able to see that I can't go on for much longer. It's just prolonging the inevitable. It's just making the process harder."

She drew in a painful breath. She'd grown fond of her husband. "I won't pretend that I agree with you," she said. "They're coming up with new methods and drugs all the time…"

"None of it will be in time for me. I spoke to the oncologist yesterday. I didn't tell you." He sat down on the side of the bed. "Maybe three months, tops, Colie. That's what he said."

She'd gone from day to day, not thinking about how inevitable things really were. Her eyes teared. "Three months?"

He nodded. He brushed back her disheveled hair. "I've enjoyed this time with you," he added. "With the baby coming." He smiled sadly. "Mary and I wanted children so much! Waiting for Ludie even made the pain bearable. But it's getting worse. Eventually, they'll have to drug me so much that I won't even know what's going on around me, to control the pain."

She winced.

"I've been privileged to have you in my life, Colie," he said. "But everything ends."

She slid her hand over his. "Thank you," she said sincerely, "for making my life bearable. For giving my baby a name."

He smiled. "It has been a daily joy. But it's time to let go."

She didn't fight the tears. "I'll be with you every minute. Right up until the end."

"I know that."

WHEN LUDIE WAS two months old, hospice had to come in to help with Darby's care. He was growing steadily weaker. At least, Colie thought, there was plenty of money to take care of whatever needs he had. After the hospital bill was paid, and all the doctors, there would be a huge hole in his savings. She didn't care. She'd always worked for her living. It wouldn't matter if there wasn't a dime left, so long as he had everything they could give him to make it easier.

A sudden phone call upset her even more. Her father had been rushed to the hospital for emergency surgery. He was in very bad shape.

Ty and Annie Mosby had gone to a dog show, or she'd have asked them for help. So Colie phoned her friend Sari Grayling Fiore, who was a sister to Ren Colter's wife,

Merrie in Catelow, and begged a seat on the Grayling jet to get to her father with the baby.

"I can get a commercial flight, but Darby can't come with me, he's so sick…!"

"Don't you even think about it," Sari interrupted. "I'll have the plane and the pilot waiting for you at the airport. How bad is it?"

"I don't know," Colie said miserably. "They said his appendix had perforated. I don't know what that means, but it sounds horrible…!"

Sari knew. She didn't say. "You just get there as fast as you can. I'll call ahead and have a car waiting at the airport in Catelow to take you straight to the hospital."

"You're so kind." Colie broke down.

"You're so kind," came the soft reply. "We all love you, Colie. I'm sorry about Darby. We heard that he's losing ground."

"Very fast," came the tearful reply. "Oh, I hate to leave him, even for a day, but I have to see about Daddy. Nobody can find Rod," she added coldly.

"Your brother?"

"My brother."

"Maybe he'll show up," Sari said slowly.

"I'll be there, anyway. Thanks so much. I owe you!"

"No, you don't. Get a cab to the airport. Morales runs one twenty-four hours a day."

"I know. I'll phone him right now. And thanks!"

"No problem."

SHE CALLED JACK MORALES, a former San Antonio policeman who'd decided that running a twenty-four-hour cab service in Jacobsville was less stressful than his former profession.

"I hate to wake you up at 2:00 a.m.," Colie began.

"That's what I'm here for," he chuckled. "I'll be there in five minutes."

"Thanks."

SHE KISSED DARBY and explained where she was going. He was foggy from drugs, but he squeezed her hand. "Be careful. Tell your dad I said hello and I wish him the best."

"I'll be back as soon as I can. I promise."

"I know. My sweet girl."

She fought tears as she gathered up Ludie and her diaper bag, and her small carry-on bag, spoke to the nurse and went out the door.

THE CATELOW HOSPITAL was quiet so early in the day. Colie sat in the waiting room with Ludie while the surgeon operated on her father.

She'd been there only a short time when he came out, smiling.

"We got it in time," he said, smiling at the baby. "He'll be fine."

"Oh, thank God," she bit off, tears rolling down her cheeks. "I was so scared!"

"He wasn't, which caused the problem," the surgeon chuckled. "He had terrible pain in his stomach, but it suddenly stopped. He tried to send the ambulance he'd called away, but when he told them how much better he felt, they loaded him up and rushed him here. As it was, they were barely in time." He leaned forward. "I scooped what was left of his appendix out with a spoon, figuratively speaking!"

"Really?"

He nodded. "The lack of pain meant it had perforated." He shook his head. "I had a patient die once, because he thought he was better and didn't call an ambulance in time. Painful lesson about the appendix and its malfunction."

"I guess so. Daddy's going to be okay?"

He smiled. "Yes, he is. When he's out of recovery, I'll let you see him." He glanced at the baby. "Boy or girl?"

"A little girl," she said. "She's two months old today."

"Pretty hair."

"I think so, too." She hesitated. "Will they let me in with the baby?"

"We'll have one of the hospital volunteers sit and hold her for you," he promised. "No worries."

SHE GOT BACK to her father while a retired nurse who did volunteer work at the hospital sat in the waiting room with the baby.

"Scared me, you know," she chided as Reverend Thompson opened his eyes and looked up groggily.

He managed a laugh. "Sorry. I guess I didn't know as much about appendicitis as I thought I did."

"Good thing the EMTs did," she pointed out.

"Got Ludie with you?"

"I have. She's in the waiting room with a nurse's aide. I had to leave Darby. He's bad. Really bad. We've got hospice now."

"Your life has been an ongoing tragedy, my darling. I'd hoped for something happier for you."

She bent and kissed his forehead. "We do things and then we pay for doing them," she said simply. "That's life."

"I suppose so. But God loves us, no matter what we do."

She grinned. "That, I did know." She laughed.

"You can't stay long," he supposed.

She nodded. "Until you come home from the hospital and I find you a nurse," she said. "Then I have to go back. We have a nurse staying with Darby."

"I know you hated leaving him. You could go now..."

"After you're home," she repeated.

"I don't need a nurse, you know. It's just an appendectomy. I asked the doctor."

She wanted to argue, but his expression told her it would do no good. "Okay, then," she said, smiling at him.

He sighed. "Rod didn't come home this week. He called and said he and his friend had business in Denver. Big business. He didn't say what it was. I'm not sure he's working at the hardware store anymore."

"He probably has other things in mind to do," was all she'd say. "Maybe he's found a new career," she added, and tried to keep the contempt out of her tone.

"I guess so."

"I'm going back to the house now, but I'll see you later in the day. I need to feed Ludie."

"That's okay."

He closed his eyes and went back to sleep.

THE HOUSE WAS just as Colie remembered it, but dustier. She unfolded the carrier that doubled as a baby bed and put the few bottles of baby food and milk that she'd brought with her in the fridge. If she was staying until her father was released—probably two days, the surgeon thought—she'd have to go shopping.

SHE PHONED LUCY, who was off on this Saturday afternoon, and asked her to take care of Ludie while she visited her father. Lucy came over, excited to see the baby.

"Gosh, she really is a little doll," she exclaimed. "Look at that hair!"

Colie grimaced.

"I guess there's a redhead in your family tree, huh?" Lucy continued, unaware of her friend's discomfort.

"Somewhere," Colie said. "I won't be long."

"That's okay. Ludie and I will get along just fine!"

"Thanks, Lucy."

"That's what friends do for one another. If I ever get pregnant, and I hope to, one day, you can do the same for me, when you're visiting your father," she said with a grin.

"Count on it," Colie promised, smiling.

"MERRIE SAYS HER SISTER, Sari Fiore, sent Colie up here on the family jet," Ren remarked while he and his security chief were having coffee midmorning.

J.C.'s hand jerked a little on the cup. Otherwise, he gave no sign that the news affected him. "Did she? Why?"

"Her father had to have an emergency appendectomy," Ren replied. He looked up. "Colie's husband is in the final stages of cancer. They have hospice for him."

J.C. grimaced. "That must be rough."

"My mother went through cancer treatment," Ren recalled. "It hasn't been long enough that I've forgotten how rough it was on her. And on us. But her prognosis was better. She recovered and the cancer hasn't come back."

J.C. nodded. He looked down at his coffee cup. "Did she bring the baby with her?"

"Yes."

He wouldn't admit, couldn't admit, how desperately he wanted to see the child. He forced his mind on to another subject. Ren obliged him by not volunteering any more information.

Later that same day, J.C. had to stop by the grocery store to pick up a loaf of bread for Delsey, the cook at Ren's ranch.

Halfway down the aisle, there was Colie, with the baby in her arms, looking at crackers.

He stopped, waited until she saw him. When she did, her whole body seemed to jump. He was so eaten up with guilt that he was blind to the involuntary joy she felt at the sight of him.

He moved a step closer, wary of people nearby. But it was midafternoon and most shoppers were at work. There were hardly any customers in the small grocery store right now.

"How's your father?" he asked.

She swallowed, hard. "He's much better. They'll let him come home day after tomorrow."

"What happened?"

"Appendicitis," she said. "His appendix perforated. He didn't realize until it was almost too late."

He nodded. His eyes were on the baby in her arms. He could hardly pry his gaze away from the child. Red-gold hair like his mother. Then she opened her little eyes and looked up at him. Even at that age, he could tell that her eyes were going to be gray, like his. Like his mother's. His face contorted.

"I can only stay until tomorrow," she said, hating the huskiness in her voice. "Darby's very bad. We have hospice helping with his care, but I still need to be there." She paused. "He's been very kind to me."

He was breathing roughly, trying to control his own

emotions. He stuck his hands in his pockets. "Kind, when I wasn't," he said gruffly.

She averted her eyes to the shelves and picked up a box of soda crackers, her father's favorite. She'd add cheese when she went to the refrigerated section. Her dad loved his midnight snacks. He'd sent her shopping.

"Have you seen Rod?" she asked, for something to say.

"If I had, it would probably be in the police report in the local papers," he gritted.

She looked up at him, surprised. Her eyes searched his. She had to drop them. The contact was shattering.

"Have you heard from him?" he replied.

"No. Daddy said he hasn't been home for over a week. He said that he and his friend had big business in Denver," she added bitterly.

"He's mixed up in something," J.C. said. "I don't know what, but there's gossip."

She put the crackers into the shopping cart. She'd had the baby resting in the top section of it, in her carrier, but Ludie had become fussy so she'd picked her up temporarily.

"You know something about Rod," J.C. guessed, and so accurately that her head came up. Guilt was written all over her. "What do you know?"

"I can't tell you," she said. She lowered her eyes. "I had planned to…"

"And you told Rod that you were going to tell me," he guessed icily. "So he found a foolproof way to get you out of my life."

Her eyes registered her shock.

He nodded slowly. His face was set in hard lines. "I finally worked it out. Not in time to do either of us any good." He drew in a long breath. "I should have told you about my childhood, Colie—about the experiences that taught me never to trust anyone."

She didn't reply. He kept secrets. She'd lived with him for several weeks, and never really got to know him at all.

His eyes narrowed. "And you should have told me that you were innocent," he added shortly, registering her scarlet blush. The blood that first time, that he'd taken for her period starting, her distaste for sex, it had all finally added up in his mind. "For God's sake," he bit off, "I could have read a book, or something. I could have learned what to do…" He stopped, self-conscious.

She'd wondered if he would ever puzzle that out. Now he had. So many revelations coming out, in a grocery store in Catelow, in the middle of a normal day. And none of it mattered. None of it made the slightest difference in her life.

He sighed. "Damn, Colie," he said half under his breath. "The only women I was ever with were experienced, and they liked it rough." He averted his eyes. "We act as we're taught."

She remembered the call girl he'd been in love with all those years ago and reasoned that such a woman probably didn't really like sex at all, but pretended to, for the money. Now things began to make sense to her.

"It's all water under the bridge, now," she said quietly. "I'm married, J.C."

His face gave away little, but his jaw tautened. He wouldn't look at her. "I'm glad that he was good to you."

"He and his first wife couldn't have children," she confessed. "He was so excited about Ludie. He was with me every step of the way, right up to the C-section…"

"C-section?" he exclaimed.

"Something went wrong. They're not sure what," she

replied. "It was rough for a few weeks, but I'm recovering. Darby had a nurse stay with us, to help with Ludie while I got back on my feet. Now she's staying because he can't be left alone." Tears threatened. "It's rare, people like him, in the world. He doesn't ask for anything. He just gives."

"My total opposite," he replied shortly. "I never gave anything. Just like my father, wherever he is."

She studied his hard face. "You don't forgive people, J.C. It was one of the first things I learned about you." She smiled sadly. "You wouldn't forgive me."

"I didn't know," he said huskily.

She just looked at him. "Rod never told the truth in his life, and I never told a lie. But when it came down to it, he was the one you believed."

"Because I was..." He paused. He wanted to say "afraid," but it was a weakness. He'd learned in his life never to show weakness to anyone else. "I didn't want a family," he corrected.

"Lucky you," she replied. "You got your wish."

He looked at the child, who was watching him. It was eerie, that there was something like recognition in those wide gray eyes. It was as if the child knew him. He shook himself mentally. Now he was having delusions.

"She's a pretty child," he remarked quietly.

"She's a good baby. She almost never cries, and when she does, it's because she's hungry or needs changing."

"You always wanted kids."

She nodded, smiling sadly. "And you never did. It would never have worked. Besides all that, my poor father had been embarrassed enough by my behavior. I expect gossip has slowed down since I left town. Especially since I married."

"Everyone thinks the child is your husband's," he said with more bitterness than he realized.

"Of course she is," she returned without looking at him.

He felt the words like a body blow, until he realized that she didn't mean them. She was behaving like a fugitive, refusing to look at him while she told the lie.

He couldn't admit what he'd worked out. He didn't want to make her more uncomfortable than she was. "I saw the wedding announcement in the paper," he said. "Lucy had photos of the baby when she was born. I was in the cafeteria. She showed them to me…"

Colie looked up with so much pain in her eyes that he stopped what he was saying and just stared down at her.

"I messed it all up," he said, half under his breath as he looked from Colie to the baby in her arms.

"It doesn't matter now," Colie said quietly. "Darby always says that yesterday is a memory and tomorrow is a hope, that all we really have is right now, today." She smiled. "He's right."

He became aware of an older man pushing a grocery cart down the aisle. "I have to go," he said, picking up the loaf of bread he'd been sent for. "Delsey ran out of bread, so she sent me in to pick up a loaf for sandwiches."

"Sari had the Grayling jet pick me up and fly me here," she remarked. "It would have been rough coming by myself with the baby and all her stuff. Diaper bag, bottles, formula," she added on a breathless laugh.

"You don't nurse her?" he asked softly. Then his face hardened. "Of course you don't. Not with a C-section."

She was curious. "How do you know about them?"

"Merrie had to have one, with their son," he replied. "Ren went wild. I had to hide all the whiskey bottles."

She managed a smile. "Darby said he was never more tempted to have a drink. He can't tolerate alcohol."

He hated the mention of her husband. He hated the whole world. There she stood, the color and light of his life, with his child in her arms, and he was an outsider, a spectator. That was all he could be now.

"Life doesn't come with a reset button," he remarked heavily. "God help me, I'd give anything if it did," he added, his eyes on Ludie as he winced.

Colie, aware of the older gentleman approaching with his cart, just smiled. "Tell Sari I said thank you for everything," she said. "And that I'm going home in the morning, early, if that's okay. She's letting her pilot fly me back in the jet."

He nodded. "I'll tell her." He moved back a step. "Be happy, Colie," he said softly. He had to pry his eyes away from her. "Tell your father I hope he does well."

"I will. Goodbye, J.C.," she said with more feeling than she realized.

He couldn't look at them. He was too cut up inside, too sick at his own behavior that had robbed him of the family Darby Howland now enjoyed.

"Goodbye, Colie," he said in what he hoped was just a pleasant tone. He nodded politely at the older gentleman, who nodded back and smiled. He walked out of the grocery store, feeling as if he was dragging his heart behind him on the ground.

Colie watched him go, all the way out the door. He never looked back once. She smiled sadly. Nothing had changed. Nothing at all.

CHAPTER ELEVEN

COLIE STAYED JUST long enough to see her father settled back at home before she took Ludie to the airport and boarded the private jet that would take them back to Jacobsville. During the long flight, she recalled the odd conversation with J.C.

Did he know that Ludie was his? She thought he must have. He hadn't come right out and said anything, but he'd insinuated it.

She allowed herself, for just a minute, to wonder what would have happened if he'd come to his senses sooner, if he'd been able to speak to Colie before she married Darby. But J.C. had been adamant about not wanting children. Perhaps if he'd known the child was his, he'd have asked her not to have it.

She looked at the sleeping child in her arms and didn't regret a thing. Ludie was so precious. Every day brought new joy, new wonder, into Colie's life. She wished she'd lived a conventional life, that she hadn't stepped out of line so badly. She wished that J.C. had been more honest, more open with her. Something had happened to him, something very bad, that had taught him not to trust people.

She wondered what it was. She knew his mother had died when he was ten, that he was placed in foster homes until he got through school. Was it in one of them that he'd had something traumatic happen? It might explain his hatred of his father, his refusal to even try to contact the man who was his only surviving relative. J.C. didn't consider that people had motivations, reasons for the way they behaved. It explained a lot. He saw things in black-and-white, never in shades of gray.

Colie was sorry for him. He'd be alone his whole life. His daughter would grow up in Texas, with another man's name. All that, because J.C. never trusted Colie. It made her sad.

Thinking about Darby made her sadder. He was losing ground. It wouldn't be much longer. But she'd make his remaining time as happy as she could, she decided.

She looked down at her daughter and smiled. Ludie's gray eyes were open, staring up at her. She made a face that looked suspiciously like a tiny smile. She wondered if babies could smile at this age. She'd have to ask the doctor when she got home.

REN NOTICED HOW preoccupied J.C. was. "Your mind's not on the job," he said drily.

J.C. shook his head. "She had the baby with her. It's a beautiful child," he added, the words almost torn out of him.

"Merrie wanted to see him, but our son's had an ear infection. She's had her hands full." He chuckled. "So have I. We both get up with him in the night, still, if he cries. They say the first two years are spent mostly in doctor's waiting rooms. Babies get sick for all sorts of reasons, despite the immunizations they give."

"Merrie had them stretch those out, didn't she?" he asked absently.

"We both did," Ren replied. "They have to have the

vaccines, but I'm not letting anyone give them all at once. Even when we take the puppy to the vet, we have them stretched out. Safety precaution," he added. "They can't predict the interactions of so many vaccines at once. At least, I'm not convinced that they can. We're erring on the side of caution."

"Parents." J.C. laughed. But his eyes were sad. "That's something I'll never know about," he added a little stiffly.

"How's Colie's dad, did she say?" Ren said, changing the subject.

"He's doing very well," he replied. He hesitated. "I'm off Saturday. Thought I might go and check on him. If he'll let me in the door."

"Reverend Thompson's not like that," Ren commented, because he and Merrie and their son all went to the local Methodist church. "He never holds grudges, and his door's always open."

J.C. thought about that. "I'll take him some fresh fruit. Colie used to say that he loved it more than anything."

Ren smiled. "Peace offering? Not a bad idea."

J.C. laughed at the idea of apples making up for all the embarrassment he'd caused the reverend. He might not get in the door. But he was going to try.

"Delsey made a big pot of soup," Ren said. "Take him a jar of that, instead of fruit."

J.C. smiled. "Okay. Thanks."

DARBY WAS GOING downhill fast. Colie hired another nurse to take care of the baby, because Darby was now a full-time job for the nurse they had.

Colie didn't need telling how bad things were. They were having to give Darby massive doses of narcotic to keep the pain at bay. He slept most of the time. When he woke, Colie was always by his bedside, night and day.

"I'll never be able to thank you enough, for all you've done for me," he said in a wispy tone during one of his lucid periods.

"That works both ways." She squeezed his hand. It was so thin and cold. "You made life bearable for me."

"I'm sorry that I have to leave you," he said drowsily. "But I'll be with Mary, you know." He smiled. "I saw her. She was here last night, sitting by the bed while you caught a couple of hours' sleep. She smiled at me." He closed his eyes, barely aware of Colie's fascinated look. "She'll come and take me home, when it's time. I'm not afraid. Not now…"

Colie had heard all her life that the person who loved you most in life would come to fetch you, when you died. She'd been with her mother when the end came, and her mother had seen her own mother, standing in the doorway, smiling, the day before she died.

It was a reminder, a sweet reminder, that life went on, even when it seemed that the person you loved was gone forever. There were other stories she remembered from childhood, other people who'd seen long-gone loved ones at the end. It was comforting. She knew how much Darby had loved his wife. It made her happy that he was anticipating a joyful reunion.

She took time to feed the baby, while the nurse sat with Darby. The other nurse had gone to the pharmacy for things she needed in Darby's care.

It had been only five minutes when the nurse entered the room, her face set in hard lines, her eyes red. She'd become fond of Darby while she'd been with them, although she was professional enough not to let a slip of emotion show, normally.

"Mrs. Howland?" she said softly. She drew in a breath. This was never easy. "He's gone."

Even though she was expecting it, Colie gasped and felt the blood drain out of her face. "But I was just with him…!"

"I'm so sorry," the nurse added quietly. "He just took a deep breath and it was over, just that quickly." She hesitated. "You know that he had a living will, that he stipulated we weren't to try and bring him back, if…" she added.

"Yes, I know. It's all right. Hold the baby, please," Colie said, getting up. She handed the bottle and Ludie to the nurse and went back into Darby's bedroom.

He looked as if he was sleeping, except for the odd tinge of color that seemed to overlay his even features. She sat down beside him on the bed. His face, when she touched it, was still warm.

"Mary came for you, didn't she?" she whispered while tears drained from her eyes and ran, salty, into the corners of her mouth. "I'm happy for you, Darby. But I'll miss you. Thank you. Thank you for all you've done for me."

She bent and kissed his forehead. It was hard to get up, to leave him. She had to remind herself that this was now just an empty shell. Darby was off somewhere in a meadow, picking wildflowers with Mary, laughing. She kept that picture in her mind as she went back to get the nurse. There would be much to do now.

THE FUNERAL WAS very nice. Darby was a military veteran, so there was an honor guard from the local Veterans of

Foreign Wars, and a twenty-one gun salute as well as an American flag draped over the coffin. It was a poignant service to Colie, whose mother's funeral was still fairly fresh in her mind, despite the years since she'd died.

Her father had told her once that funerals became harder as people aged, because each new one brought back memories of all the old ones. They piled up in the mind like a nightmare, echoing the pain of past losses. Even when you believed in an afterlife, as he did, it was still rough. He presided over almost every funeral of people in his congregation.

He was sitting beside Colie now, in the front pew, while another minister, Jake Blair, spoke about Darby and his importance to the community and its people.

Colie had the baby in her lap. Ludie was very quiet, playing with a baby rattle, not making a sound, as if she understood even at that tender age that she was supposed to be quiet in church. Her pale gray eyes looked up into her mother's green ones, curiously, watching as Colie cried. She dropped her rattle and reached a tiny hand up toward her mother's face, as if she sought to comfort her.

Colie took the little hand and kissed it. Darby had loved Ludie so much. She owed him a debt that she could never repay. Her eyes went back to the casket and she remembered the man inside it with great affection and deep loss.

THEY BURIED HIM on a hill in the Jacobsville cemetery, beside Mary. Colie had already ordered the tombstone, which would be identical to Mary's, so they'd match. She'd remember to put flowers on both graves, she thought, at every holiday.

After the memorial service, her father had to go home.

Once again, Sari Fiore had organized transportation for Colie's father, so that he didn't have the hassle associated with public air travel. The jet was waiting for him at the Jacobsville airport, and Jack Morales was loading his suitcase into the cab as he parted with Colie and Ludie on the front porch.

"I hate to leave you alone," he said solemnly.

"I'm not alone," Colie told him sadly. "I have Ludie. We'll come up to visit you at summer vacation," she added. "I have my old job back at the law firm, so finances aren't going to be a problem. Darby had paid off the loan on the house, so it's mine free and clear. I just have to make enough to maintain it," she said with a smile.

"He was well-to-do," her father began.

"Was, yes," she replied with a gentle smile. "Cancer is a very expensive disease, and he was years too young for Medicare," she added. "It took everything he had. I don't mind, you know that. I never married him for his money."

"Everybody knew that. But only we know the real reason," the reverend added quietly. "It was a noble, kind thing he did for you, giving Ludie a name."

"Something J.C. would never have done," she replied sadly.

Reverend Thompson didn't reply immediately. He knew things about J.C. now that he wished he'd known a year ago. He couldn't tell Colie. It would only hurt her more. "I'll miss you, sweetheart," he said, and hugged her tight.

"I'll miss you, too."

He let her go with a sigh. "I wish your brother had been like you."

"Immoral…?" she teased.

"Stop that. I mean good-hearted and kind and respon-sible," he said. "I never see him. Colie, I think he's mixed up in something very bad."

"If he is," she said suddenly, and emphatically, "don't you get involved. You have to trust that I know more than I can ever tell anybody. Just pretend you have no idea what he's doing. Please. For my sake, and Ludie's!"

He was surprised at her response. He hadn't expected that she knew much about Rodney and his habits. Then he remembered what she'd said, about Rod going to see J.C. and telling a lie about the baby.

"Your brother needs help," he said.

"He'll never get it," she said back. "He doesn't think he needs it. We can't do anything for him until he realizes that he has a problem and wants to do something about it. I don't think that will ever happen, Daddy."

He searched her green eyes. "Miracles happen every day."

"They do, for many people."

He smiled sadly. "Sometimes, hope is all we have. Take care of yourself and my granddaughter."

"Call me when you get home, so I'll know you got there okay."

He laughed. "I will." He kissed the baby's forehead. "Take care of each other. I'll see you soon, I hope."

"Me, too. Have a safe trip."

She watched him climb into Jack's cab and wave. They drove away. She was still watching, tears in her eyes. She'd never felt so alone.

TIME PASSED. Colie and her father talked on Skype at least twice a week. It wasn't as good as a true visit, but it made up for the distance.

Meanwhile, unbeknownst to her, the reverend had someone else watching over him.

It had started unexpectedly. Reverend Jared Thompson had gone to the door one evening just after he'd come home from the hospital to find J.C. Calhoun standing outside with a large bag in his hands.

The younger man seemed unusually insecure. He handed Jared the bag. "Merrie and Delsey have been in the kitchen making soup. It's really good. Ren and Merrie thought you might like some, while you're recovering from surgery."

"That's very kind of them," Jared said, and smiled. "Thank you for bringing it."

"No problem. I was on my way home."

He didn't leave, though. His eyes were on a chessboard in full view of the door. "You play?" he asked abruptly.

"I do," the reverend said. "Do you?"

"I was part of a chess team in my unit, when I was in the service. I still play with Ren."

The reverend pursed his lips. "You busy?" he asked.

J.C. seemed surprised. "Well, no. Not really."

"Up to a game?"

The younger man returned the smile. "If you are. I wouldn't want to tire you. I heard from Ren what a rough time you had, with the appendicitis."

"I'm much better. And I'd enjoy the company."

J.C. drew in a worried breath. "Listen, about all that happened…"

"Come in. I'll make coffee."

J.C. only hesitated for a few seconds. "Okay."

THEY PLAYED TO a draw twice.

"You're very good at this," the reverend remarked.

J.C. laughed softly. "My mother taught me. She worked for the government in British Columbia for a time. She was from Ireland. Redheaded and gray-eyed. Smart and kind and loving." His face set. "My father's exact opposite."

The reverend didn't speak. He just listened, which made the younger man relax.

"When I was young, he was driving her to a meeting at my school. He'd been drinking, as usual, but she said they should both go. The car went off the road and she died. They would have taken him to jail, if they could have found him. They couldn't. He ran. Nobody knew where he was." His face set in hard lines. "I was put in temporary homes, foster homes."

Reverend Thompson still didn't speak. He cocked his head to one side, just waiting.

J.C. drew in a long breath, his eyes on the chessboard. "In the second one of those…homes," he said, "my foster mother decided that I needed a firsthand look at the facts of life. I was twelve. She was repulsive to me. Even if she hadn't been…" He stopped, swallowed. "So I went to talk to her husband about it. I hoped he'd at least listen to me. Well, he listened." His face hardened. "He closed the door and locked it, and said that if I didn't like her, maybe I'd like him."

The reverend read between the lines very well. "Dear God," he said softly. "I'm so sorry."

J.C. had never spoken of it. Sympathy was the last thing he'd expected from this kind man, whose life he'd made miserable by his treatment of Colie.

"When I got away from him, sick and scared, I climbed out my window—he'd locked me in, you see—and I ran until I couldn't run anymore. I ended up outside a hotel. I was too ashamed to tell anybody what had happened. But I was a kid, and alone. I was panhandling, getting just enough coins to eat and avoiding the police. A mining foreman and his wife were in town for a reunion. They were kind. I told them my parents had just died and I had no place to go."

"And?" Jared prompted gently.

"They lived in the Yukon, several hundred miles from Whitehorse. Far enough away that I thought maybe the authorities wouldn't come after me. They said they'd take me in. They had no kids and I guess they felt sorry for me," he said. "I don't know how he managed, but he got papers for me so that he could take me out of Canada. I lived with them for almost a year. He and his wife were going to adopt me." He laughed hollowly. "I'd just come home from school. I saw the flames when the bus stopped about a quarter mile from their house. I remember that I threw down my book bag and ran the whole way. I tried to get them out, but the fire was so intense that I couldn't get near the front door. The firemen were nearby, but it was already too late. A neighbour actually sat on me to keep me from trying to get to them. By then, of course, it was all over, anyway."

"Tough luck," the older man said softly.

"The firemen told their chief, who did some digging and found out that I'd run away from my former home. I tried to tell him what had happened there, but he said I was exaggerating because I didn't like the couple I'd lived with." He fiddled with a chess piece. "He called the authorities and they sent someone to drive me back. But halfway, I told the man I needed to stop at a restroom. He was getting gas when I ran out the back way and hid. It was dark. He couldn't find me, so he drove off, presumably to get the authorities. But by then, I'd hitched a ride with a couple of loggers. They were going to Juneau by boat. You can't drive to Juneau," he added with a faint smile. "Only way in is by air or sea. So I told them my parents were there, that I'd been staying with a cousin and my family thought I was on another boat, but I'd missed it."

"So you ended up on your own again," the reverend said quietly.

J.C. nodded. It was so easy to talk to the man. He'd never told a soul about any of this.

"I was on the streets, there, trying to find anything to do that would make me some money. I fell in with a gang," he added on a short laugh, shaking his head. "They were like me, homeless kids that had been kicked around a lot. They worked for a local crime boss. I became an errand boy. Illegal, but not as bad as killing people or stealing, which I refused to do."

"At least, you had a place to stay."

"Yes. I lived on the streets until I graduated from high school. I'd managed that in spite of some teasing by the other kids about how stupid it was to go to school every day. I had it down pat—I invented parents, had one of the older kids let me use his internet for report cards and to have my 'parents' communicate with my teachers. I knew that without an education, I'd end up like a lot of the street people. I wanted something better than that. The kids I hung around with were ice-cold, some of them, but they were kind. We had a network, and they went to bat for me, making sure the police didn't find out that I'd run away from foster care. Living on the streets is a tough way to get by," he added. "If I had any softness left in me by then, the lifestyle beat it out of me. I had American citizenship through my mother, who was a naturalized citizen, and when I graduated, I found a way to get my birth certificate and my mother's, to prove American citizenship. I had nothing against the Yukon, but I wanted a fresh start. I wound up in Billings, where I joined the police force."

This, the reverend hadn't known. His eyebrows went up.

"I spent two years there," J.C. continued. "It was a tough job sometimes, but I was used to violence and rough people. I seemed very well suited to the job. But I wanted to see the world, and I didn't have any money, so I went into the Army." He laughed. "I seemed to fit in a structured, military environment. But I couldn't settle in a regular unit. I ended up in spec ops, where I did even better. That's where I met Ren. I kicked around the world for several years, doing freelance work. I ran into him again when we were both doing jobs overseas in the Army Reserves, and he offered me a job. I was skilled at surveillance, and I'd studied computer programming. So I ended up working on a ranch in Wyoming."

"You don't like women," the reverend said unexpectedly.

J.C. winced.

The reverend just waited.

"I was grass green about women. When I was in the gang, a lot of the boys had girlfriends, but they were raw things, casual things. My mother had raised me to believe in something more than that. After what happened to me, I was even less interested in that part of life." He leaned back. "After I enlisted in the Army and got through basic training, I met Cecelia. She was sophisticated, smart, well-to-do. I met her in a nightclub, a rare evening out. She seemed really fascinated with me. She knew one of my buddies. I didn't realize it at the time, but he knew that I always had money and she was out for anything she could get."

He picked up the chess piece and looked at it with eyes that were focused on the past. "I went crazy for her. I bought her expensive presents, took her out almost every night. She was…amazing," he concluded, not volunteering that she was everything a man could want in bed. "What I didn't know was that she was a call girl," he added from between clenched teeth. "I found it out in the worst way. I'd bought a bouquet and I went to her apartment to surprise her, on her birthday. The door was standing half-open, so I walked in." He laughed hollowly. "She was talking to one of her clients, telling him she had a soldier on the string who was so stupid he didn't even realize that she sold herself for money. He bought her all sorts of expensive things and he was so besotted that she could make him do anything she liked."

The reverend winced.

J.C. managed a smile. "I was naive. I didn't know anything about women, except that I'd already formed a pretty bad opinion of them. That pretty much burned me out on the idea of a home and a family. From that day forward, I took what was offered and walked away." He hesitated. "Until Colie came along." His eyes closed. "Her friend Lucy said that life doesn't come with a reset button. That's true. But if it did…" He looked at the reverend with anguish on his face. "I believed a lie. I think I knew better, even then. But she had such a hold on me, and I'd been sold out so much." His voice trailed away.

"You never told her any of this," the older man surmised.

"None of it," J.C. agreed. "I didn't trust her enough."

"Where was your father all this time?" the other man asked.

"I don't know. I don't care. He killed my mother."

"J.C.," the reverend said gently, "people always have motivation for the things they do. Some act out of anger, others out of a weakness in character, some as a result of substance abuse. But there's always a reason."

"Mother said he wanted a ranch of his own, but when I came along, he had to work in the mines to make enough to support us. She had a good job with the government, but she had weak lungs and she was sick a lot. He was never the loving father you hear about in stories." He laughed coldly. "If I got in his way, he'd knock me down. I can't count the number of times the police came to our door because he'd beat up my mother. I don't think I ever saw him sober."

Reverend Thompson had, by now, a painful portrait of the man his daughter loved. He wished with all his heart that J.C. had come to him years earlier, just to talk. What a load of misery he carried on his broad shoulders.

"So you decided that there was no such thing as a good marriage."

J.C. looked up with a wistful smile. "Or a good woman," he added. "I only had my mother's example of what a woman should be. But the kind I encountered were a far cry from her."

"My parents were missionaries," the reverend said. "They married in their teens and lived together for forty years before they died, in a tornado. It was just as well, because I don't think one could have survived without the other. I had the same sort of marriage. I loved my wife until the day she died, and I still mourn her."

J.C. searched his eyes. He was thinking that if he'd had such an upbringing, his own life might have settled into something more conventional than it had.

"Colie loves you very much," J.C. said. He drew in a troubled breath. "I wish that I'd made better choices. I never considered what living with me would do to her, or to you."

"Actions have consequences," the older man said simply. "Life is all lessons. We make mistakes, but we learn from them." He smiled. "Faith teaches us that the greatest gift is forgiveness." He cocked his head again. "J.C., don't you think it's time you forgave yourself?"

J.C.'s lean hand jerked. He almost dropped the chess piece. He righted it and placed it with deliberate care back on the board. "Excuse me?"

"It's something I see often in abused children." He noted the other man's surprise. "Oh, yes, it happens in the best of families. I've seen far too much of it in my life. One thing the children all have in common is that they blame themselves for what happened to them. They think it's some evil in themselves that caused it. That's not true."

J.C. didn't speak. But he was listening, intently.

"Abusers were, in many cases, themselves abused children. The prisons are full of them, kids who lived in anguish, in secrecy, afraid to tell anyone for fear of not being believed, of making a bad situation worse."

"I know the feeling."

"Of course you do. The thing you have to understand is that you're punishing yourself. You have to let go of the past, and go ahead. Looking behind you is never a good option."

"Well, unless you're being shadowed by someone in an

enemy uniform carrying an AK-47," J.C. offered, tongue in cheek.

The reverend laughed. "I was in the Army Reserves when Desert Storm came up. I went overseas with my unit as a chaplain." His eyes, green like Colie's, were full of sadness. "I know the face of war, and its consequences."

J.C. nodded. "I was always in the front lines," he confided. "It never got easy, and all of us were afraid."

Reverend Thompson chuckled. "Anybody who tells you he hasn't felt fear in combat is lying," he replied. "But courage isn't the lack of fear—it's having the guts to act even when you're most afraid. That's true heroism."

J.C. toyed with the chess piece again. He didn't look up. "I wish I'd talked to you before."

"I wish you had, too, J.C.," Reverend Thompson said quietly. "Holding resentments inside is like ignoring an infected wound. It only festers and then inflames."

"Not a bad analogy."

"Thank you, I worked on it for years," came the amused reply.

J.C. chuckled.

"In case you wondered, I never repeat anything I'm told in confidence, even to my family," he added. "I keep confidences."

"I wouldn't have asked. But, thanks."

"You're welcome." The older man's eyes twinkled. "Best three out of four?" he added, nodding at the chessboard.

J.C. chuckled. "Okay. If you've got some more black coffee. I'm out."

"So am I," came the laughing reply.

J.C. WAS RELUCTANT to leave. "I wasn't sure that you'd let me in the door," he confessed as he stood on the porch. "I've done a lot of damage to your reputation."

The older man shrugged. "I've weathered worse storms. It was Colie who was hurt the most."

J.C. winced. "I know." He shoved his hands into the pockets of his jeans. "It all went wrong in one day," he added heavily. "I had a set of rings in my pocket when I came home," he said gruffly. "Emeralds. Green, like her eyes."

The reverend's heart jumped.

J.C. looked up, recognizing the other man's surprise. "I was ready to take a chance, even though I still had doubts." He looked away. "Don't tell her," he said huskily. "It would only hurt her more."

The reverend was at a loss for words. He didn't know what to say. Poor Colie! After a minute, he regained his composure.

He frowned. "Colie said that Rod met you at the airport," he said unexpectedly.

J.C. hesitated. He'd damaged Colie. He didn't want to wound this kind man by speculating on what Rod was into, or why he'd deliberately told a lie about Colie.

"I see," the reverend said softly. "You're trying to protect me. I know how people behave when they use drugs, J.C. I see it all the time when I'm counseling young people at the detention center, many of whom are still under the influence when I'm asked to intervene."

J.C. bit his lower lip. "Rod was my friend," he said.

"He's lost his way," the older man replied sadly. "But I won't give up on him. One day, he'll realize that he's destroying himself. I'll be there, whenever it is. You never give up on people, whatever they do, and you always forgive." He smiled. "That's what religion is all about. Forgiveness. It's in short supply in the modern world, where a hunger for things has replaced a hunger for faith."

"All too true," J.C. agreed. He still hesitated.

"I like chess."

J.C. smiled. "Me, too."

"Next Friday night? If I don't get called out. I do, sometimes."

J.C.'s heart jumped up into his throat. "I'd like that. I don't have a social life anymore."

"Chess is a social life," the other man pointed out. "So, about six? I'll make chili and corn bread."

J.C. chuckled. "I'll bring a jug of buttermilk."

"How in the world did you know that I loved it?"

"Colie." J.C.'s high cheekbones flushed. "I'm truly sorry, for what I did to Colie's reputation and to yours," he blurted out. "I guess I'd lived in cities for so long that I forgot how clannish small towns are. At least about gossip."

"I don't hold grudges," the other man pointed out. "Besides," he added with a twinkle in his eyes, "I don't know many people who play chess."

J.C. chuckled. "Neither do I."

"See you next Friday, then."

"I'll be here at six." He hesitated. "Thanks," he bit off, without meeting the other man's eyes. He meant, for listening, but he couldn't manage that.

The reverend knew, just the same. "You're very welcome."

J.C. could have kicked himself for all the mistakes he'd made. But it was a new start, with Colie's father. He couldn't give up hope that one day, he might get a new start with Colie, as well. And with his little girl.

CHAPTER TWELVE

REVEREND THOMPSON HAD hoped that Colie might come home after her husband died. But she'd said that she liked living and working in Jacobsville, that she had family and friends there. He knew why she wouldn't come home. She didn't trust herself around J.C. and she didn't want to make things worse for her father. But she was lonely. Ludie made up for a lot. The child was the color in her life now. She lived for her daughter.

J.C. asked about Colie from time to time. The reverend shared the videos she sent of Ludie, as she grew. It was one of the few things that made J.C. laugh, seeing the child take her first steps, say her first words. Underneath it was a terrible sadness, though. J.C. would never know the child.

The reverend hadn't mentioned the Friday night chess games to Colie. He was growing quite fond of J.C., but she never spoke of him. She went on with her job and seemed perfectly happy where she was. One day, he reasoned, she might come home again and make things up with J.C. The man he was coming to know had some wonderful qualities, behind that mask he wore.

But it had been two years since her husband's death, and now the reverend went to Texas to see his daughter and granddaughter. Colie was reluctant to come back to Wyoming, especially with Ludie, when everyone re-

membered how things had been with Colie and J.C. As
the child grew, her hair became a riot of red-gold curls
and she had pale gray eyes that were a mirror of J.C.'s.
It would start gossip all over again, unsettle her father.
And Rod was still around with his so-called friend, who
would think Colie was coming home to tell people what
she knew. She couldn't risk it. Her father was precious to
her. She wouldn't put his life on the line. Or her daughter's. J.C. had said that he had regrets, but he'd never mentioned any possibility that he might want to get married
even now. Without all the complications, it would still be
painful for Colie to be around him, knowing that she'd
just eat her heart out with every sight of him. Better to
stay in Jacobsville, where she had a good job, relatives
and friends.

"YOU'RE PANTING LIKE an underfed steam engine," J.C.
commented during one of their Friday chess matches.
"You should see a doctor."

The reverend made a face. "It's pollen," he commented. "It's autumn. I always get shortness of breath
when the fall flowers come out."

J.C. didn't believe that. He'd been around the reverend
for over two years, now. He saw Ludie as she grew, on
the videos Colie sent her father. It had been a revelation,
how much he enjoyed those simple, poignant glimpses of
the child he wasn't supposed to know was his.

He'd wanted to go and see Colie, but he had cold feet.
He'd caused her too much pain. He wasn't certain that she
could forgive it, and his pride stood up and rattled whenever he thought of lowering it to ask for a second chance.
J.C. had never asked for anything in his life.

He knew why Colie wouldn't come home. It was for

Ludie's sake, because people would see her and speculate, knowing that Colie had lived with J.C. for several weeks. Perhaps she also thought that J.C. was of the same old mind-set, that he'd never offer commitment. He couldn't blame her. He'd never given her any reason to think he'd changed. But he had.

It was pride that kept him from going to Texas and pleading with her to come home. She stayed away out of choice. He could only assume it was because of him. She loved her father and the local law firm would have created a job for her. But she didn't want to come back. Maybe the possibility of gossip stopped her. More than likely it was the fact that J.C. had managed to kill the love she'd had for him. She didn't care enough to come back.

Still, photos and occasional videos were better than nothing. He laughed as they watched a video made four months ago of Ludie scooping up a spoonful of ice cream at her second birthday party and flinging it across the table at a little boy who called her a name. It was one they'd watched several times since Colie had sent it to her father.

"She's got a temper," the reverend chuckled as he watched the video with J.C.

"Justified, in this case," J.C. replied. His face had hardened. "I hate having her called a witch. Colie was like that, she saw things that other people didn't…"

"Yes, like Tank Kirk's wife does," the reverend interrupted. "In any community, there are people with gifts that set them apart from other people."

J.C. studied the older man curiously. "Shouldn't you be disturbed by paranormal things?"

The reverend just smiled. "Most gifts come from God, my son," he said simply, noting the effect that last word had on a man who'd barely known his own father, and not in a good way. He and J.C. had become close. "You look at the fruits. If they result in good things, how can that be evil?"

J.C. drew in a long breath. "I suppose so." He smiled reminiscently. "My paternal grandmother saw far. My father's father was a shaman in the Blackfoot nation. I suppose such gifts are taken for granted among native peoples."

He was insinuating that Ludie's gift came from his side of the family. He knew Ludie was his. The reverend had long since realized that, but he didn't comment on it.

"Will Colie ever come home, do you think?" J.C. asked after a minute while he concentrated on a chess move.

"I don't know, J.C.," came the sad reply. "People gossip. Even though she was married, most folks around Catelow know that she spent most of her time with you…" His voice trailed off.

J.C. let out a long breath. "Ludie would suffer for it," he finished for the reverend. His chiseled mouth curved down. "She's a beautiful child." He looked up. "You don't know how much it's meant to me, seeing her through the photos and videos. She's…" He searched for a word past the lump in his throat. "She's exceptional."

"Yes, she is." He leaned back in his chair. "You never thought about going to Texas and telling my daughter that you know the truth about Ludie?" he asked after a minute, revealing that he knew J.C. had worked that out.

"I did. I thought about it a lot," he replied. "But I've hurt her too much already. She seems very happy where she is." He looked up with troubled silver eyes. "I'm a bad risk," he said suddenly. "I don't know what a good home life is. I come from a badly broken home. I have trust issues." He looked down. "It's helped, having you to talk to," he confessed. "But the wounds are deep. I'm not…sure," he said finally, "that I wouldn't hurt her all over again. I couldn't bear to do that. Not when she has Ludie to care for."

"Ludie is growing up without you," the reverend said gently.

J.C. actually winced. Yes, she was, and it hurt him. His child had another man's name. She didn't know her real father. She might never know. "Colie doesn't want me to know about Ludie." He looked up in time to see the flash of pain in the older man's face. "You know that."

The reverend leaned forward. His color was high. Odd, that he'd be flushed when the room was so cool. "There's a reason Colie hasn't come home, and it has nothing to do with you," he said suddenly.

J.C. was interested. He raised both dark eyebrows.

Reverend Thompson fought to get a breath of air. Odd, how difficult it was to breathe. His chest felt as if someone was sitting on it. He was nauseous, as well. Must be the chili he'd had for supper, he reasoned.

"Have you seen my son lately?" Reverend Thompson asked suddenly.

"Rod avoids me," came the terse reply. "You can probably guess why."

"Because you were a policeman," the older man said. "You still have those sterling ideals of what the law should be, despite your troubles. It's one of the things I admire about you."

J.C. was touched. "Thanks."

"My son has learned to live without…scruples," the other man said heavily. "I know he's mixed up in something illegal, J.C. He hardly ever comes home now. He only calls at holidays, and then it's just a terse greeting and nothing more." His eyes held a faraway look. "He's never far from that friend of his from Jackson Hole. He hasn't worked for the hardware store for a long time, but people I know say that he's driving a new Jaguar and wearing handmade suits. We both know he doesn't make that kind of money selling tools."

J.C. just nodded.

The reverend put a hand to his chest. "If anything happens to me," he said quickly, "you have to make sure… that Colie's safe," he said urgently, his eyes full of worry. "That Ludie's safe, as well."

J.C. frowned. "What do you know, sir?" he asked respectfully.

The older man was struggling for breath. "Colie mentioned a case the lawyers at her job are working on. It has ties to a notorious drug lord in Jackson Hole. They're defending a member of a gang who has ties to it, and… evidence they've gathered may expose the man. Their client has a friend who is going to name the dealers and suppliers, turn state's evidence, to defend the client Colie's employers are representing. There have already been threats."

J.C.'s heart jumped. "Rod's involved." It was a statement.

"I believe so. Please, do whatever you can to protect my daughter and granddaughter."

"I'll never let anyone hurt Colie, or the child," the younger man promised. "I swear it."

"Thank you." The other man looked pale now, where he'd been flushed before. "You're like a son to me, J.C.," he said unexpectedly. "I wish… Why does it hurt so much?" he broke off, gasping for breath.

J.C. had been too mesmerized by what the older man was saying to notice the symptoms of a heart attack.

"Dear God," he whispered huskily. He got up and eased the other man to the floor. He whipped out his cell phone and called 911.

"Take care...of Colie! Tell her, I love her..." the reverend managed before he lost consciousness.

COLIE WAS HAVING supper with her cousins, Annie and Ty Mosby. Ludie, in her high chair, had been given her baby food and was playing with a teething ring when she suddenly dropped the plastic toy and looked at her mother with wide gray eyes.

"Gimpa," she said. "Gimpa sick!"

Colie lost color. She'd felt that something bad was in the offing, but with no idea what. She grabbed for her phone and pressed in her father's number. The phone rang and rang.

It was Saturday night. Her father almost never left the house then. But a member of his congregation might be sick. Or he might be working on his sermon and not realize that the phone was even ringing...

There was a click. "Colie?"

It was J.C.'s voice. Or was it? What would J.C. be doing at her father's house? "I was calling Daddy..."

"The ambulance just came. I'm riding in to the hospital with him. You need to get here as quick as you can, honey. I'm sorry. I think it's a heart attack."

"Oh, dear God," she choked.

"He'd tell you that there's a reason for everything," he managed. It was choking him up, too. He loved her father. "He said to tell you he loved you." He paused. "Come as

fast as you can, okay? Call me when you have an ETA,
I'll meet you at the airport."

"I will," she choked. She bit her lip. "Thanks, J.C."

"Hurry." He hung up.

She turned to her cousins, white in the face. "It's
Daddy. J.C.'s with him. A heart attack, he thinks… I
have to go to Catelow!"

"I'll have them prep the jet right now," Ty said, getting up.

"I'll help you pack," Annie volunteered.

"I have to call the office," Colie began and then realized it was Saturday. "I'll call Mr. Donnally at home,"
she amended. "I don't know if I can get back by Monday. I have vacation days that I haven't used, they can
get a temp," she rambled as she followed her cousin to
the bedroom with Ludie in her arms.

Ludie reached up a little hand and touched her mother's
wet face. Her gray eyes were wet, too. "Gone," she said in
her clear, soft little voice. "Gimpa gone, Mommy."

Colie felt the pain all the way to her soul. But maybe
her daughter was wrong. She discounted all the times
she'd been right in her young life. "We'll go see him," she
assured her daughter. "He'll be fine. Of course he will!"

"Gone," Ludie repeated and burst into tears.

Her cousin winced. She knew, as Colie did, that the
child had an uncanny knowledge of future events. "We'll
get you packed and on the jet," she said. "I can go with
you, if you need me."

"J.C.'s meeting me at the airport," Colie said huskily.

Her cousin's eyebrows arched. "He was with your
father. I didn't think they got along."

"Neither did I. Maybe Ren sent J.C. over to Daddy's
house with soup or something. Merrie makes it for him

when he's not feeling well." Tears were pouring down her cheeks. "My coat. I'll need my coat. It gets cold in Wyoming in autumn. Ludie will need hers, too."

Her cousin hugged her. "We'll get it all together. Try not to worry."

Colie wanted to. But her daughter's eyes were pouring tears…

J.C. WAS WAITING for them at the concourse. He looked older, worn. His face was taut with emotion as he saw Colie for the first time since her father had had the appendectomy, over two years earlier.

His eyes went from Colie to the little girl in her arms. He actually winced when he looked at the child. Her red-gold curls bounced as her mother walked, and her pale silver eyes sought his and held there, as if she knew him.

"How's Daddy?" Colie asked at once.

He tried to find words and failed. "I'm so sorry," he said roughly.

"Gimpa gone," Ludie said, her lower lip trembling.

J.C. actually gasped as he looked at her.

"She knew that something had happened to him before I tried to call him," Colie said, swallowing hard. Tears rained down her pale cheeks. She was never going to see her father again. It had been so sudden!

He reached out and touched Colie's face, brushing away the tears. The child caught his big fingers in hers and looked at him with his own eyes.

"You play with Gimpa," she said in her clear, sweet childish voice.

J.C. was reeling. "Yes."

"Play?" Colie asked.

"Chess," he said shortly. He reached for the wheeled

suitcase and the carry-on bag that held all the things she needed for Ludie. "We should go."

"My brother," she managed.

"Haven't seen him," he bit off. "I tried to call him, but he's changed phones. I called Jackson Hole and talked to the police chief. He'll find him and notify him about your father."

"Is he still at the hospital?" she asked as they moved down the concourse toward the exit.

J.C. ground his teeth together. "No. They've transported him…"

"Yes," Colie interrupted. She didn't want to hear him say "to the funeral home," even though she knew that was coming.

"There's a bad man, Mommy," Ludie said as they went out toward the parking lot. "A bad, bad man. Coming to see us."

J.C. exchanged a stunned glance with Colie.

"What bad man, sweetheart?" Colie asked the child.

"Bad man. Got a gun."

Colie bit her lower lip, hard.

"Does she do this often?" J.C. asked curtly.

"All the time." She held Ludie closer. "It's all right, honey," she said softly, kissing the wet little cheek. "It's okay."

Ludie clung to her. "Mommy," she wailed.

J.C. was disturbed by the child's gift. He hadn't known it was so developed. She was only, what, a little over two years old? He wondered if his grandmother had been able to do this when she was two.

The familiar black SUV was parked near the entrance. Except that it was a newer model.

Colie managed a smile. "Nothing changes."

He chuckled. "I like black."

"Oh, gosh, I forgot the car seat!" Colie groaned. "I was going to bring it, but I was so upset…" Her voice trailed away as she noted the child's car seat, a very expensive model, already strapped into the back seat when he opened the door.

"I planned ahead," he remarked simply.

Colie was too shocked for words.

"You're nice," Ludie said to the tall man and smiled at him. She had dimples. Her silver eyes gleamed with something like affection.

"You're nice, too, little one," J.C. said huskily.

Colie strapped her into the seat. "We'll be home, soon, okay?" she asked the child, handing her the teething ring that she loved.

"Okay, Mommy."

Colie shut the door and let J.C. put her up into the high seat. She was wearing jeans and a white sweater with her red Berber coat. Ludie had a white down jacket that she'd begged for in the children's shop back in Texas.

"At least you two dressed for the weather," J.C. remarked as he started the engine. He had on jeans, too, and a new shepherd's coat. No hat. Just like old times, Colie thought with a stab of pain.

"I remembered how cold it got," she said simply.

THEY DROVE THROUGH town on the way to her father's house.

She looked at the new construction. "What's that going to be?" she asked.

He chuckled. "A new fish place. The old one burned down last year."

"They had good food," she said before she thought.

"Yes. I miss it."

She glanced at him, noting the hard lines in his handsome face. "Why were you with Daddy?" she asked suddenly.

He managed a faint smile. "We missed our usual Friday night chess match because he had to go see a member of his congregation who was in the hospital. We postponed it until last night."

"Usual chess match," she faltered. Her father hadn't told her any of this.

He nodded. "Sometimes he'd cook, sometimes I would." He stopped, because he was choking up.

Colie saw that, fascinated. The man she remembered was all but incapable of emotion. At least, any that showed.

He drove without speaking for a long time, until he came to the turnoff that led to her father's house.

The trees were dropping leaves, but the glorious colors of autumn were much in evidence all around the house. Colie felt such pain as she saw the house and remembered all the good and bad memories that dwelled in it.

J.C. pulled up at the front door and helped her get her suitcases inside. She noticed that the chessboard was still set up, pieces out of order as they'd been when the attack had come.

"He said that it felt as if someone was sitting on his chest. I knew what it was at once," J.C. said, his pale eyes riveted to the chessboard. "I got him on the floor and called for an ambulance. I did CPR until it arrived. But I knew before they got him on the gurney that it was too late." He shoved his hands into his pockets. "Not the first heart attack I've ever seen," he added quietly. "This one would appear to have been massive."

"They show things like that on TV," she faltered. "They do CPR and then they put in stents…"

He turned to her. "Honey, a severe heart attack kills most of the heart muscle almost at once. Necrosis of tissue, massive necrosis," he said gently. "If he'd been sitting in the emergency room with a trauma team it would have made no difference. As he liked to say, when your time comes, nothing will stop it… Colie," he whispered, wincing as she wept.

He pulled her into his arms, with Ludie in hers, and held her close, rocking them both in the shelter of his embrace. "I'm sorry. I'm so sorry. He was the kindest man I ever knew," he added, almost choking on the words.

She drank in the familiar smell of J.C. that she'd never been able to get out of her mind. Even after all that had happened, the closeness was like a drug. She couldn't get enough of it.

His arms tightened. "I called Lucy while I was waiting for your plane to get in," he added. "She'll be over soon."

"Thanks," she whispered.

"I called the youth minister, as well. He said he'll organize everything."

"The funeral home," she choked.

"He told me some time ago exactly what he wanted," he said over her head. "I already called them. I'll drive you over in the morning and you can finish the arrangements."

She drew back and looked up at him from tear-wet green eyes. "Thanks," she managed.

His lean fingers drew down her wet cheeks. "It was little enough to do. He loved you both very much. I'm sorry that I couldn't save him," he bit off.

Why, he loved her father! She was surprised, not only

at the revelation that he'd been a frequent visitor here, but that he cared so much.

"He was kind to me," he said after a minute. "When he probably shouldn't have been."

She nodded. "He said that life was useless unless we forgave people. It's what faith is supposed to be all about."

He smiled gently. "Life goes on. Death is just another step in the journey. He's out picking wildflowers with your mother right now," he added.

It was so close to what she'd been thinking about Darby and his late wife when he died that she drew in her breath.

"You're the one who should have said that, by the way, not me," he added.

She searched his pale eyes. "You're not the same."

"Time changes us. Sometimes, it actually changes us for the better." He looked over her head at the chessboard and sighed. "I'll miss him, Colie."

"Me, too."

J.C.'s phone rang as he was trying to find the right words to tell Colie just how much time had changed him.

He answered the ring. "Calhoun," he said.

"It's Chief Marcus," came a deep voice over the line. "I found Mr. Thompson and told him about his father. He said he'll be there later today."

"Thanks," J.C. replied. "I owe you one."

"You know much about him?" came the quiet reply.

"A little too much," he said.

"Well, he's got a friend who's just a few inches short of the FBI's Most Wanted list, if you get my drift," the other man said. "The friend's attached to him like a tick. Something's going down pretty soon, and your buddy may be right in the middle of it. I gather that he's viewed as a security risk by the friend. Just a word to the wise."

"I was a policeman for two years. I still teach them, over in Iraq," J.C. told him. "I know how to watch my six."

"Be sure you do. Big money involved in this. People get itchy when their ill-gotten gains are threatened. We've got feds here investigating. Court case coming up in Texas that could blow this whole thing sky-high."

"I'm aware of that. Thanks for the heads-up."

"Come by when you're in the area," the other man said on a chuckle. "We can talk over old times."

"I'll do that. Thanks again."

Colie was watching him with curious eyes.

"The police chief in Jackson Hole was in combat with me," he explained. "He found your brother. Rod said he'd be here by the end of the day. And his friend's coming with him." His eyes went to Ludie, who was now sitting on the sofa playing with her teething beads. He looked worried.

"He's not staying here," Colie said curtly. "I won't let him in the front door."

J.C.'s pale eyes went back to her. "I'm not leaving you here alone," he said shortly.

She started to protest.

He held up a hand. "I worked it out with Lucy," he interrupted. "She's coming over to stay with you until after the funeral."

Her expression was more eloquent than words. She was relieved that J.C. hadn't announced he was going to stay there with her. It hurt him, but he hid it. He was used to hiding wounds.

"Cody Banks is our sheriff, and he'll come at the drop

of a hat if he's needed." He paused. "I had a talk with him about Rod. But I didn't tell him anything he didn't already know."

"About...?" she asked hesitantly.

"Your law firm is defending a client who has ties to Rod's operation, Colie," he replied. "I can't believe you didn't already know that."

She lowered her eyes to Ludie. "Yes. I knew," she said sadly.

"So did your father. He was concerned about the two of you, although he held out hope that one day Rod might see the light."

She looked up. "You and my father, playing chess," she said, and her tone was wistful. "I can hardly believe it."

"Neither could I, the first time I came over, after you were here for his surgery," he added. "He invited me to play chess." He smiled sadly. "It was a beginning. Years too late, of course."

She was thinking of a poem, about the saddest words being *it might have been*. It was absolutely true. "How are Merrie and Ren?" she asked, for something to say.

"Doing well. They'd love to see you, if you're going to stay for a few days before you go back home."

"I don't know how long it will take, to wrap things up." She was fighting tears again.

"I'll do anything I can to help. He was a good man. The best I've ever known," he added curtly.

She searched his eyes, those pale gray ones that looked so much like Ludie's. She wondered if he'd ever suspected that the child was his. He probably wouldn't have believed it if she'd told him.

"Well, I'll get home," he said after an awkward silence. "If you need anything, you can call me."

"Thanks for bringing us home," she said.

"It wasn't a problem." He glanced at Ludie, who was still watching him with open curiosity. The sight of her was painful. He'd missed so much of her life.

Colie saw the pain he couldn't hide, but she wasn't admitting anything.

"If Rod shows up here, you call me," he said abruptly. "Or you call Cody Banks. Don't play with fire."

She drew in a breath. "He's in a bad place. I'm not sure he can dig his way out, or that he wants to. But I meant it. I won't let him in the front door."

She didn't realize, and he didn't tell her, that a determined man would barrel right past her and Lucy. Verbal threats would be useless from a woman.

"Keep your cell phone handy."

"I always do."

He walked out, reluctantly. As he drove away, he saw Colie, holding Ludie, standing in the doorway. It was a poignant sight, the family he might have been part of. Now, his only thought was to protect them, to keep them safe.

On the way home, he phoned Cody Banks.

"I spoke with the police chief in Jackson Hole, who said Rod was mixed up in some bad company," he said, after revisiting Rod's excessive lifestyle. "If he comes back here, Colie says she won't let him stay in the house. But the police chief seems to think he's bringing his friend with him—the drug supplier."

"If he comes here looking for trouble, he'll find some," Cody said simply.

"Colie and Ludie are going to be alone, except for her friend Lucy," he replied. "I would have offered to stay, but it would start gossip all over again. I don't want to hurt her reputation any more than I already have."

"Noble thought, but a man in the house would be more help than a dozen cell phones with 911 preprogrammed."

"I know that," J.C. said abruptly.

"Sorry." There was a pause. "Don't we know a man she might trust to stay with her?"

"Ren might volunteer, if I asked him," J.C. said after a minute. "Or even Willis. He could bring his wolf," he added with faint humor.

"Oh, I can see it now, a little girl who liked bologna sandwiches and a three-legged wolf hungry for meat…"

"Stop that," J.C. chuckled. "You know the wolf's tame."

"No wild animal is ever tame, and you can quote me. Or have you forgotten my one experience with trying to raise a tame fox?"

"Ouch," J.C. replied, and tried not to laugh.

"Damned thing almost took my thumb off, and I'd raised it from a kit," he sighed. "I guess dogs are better, anyway. My Siberian husky is five years old now. My wife gave her to me for Christmas, the year before she died," he added quietly.

J.C. didn't reply. He knew the story, as most local people did. Cody's wife, a doctor at a hospital nearby, had died of a contagious illness some years back. He'd mourned her and never remarried.

"I had a husky when I was a boy," J.C. commented. "I'd take him on the toboggan with me and we'd go down the most dangerous hills I could find. He was a great pal."

"They usually are. Except that if you're ever burgled, the husky will follow the thieves around to show them the best stuff and then help them carry it out to the get-away car," he added, laughing. "A watchdog, he is not."

"True, that."

"Tell Colie that if she needs me, she can call any-time," the sheriff added. "I don't sleep much and I'd love a chance to put her brother where he belongs. Don't tell her that last bit," he added.

"I won't. But I feel the sentiment, just the same. He's mixed up in dangerous company. It's just a matter of time until he's called to account for his crimes."

"Now you sound like a cop again," Banks chuckled.

"I guess I do. Thanks for the backup."

"No sweat. Is Colie staying long, or did she say?"

"She's got a job back in Texas," J.C. replied heavily. "And she seems to be happy there."

"Too bad, about the husband."

It stung J.C. to think about the man who'd followed him in Colie's life. "She said he loved the little girl."

"What did he look like?" Banks asked suddenly.

"Her husband? I'm not sure."

"Doesn't matter. Just a sec…" There was a pause and some static. Banks came back on the line. "We've got a pileup on the interstate. I'm en route. Talk to you later."

"Sure."

He hung up. For the first time, he wondered what Co-lie's husband looked like. He'd assumed that the child was his. Apparently, so had Reverend Thompson. But what did the man look like? Was he redheaded? Did he have light eyes? If he did, then all J.C.'s imaginings about the child might be completely wrong.

He was surprised at how disappointing the thought was.

CHAPTER THIRTEEN

COLIE CRIED IN Lucy's arms. The other woman just rocked her, crooning soft words.

"I'm so sorry, Colie," she said gently. "So sorry. I know how much you loved your dad."

"He was hardly ever sick. He had the appendectomy, but other than that…" She choked back a sob and moved away to wipe her eyes. "I still can't believe he and J.C. played chess together every week."

"They were close," Lucy said, to her surprise. "J.C. looked out for your father. He was always around, anytime he was needed. The reverend put him to work passing out donated groceries to poor families. He said J.C. was a natural at volunteer work."

"The things we don't know," Colie said sadly. She paused to peek into her old bedroom, where Ludie was taking a nap. She came back into the living room. "She's tired out. She told me that my father was sick," she added. "She said he was gone before we ever got to the airport and J.C. told me."

"A truly amazing gift," Lucy said. Her eyebrows lifted. "J.C. met you at the airport?"

"Yes. With a car seat in the back seat of his SUV for Ludie." She smiled and shook her head. "The old J.C. would never have done such a thing."

"Or maybe he would have, and you just didn't know."

"That's possible."

"Your father said J.C. had a ball watching the videos of Ludie that you sent home." She bit her lower lip at Colie's expression. "Oops. Sorry. That just slipped out."

"It's okay. I know J.C. suspects the truth. But I've never confessed it. Unless Daddy told him…"

"If he had, I think we'd have all known," Lucy said, grimacing. "I'm so sorry!"

"I had no idea that he and my father were that close…"

"What tangled webs we weave," Lucy said quietly.

"Indeed."

"Is your brother coming over for the funeral?"

"Yes. But he's not staying here," Colie said curtly. "I won't have him in the house. If he shows up with his friend, the only thing he'll be interested in is how much he's getting from the will and whether or not I've kept my mouth shut."

Lucy grimaced. "That's why you stayed gone."

"Yes. I couldn't even tell my father. I was afraid he'd say something to Rod and his friend would cause problems for Daddy. I agonized over it. I wanted to be here. But there were just too many reasons why I couldn't come home."

"J.C. being at the top of the list."

Colie nodded as she led the way into the kitchen to make coffee. "I didn't want to subject Daddy to any more malicious gossip. I caused him such heartache." Tears threatened again. "If I could just go back and relive that part of my life…!"

"And if you did, you wouldn't have Ludie," came the reply.

Colie turned, glancing at her friend through red, wet eyes. "No. I guess I wouldn't."

"You don't think your brother would actually harm you?"

Colie hesitated. She turned back to the coffeepot and pulled down a box of white coffee filters. "I don't know," she said after she'd filled the pot and started it going. "I really don't. The big brother I loved was a different man when he got out of the military. He's turned into someone I don't know—into someone I'd rather not know."

"Drugs do that."

"It's such a waste," she said as she sat down heavily at the table. In the dining room, she could see the chessboard her father and J.C. had played on. She forced her eyes back to Lucy. "He was a good man. He was just weak. He'd do whatever anyone asked him to, whether it was bad or good. He was a follower."

"They usually end badly," Lucy replied. "We've both seen the results of that personality trait in clients who come through the law office."

"Yes. It's just sad."

"I hope my son will have the guts to stand up for what's right, not what the crowd wants," Lucy said on a sigh. "He's just a year old now, but we're going to do our best with him."

"Me, too, with Ludie," Colie agreed. She smiled. "You know…" She paused because the front door opened suddenly.

Her brother, Rodney, walked in with his smarmy friend Barry, from Jackson Hole.

"Sis," Rodney said hesitantly when he spotted Lucy at the table with his sister. "I'm so sorry…!"

Colie stood up. She was no longer the shy, helpless girl she'd once been. She pulled out a cell phone and showed it to her brother. "You can leave, or I can have Cody Banks escort you out."

"This is his home, too, now," the drug lord said haughtily, wearing a suit that cost more than Colie would make in two years.

"Not until the will is probated. You do know the law, I presume?" Colie added coldly, and she didn't back down an inch.

The man gave her a hot glare. Of course he knew the law. He'd been running from it most of his life.

Rod flushed, looking from one to the other. "Sis, I've got no place else to stay," he began in a plaintive tone.

"Hock your new Jaguar and get a motel room," was Colie's reply.

The flush became redder. "It's just a demo model," he protested. He stuck his hands in his pocket and gave his friend a very nervous look. Some sort of signal passed between them. "Look, we need to talk."

"Not now," she said flatly. "I have a funeral to arrange, and my daughter is asleep."

"Oh. You brought the little girl?" Rodney seemed disconcerted. He darted another nervous glance at his companion. "I thought she'd stay with your husband in Texas…"

"My husband is dead."

"Oh." He shifted restlessly. "Oh, I see. I'm sorry."

"He had cancer, Rod. He was ready to let go."

He grimaced. "You've had a hard time, I guess," he conceded.

"A hard time," Lucy scoffed. Her eyes glared at him. "Like you'd know what a hard time was, Rodney Thompson!"

He averted his eyes.

"Let's go," the friend told Rodney, glaring at the women. "We can come back later and talk to your sister. When she's alone," he added in a low, faintly threatening tone.

"J.C. knows I'm here," she told Rodney, watching his reaction. "In fact, he met me at the airport. It was very different, the way that went this time, since you weren't there to fill his head full of lies," she emphasized.

"Don't get too cocky," the friend said shortly. "J.C. Calhoun is no threat, whatever you may think."

"Cody Banks will be," she shot back. "And I promise you, he'll know the minute you walk out that door." She indicated the cell phone.

"Sis…" Rodney began worriedly.

His friend took him by the arm and propelled him outside, slamming the door behind him.

"You call Cody right now," Lucy told her best friend. "That man made threats."

"He certainly did."

She called the sheriff and told him what had just happened.

"If I had a man I could send over, I would," the sheriff replied tersely. "You call if you need me. Dispatch can find me, wherever I am. Does J.C. know Rodney's back?"

"Not yet," she said.

"I'll call and tell him," the sheriff told her. "He and your father were close. He'll help us keep an eye on things."

She felt a twinge of worry. "Don't…don't tell him," she asked softly. "I'll call him and let him know. Okay?"

He chuckled. "Okay." He hesitated. "They said your husband had cancer."

"Multiple myeloma," Colie confessed. "It was hard

to watch." She hesitated. "J.C. played chess with Daddy every week," she added on a laugh. "Talk about shock!"

"People change, Colie," he told her gently. "You might not believe it's possible, but I work in law enforcement. I see those changes every day, in some people that the whole world gave up on."

She smiled. "I guess you'd know."

"I certainly would. Sorry about your husband. But life goes on. I thought I'd die when my wife did. I kept on. I'm still keeping on. It does get easier. And you have a beautiful little girl to remember him by."

It had almost the tone of a question. "I certainly do," she said. "He was very proud of Ludie."

"Ludie," he said softly. "She was named for your mother, wasn't she? Her name was Louise, but everybody called her Ludie."

"She was. I miss my mother. But it's kind of comforting to know that Daddy's with her now," she added. She was choking up. "It's hard to talk about it."

"Get some rest," he said quietly. "And if you need me, you call. You tell J.C., too. Okay?"

"Okay, Sheriff. And thanks."

She hung up. She turned to Lucy. "He was going to tell J.C. But you heard what that man said. If I tell J.C., if I involve him and they know it, he could wind up dead."

"Honey, you could wind up dead," Lucy emphasized. "J.C. trains policemen. He was a policeman, for heaven's sake. He's used to dealing with violent people. You've got a real situation here. You can't handle it alone!"

Still, Colie hesitated. Surely her own brother wouldn't harm her. He wouldn't let that slinky man harm her, either.

"You're thinking Rod won't hurt you," Lucy said,

reading her friend's expression very well from long acquaintance, nodding when Colie started. "But his companion would. And Rod's not forceful. He'll go belly-up at the first sign of trouble. You never knew what happened to him overseas, did you?" she added suddenly.

"What? To Rod?" Colie asked.

"Yes. To Rod." Lucy's teeth clenched. "Nobody had the heart to tell your father, or you, in case you told him. But Rod's squad went up against an insurgent group. And he threw down his rifle and ran away and hid. Two members of his squad were killed. He was permitted to take a dishonorable discharge before his tour of duty was up, in lieu of a court-martial, because his commanding officer knew your father and went to bat for him."

"Dear God!" Colie exclaimed, horrified. "He never said a word about it!"

"No wonder." She sighed. "J.C. knows. He didn't throw Rod under the bus, like some other ex-military people did. He's loyal to a fault. But once Rod got mixed up in the drug trade, J.C. had nothing more to do with him."

Colie sat down, hard. "The shocks just keep coming," she said.

Lucy made more coffee and served it before she sat down, too. "You have to keep your doors locked and your cell phone handy. Why don't I call J.C. and let him come over and spend the night…?"

"And start gossip all over again?" Colie interrupted with a sad smile. "If it was just me, I might do it. But I have a little girl who'll suffer for my indiscretions. Besides, there's Daddy's congregation." She fought tears and swallowed down the pincushion in her throat. "I'll manage. I can call Sheriff Banks if anything happens. Rod doesn't have a key to the door. The only reason he was able to get in a few minutes ago was that it's not locked."

"Put on the chain latches, too. I wouldn't put it past either one of them to pick a lock," Lucy advised.

"Rod wants people to think he came because of Daddy, but he's really here with his friend because my employers have a client whose friend is turning state's evidence in a huge drug distribution case that has ties to Jackson Hole," she replied. "If he does, the feds will have a field day invoking the RICO statutes and many drug lords—presumably including Rod's friend—will be running for the border, penniless."

"How does that involve you?"

Colie stared at her friend. She couldn't admit that she'd actually seen Rod take possession of a suitcase full of narcotics from the very friend who'd accompanied him today—that the reason she'd had to leave Catelow in the first place was to protect her father, to prove that she wasn't going to tell anyone what she'd seen. It was the only way she could keep her father alive and protect herself and the baby she was carrying.

"I can't tell you," she said gently. "I won't put you in the crosshairs, too. Just believe me when I say there's a real threat. Tomorrow, I'm going to call my bosses in Texas and ask for help. They have a top-notch investigator. If I ask, they'll send him up here. He's a former Green Beret."

"Then you do that. First thing in the morning," Lucy said firmly.

Colie hugged her. "Thank you for being my friend."

Lucy smiled against her shoulder. "Remember that old saying? When the going gets tough, the tough get going?"

"That's me," Colie sighed, drawing back. "Tough." And she smiled.

IT WAS A long night. Ludie, who usually babbled at bath time and bedtime, was oddly silent. She kept looking at her mother in a troubled way. So young, but she was far wiser than her years.

"Bad man," Ludie said just before she went to sleep. "Bad man, Mommy. He hurts people."

"He won't hurt us. We're going to have help," Colie assured her with a smile and a tender kiss.

"I want my daddy," Ludie said, her gray eyes brimming with tears.

Colie grimaced, leaning over to brush the red-gold curls away from tearstained little cheeks. "Ludie, your daddy is dead," she began.

"Not my real daddy," the child said in a soft voice. "I want my real daddy."

Colie just sat there, searching for words.

"He came with us. He carried me in the house."

Colie knew the blood was draining out of her cheeks. J.C. The child was telling her that J.C. was Ludie's daddy. She couldn't know! It wasn't possible. Colie had been so very careful not to say anything about J.C. or her past with him around the child, who was precocious to a fault.

"Ludie," she began, not knowing what to tell her.

"He loved Gimpa," she added, using the name she'd always called her grandfather.

"We all loved him," Colie managed.

"My real daddy will make the bad man leave us alone." Her eyes closed. "I like my real daddy…"

Her voice trailed off.

Colie sat with her, fingers loosely touching the blanket that covered her child, with the weight of the world on her shoulders.

THE NEXT MORNING, she made breakfast and fed Ludie, who was still far too quiet. As soon as they finished, and she cleaned up her father's kitchen, she was going to call the law firm where she worked and ask them to send the investigator.

She never made the call. Before she could put away the breakfast dishes, she heard the sound of a key being inserted in the locked front door. The chain latch was on, but a hard shoulder broke it. Colie barely had time to gasp before two men had her cornered, with Ludie, in the kitchen...

THE SNOW WAS coming down on Skyhorn, Ren Colter's Wyoming ranch. J.C. Calhoun drove through it without blinking an eye. It reminded him of wild days in the Yukon Territory, when he was a child. He wasn't from Wyoming, but an ancestor was from nearby Montana. He thought about the ancestor with a grin. He'd have to tell Ludie about him one day, about the Blackfoot warrior who rode with Crazy Horse, an Oglala Lakota, in the Battle of the Rosebud up in Montana.

Ludie. His child. He sighed. He wondered if Colie would ever tell him the truth. He had suspicions, but no facts. He hoped she still had Lucy with her, and that Rod hadn't shown up with his friend. Later, he was going over to check on them, to make sure.

He spotted a big white blob near the ranch road, next to a fence bent down by a broken tree. Probably the weight of snow and ice had brought down the lodgepole pine. He pulled the truck to the side of the road and got out. Snow peppered down on his short, jet-black hair. He hated hats. Ren was always on him about it. But J.C. had grown up in Yukon Territory, the only son of a Blackfoot father and a redheaded Irish mother. He was something of a rebel. He'd never really tried to settle down. Not until now.

It still hurt J.C. to remember poor Colie, when he'd confronted her three years ago with what Rodney said she had done. She hadn't said a word. She'd just sighed and looked at him with those soulful green eyes that could say so much in silence. She wasn't a forceful woman. Perhaps that was why he'd become involved with her in the first place. She simply accepted what little affection he was capable of, without wishing for more. She'd wanted marriage, but an engagement was all he'd been willing to give her. It was his terms, all the way.

Since childhood, it had been that way. His adoring little Irish mother had protected him from his father's rages. She loved his father, alcoholic binges and all. Sad to see an educator, a brilliant man, end up so addicted to whiskey that he couldn't even function in the world. He'd given up teaching for mining, because there was more money in it. And the money and a child, J.C., had killed his dreams of a ranch of his own. No matter how bad it got—and it got bad—his mother wouldn't leave him. You didn't desert people you loved, she told him once. You stood by them, no matter what, and never gave up trying to save them.

J.C. had survived a horror of a childhood. He'd grown up and tried to settle into the military, but he was too much of a maverick for the regular Army. He ended up in spec ops. He was working in Iraq when he met Ren Colter, an officer, after a devastating incursion against militants. They'd become friends. Ren had offered him a job, which he accepted.

He liked Ren. The man was as much a maverick as he was, himself. Of course, Ren had married, so the occasional bar fight was now going to become a thing of the past. He liked Ren's wife. She had an unnatural affinity for animals. Like Colie.

His face tautened as he remembered Colie, weeping without making a sound, tears rolling down from her green eyes like silent streams while he raged at her. Colie, her wavy, dark brown hair soft in the light of his cabin, her pale face drawn from the ravages of morning sickness. He'd finally run out of names to call her. She never said a word. Not even when he put her on the porch in the snow and closed the door.

He shook himself mentally. Looking back accomplished nothing. It only made him sadder. He hadn't looked at a woman since Colie. He probably never would again. He could see himself as he would be in a few years, grizzled, living alone, at war with the world and himself. It was a lonely life, but it suited him. He had a small cabin on a few hundred acres of land that adjoined Ren's property, and a few head of purebred Black Angus cattle of his own. Ren paid him a princely salary for heading up the security of the ranch, but he had a sideline of his own. Twice a year he still went overseas to train policemen in some of the most dangerous areas in the Middle East. What he earned, he invested. He was quite comfortable now. But he kept the job, because it challenged him. It was about the only thing in life he still enjoyed.

He got out of the truck and went down on one knee near the cow. She was one of the pregnant heifers, a first-time mother. He grimaced. She was tangled in the wire.

"Just sit still, Bessie, I'll get you out," he said, his voice soft and deep. He patted her softly on the head. He went back to the truck to call in her position on GPS and get a pair of wire cutters.

"Better send the sled out," he told Willis, the foreman. "She looks okay except for the cuts, but better safe than sorry with purebreds."

"I hear that," Willis chuckled. "I'll send Grandy."

"I'll wait for him."

He cut the heifer out of the wire and eased her to her feet. She was wobbly. He felt for breaks in her legs, but he didn't find any. She was very pregnant. He scowled. He hated the memory of pregnant human females. It brought back so much pain.

He hadn't thought he cared that much. Not until it was too late. He drew in a breath, feeling the icy fingers of it as it went down his throat.

"You'll be okay," he told the heifer in a soft voice. "Just stand…"

He stopped abruptly. He heard a sound. It was an odd sound. Like a child whimpering. He shook his head. He was hearing things. Maybe Ren was right, and he did spend too much time alone.

He went back to put up the cutters. That was when he saw it. Tire tracks. He frowned. Why would there be tire tracks here, on a ranch road, when he knew that nobody had come this way all day? They weren't covered with snow, which meant they were recent.

He went down on one knee and studied them. Car tires. He knew the difference. He'd worked as a police officer before he went into the military. One of his duties had been accident investigation. He scowled as he saw something else. Blood!

He looked around, alert now. He went back to the truck and opened the pocket, pulling out the .44 Magnum he always carried around the ranch. He stuck the holster on his belt and shoved the sidearm into it. His odd, pale silver eyes narrowed in his olive tan face as he looked around for signs.

There were tracks, leading off the road, near where the cow had tangled herself in the downed fence.

He followed them. Strange tracks. Very small, like a child's. What the hell would a child be doing here, on a ranch road in the middle of a blizzard? He was getting fanciful. Probably it was some small animal. Still, there were the blood traces...

It came again. Just a whisper of sound, a whimper.

His ears were as keen as his eyes. His head turned. He closed his eyes, so that all his attention was focused on what he heard. There. To the left.

There was a small stand of baby lodgepole pines and snow covering a bush. Under the bush he spotted a white hooded jacket, puffy, like those made with goose down that he'd seen on Colie's little girl. It was the blob he'd thought was a pile of fallen snow.

He went closer and knelt. He reached out a hand and lightly touched the shoulder of the bloodstained jacket. Eyes the pale gray of a winter sky looked up into his, in a frame of curly reddish-gold hair, in a pale face with red, rosy cheeks and a rosy mouth that looked like a little bow. Tears had rolled down the cheeks.

"Ludie!" he exclaimed. "Dear God, what happened? What are you doing out here, baby?" he asked huskily.

She bit her lower lip. She had eyes that should have held no place in a tiny child's face. They held the same horror he'd seen in combat veterans' eyes.

"Can you tell me?" He noted the front of the jacket, where blood was smeared. He scowled. "Are you hurt?"

"N-no," she whispered. She shivered.

He felt a sudden coldness. "Where's your mother?" he asked suddenly.

"I don't know." The tears came again, hot and copious. She brushed at them with a tiny fist. "Mommy put me out of the car and told me to run and hide. That was before."

"Before what?"

She sobbed. "Before he…shot her."

His breath caught. "Who shot her?"

She didn't answer him. She shivered.

"Who shot her, baby?" he repeated softly.

She seemed to be in shock. "He shot my mommy. I ran and ran. He shot my mommy!"

"Dear God." There was trace evidence all over her. He didn't care. No human with half a heart could have left her sitting there in the snow. He pulled her up into his arms and rocked her, kissing her red-gold curls. "It's all right, honey," he whispered. "It's all right, you're safe."

He jerked his phone out of the holder and called the county sheriff, Cody Banks.

"Good God!" Cody exploded when J.C. told him what he'd found. "I'll be right there. I'm less than two miles from your position. Thank God you have GPS. Don't touch anything. I'll have Davis meet us here." Davis was his investigator.

"She said someone shot her mother," he added. "You have to find Colie!"

"We're on it. Is the child all right? Should I send an ambulance?"

"Please."

"We're on the way."

J.C. hung up. He brushed back the child's hair while his heart felt as if it had turned to stone as he thought about what she'd said, about Colie. "You're going to be okay. Nobody's going to hurt you. I promise."

She was still biting her lower lip and the tears hadn't stopped. "I want my mommy," she sobbed.

"We'll find her, Ludie," he said in a soft, deep tone. "I promise, we will."

She looked up at him with his own eyes. "Uncle Rod helped the bad man."

He consigned Uncle Rod to the devil. There would be retribution. God help Rod if Colie was dead.

J.C. stood up with the child in his arms, looking around warily. He'd seen the direction the tire tracks went, toward the Thompson place. How in the world had the child ended up here, and where was Colie? The child said she was shot. What if she was dead? His eyes closed. He felt a shudder go through him.

The child seemed to sense his pain. Her small hand touched his lean, hard cheek. The pale gray eyes, his eyes, looked up at him. "Oh," she said. She hesitated. "Okay." She nodded, shaking the long, red-gold curls. She reminded him so much of Shirley Temple dolls he'd seen. She was a beautiful child. "Okay. Mommy's okay."

He remembered at the airport when Colie and the child had come back for Reverend Thompson's funeral. Ludie had been crying. She'd told her mother that her grandfather was dead even before she arrived and J.C. had to break it to her.

"You know things, don't you?" he asked very softly.

She nodded again. Her small hand was still on his cheek. "You're my daddy," she said in her clear, pretty little voice.

His caught breath was audible. She cocked her head

and looked up at him. "Bad man hurt my mommy," she said. "She's at the house. The house where Gimpa lived."

J.C.'s heart jumped. He pulled out the phone and called Banks back. "Can you check at Reverend Thompson's house and see if Colie's there?" he asked. "Never mind how I know," he added, glancing at Ludie, who was clinging to him. "Just check." He sighed. "Sure. Thanks." He hung up again.

"I want my mommy." Her little voice broke.

He drew her closer, held her, rocked her, kissed the damp red-gold curls and fought a mist in his pale eyes. Please, God, let Colie be all right, he thought. Please!

Her little arms curled around his neck and she held on for dear life. "I'm so scared," she whispered. "He hurt my mommy. He said he would hurt me, too…!"

His arms tightened. "Nobody's ever hurting you. Not while I'm alive. I swear it!"

He felt her relax, just a little, but she was still sobbing.

Sirens burst like bombs onto the snow-muffled silence of tall pine trees and distant mountains.

Sheriff Cody Banks slammed out of his patrol car, followed closely by his undersheriff, Matt Davis, in a second car.

Cody grimaced when he saw J.C. holding the child.

"Don't you say a word," J.C. muttered, standing with the child still close. "There's trace blood by the road, in the depression there where she's been lying, and on her jacket. More than enough for evidence, despite the fact that I moved her from her hiding place. She says a man shot her mother. She was crying." He swallowed. Hard.

"I wasn't going to say anything," Cody replied gently, wincing as the child lifted her face and he saw the tears and the swollen redness of those pale wintry eyes. "The EMTs are right behind me."

Even as he said it, the ambulance rolled up with its lights flashing and two uniformed men exited the vehicle with a case.

They examined Ludie while the sheriff's investigator gathered trace evidence and took photos of the scene, including the tire tracks and evidence that the child had exited a car there.

"She seems okay," one of the EMTs said, smiling at the child. "But it would be a good idea to take her to the emergency room and get her checked out…"

"No!" Ludie clung to J.C. when the EMT reached for her.

J.C. felt a jolt of possession all the way down his body when she did that. He, who hadn't ever wanted children, wanted this one with his whole heart.

"I'll take her there," J.C. said.

"We can place her in a temporary home," Cody tried again.

"No!" she wailed, and started sobbing and clinging even closer.

J.C. took a deep breath. "Her mother and I were engaged once," he told Cody. "I'm family, as near as not. She can stay with me for the time being."

The child's arms tightened.

"We'll work it out with the court," Cody said, laughing softly as he noted the interaction between the child and the man who hated children. "We'll need to get her to a psychologist as soon as possible, too. She's been traumatized. Davis, let's get to work."

"Have you checked at Reverend Thompson's house yet?" J.C. asked.

"My deputy headed there when I started over here," the sheriff said. "We'll know something soon."

J.C. just nodded. He felt sick all over. He couldn't picture a world without Colie. He didn't want to.

THEY FOUND ENOUGH evidence for the crime lab to begin with. By the time it was collected, Cody had the model and make of the car Colie Thompson Howland was in. A surveillance camera that was placed near the highway, on Ren's land, had recorded the car stopping, the child running away from it. The car belonged to Rodney Thompson, J.C.'s best friend.

Since he and Rodney had parted ways, he'd heard plenty of gossip about the man. The ex-military man had gone from a responsible salesman at the local hardware store to a worthless layabout, a man who dealt drugs and had multiple arrests for possession. J.C. had loved him like his own brother when they first became friends. So quickly, that closeness had disappeared.

Who had shot Colie? The child hadn't said so, but it was painfully obvious. She'd come out of her uncle's car. Presumably her mother was still in it, somewhere, dead. Had Rodney shot his own sister? His face hardened. He wanted the man locked up for life. He didn't realize he'd said it aloud, or with such passion, until Cody answered him.

"My idea, exactly, if we can prove it. I've got a man headed at his house right now, in fact," Cody said quietly. "I want to impound the car before he has time to remove any evidence. And there's still the issue of finding…" He stopped when he noticed the child looking at him. He didn't want to add "…the woman's body," in front of Ludie.

"I'll take Ludie to the emergency room," J.C. said curtly. He wanted desperately to go to the house, to see if Colie was there. But she might not be, and Ludie had to come first. "I know I can't have any part in the investigation, but her mother and I were engaged." He bit down hard on his emotions as the words slipped out. "I played chess with her father every Friday night for almost two years. First him, now her... God, it's just too much!" He drew Ludie closer and looked over her head at Banks. "Call me, as soon as you know something. Will you?"

"I'll do that," Cody promised gently. "I'm sorry," he added, wincing as he looked at the child's tearstained face.

J.C. was trying hard to contain his own fear and it wasn't easy. "We'll go on to the hospital."

CHAPTER FOURTEEN

COLIE HAD BEEN making breakfast when she heard a key in the lock of the front door.

Ludie looked up at her mother and winced. "Bad man, Mommy, bad man!" she said urgently.

Before Colie had time to react, Rodney and his friend Barry came in the door. Rodney's expression was one of regret and apology. His friend, holding a pistol in his hand, was arrogant.

"Colie, you have to call your bosses and tell them not to go ahead with that drug case," Rodney said quickly. He darted a glance at Barry. "She'll do it, I know she will," he added. "You don't need the gun…!"

"She'll never do it," Barry said, reading with accuracy the look on Colie's face. "She doesn't care if you go to prison."

"That's not true…" Colie began, playing for more time to think, to do something. Let him shoot her, if he had to, but she must save Ludie. If only she'd asked J.C. to stay with them. Too late now.

"But," Rodney protested, and looked as if it actually mattered to him that his sister wasn't harmed. For once, his eyes weren't bloodshot. He looked like the brother he used to be, not under the influence of drugs.

"Shut up, Rod," Barry said. "It's too late. Get the kid. You're coming with me," he told Colie.

"No," she said, and reached for a butcher knife on the counter.

Barry simply pointed the .45 automatic at Ludie's head. "Your choice," he drawled.

Now Colie was terrified. The man didn't seem to be bluffing. If the court case went ahead, he'd be in federal prison in no time, and he knew it. He was desperate enough to do anything; even shoot a helpless toddler.

"All right," Colie said quickly, putting the knife down. "All right, I'll do whatever you want. Just don't hurt Ludie."

"Bad man," Ludie said, staring at Barry. "Bad man."

"Bad enough," Barry said with an arrogant smile. "Let's go." He pointed the gun at Colie. "Get the kid and come on."

"Where are you taking them?" Rodney asked, worried.

"Just out for a ride, and a little conversation. You stay here and wait until I get back," he instructed. "Give me your car keys."

Rodney did, primed to do anything this man said, because he was up to his neck in trouble and he knew Barry wouldn't hesitate to shoot him, too. But he honestly didn't realize for precious minutes what the man had said. "Until I get back." Barry meant that he'd be returning alone.

"Do anything you like to me, just don't hurt my daughter," Colie pleaded as Barry drove up the road to a deserted stretch that ran alongside Ren Colter's ranch.

"You told them what you saw three years ago, didn't you?" Barry asked as he drove. "You told them you saw me bring Rod a suitcase of drugs. You're the only witness who can testify to that."

She caught her breath. So this was what it was really about—not the court case at all. "I never told a soul," she protested.

"Sure, you didn't," he said hotly. "But you won't testify."

"No. I won't. I promise," she said, bargaining for their freedom. She held Ludie tight. There was no car seat, so Ludie was in her lap.

"Too late for that." He stopped the car and produced the gun. "This is a nice, private spot. No witnesses."

Colie had seconds to act. She threw open the door and put Ludie out on the snow-covered ground. "Run!" she told the child. "Run like the...wind!" Her voice broke as the man beside her pulled the trigger. Blood went everywhere, splattering even onto Ludie's white jacket.

Ludie screamed as she heard the shot. She tried to look back, but her mother cried, "Run!" one last time.

She ran toward the fence, found an opening under it where some large animal had dug an entrance through the snow and crawled through it. With tears staining her cheeks, she ran as fast as she could into the sheltering woods.

"You won't hurt...my child!" Colie said, struggling with the man. She wasn't big-boned, but she was strong. Even with adrenaline pumping through her, the wound was weakening her. She could barely get a breath and she was light-headed. She felt the life draining out of her through the hole in her chest. "You...won't!"

"She'll freeze to death out there before too long," Barry said harshly, "and she won't be a witness, anyway."

"Witness..." He was blurring in her eyes. The chest wound was making odd sounds. She struggled to get a tiny breath of air.

It had felt like a fist slamming into her rib cage, but now the pain was starting. If only Ludie made it to safety! She must try to stay conscious…

She took a last, labored breath and passed out. Barry thought of pushing her out, but it might lead someone to the child, if they spotted small footprints in the snow. He didn't want the child found. The dying woman beside him wouldn't be able to tell where she was, anyway.

He drove the car back to Rodney's house.

ROD WAS WAITING on the front porch, pacing. He ran toward Barry. "What did you do… Sis!" he exploded when he saw her.

"Just what was necessary," Barry told him nonchalantly. "Now there'll be no witness to testify against me for a drug deal, even if her law firm does pull the rug out from under the dealers. I can beat that rap. But an eyewitness to drug distribution could have put me in federal prison. I couldn't take the chance."

"My sister." Rod lifted her gently out of the car, tears running down his face. "My sister!"

"Your car, her blood, guess who'll go up for murder one?" Barry drawled.

Rodney wasn't hearing him. He laid Colie gently on the floor of the porch. "You killed my sister!" He looked into the open passenger door and his blood ran hotter. "Where's Ludie?"

Barry just shrugged. "Lost in the woods. You'd better think about what you're going to do," he said easily. "Me, I'm driving back to Jackson Hole. I may go to Aruba. You're on your own. You were a lousy dealer, Rod. Just as well I don't have to keep an eye on you anymore to see what your sister's up to." He looked at the dying woman. "She won't be a problem anymore."

"Murderer!" Rod raged, and rushed him.

Barry easily put him on the floor, adjusted his expensive suit and walked to his own luxury car. He got into it and drove away. Even if Rodney called the cops, Barry was in the clear. There were no witnesses, and the blood and the body could be traced to Rod's car. It wasn't Barry who'd go to jail for murder. Meanwhile, he could relax. There were no witnesses to what he'd done. And who knew, with the snow falling so hard, they might not find the kid's body for a long time.

RODNEY CALLED 911 from one of his throwaway phones. He didn't dare stay. Barry was right. He'd be on the rack for murder one if Colie died. His sister. He'd left her on her own, been reluctant to leave Barry and the quick money, sold out his own flesh and blood. His father was dead. His sister was dying. And Ludie. What about Ludie? He had no idea where she could be. Barry hadn't been gone long, but it was a big area. He'd never be able to find the poor child, even if he had time to look for her.

He smoothed back Colie's hair. She had a sucking chest wound. It would kill her soon if she didn't get help. He told dispatch where the house was, but he hung up almost immediately. He went into the house and got a big plastic bag from the kitchen. He put it on the chest wound and wrapped a blanket tight around her to hold it in place. During his term in service, he'd seen makeshift treatments for all sorts of wounds. Thank God he remembered this one.

But she was still in bad shape and he didn't dare stay. He wanted to leave a note, implicate Barry, tell Colie he was sorry he'd brought this on her and her child. Her child! His blood ran cold. It was J.C.'s child. He knew. Most people knew that Colie had only ever had one lover, and it was J.C. He was certain that no other man had fathered that little girl, and he could only imagine what J.C. would do when she was found dead. Or when Colie was found dead, if she didn't survive.

The safest place was going to be somewhere out of the country. Rod had money. He could get away. But only if he acted quickly.

He jumped into the car, wincing at the blood on the passenger seat, and shot off into the distance down the road. He could stop at a service station and get some paper towels to clean up the mess. He'd find some rural one, on a less traveled road, to do that. Meanwhile he sent up a silent prayer that Colie would be found in time, even if she lived to testify and put him in prison. He'd been responsible for it all. His father had raised him to be a good boy, but he'd been weak and easily led with tragic results. His father would be ashamed of him. He was ashamed of himself. But he kept driving, just the same.

THE DEPUTY FOUND Colie on the porch and radioed for the EMTs. They were less than a minute away, having just checked out Ludie up the road where J.C. had found her.

"Look at this," one EMT told the other as they stabilized Colie, noting the makeshift bandage. "Somebody tried to help her."

"Maybe the person who shot her," his companion said. "We've got something better than that, thank God. Let's call it in and get her ready for transport."

"I'm way ahead of you," the woman said, rushing back to the truck for supplies.

J.C. HAD JUST finished with Ludie in the emergency room. Except for some emotional trauma, the resident told him, the child would be fine. She was unharmed, even by the snow she'd been found lying in. Lucky, the man added, because frostbite would have been an issue if she'd stayed out in the cold much longer.

J.C. thanked the man and cuddled Ludie close as they left the cubicle.

"Mommy over there," Ludie said, pointing.

J.C. looked and then smiled. "No, baby, she's not. They're looking for her..." He didn't have much hope that she'd be found alive. It was like acid, eating his heart, knowing that. He had to be calm, for Ludie's sake.

"Mommy," the child insisted.

J.C. looked again, and EMTs were rushing in with a woman on a stretcher.

"Colie!" J.C. burst out. He ran to the stretcher with Ludie in his arms.

"This is her child," he told them as he followed. "Will she live?"

"It's a GSW," one EMT said, meaning a gunshot wound.

"It's a sucking chest wound," the female EMT added, not breaking stride on her way through the swinging doors to surgery. "She's in bad shape. The doctor will have to evaluate her and give you a prognosis. Are you a relative?"

"Her fiancé," he said.

"That's my mommy," Ludie told them, crying again. "Mommy be okay?" she asked.

"We'll do everything we can," the man assured her.

"This my daddy," Ludie added, patting J.C.'s face.

The EMT, who was local, just grinned at J.C., who looked at the child with mingled pride and delight.

"We'll wait out here," J.C. told them.

They rushed Colie back into the emergency section.

IT WAS A long time before a man in surgical gear came to talk to them, pulling down his mask as he walked.

J.C. was on his feet immediately, with Ludie in his arms. "How is she?" he asked quickly.

"She'll live," the man said, noting the horror that had been contained in the two pairs of eyes that were identical, a pale, shimmery gray.

"Thank God," J.C. said heavily. Ludie just smiled at the surgeon, who grinned at her.

"There was some damage to the lower lobe of her lung. The bullet ricocheted and nicked her colon. It lodged in her back, in a place where it would be more dangerous to remove it than to leave it," he added quietly. "The body will react by building a fleshy shield around it. She won't know it's there."

"I've got one in me somewhere," J.C. replied. "Combat in the Middle East. It's not a souvenir I really wanted, but my combat surgeon told me the same thing you just said about Colie."

"I've had some royal battles with policemen over removal of bullets for evidence. Went to court one time to make sure I wasn't pressured into doing something I deemed an unnecessary risk. The policeman had to search for other evidence. He did find it, in case you wondered."

"Can we see Colie?" he asked huskily.

The surgeon was reluctant until he looked into Ludie's

eyes. He relented. "Okay. Just for a minute, though. She isn't out from under the anesthesia just yet."

They followed him back to the recovery room, where a nurse was overseeing two postsurgical patients.

"Her daughter," the surgeon told the hovering nurse, who took one look at Ludie's little tearstained face and couldn't help smiling.

"Mommy!" Ludie exclaimed.

J.C. moved to the still, white form under the sheet. "Dear God, I've never prayed so much in my whole life," he said under his breath.

"It was a close call," the surgeon affirmed. "If she'd been found just a little later, and if someone hadn't rigged a plug for the wound…"

"A what?" J.C. exclaimed.

"Somebody treated her before the EMTs arrived," he said. "There was a makeshift bandage, a plastic one, over the sucking chest wound. Very effective. Probably saved her life."

"Yes." J.C. hefted Ludie closer and reached down to touch Colie's white face. He brushed back her thick, soft dark hair tenderly. "Colie," he whispered huskily.

Her eyes shot open. She looked up at them through a layer of mental fog brought on by the anesthesia. She blinked. She winced.

"Mommy!" Ludie called.

She looked at the child and managed a smile through the pain that was slowly returning. "Ludie. My baby," she whispered.

"Who shot you?" J.C. asked quickly.

"Barry. He was going to kill…both of us. I put Ludie out. Told her…to run." Tears threatened. "I was afraid… she could have frozen to death!"

"She's fine. I'll take her home with me," J.C. said gently. "You'll be fine, honey. Just fine."

She looked up at him with pain-filled green eyes. "Thanks…J.C." she managed.

His big hand smoothed her hair. "We'll come back to see you tomorrow. Okay?"

She managed a smile. "I love you, Ludie," she whispered.

"I love you, Mommy," the little girl replied. "Bad man ran away!" she added.

"He won't get far," J.C. said curtly. "Half of Wyoming law has him in their sights."

"I want five…minutes alone with him," Colie whispered. "With a tire iron…" She tried to laugh and drifted away instead.

"She'll sleep now," the surgeon assured them. "You have to leave. So do I. I have another case waiting."

"Thanks for letting us in," J.C. said with a wistful, relieved glance back at Colie. "We were scared to death."

"Mommy okay now, Daddy," Ludie said, nuzzling close to him.

He smiled over her head at the surgeon and walked out to the SUV.

HE CALLED SHERIFF BANKS from his cell phone when he and Ludie got back to Skyhorn, but the sheriff had been too busy to answer. He left a callback number. Banks needed to know what Colie had told him.

He left Ludie with Ren's wife, Merrie, with a plea to bathe her and wash her clothes while he went back to town to buy some clothes and a toy or two for the little girl, who was going to stay in his cabin with him. Merrie assured him that she'd take care of the child. It amused her to see the very real bond between father and daughter that had already appeared.

Banks called him when he'd just pulled up in front of a clothing boutique that catered to children, in downtown Catelow. "I talked to Colie at the emergency room," he told Banks. "She said Barry Todd shot her. He was going to kill Ludie as well, but she pushed Ludie out and told her to run."

"I figured that. She must have something on Barry Todd, for him to have tried to murder her and the child, as well."

"Something she's never told anyone," J.C. agreed. "I thought it was because of the court case back in Texas. They have an informer who's ready to blow the drug distribution network apart, and apparently it involves Barry himself."

"So maybe he had two reasons."

"Somebody dressed the wound. Somebody who knew how. It was a sucking chest wound. The surgeon said it saved her life."

Banks let out a sigh. "Thank God for small blessings. Todd wouldn't have done that," he added.

"I know. I'm pretty sure it was Rod. He was in combat. I know he'd have some idea of what to do for a wound."

"Yeah. I've got a BOLO out for him, and for Todd. If we can find him, Todd will go up for attempted murder. And since he literally kidnapped Colie and her child from their home, I can bring in the feds to help. Federal offense, kidnapping. Todd's sealed his own coffin."

"We can hope so," J.C. said coldly. "I left Ludie with Merrie while I get her some clothes and I'm going to get her a kid's meal from the local fast-food joint. I can cook, but I'm not in the mood right now. It's been a damned long day."

"Tell me about it," Banks laughed hollowly. "I'm out after a bank robber, believe it or not. He took several hundred dollars from a dry goods store at gunpoint and ran for his life. We've got him cornered at his grandmother's house, but he's threatening to kill her if we don't back off. That's why I haven't been to the hospital to question Colie. She's going to be all right, then?"

"That's what the doctor says. He had to leave the bullet in."

"Hey, I've got one of those, too," Banks said.

J.C. laughed. "Me, too. Maybe we'll form a club or something."

"I have to get back to my men. I'll let you know if we turn up Todd or Colie's brother."

"Thanks, Cody."

"No problem."

J.C. hung up. He walked into the children's shop. The clerk, who knew about him from Lucy, who shopped there for her son, eyed him with shock.

"I need some things for my daughter," he said, and the words ran through him like liquid joy.

The woman smiled. "Tell me what you want."

IT WAS AN ADVENTURE, shopping for a little girl who was little more than a toddler. He had no idea of what size things to buy, so he just guessed. If some of the things didn't fit, the saleslady assured him, he could bring them back and return them. He got pajamas and a couple of pair of pants and two shirts, plus some underthings and a new jacket with a hood. He didn't like the idea of having his child in a bloodstained garment.

He gave the woman his credit card and thanked her when she had it all packaged. He took it out to his big black SUV.

There was a tearstained woman standing there, looking at him with fear and hope. "Colie," Lucy said huskily. "How is she? Is Ludie okay?"

"They're both going to be fine," he assured her. "Colie had a chest wound. Ludie was only traumatized. She got away in time."

"Who did it?" Lucy asked coldly. "It was that slimy friend of Rodney's, wasn't it? That Barry Todd!"

"Colie identified him as the shooter. I still don't know why he'd target her, just because her law firm was involved in court case over drugs."

"Neither do I," Lucy agreed. "Colie said there was something more, a secret she'd kept for a long time. She wouldn't even tell me, because she said it would put me at risk. But I'm pretty sure it's why she's stayed in Texas all this time. You know she'd have been here with her father, if there hadn't been a good reason for her to keep away from Catelow."

He sighed. "I think it's why Rodney and his friend Barry met me at the airport and told me Colie had cheated on me." His face closed up. "I should have laid them both out on the floor and trusted Colie instead. I had issues," he added, averting his eyes.

"Sometimes we get second chances," Lucy replied.

He managed a smile. "Sometimes we hope we won't mess those up, too. I'm just grateful that they're both still alive. It was a close call."

"If Colie needs me to help her with Ludie, I'll be glad to stay with her," Lucy offered.

"Thanks. I'll tell her. But for the time being, Ludie's

staying with me at Skyhorn. In case that deranged drug lord finds out she's alive and decides to try again." His face hardened. "I'll ask Banks to post a man at the hospital as well, to make sure Colie's kept safe." They both knew that since the crime had taken place outside the city limits, Banks would have jurisdiction. Not to mention that the hospital was located outside the city limits, as well.

"Good idea. I'll get back home," Lucy said. "I heard about the shooting on the radio and I spotted your truck on my way to the hospital. I figured you'd know what happened."

"I do know. Colie's in intensive care," he added. "I doubt they'll let you in. But the surgeon said that they may be able to move her into a room tomorrow. She came out from under the anesthetic while Ludie and I were in the recovery room with her. The surgeon made an exception for us."

"I'm so glad she's going to be okay," Lucy said huskily. "I don't make friends easily. I've missed Colie since she's lived in Texas."

"A lot of us have missed her," he said. He glanced at his watch. "I'd better get back to the ranch. Merrie's giving her a bath for me." He laughed softly. "I imagine I'll get a crash course in child raising tonight."

Lucy studied him quietly. "She's a precious little girl. She does have some very unusual skills, for such a young person."

"She sees things," J.C. replied. "My grandmother had the same gift. It's fairly rare."

"It amazes me. She amazes me. She's very mature for a child who's just over two years old."

He nodded. "Colie said that Ludie told her at the airport that her father was gone, before I spotted them on the concourse."

"An exceptional child," Lucy said.

"And very sweet, like Colie," he replied. He sighed. "I've got so much to make up to them that I hardly know where to start."

"One day at a time," she advised.

He just nodded.

LUDIE WAS DELIGHTED with a toy J.C. had bought her in the little boutique in town. It was a fuzzy bear that repeated everything the child said.

"He's so cute!" Ludie enthused. She ran to J.C. to be swung up in his arms, bear and all. He kissed a rosy cheek. "Thanks, Daddy," she said with twinkling eyes.

He was still getting used to that word. It filled him with pleasure, every time she said it. He was beaming from ear to ear when he noticed the looks he was getting from Ren and Merrie and Delsey.

He grimaced. "I suppose it's an open secret already, right?" he asked with resignation.

"Not much guesswork, you know," Merrie commented. "Everybody knew that Colie would never have let another man touch her. She was so crazy about you."

His high cheekbones flushed. It reminded him that he hadn't believed Colie. He'd preferred Rod's lie to the truth. It was still hard to live with.

"What about Colie?" Ren asked. "Barry Todd is still on the loose. If he knows she survived the shooting…"

"Banks has a man stationed inside the hospital, near the ICU where she's spending the night," J.C. revealed. "I spoke to him just a few minutes ago. He was concerned, as well."

"I hope they can nail Barry Todd and Rodney Thompson to a big, hard wall," Merrie muttered.

"By the ears," her husband agreed with a cold smile.

"Barbarians," J.C. scoffed.

"Daddy, what's a bar…bar…that thing?" Ludie asked him.

The others smiled at her.

"Barbarian," J.C. replied. "And you need to grow a bit before you ask me for that answer. Okay?"

She nodded solemnly. "Okay, Daddy," she promised.

He shifted her in his arms. "I'd better get her to bed. It's been a long day." He hesitated. "Thanks for bathing her and feeding her," he added. "I had no idea what to buy."

"You're just lucky that she's on the same level of food that our son is, and that I always have extra jars of it," Merrie chuckled. "But you're very welcome."

"We'll go and see Colie when she's better," Ren promised. "But right now, our only mandate is to keep her breathing."

"Amen," J.C. added.

COLIE WAS BREATHING much better when J.C. went to see her at the hospital the next morning. They had her in a semiprivate room, propped up in bed in one of those strange-looking hospital gowns. She had a worn look on her pale face. Her hair was disheveled and she was bandaged on the left side of her chest, where the bullet had gone in.

"Is Ludie all right?" she asked quickly.

"She's fine," he said softly. "I borrowed a rollaway bed from one of the married cowboys and kept her right next to my bed all night. She only woke once."

"Thanks," she said.

"I'm enjoying it," he replied. "It's not what I expected. Having a child around, I mean," he added as he stood beside the bed. "I always thought of kids as a nuisance."

"It's different when they're...when you know them," she amended.

He knew that she meant "when they're yours," but she wasn't admitting that just yet. He couldn't blame her. He'd done nothing to earn her trust. He hoped he could manage that in time to keep her from going back to Texas when the situation resolved itself.

"Lucy was on her way to the hospital when she spotted me at the children's boutique yesterday," he added. "I told her how you were. She was worried. She'll be over today."

"She's the only real friend I have," Colie confided. It was still difficult to talk. The wound was taking a toll on her. She winced as she moved. "It didn't hurt so much... yesterday."

"You were numb and in shock yesterday," he said. "The first few days after a wound are pretty bad. But you'll get through it. Take your meds and do what they tell you."

"There's a man in a uniform outside," she remarked. "I got...a glimpse of him when the nurses came in."

"It's one of Banks's men," he replied. "We're taking no chances that Rod's friend Barry might try again."

"He's probably halfway around the world by now," she said heavily.

"There's a BOLO, as well," J.C. told her. "One for your brother, too. Although he's the reason you're probably still alive."

"What?"

"He did a makeshift bandage," he explained. "You

had a sucking chest wound. It could have killed you very quickly if it had gone untreated for any length of time."

"Maybe Daddy was right," Colie said. "Maybe Rod still has a little good in him."

"I read about a serial killer who carried an old woman's groceries in the house for her and repaired a disabled man's porch steps," he commented.

She just looked at him.

"One trait doesn't rule out another, worse, one," he said simply. "Someone can do a good deed and go right out and commit murder. That's hard for people to understand. It's why some killers go free."

She frowned. "I see."

"I spoke to the surgeon on my way in here," he said. "He thinks you'll recover nicely. It will take time," he added firmly. "That means, you won't jump up and run back to Texas within a few days."

"I figured that. My job," she said, and winced. "I'll be letting them down."

"Have Lucy call them for you and explain what's going on."

"I can do that."

"Meanwhile, I'll take care of Ludie."

"How will you work?" she worried.

He laughed softly. "Most of what I do is around the ranch. I'll just take her with me. She's fascinated by the horses and cows and dogs."

"She loves animals."

"You always did, too," he replied. "Your father dreaded telling you when Big Tom died," he added. "He said you took it hard."

"I loved him," she said simply.

"I remember."

She drew in a painful breath. "Pain's coming back." She touched a control and a painkiller was triggered to counteract it. "Modern technology is awesome."

"It truly is."

She looked up at him. "What if Barry comes back to finish the job?" she worried.

"When you leave here, you're coming to Skyhorn," he said simply. "Merrie says they have two spare bedrooms. You and Ludie can have one until it's safe for you to go home."

"Oh, that's so kind of her!" Colie said, fighting tears.

"I would have invited you to stay with me, but I've given Catelow enough reason to gossip about you and Ludie. Never again."

She searched his pale eyes, so much like Ludie's.

"I've made a mess of both our lives." He paused. "Do you remember long ago, when we compared the fortunes we were told?"

She thought back. "Yes."

"In hindsight, I think I could say they were eerily accurate."

"Too much so."

He reached down and brushed back her disheveled hair. "Yours had something about joy following sorrow, didn't it?"

"I believe so."

"Mine, as well." He bent farther and brushed his mouth tenderly over hers. "So when you get out of here, we might consider going in search of some of that. Joy, I mean."

"Joy." She was staring up at him with her heart in her eyes.

His lips teased hers gently in the long silence. "I never believed in miracles. Before."

"You didn't...?" She was trying to lift closer to that hard, sensuous mouth. It had been so long! Even through layers of pain and painkiller, she was dying for him, all over again.

"I didn't," he whispered as her lips parted. "But, now..."

The door opened and he jerked erect, actually flushing as the nurse came in to check Colie's vitals.

"You look flushed. We'd better check your temp," the nurse said gently.

Colie looked past her to J.C. and they exchanged helplessly amused smiles. Colie actually felt the joy, pulsing through her veins like molten honey. J.C.'s eyes were promising heaven.

CHAPTER FIFTEEN

BY THE TIME the nurse was finished, Lucy had walked in the door. J.C. touched Colie's cheek with his fingertips.

"Do what the doctor says. I'll bring Ludie to see you later, okay?"

"Okay, J.C.," she said with a sleepy smile.

"I'll phone you if she tries to escape," Lucy promised him.

He chuckled as he left. But this time, he turned at the door and looked back at Colie, his pale silver eyes alive with pleasure.

"That's a first," Colie remarked when he was gone.

"What is?" Lucy asked, putting down her purse and coat in the second of two chairs by the bedside.

"He used to never look back," she explained.

Lucy smiled. "He's not the same man he used to be, Colie. Not at all. Imagine the old J.C. shopping at a child's boutique!"

"I can't."

"Honestly, neither can I." She moved close to the bed. "How are you? I almost had a heart attack when I heard about the shooting on the news. I was rushing to the hospital when I saw J.C. outside the shop and pulled over. I figured he'd know more than the news about what happened."

"He always did," Colie recalled with a wan smile.

"What happened? It was that friend of Rod's, wasn't it?" the other woman asked belligerently.

"Exactly," she replied on a short breath. "I saw something three years ago that put him and Rod into a panic. Rod and his friend Barry had a suitcase of drugs. I went away partly to show Barry that I wasn't going to tell what I knew. But he thinks I'll do it, now that the law firm where I work is going after a distribution network. He said he could beat that rap, but what I knew could put him in federal prison for conspiracy to distribute illegal drugs. I was expendable. So was my child." Her eyes closed and she shivered. "He was going to kill us both. He got us in Rod's car at gunpoint and drove us to a lonely stretch of road. I opened the door and pushed Ludie out and told her to run, just as he pulled the trigger. God bless her, she did exactly what she was told, or she likely wouldn't be alive now. If it hadn't been for Rod, I imagine I'd be dead, too."

"What do you mean?"

"J.C. said that someone put an emergency bandage on me that saved my life. Barry wouldn't have cared, but Rod would, and he was in combat. He knew how to treat wounds."

"He ran and left you on the porch," Lucy said icily. "I heard that from my coworker, whose cousin is one of the EMTs who went to your house after you were shot. They said you were barely coherent, but you knew you were in Rod's car, and afterward it was gone. They put two and two together."

"How did they know to go there?" she wondered.

Lucy hesitated. "I guess Rod called them. Otherwise, they wouldn't have known until it was too late."

"That's what I was thinking."

"Rod may have good points, but there's no way he'll avoid jail time if he's ever caught, you know," Lucy said gently as she dropped into a chair. "At the least, they'll get him for conspiracy to distribute drugs. That's a tough sentence."

"I know." Colie closed her eyes. "Rod was always so easily led. He never learned."

"That's a shame," Lucy said. "He's the last living close relative you have."

Colie agreed. "We can't choose our kinfolk."

Lucy's lips pursed. "Pity."

Colie managed to laugh.

J.C. HAD TO help the men get the pregnant heifers to pastures close to the house. It could be dangerous work, but he took Ludie with him, cautioning her to stay in the SUV until he came to get her. She could watch through the window.

Willis rode up on his sorrel mare and paused by the truck. "I see you have help today," he said with a chuckle.

"Wolf!" Ludie exclaimed, having powered the window down. "Wolf man. Can I see the wolf? Oh, please?"

Two men stared at the child with changing expressions. "You told her?" Willis asked.

J.C. shook his head. "No."

Willis whistled through his teeth. "You'll have to tell Tank's wife about that," he said.

J.C. smiled. "I will, as soon as they get back from that conference they went to."

"Yes, young lady, you can see the wolf. J.C., want to drive her up to my cabin? She can look at him through the screen. They're sort of unpredictable," he added warily. "I'll ride up with you."

"We'll go right now." He phoned Ren, explained Ludie's request and got a laughing affirmative for the trip.

WILLIS'S CABIN WAS set back in the woods, like J.C.'s. All of Ren's huge ranch bordered on the Wapiti National Forest, so it was far away from Catelow.

J.C. pulled up at the front door and lifted an excited Ludie down. "You can't go inside," he cautioned.

She looked up at him with his own eyes. "Please, Daddy?" she asked.

He felt the words all the way to his toes. Willis came up on the porch after tying his mount to one of the posts.

"He has moods," Willis chuckled. "Let me go in and see if he's sociable today."

The man and the child waited on the porch. A minute later, the wolf came loping out from the back of the house to stand on his three legs near the screen. He sniffed Ludie and whined.

"Please?" Ludie persisted.

"Honey, it's not safe…"

"Please?!"

"Colie's going to kill me," J.C. murmured under his breath, but he opened the screen door.

Ludie ran in and caught the wolf around the neck and hugged him and hugged him. The wolf laid his big head on her little shoulder and sniffed her and whined softly. He made no sort of aggressive move toward her.

"Pretty boy," Ludie purred. "Sweet wolf."

The wolf whined some more. His gray eyes were closed and he was almost purring himself.

"Not since Merrie came in here, and he did that, have I ever seen him so docile with another person except me," Willis said, shaking his head.

"She has…gifts," J.C. said finally.

"Oh, yes," Willis agreed soulfully.

LATER, J.C. TOOK Ludie to the hospital to see her mother. Colie had just finished a light lunch. Her green eyes brightened with joy as her daughter ran up beside the bed.

"Careful, honey," J.C. cautioned. "Mommy's sore."

"I know, Daddy," she said, smiling up at him. "Mommy, I hugged the wolf! He liked me!" she exclaimed.

J.C. grimaced and waited for the storm.

But Colie didn't jump at him. She just smiled. "She found a dog beside the road near Jacobsville, where we lived," she explained. "It was big and known to be dangerous. I tried to stop her, but she ran right to it, sat down beside it and started talking to it. The dog stretched out, whining in pain, and didn't even show his teeth. Cousin Ty helped us get it to the vet, and we adopted it. The vet said she had a gift. I've heard that Tank Kirk's wife has one, as well. She picked up a rattlesnake and took it to a wildlife rehabilitator," she laughed.

J.C. let out a sigh of relief. "How do you feel, honey?" he asked Colie, his deep voice soft and caring.

"Still hurts," she told him. "But I'm getting better. Have you heard anything from the sheriff?"

"Not yet. I left a message with dispatch…" His phone rang. He paused to answer it. Sure enough, it was Banks. He put it on speaker so Colie could hear, too.

"We called in the feds and they tracked Barry Todd to the airport in Atlanta," he told J.C. "He was apparently on his way to South America. They've sent federal marshals to transport him back to Denver for trial. We hear that Colie's bosses in Jacobsville have enough to hang him."

"I have something to help hang him," Colie said. "Hi, Sheriff."

"Hi, Colie. Getting better?"

"Much." She drew in a breath, aware of J.C.'s big hand linking with hers on the bed. "I saw Barry give my brother a whole suitcase of illegal drugs and I heard him instructing Rod in their distribution."

"Good God!" Banks exploded. "You actually saw it?"

"Yes," she said, noting J.C.'s thunderous expression. "I went away so that Barry would think I was going to keep my mouth shut. I stayed away, to protect my father and my child."

"I wish you'd come to me," Banks said. "I'd have managed to get protection for you."

"I was afraid," she said. She lowered her eyes. "Besides that, I'd just had a sort of traumatic personal experience. I was reeling from it, and not really thinking straight. I just ran."

J.C.'s eyes closed. He knew what she meant. He'd thrown her out of his life on the word of a thief and a drug lord. He'd have to live with the memory of his betrayal all his life.

"I can understand that," Banks was saying. "Would you be willing to testify to that in court?" he added. "I can assure your safety."

Colie knew that it was wind, air, that nobody could save her if Barry wanted retribution. But she was certain that J.C. would keep Ludie safe, whatever happened. And it was time to stop running. "Yes," she said. "I'll testify."

"I'll tell the feds," he replied. "You'll also have to testify to the shooting. You understand?"

"Yes, sir," she said respectfully. "I'm just sorry that my brother got mixed up in this. Has he been found?"

"No," Banks said, his voice gruff. "But we're tracking him. We have an investigator who'll follow a suspect all the way to hell to get him. Your brother won't escape. I'm sorry, Colie, but we break the law, we have to pay the price."

"I know that," she said. "It's just that he's my only living relative. Besides Ludie."

"I had a cousin who went up for murder one," Banks replied. "It hurt me, because we were best friends. But the law is the law."

"Yes. I've worked for lawyers for several years," she reminded him. "You do get a good picture of the criminal justice system."

"Indeed so. I'll be in touch when I learn more," Banks promised.

They thanked him. J.C. put the cell phone back in its holder.

Ludie was looking from one parent to the other with soft, loving eyes. "Gonna be okay," she said softly. "Bad man won't hurt us ever again."

Colie looked up at J.C. "Oh, I hope you're right, Ludie," she said. She held out her arm and Ludie got as close as she could.

"I love you, Mommy."

"I love you, too, honey." Colie was fighting tears. The pain was still bad, and she was fighting nausea, as well.

"We should go and let Mommy rest, okay?" J.C. asked, bending to lift the child with the strawberry curls into his arms. He kissed her little cheek. "My very own living Shirley Temple doll," he teased.

"Who's Shirley Temple?" Ludie wanted to know.

"I'll find a movie on YouTube and you can watch it and see," he promised.

"J.C., thank you. For everything," Colie said.

He bent and kissed her softly. "I have to take care of my own," he said in a husky whisper. His eyes said more than words.

Colie reached up, grimacing as the action pulled the wound, and touched his hard face. "So many years," she said.

"After the cut, the kiss," he replied. He smiled tenderly. "Think about it."

She understood. Life taught painful lessons, but they were almost always followed by periods of great joy. She had a feeling that she was headed for one.

"Something else to tell you," J.C. added with twinkling pale gray eyes. "I've been reading books!"

"Books." She stopped, looked at him, realized what he was telling her, and flushed.

"Good books," he added, and showed perfect white teeth as he grinned at her. "We can discuss that when you're better."

"Well…" She grimaced. "My bosses!" she exclaimed. "They won't know what's going on…!"

"I'll call them today and explain. I need the number and the name of someone I can talk to," he added.

"It's in my cell phone, in the drawer, in my purse." She directed him to the chest next to the bed.

He pulled the phone out of her purse and gave it to her.

"It's this one," she said, pulling up a contact. "That's Mr. Copeland. He's head of the law firm, now that…now that Darby's gone." It was still hard to remember Darby without tears. He'd been so kind.

"I'll explain everything," J.C. promised, copying the information and putting her phone and purse back in the drawer.

"You be good for J.C.," Colie told her little girl with a warm smile.

"I'll be good, Mommy. That nice lady drew us," she added suddenly.

"Drew us?" Colie asked.

"Merrie sketched us when I first brought Ludie over," he replied. "She has a masterful touch. She's doing a painting. It will be a revelation, I promise. She saved her own life by painting a mobster from back East," he added, chuckling. "He actually gave her away when she married Ren."

"I like Merrie," Colie said. "She's always been kind to me."

"They've got your room ready, as soon as you're able to come home," J.C. assured her. "I'll bring Ludie back tomorrow. We're having another storm, so all the hands are working against the clock to get the pregnant heifers and cows close to the barn."

"You be careful," she said.

He smiled. "Yes, ma'am," he replied.

She felt born anew as she looked at him. It was different than before. There was less violent physical attraction, more deep and tender affection. She couldn't wait to see how things went.

Then she remembered her brother and her face fell.

"Uncle Rod coming back," Ludie piped up. "Gonna tell on bad man, Mommy."

Colie looked at J.C. If Ludie was right this time, things might work out well. At least, Rodney might be able to make a deal for a lesser sentence. Only time would tell.

"Get better," J.C. told her. "I'll take care of Ludie."

She smiled drowsily. "I know that."

"Bye, Mommy," Ludie called back from the doorway.

Colie was asleep before they got to the elevator.

COLIE WAS WELL enough to leave the hospital three days later. J.C. and Ludie went to get her.

"They were good to me, but I'm happy to get back to normal," Colie said as they drove away. Ludie was in her car seat in the back seat, while Colie was strapped into the passenger seat beside J.C.

"Still feeling okay?" he asked as they drove off.

"A little sore," she said. "The doctor said that was normal." She was holding a sheaf of papers in a folder in her lap.

"We'll stop by the pharmacy and give those prescriptions to the pharmacist on the way home," he told Colie. "I'll go back and pick them up when they're ready."

"Medicine is so expensive," she began.

"Honey, I can afford most anything you want," he said gently. He smiled at her as he glanced in her direction when they came to a stoplight. "Anything at all."

"Can you buy me a peaceful life without any wild-eyed drug lords roaming around it?" she wondered.

He chuckled. "The criminal justice system will take care of that."

"It doesn't always work," she replied. "Juries cut people loose sometimes."

"You do something bad, something bad happens to you," J.C. said simply. He shrugged. "Your father rubbed off on me," he added quietly.

She fought tears. It was so much. Her father's death, the anguish over Rodney, the shooting...

She felt J.C.'s big hand clasp her own. "Something

else he taught me. You have to have faith, Colie," he said softly.

She could almost hear her father saying the same thing. She returned the soft pressure of his hand. "Okay," she said simply.

SHE WAS SURPRISED when J.C. pulled up at his own cabin instead of Ren's big house.

"But…" she began.

He put a soft velvet-covered box in her hands. "Story's in the newspaper already. I expect when you check your cell phone, you'll have a lot of messages." He grimaced. "Probably the first one will be from Lucy, raising Cain because you didn't tell her first."

"Lucy…?"

She pulled her cell phone out of her purse while J.C. was getting the luggage into his cabin. There was a message from Lucy. Congrats! And why in the world didn't you tell me?!

She looked up as J.C. was getting Ludie out of the back seat. "Why didn't I tell Lucy what?" she asked.

"Open the box," he said simply.

She did. Inside were a diamond-and-emerald engagement ring, and an emerald-studded gold band that matched it exactly. The stones were inlaid. It was a very expensive set.

He deposited Ludie inside and came back to get Colie. She just stared at him.

"I bought those three years ago," he said quietly. "They were in my pocket when your brother and his friend met me at the airport."

She bit her lower lip. J.C. had never made any declaration of love, any hint of what he had in mind for the future. This was a revelation. If. If. If!

Tears ran down her cheeks.

He picked her up gently in his arms. "I screwed up, Colie," he said softly. "I was running scared. I wanted you, but my own home life was the pattern I judged the world by. I didn't have a normal childhood. Mine was violent and tragic." He drew in a breath as he carried her to the cabin. "I've kicked myself mentally a dozen times for ever listening to Rod in the first place. But we can't go back, honey. We have to try to move ahead."

He put her down inside the cabin and looked into her soft green eyes. "Can you forgive so much hurt?" he asked. "Can you move past what I did to you?"

She drew in a breath. Tears were still threatening. "I can," she said.

"You won't ever have a reason to distrust me again," he promised.

"Daddy, want cheese," Ludie piped up, looking at him with his own pale gray eyes.

He chuckled. "Cheese fanatic," he murmured. "My fridge is full of it, every kind under the sun. She discovered it and now it's cheese every meal."

"I like it, too," Colie remarked, moving slowly toward the kitchen. "Honestly, I'm so tired of gelatin!"

J.C. laughed out loud. "I've been in the hospital a time or two. I know exactly what you mean."

He got out dishes and started slicing cheese. He put crackers of all sorts out with them and poured milk for Ludie and soft drinks for himself and Colie. He remembered the cold ginger ale she liked.

She smiled as she sipped it. "This was my favorite."

"I know," he replied. He leaned back in the chair, his eyes on his child. "She's very bright," he remarked.

"Almost too bright," Colie laughed. "She scares people sometimes with those things she blurts out."

"She'd be right at home here in Catelow, with Tank Kirk's wife not too far away."

"The clairvoyant," Colie recalled. "I'd love to meet her."

"I'll make a point of introducing you. Ren bought some livestock from him just recently. Tank's a good guy. He was border patrol a few years back. Got shot up pretty badly. But he recovered. And his brother Mallory is married to a Texas girl—King Brannt's daughter."

"Goodness, I know about her from cousin Annie," Colie told him. "She knows everybody in South Texas. Or sometimes it seems so."

He cocked his head and studied her. "Could you live here, Colie?" he asked.

She paused with her ginger ale halfway to her mouth. It was a profound question. It went with the set of rings she still had, clutched tightly in her free hand. She looked at the only man she'd ever loved, and felt the old hunger burning deep down inside her. Except that this time, it wasn't raw passion. It was deeper. Sweeter. He was offering her a new life. If she had the will to take it.

"Yes," she said finally, and watched his face light up with the words. "Yes, I could live here, J.C."

"John Calvin," Ludie corrected as she munched cheese.

J.C.'s high cheekbones colored.

"You told her?" Colie asked.

"No," he said flatly. "I've never told anyone. My

mother was Irish, but her parents were from Scotland. They were staunch Presbyterians who revered John Calvin, one of the founders of the Protestant faith. I was named for him. My mother converted to Roman Catholicism when she married my father."

"It's a noble sort of way to name someone," she remarked. "I was named Colleen Mary, for a great-aunt who was a pioneer newspaperwoman in Wyoming."

"I never knew your real name," he remarked with a smile.

"We didn't talk much. Not really," she said.

"We have all the time in the world to talk now," he told her. "But first," he added heavily, "there's a sad duty to perform, for both of us. I talked with the assistant minister and he agreed that Saturday would be a good day for the service. He thought it would give you enough time to get out of the hospital and rest for a day or so."

She nodded. "He's a good man. Daddy loved him." She looked up. "He and his wife came by to see me last night, after you left. They're a cute couple."

"She plays tennis," he said. He laughed. "Beats her husband every single match."

"I know. He thought it was awesome."

He sighed. "But you should always let the man win, you know," he said with pursed lips. "It feeds his ego and makes him feel important."

"Bull."

His eyes sparkled. "Okay, no more propaganda. Do you still like the new *Sherlock* series?" he asked.

"Oh, yes!" she exclaimed.

"In that case, when little bit goes to sleep, I'll play the instant video shows for you."

"I'd love that."

"Who's little bit, Daddy?" Ludie wanted to know.

He bent over and kissed her little nose. "That's you, tidbit."

She laughed. "Oh, you're funny, Daddy!"

"I'm happy," he said. He touched her strawberry curls. "My sweet girl. Daddy's girl," he added proudly.

She linked her little arms around his neck and held on tight. "I love you, Daddy."

"I love you, too. Time for bed very soon."

"I'll go get into my jammies," she said, climbing down from the chair.

"I never knew a child her age could dress herself, until she came along," J.C. remarked.

"She's precocious," Colie laughed. "She constantly amazes me. She knows her alphabet and her colors and numbers already. She's in prekindergarten back in Texas…" Her voice trailed off. There were so many connections back there.

"They have a very good Presbyterian preschool right here in Catelow," he pointed out. "And you can Skype with your cousins."

"Yes. I can do that."

He caught her hand in his and kissed the palm hungrily. "I'll never let go again, Colie," he said huskily. "I promise you that!"

She touched his lean cheek with the tips of her fingers. "It's been so long, J.C.," she said sadly.

"Too long," he agreed. "Your father missed you, too. He thought I was the reason you wouldn't come back, at first. But then, he paid more attention to Rodney and what he was up to, and he came up with another scenario.

He thought you'd been threatened, and that's why you didn't come home."

"He was right. I couldn't tell him," she said, her eyes sad. "It would have put him right on the firing line. I would have told you, if things had been different. That's what I planned to do, but Rodney made sure I couldn't."

J.C.'s silver eyes flashed. "I did finally realize that you'd never have sold me out like that." He winced. "But by the time I came to my senses, you were already married. If it hadn't been for your father, I think I'd have gone mad."

"Playing chess with Daddy," she said, and laughed. "I didn't believe that, at first."

"He figured I wasn't a complete lost cause, and he got to work on me." He shook his head. "I never knew anyone like him. He was the closest thing to a father I've ever known. I'd have done anything for him. Anything in the world."

"He was very special," she agreed.

There was a brief silence of shared grief. He pulled her up into his arms and held her as closely as he dared. He didn't want to make her any more uncomfortable than the wound already did.

"We start over, right here," J.C. said softly. "And from now on, if you tell me the sky is green with cherry blossoms in it, I'll believe you without proof."

She grinned. "Okay."

He bent his head and brushed her soft lips with his hard ones. "And I will love you," he whispered into her mouth, "until the stars go out. And forever after, Colie."

Tears rained down her face. "I never stopped loving

you," she whispered back. "I couldn't. It was only you. Only you, my whole life…!"

His mouth stopped the words. He held her face between his warm hands and kissed her until her mouth was sore and her face flushed.

He lifted his head and looked into her eyes, the tension so sweet and thick that it was almost tangible.

And in the middle of that soulful exchange, a little voice called from the next room, "Mommy, I dropped my sock in the cubbymode!"

"So now you know all about parenthood," Colie teased him.

He shrugged. "It's just a sock. We can buy her lots of new ones."

"Last week, she flushed two washcloths down the 'cubbymode,'" she informed him. "It took the plumber fifteen minutes to get the toilet working again."

"Scientific curiosity," he said, defending his child. "She likes to experiment."

She grinned. "In that case, since you're in a nesting mood, suppose we go to the courthouse in the morning and get one of those license thingies?"

"I would love that," he said.

She sighed, pressing against him. "I would, too. But before we can get married, we have to have a funeral. And somewhere out there is my brother, running from the law. There's also a drug lord who may have a very long reach, even in prison."

"Worry about tomorrow, tomorrow," he advised, kissing her forehead. "Tonight, we have a sock in the cubbymode to handle."

"You first," she offered.

He laughed and went to fish out the offending object. Inside, he felt like a man who'd won the lottery. He'd never expected her to feel the same way she had about him, much less agree to take a second chance on him. He was never going to fail her again, no matter what!

CHAPTER SIXTEEN

THE FUNERAL WAS quiet and dignified, just as Jared Thompson himself had been. The assistant minister at the Methodist church led the service. He spoke of Jared's kindness, his love for his congregation, his love for the church.

There were songs, the ones Jared had loved most. When the choir sang "Amazing Grace," Colie burst into tears. J.C. slid an arm around her shoulders and drew her close. Ludie, on his other side, was also pressed close. It was the nearest thing to a family J.C. had ever known. He missed her father. He'd turned J.C.'s life around with his quiet, patient counsel. Now, looking back, J.C. would have given anything to be able to start over with Colie, at the very beginning of their turbulent relationship, when he went to supper at the Thompson home and asked her out for the first time. But that wasn't possible. He had to move forward, and do all he could to take care of her and his daughter.

Colie seemed to feel that regret in him. She looked up at him and smiled tenderly through her tears. He smiled back.

Her father had been a military veteran, so there was an honor guard and a flag, which was reverently folded up when it was removed from the casket. The officer handed it to her, with his condolences.

THEY BURIED JARED on a hill overlooking the distant peaks of the Teton Mountains, snowcapped and beautiful.

Little Ludie didn't even fidget during the graveside service. She sat between her mother and father and listened quietly to the brief prayers.

The new minister, the former assistant pastor, Marvin Compton, paused beside Colie to offer condolences.

"He was a wonderful man," he told her. "It was a privilege to be in his life."

"It was for me, too," Colie said with a sad smile.

"Gimpa in heaven," Ludie said. She smiled at the minister, too. "Gimpa with Grandma."

"That's what I think, too, little lady." He smiled back. "You two planning to come to Sunday services?"

"I am," Colie said. "I don't know about..." She looked at J.C. warily.

"I meant you and Ludie," the minister chuckled. "J.C.'s in the front pew every Sunday," he added, surprising Colie, who just stared at him.

"Second row," J.C. corrected. "Your kids take up most of the front pew," he teased.

Marvin chuckled. "Well, them and my wife and my mother and my mother-in-law," he agreed. "We think it's a great church."

"So did Daddy," Colie replied. "And, yes, Ludie and I will be coming with J.C. from now on. I joined the church when I was just fifteen," she added.

"Your father told me," the minister said. "J.C. joined two years ago."

That was news. Faintly shocking news. She looked up at the man beside her with the surprise in her face.

He shrugged. "Your father was very persuasive," he said simply.

She grinned.

There was a faint, ruddy flush on his high cheekbones, but he smiled, too.

"Then we'll see you Sunday. And again, I'm so sorry, Colie," Marvin repeated.

"Thanks, Reverend."

The family left first, but they didn't go far. There were friends and neighbors who wanted to express their own condolences. Among them were J.C.'s boss, Ren Colter, and his wife, Merrie, and their little boy, barely walking now.

"He was a fine man, Colie," Ren said gently. "We all know where he went."

"Yes, we do," Merrie agreed. She grinned at Ludie and wrinkled her nose. "I'm painting you," she said, "with your dad."

"I know! It's so pretty," Ludie added to her mother. "She draws nice!"

"I knew that already," Colie told the child. "I can't wait to see it," she said to Merrie. "It's so kind of you. The one you did of J.C. is just awesome."

"He was a fascinating subject," Merrie said.

"Not on a par with the East Coast gangster, however," Ren said, tongue in cheek. "Saved her life, painting that one."

"I remember," J.C. said. "Those were dark times."

"So. Are we invited to the wedding?" Ren teased.

"You know you are. This Sunday, at 2:00 p.m. at the church."

"Yes," Marvin said, clapping Ren on the shoulder. "I'm officiating."

"We expect half of Catelow to show up," Ren added. "Nobody could believe that he was actually going to get married," he said, nodding toward J.C.

J.C. caught Colie's hand in his. "Instant family, just add rings," he chuckled, looking down at his daughter, who was beaming at him.

"Where does she get that red hair?" Marvin wondered.

"From my mother," J.C. replied. "She was from Dublin. She had curly red-gold hair, just like Ludie's, and pale gray eyes. I inherited the eyes."

"Your father had dark hair, I presume?" Marvin asked innocently.

Colie braced herself for his response. J.C. didn't speak of his father.

But J.C. didn't blow up at the man. "He was Blackfoot," he told the man. He hesitated. "I've blamed him for everything that went wrong in my life. Colie's father taught me that vengeance is a dead end, that resentment is a wound that festers." He shrugged. "I've had a private detective looking for him," he confessed. "I'd like to mend fences, before he dies, if he hasn't already."

"My other gimpa got collar," Ludie interrupted. "Got a collar." She yawned.

J.C. shook his head. The child was tired and not making sense, either. "We'd better go. Somebody needs a nap."

"I noticed." Marvin shook hands with them. So did Ren. Merrie hugged everyone. "We'll see you Sunday at church," Merrie said, "and we'll stay for the wedding," she added with soft laughter.

"We'll be there," Colie promised. "All of us," she added, looking up at J.C. with adoring eyes.

THE WEDDING WAS not only well attended, there was a newspaper reporter and a photographer there to record the ceremony.

Colie, in a neat white suit and a hat with a veil, was surprised at the coverage. She saw Ren Colter grinning and figured he had something to do with it. But she was too happy to care about any publicity. After all, they lived in Catelow. It was natural that the community would want to know that one of their own—two, if you counted J.C.—was getting married.

Lucy served as matron of honor, along with Ren's wife, Merrie, and Ludie was the flower girl, precious in a lacy white dress carrying a basket of white rose petals. As Colie stood beside J.C., resplendent in a dark suit, she thought over the past few years of her life and how sad they'd been. She couldn't help remembering the prophecy her grandmother had told her, the one that meshed so perfectly with the one J.C.'s grandmother had given him years ago. A long sadness, followed by great joy. She looked up at him and felt the joy, like a silky wrap around her body. It was reflected in the green eyes that met J.C.'s loving gray ones.

The minister pronounced them man and wife. J.C. bent and lifted the veil. He looked into her eyes for a long moment before he bent and kissed her reverently, one big hand caressing her rosy cheek.

Her fingers brushed over his. She smiled with her whole heart.

The strains of the "Wedding March" began again, the signal for them to leave the church, down the aisle, where a group of people were waiting to congratulate them. Colie couldn't have stopped smiling to save her life.

"Happy?" J.C. asked on the way to the fellowship hall where the reception was being held.

"So happy," she said softly. "It's been a long, long road here, J.C."

He nodded. "But a sweet rest at the end of it." He glanced down at his daughter, grinned and lifted her up into his arms. "Instant family, just add rings," he chuckled, echoing what he'd said before.

"My daddy." Ludie sighed, and rested her little cheek on J.C.'s broad shoulder.

J.C. hugged her close. "My angel," he replied, kissing her red-gold curls.

Watching them together, Colie could hardly believe the expression on the face of a man who'd sworn he wanted nothing to do with kids.

"Congratulations, you two," Lucy said with a grin. She had her son in her arms. Her husband, Ben, beside her, was smiling as he echoed her sentiments.

"Thank you for everything, Lucy," Colie said softly.

"You're very welcome. I hope..." She stopped and looked past them at an approaching figure. It was Cody Banks, in his sheriff's uniform. He looked grim.

"Oh, dear," Lucy murmured.

Colie turned and ground her teeth together. She searched for J.C.'s free hand and held it tight.

"Sorry," Cody said gently as he approached them. "It's a happy occasion and I don't want to taint it, but I'd rather you heard this from me before you saw it on Facebook, or Twitter," he added.

"Shoot," Colie said, steeling herself.

"We have your brother in custody."

She grimaced.

"It's not quite as bad as it sounds," he added quickly. "He actually turned himself in, and he's turning state's evidence against Barry Todd."

"Rod?" Colie exclaimed.

"That's the Rod I knew overseas," J.C. said quietly. "He lost his way. But it seems he's found the path again."

"Yes, he has," the sheriff agreed. He smiled at Colie. "He'll still have to serve time," he told her, "but he's sure to get a reduced sentence. It will help us get Todd off the streets for good."

"What a lovely thought." Colie sighed. She smiled at Banks. "And I didn't get you anything," she teased.

"I love chocolate pound cake," he suggested.

"That will be the first thing on my list after my job interview tomorrow," she promised.

"What job interview?" J.C. asked.

"Lucy's bosses are going to try and fit me in doing my old job," she explained, as Lucy nodded enthusiastically. "Their other administrative assistant has an aging mother in Montana and wants to go and take care of her. That will leave a job available."

J.C. smiled. "You can stay home, if you want to," he told her. "It wouldn't work a hardship on the family budget."

"You're sweet, but I've always worked," she pointed out. "It makes me feel useful, to do a job like I do. People who come into law offices are usually scared or sad or angry. I like helping them get through the process."

"She's very good at consoling terrified people," Lucy said.

"Whatever you want to do, honey," J.C. said gently, smiling down at her. "I'm behind you, all the way."

She leaned against him and rested her head on his broad chest. "That goes double for me," she replied.

"Want cake, Mommy," Ludie said. "Please?"

They all chuckled. "Okay, sprout, let's see what kind they've got," J.C. agreed, leading the way into the fellowship hall.

IT WAS A NOISY, joyful reception, even with the sad news about Colie's brother.

"At least he's finally doing something right," Colie mentioned to J.C. as they were sipping champagne for photographs.

"I like the idea of Todd going away for a hundred years or so," J.C. said icily.

"Me, too, but it's probably going to be more like ten." Colie sighed.

"I wish we could go back and start over, sweetheart," J.C. said with heartfelt emotion. "I'd give anything to start over with you."

She touched his chin with her forefinger. "We're starting over right now," she pointed out. "One day at a time."

He sighed and drew her close. "I wish we had time for a honeymoon…"

"Every day will be a honeymoon, for the next forty years or so," she interrupted. She smiled up at him. "Honest."

He laughed. "Okay, then."

IT WAS LATE when they got back home. Snow was falling lightly. Ludie was asleep in the back seat and had to be carried inside. She woke only briefly, when Colie was changing her into a gown before she slid the sleepy child under the covers.

"Gimpa got collar," Ludie repeated sleepily.

Colie had no idea what she meant. She just smiled and kissed the rosy little cheeks. "Sleep tight, my baby."

Ludie smiled and went right back to sleep.

A FEW WEEKS LATER, when she was released by her doctor after the surgery following the gunshot wound, Colie was steeling herself to cope with what was going to happen next.

In spite of the tender kisses and caresses that accompanied her path to healing, she was still a little apprehensive when the lights went out in J.C.'s bedroom. She loved J.C., but this had been an unpleasant part of their relationship, just the same.

"It's okay," he said softly as his mouth found hers. "You have to trust me, this once."

She felt stiff and unresponsive, but she forced her rigid body to relax. "It won't hurt?" she blurted out.

He laughed softly. "I told you. I've been reading books…"

She gasped as he touched her in a new way.

"Just relax," he whispered. "Come on, now, honey. Relax, that's it."

The things he was doing to her made her body sing. She'd never even read about some of them in her romance novels. Of course, the books she liked weren't the wild permissive ones with graphic details. She liked sweet romances…!

Her body arched off the bed and she made a sound she'd never heard come out of her own throat. She writhed under the slow, deep caresses. All the while, his mouth teased hers, coaxed it open, penetrated it in slow, deep thrusts.

It echoed what his body was already doing to hers. She felt the cool air in the room on bare skin. Closer, she felt the heat and power of his body, warm and muscular where his skin brushed against hers, abrasive where the thick hair on his chest and stomach dragged against hers.

By the time he finally went into her, she was writhing on the sheets, arching up to him, begging silently for an end to the slow, sweet torment of tension that built suddenly to flash fire.

She felt one big, warm hand catch her upper thigh and position her. But he was teasing more than taking in the heated seconds that followed.

"Oh…please," she pleaded in a hoarse whisper. "Please!"

"Yes." He moved down against her, slowly impaling her. He was more formidable than she recalled, but no longer rushing or impatient. He made sure that she went with him every step of the way, feeling her shiver and cling as he intensified the heated power of his thrusts.

Tears were rolling down her cheeks as she strained up to meet each downward motion of his hips. Her nails bit into his hips. She sobbed, finally, as the fever of it caught her up and made her shudder every time he thrust down into her body.

And then, so suddenly, there was no time left. She was dying. She couldn't live if the tension lasted much longer. She pleaded with him, twisted up to him, bit his shoulder in her agony of passion.

He indulged her then, his body pressing her hard into the mattress as the rhythm and fever caught them both up in a whirlwind of ecstasy and dashed them into infinity for a space of exquisite, anguished seconds that, all too soon, fell away.

SHE WAS WET with sweat. She couldn't get a single breath. She lay against his damp body, quivering in the aftermath. She felt a shudder go through him and her arms pulled him closer.

"Better?" he asked at her ear.

"Oh…gosh…!" she ground out. She shivered again. "I never knew…!"

"Neither did I, honey," he said quietly. He smoothed her dark hair. "I only knew one way, you see. The women I had were very experienced, demanding, wildcats in bed. They didn't want tenderness, so I never learned it." He drew in a long, satisfied breath. "But I think I'm getting the hang of it now," he added on a chuckle.

"I'll say!" she exclaimed.

He kissed her damp hair. "We haven't discussed birth control," he said after a minute.

"I like little boys," she said simply. "We should have at least one, while we're still young, don't you think?"

He laughed softly, delighted. "We'll take whatever we can get. But, I agree. A boy would be nice." He kissed her closed eyelids. "I'm sorry about Rod," he added tenderly. "We'll get him a good attorney and do whatever we can for him."

"Yes. I'm sorry, too. But I'm so proud of him," she whispered, and her voice broke.

"Me, too," he said.

He held her close, in the warm silence of the dark room. Outside, snow was falling harder.

THEY WENT TO see Rodney at the county detention center. He was quiet, contrite. For once, he looked like the brother Colie remembered from their childhood.

"I'm so sorry, sis," he said as they spoke over telephones on either side of a glass partition.

"I'm sorry for you," she replied. "I'm so proud of you!"

He flushed a little. "Too little, too late. I've done so much harm…"

"You're my brother," Colie said. "I love you. It doesn't matter what you've done. I just want to help you, however I can. You saved my life, Rod."

He grimaced. "I should have stayed. I just ran." He made a face. "It's what I'm best at—running. But I'm going to try to turn my life around. Daddy would have wanted that." He fought tears. "I'm so sorry. He'd be ashamed of me!"

"He'd understand, Rod," she returned. "You know how he was. He never looked down on people, no matter what they did."

He nodded. "He was one of a kind."

"Yes."

They shared the grief of the loss of their parents. After a minute, Rod glanced behind her at J.C. "I'm sorry for the lies I told you, too, J.C.," he said. "If it hadn't been for me, you'd have been in your daughter's life the whole time."

J.C. put his hands on Colie's shoulders. "Your father turned my life around," he said. "He had this great attitude, that everything happens for a reason. He'd say that things happened the way they were meant to."

"He would," Rod agreed. He managed a smile. "At least Barry won't be gloating," he added. "They've got him in solitary confinement. He hit a guard."

"Bad move," J.C. observed.

"Very bad," Rod agreed. "And it's just the beginning of his troubles. He was skimming off the profits. By now, someone's surely noticed. Even in prison, he won't be safe from retribution."

"I've read about that sort of thing," Colie replied. "He may not even get to trial."

"You never know," Rodney replied.

IN FACT, BARRY TODD was found dead in his jail cell three days later of an apparent opioid overdose, despite the known fact that he never used the drugs he distributed. It was thought that he'd run afoul of some very dangerous people in the organization he'd belonged to. But nobody missed him.

Colie got her job back at the law firm, sharing administrative chores with Lucy. She and J.C. took turns dropping Ludie off at pre-K and picking her up after classes. Colie was so happy that she radiated joy. Marriage suited her. It seemed to suit J.C. as well, because he never stopped smiling. He loved to show his small family off, everywhere from church to the grocery store. Even people who'd been critical of him years before now found things in him to admire. He was a tireless worker with the soup kitchen and the homeless shelter. So was Colie. They carried on the work her father had started.

The story of the marriage was in the local paper, but it was a slow news week and it was picked up by one of the larger dailies up in Montana a week or so later. Where it would eventually be seen by an unexpected reader.

One Saturday afternoon a couple of weeks before Christmas, a sedan drove up in J.C.'s front yard and stopped just as J.C. and Colie were getting Ludie into the house after a Christmas shopping trip to the nearby Walmart.

Wary, J.C. motioned Colie with Ludie onto the porch. He waited while a tall, white-haired man with dark olive skin got out of the car. He was wearing a black overcoat. He looked both dignified and solemn.

"Can I help you?" J.C. asked, standing unobtrusively between his family and the visitor.

The old man cocked his head and looked at J.C.

for a long time. He managed a terse smile. "You don't know me."

J.C. frowned. The voice was oddly familiar, but he couldn't place it. "No," he said tersely.

The old man moved a step closer. His eyes went to the porch and he smiled suddenly. "I read about the wedding in an old Montana paper that a parishioner brought by. It had a story on a missionary. But there was a story about you and your new wife, as well. That's where I live, up in Billings. You'd be Colleen, I suppose?" he said to Colie. "And that would be Beth Louise. Ludie?"

"Gimpa!" Ludie called out, laughing. "Gimpa got collar!"

J.C. felt the blood draining out of his face. That was his father? After all the long years of neglect, of anguish, of pure hell in foster homes...!

He started to speak, but before he could, his father unbuttoned his overcoat. It was there. The collar. The mark of a Roman Catholic priest.

J.C.'s jaw actually dropped.

Colie came closer with Ludie by the hand. "She said you had a collar, weeks ago," she told the old man, almost in a daze.

The man looked down at the pretty little girl. "You look like my wife," he said softly. "She had curly red hair and gray eyes. She was beautiful."

"Gimpa!" Ludie exclaimed and pulled away from her mother, to hold her arms out to the newcomer.

He picked her up and hugged her, fighting tears. "Beautiful child," he whispered brokenly.

J.C. was still standing there, lost for words, fighting hatred and rage and curiosity, all at once.

Donald Six Trees looked at him from serene dark eyes.

"I have so much to say to you," he began. "I hardly know where to begin. I feel that I should apologize for ten minutes before I even try to explain the wrongs I've done you."

J.C. was rigid, but he didn't order the old man to leave. He just looked at him.

"Your father was a minister, yes?" he asked Colie.

"Yes," she said with a sad smile. "I lost him—we lost him," she corrected, "a few weeks ago."

"I heard a lot about him, from a mutual friend, a Methodist minister who lives in Billings. I'm very sorry for your loss."

"Would you like coffee?" Colie offered with a wary glance at J.C.

"I would," the old man said. "If it's all right with you," he added, looking into J.C.'s turbulent eyes.

"Remember what Daddy said," Colie told her husband.

He drew in a long breath. "I remember," he said after a minute. He averted his eyes. "I could use a cup of coffee, as well."

"Come in," Colie invited, and she smiled.

The old man, still holding Ludie, followed her and J.C. into the cabin.

"MY FATHER-IN-LAW SAID that people have motivations for every single action," J.C. said when they were sipping coffee at the kitchen table.

"Some are more painful than others," his father returned. He set down his cup. "There was a reason that I was drinking, when I wrecked the car and your mother died," he said heavily. "I'd been working in the mines with my brother. I set off a charge too soon. There was a cave-in, and he died." His face was set in hard lines.

"I'd been drinking before that. But I really tied one on after I saw my brother's body. His wife was collapsed on his body. She looked at me and called me a murderer." He grimaced. "It was no more than what I'd been calling myself, but words have power. I left work and started drinking in a local bar. I was stoned when I got home. Your mother was very big on school meetings. I didn't want to go, but she insisted. I told her that I was too drunk, but she said it was only two miles, it wouldn't matter. She'd sprained her ankle two days before, and she couldn't drive." His eyes closed. "I was too drunk to reason. I just got behind the wheel and started driving. I missed the turn and went off the bridge." He shook his head. "I ran. I ran and ran and ran some more. I knew she was dead at the scene and that I'd go to jail if they caught me." He looked up at his son with agony in his face. "Running never solves a problem. It only makes it worse. It took me years to face what I'd done, to admit fault. I'd not only killed your mother, I'd deserted you at a time when you needed me most. I did go looking for you, after I sobered up, but they said they'd already placed you in a good home…"

"Good home." J.C. said the words with icy contempt. "Sure."

The old man saw more than J.C. realized. "I headed East. I worked at laboring jobs for a long time, until I was taken in by a Benedictine priest. He got me back into the church, taught me that I had to forgive myself before I'd be of any use to anyone else. He made me realize that all my life it had been me, what I wanted, what I needed. I'd never put anybody else first." He grimaced. "Needless to say, it was a painful adjustment. But I made it. I trained as a priest and started working in the parish with the priest who'd saved me. He died last year and I took over his duties. But I never stopped looking for you," he added, his dark eyes steady on J.C.'s strained face. "I'd given up until I saw a photo of the two of you in the paper, in the wedding announcement. I knew it was you when I saw you." He shrugged. "You're the image of me, when I was your age. Your mother named you John Calvin, and your mother's father was a Calhoun. The newspaper said you'd lived in the Yukon Territory as a child." He smiled sadly. "It wasn't much guesswork to puzzle it out, after that."

J.C. started to speak, stopped, tried again.

"You have to make up, Daddy," Ludie piped up, leaning against her father's long legs. "Gimpa's my only gimpa, now."

"She does have a point," Colie said softly, smiling at him.

He looked torn. But after a minute, he smoothed his hand over his daughter's curly head. "She has a point," he agreed finally. "Hatred serves no purpose, except to propagate itself," he added.

The old man smiled. "And forgiveness is divine," he added.

"Divine." J.C. looked at the man he'd spent his life hating, and realized that the only person he'd hurt was himself. As Jared Thompson had said, everyone had reasons for the way they behaved, for the hurtful things they did. "Well, it's a start," he said absently.

"The longest journey begins with a single step," the old man replied. He hesitated. "I'll try, if you will."

J.C. thought about it for a minute. Finally, he nodded. "I'll try, too."

The old man's dark eyes lit up, like fires on a cold night.

IT TOOK TIME, but J.C. and his father finally reached an accord. As Ludie said, she had only one grandparent living. The old man wasn't the same person J.C. remembered from his fraught childhood. It was obvious that this priest had found redemption, and that he loved his son. J.C. agreed with Colie that forgiveness was more important than retribution. The old man, like J.C., had paid a high price for his past. It was time to let it go.

A FEW WEEKS after they were married, Colie met J.C. at the door when he came home late one night and excitedly held his hand to her still flat stomach.

She didn't say a single word, but J.C. knew what had happened immediately. He gave a whoop and whirled her around and around before he stopped and kissed her until her mouth was sore.

"Gonna get a baby brother!" Ludie piped up nearby. She was grinning from ear to ear.

"It will probably be another girl," J.C. teased. "I love girls."

Ludie shook her little head. "Gonna be a boy!" she said, and giggled.

EIGHT MONTHS LATER, J.B. and Colie Calhoun announced the birth of a new family member: a little boy, whom they named Jared Rodney Thompson Calhoun. Ludie didn't even gloat.

* * * * *

CHRISTMAS COWBOY

To the men and women
of the Cornelia Police Department.

CHAPTER ONE

IT WAS THE holiday season in Jacobsville, Texas. Gaily colored strands of lights crisscrossed the main street, and green garlands and wreaths graced each telephone pole along the way. In the center of town, all the small maple trees that grew out of square beds at intervals along the sidewalk were decorated with lights, as well.

People were bundled in coats, because even in South Texas it was cold in late November. They rushed along with shopping bags full of festively wrapped presents to go under the tree. And over on East Main Street, the Optimist Club had its yearly Christmas tree lot open already. A family of four was browsing its sawdust-covered grounds, early enough to have the pick of the beautifully shaped fir trees, just after Thanksgiving.

Dorie Wayne gazed at her surroundings the way a child would look through a store window at toys she couldn't afford. Her hand went to the thin scar down an otherwise perfect cheek and she shivered. How long ago it seemed that she stood right here on this street corner in front of the Jacobsville Drugstore, and backed away from Corrigan Hart. It had been an instinctive move; at eighteen, he'd frightened her. He was so very masculine, a mature man with a cold temper and an iron will. He'd set his sights on Dorie, who found him fearful instead of

attractive, despite the fact that any single woman here-
abouts would have gone to him on her knees.

She recalled his jet-black hair and pale, metallic eyes.
She'd wondered at first if it wasn't her fairness that at-
tracted him, because he was so dark. Dorie had hair so
blond it was almost platinum, and it was cut short, falling into natural thick waves. Her complexion was deli-
cate and fair, and she had big gray eyes, just a shade
darker than Corrigan's. He was very handsome—unlike
his brothers. At least, that was what people said. Dorie
hadn't gotten to meet the others when she left Jacobsville. And only Corrigan and three of his brothers lived
in Jacobsville. The fifth Hart male wasn't talked about,
ever. His name wasn't even known locally.

Corrigan and three of his four brothers had come down
to Jacobsville from San Antonio eight years ago to take
over the rich cattle operation their grandfather had left
to them in his will.

It had been something of a local joke that the Harts
had no hearts, because they seemed immune to women.
They kept to themselves and there was no gossip about
them with women. But that changed when Dorie attended
a local square dance and found herself whirling around
the floor in Corrigan Hart's arms.

Never one to pull his punches, he made his intentions
obvious right at the start. He found her attractive. He was
drawn to her. He wanted her. Just like that.

There was never any mention of marriage, engagement
or even some furtive live-in arrangement. Corrigan said
often that he wasn't the marrying kind. He didn't want
ties. He made that very clear, because there was never
any discussions of taking her to meet his brothers. He
kept her away from their ranch.

But despite his aversion to relationships, he couldn't seem to see enough of Dorie. He wanted her and with every new kiss Dorie grew weaker and hungrier for him.

Then one spring day, he kissed her into oblivion, picked her up in his arms and carried her right into her own bedroom the minute her father left for his weekly poker game.

Despite the drugging effect of masterful kisses and the poignant trembling his expert hands aroused, Dorie had come to her senses just barely in time and pushed him away. Dazed, he'd looked down at her with stunned, puzzled eyes, only belatedly realizing that she was trying to get away, not closer.

She remembered, red-faced even now, how he'd pulled away and stood up, breathing raggedly, eyes blazing with frustrated desire. He'd treated her to a scalding lecture about girls who teased. She'd treated him to one about confirmed bachelors who wouldn't take no for an answer, especially since she'd told him she wasn't the sleep-around sort.

He didn't buy that, he'd told her coldly. She was just holding out for marriage, and there was no hope in that direction. He wanted to sleep with her, and she sure seemed to want him, too. But he didn't want her for keeps.

Dorie had been in love with him, and his emotional rejection had broken something fragile inside her. But she hadn't been about to let him see her pain.

He'd gone on, in the same vein. One insult had led to another, and once he'd gotten really worked up, he'd stormed out the door. His parting shot had been that she must be nuts if she thought he was going to buy her being a virgin. There was no such thing anymore, even at the young age of eighteen.

His rejection had closed doors between them. Dorie couldn't bear the thought of staying in Jacobsville and having everybody know that Corrigan Hart had thrown her aside because she wouldn't sleep with him. And everybody would know, somehow. They always knew the secret things in small towns.

That very night Dorie had made up her mind to take up her cousin Belinda's offer to come to New York and get into modeling. Certainly Dorie had the looks and figure for it. She might be young, but she had poise and grace and an exquisite face framed by short, wavy blond hair. Out of that face, huge gray eyes shone like beacons, mirroring happiness or sorrow.

After that sordid evening, Dorie cut her losses and bought a bus ticket.

She'd been standing right here, on this very corner, waiting for the bus to pick her up in front of this drugstore, when Corrigan had found her.

Her abrupt withdrawal from him had halted him in his tracks. Whatever he'd been going to say, her shamed refusal to look at him, combined with her backward steps, stopped him. She was still smarting from his angry words, as well as from her own uninhibited behavior. She was ashamed that she'd given him such license with her body now that she knew there had only been desire on his part.

He hadn't said a single word before the bus stopped for her. He hadn't said a word as she hurriedly gave her ticket to the driver, got on the bus and waited for it to leave without looking his way again. He'd stood there in the trickling rain, without even a raincoat, with his hands deep in his jean pockets, and watched the bus pull away from the curb. That was how Dorie had remembered him all the long years, a lonely fading figure in the distance.

She'd loved him desperately. But her own self-respect wouldn't let her settle for a furtive affair in the goldfish-bowl atmosphere of Jacobsville. She'd wanted a home, a husband, children, everything.

Corrigan had only wanted to sleep with her.

She'd gone, breathless and sick at heart, all the way to New York City, swearing her father to absolute secrecy about her movements.

There had been a letter, a few weeks after her arrival, from her father. In it, he told her that he'd seen Corrigan only once since her departure, and that he was now hot in pursuit of a rich divorcée with sophistication dripping from her fingers. If Dorie had any parting regrets about her decision to leave town, that was the end of them. Corrigan had made his feelings plain, if he was seeing some woman already.

Dorie wondered if her father hadn't said something unpleasant to Corrigan Hart about his daughter's sudden departure from home. It would have been like him. He was fiercely protective of his only child, especially since the death of her mother from heart disease some years past. And his opinion about philandering men was obvious to everyone.

He believed in the old-fashioned sort of courtship, the kind that ended in marriage. Only a handful of conventional people were left, he told Dorie over and over. Such people were the cornerstones of social order. If they all fell, chaos reigned. A man who loved a woman would want to give her, and his children, his name. And Corrigan, he added, had made it clear to the whole town that he wanted no part of marriage or a family. Dorie would have been asking for heartbreak if she'd given in to Corrigan's selfish demands.

Her father was dead now. Dorie had come home for the funeral as well as to dispose of the house and property and decide her own future. She'd started out with such hopes of becoming a successful model. Her eyes closed and she shivered unconsciously at the memories.

"Dorie?"

She turned at the hesitant sound of her name. The face took a little longer to recognize. "Abby?" she said. "Abby Clark!"

"Abby Ballenger," the other woman corrected with a grin. "I married Calhoun."

"Calhoun!" Dorie was momentarily floored. The younger Ballenger brother had been a rounder and a half, and he was married? And to Abby, of all people, the shy and sweet girl for whom Calhoun and Justin had shared guardianship following the death of their parents.

"Surprising, isn't it?" Abby asked, hugging the other woman. "And there's more. We have three sons."

"I haven't been away that long, have I?" Dorie asked hesitantly.

"Eight years," came the reply. Abby was a little older, but she still had the same pretty gray-blue eyes and dark hair, even if it had silver threads now. "Justin married Shelby Jacobs just after I married Calhoun. They have three sons, too," she added on a sigh. "Not a girl in the bunch."

Dorie shook her head. "For heaven's sake!"

"We heard that you were in modeling…" Her voice trailed away as she saw the obvious long scar on the once-perfect cheek. "What happened?"

Dorie's eyes were all but dead. "Not much. I decided that modeling wasn't for me." She laughed at some private joke. "I went back to school and completed a course in business. Now I work for a group of attorneys. I'm a stenographer." Her gaze fell. "Jacobsville hasn't changed a bit."

"Jacobsville never changes," Abby chuckled. "I find it comforting." The laughter went out of her eyes. "We all heard about your father. I'm sorry. It must have been a blow."

"He'd been in the nursing home near me for some time, but he always said he wanted to be buried here. That's why I brought him home. I appreciated so many people coming to the funeral. It was kind."

"I suppose you noticed one missing face in the crowd?" Abby asked carefully, because she knew how persistent Corrigan Hart had been in his pursuit of Dorie.

"Yes." She twisted her purse in her hands. "Are they still making jokes about the Hart boys?"

"More than ever. There's never been the slightest hint of gossip about any of them and a woman. I guess they're all determined to die single. Especially Corrigan. He's turned into a recluse. He stays out at the ranch all the time now. He's never seen."

"Why?"

Abby seemed evasive. "He doesn't mix and nobody knows much about his life. Odd, isn't it, in a town this small, where we mostly know each other's business, that he isn't talked about? But he stays out of sight and none of the other boys ever speak about him. He's become the original local mystery."

"Well, don't look at me as if I'm the answer. He

couldn't get rid of me fast enough," she said with a twinge of remaining bitterness.

"That's what you think. He became a holy terror in the weeks after you left town. Nobody would go near him."

"He only wanted me," Dorie said doggedly.

Abby's eyes narrowed. "And you were terrified of him," she recalled. "Calhoun used to joke about it. You were such an innocent and Corrigan was a rounder. He said it was poetic justice that rakes got caught by innocents."

"I remember Calhoun being a rake."

"He was," Abby recalled. "But not now. He's reformed. He's the greatest family man I could have imagined, a doting father and a wonderful husband." She sobered. "I'm sorry things didn't work out for you and Corrigan. If you hadn't taken off like that, I think he might have decided that he couldn't live without you."

"God forbid," she laughed, her eyes quick and nervous. "He wasn't a marrying man. He said so, frequently. And I was raised…well, you know how Dad was. Ministers have a decidedly conventional outlook on life."

"I know."

"I haven't had such a bad time of it," she lied, grateful that her old friend couldn't read minds. She smiled. "I like New York."

"Do you have anyone there?"

"You mean a boyfriend, or what do they call it, a significant other?" she murmured. "No. I…don't have much to do with men."

There was a strangely haunted look about her that Abby quickly dispelled with an offer of coffee and a sandwich in the local café.

"Yes, thanks, I'm not hungry but I'd love some hot chocolate."

"Great!" Abby said. "I've got an hour to kill before I have to pick my two oldest boys up at school and the youngest from kindergarten. I'll enjoy your company."

The café was all but empty. It was a slow day, and except for a disgruntled looking cowboy sitting alone at a corner table, it was deserted.

Barbara, the owner, took their orders with a grin. "Nice to have pleasant company," she said, glaring toward the cowboy in the corner. "He brought a little black cloud in with him, and it's growing." She leaned closer. "He's one of the Hart employees," she whispered. "Or, he was until this morning. It seems that Corrigan fired him."

The sound of the man's name was enough to make Dorie's heart race, even after so many years. But she steeled herself not to let it show. She had nothing left to offer Corrigan, even if he was still interested in her. And that was a laugh. If he'd cared even a little, he'd have come to New York looking for her all those years ago.

"Fired him?" Abby glanced at the man and scowled. "But that's Buck Wyley," she protested. "He's the Harts' foreman. He's been with them since they came here."

"He made a remark Corrigan didn't like. He got knocked on his pants for his trouble and summarily fired." Barbara shrugged. "The Harts are all high-tempered, but until now I always thought Corrigan was fair. What sort of boss fires a man with Christmas only three weeks away?"

"Ebenezer Scrooge?" Abby ventured drily.

"Buck said he cut another cowboy's wages to the bone for leaving a gate open." She shook her head. "Funny, we've heard almost nothing about Corrigan for years, and all of a sudden he comes back into the light like a smoldering madman."

"So I noticed," Abby said.

Barbara wiped her hands on a dishcloth. "I don't know what happened to set him off after so many years. The other brothers have been more visible lately, but not Corrigan. I'd wondered if he'd moved away for a while. Nobody even spoke of him." She glanced at Dorie with curious eyes. "You're Dorothy Wayne, aren't you?" she asked then, smiling. "I thought I recognized you. Sorry about your pa."

"Thanks," Dorie said automatically. She noticed how Barbara's eyes went to the thin scar on her cheek and flitted quickly away.

"I'll get your order."

Barbara went back behind the counter and Abby's puzzled gaze went to the corner.

"Having a bad day, Buck?" she called.

He sipped black coffee. "It couldn't get much worse, Mrs. Ballenger," he replied in a deep, pleasant tone. "I don't suppose Calhoun and Justin are hiring out at the feedlot?"

"They'd hire you in a minute, and you know it," Abby told him. She smiled. "Why don't you go out there and…"

"Oh, the devil!" Buck muttered, his black eyes flashing. He got to his feet and stood there, vibrating, as a tall, lean figure came through the open door.

Dorie actually caught her breath. The tall man was familiar to her, even after all those years. Dressed in tight jeans, with hand-tooled boots and a chambray shirt and a neat, spotless white Stetson atop his black hair, he looked formidable, even with the cane he was using for support.

He didn't look at the table where Dorie was sitting, which was on the other side of the café from Buck.

"You fired me," Buck snapped at him. "What do you want, another punch at me? This time, you'll get it back in spades, gimpy leg or not!"

Corrigan Hart just stared at the man, his pale eyes like chrome sparkling in sunlight.

"Those purebred Angus we got from Montana are coming in by truck this morning," he said. "You're the only one who knows how to use the master program for the computerized herd records."

"And you need me," Buck agreed with a cold smile. "For how long?"

"Two weeks," came the curt reply. "You'll work that long for your severance pay. If you're still of a mind to quit."

"Quit, hell!" Buck shot back, astonished. "You fired me!"

"I did not!" the older man replied curtly. "I said you could mind your own damned business or get out."

Buck's head turned and he stared at the other man for a minute. "If I come back, you'd better keep your fists to yourself from now on," he said shortly.

The other man didn't blink. "You know why you got hit."

Buck glanced warily toward Dorie and a ruddy color ran along his high cheekbones. "I never meant it the way you took it," he retorted.

"You'll think twice before you presume to make such remarks to me again, then, won't you?"

Buck made a movement that his employer took for assent.

"And your Christmas bonus is now history!" he added.

Buck let out an angry breath, almost spoke, but crushed his lips together finally in furious submission.

"Go home!" the older man said abruptly.

Buck pulled his hat over his eyes, tossed a dollar bill on the table with his coffee cup and strode out with barely a tip of the hat to the women present, muttering under his breath as he went.

The door closed with a snap. Corrigan Hart didn't move. He stood very still for a moment, as if steeling himself.

Then he turned, and his pale eyes stared right into Dorie's. But the anger in them eclipsed into a look of such shock that Dorie blinked.

"What happened to you?" he asked shortly.

She knew what he meant without asking. She put a hand self-consciously to her cheek. "An accident," she said stiffly.

His chin lifted. The tension in the café was so thick that Abby shifted uncomfortably at the table.

"You don't model now," he continued.

The certainty in the statement made her miserable. "No. Of course I don't."

He leaned heavily on the cane. "Sorry about your father," he said curtly.

She nodded.

His face seemed pinched as he stared at her. Even across the room, the heat in the look was tangible to Dorie. Her hands holding the mug of hot chocolate went white at the knuckles from the pressure of them around it.

He glanced at Abby. "How are things at the feedlot?"

"Much as usual," she replied pleasantly. "Calhoun and Justin are still turning away business. Nice, in the flat cattle market this fall."

"I agree. We've culled as many head as possible and we're venturing into new areas of crossbreeding. Nothing but purebreds now. We're hoping to pioneer a new breed."

"Good for you," Abby replied.

His eyes went back to Dorie. They lingered on her wan face, her lack of spirit. "How long are you going to stay?" he asked.

The question was voiced in such a way it seemed like a challenge. Her shoulders rose and fell. "Until I tie up all the loose ends, I suppose. They've given me two weeks off at the law firm where I work."

"As an attorney?"

She shook her head. "A stenographer."

He scowled. "With your head for figures?" he asked shortly.

Her gaze was puzzled. She hadn't realized that he was aware of her aptitude for math.

"It's a waste," he persisted. "You'd have been a natural at bookkeeping and marketing."

She'd often thought so, too, but she hadn't pursued her interest in that field. Especially after her first attempt at modeling.

He gave her a calculating stare. "Clarisse Marston has opened a boutique in town. She designs women's clothes and has them made up at a local textile plant. She sells all over the state."

"Yes," Abby added. "In fact, she's now doing a lot of designing for Todd Burke's wife, Jane—you know, her signature rodeo line of sportswear."

"I've heard of it, even in New York," Dorie admitted.

"The thing Clarisse doesn't have is someone to help her with marketing and bookkeeping." He shook his head. "It amazes me that she hasn't gone belly-up already."

Abby started to speak, but the look on Corrigan's face silenced her. She only smiled at Dorie.

"This is your home," Corrigan persisted quietly. "You were born and raised in Jacobsville. Surely having a good job here would be preferable to being a stenographer in New York. Unless," he added slowly, "there's some reason you want to stay there."

His eyes were flashing. Dorie looked into the film on her cooling hot chocolate. "I don't have anyone in New York." She shifted her legs. "I don't have anyone here, either, now."

"But you do," Abby protested. "All your friends."

"Of course, she may miss the bright lights and excitement," Corrigan drawled.

She looked at him curiously. He was trying to goad her. Why?

"Is Jacobsville too small for you now, city girl?" he persisted with a mocking smile.

"No, it isn't that at all," she said. She cleared her throat.

"Come home," Abby coaxed.

She didn't answer.

"Still afraid of me?" Corrigan asked with a harsh laugh when her head jerked up. "That's why you left. Is it why you won't come back?"

She colored furiously, the first trace of color that had shown in her face since the strange conversation began.

"I'm not...afraid of you!" she faltered.

But she was, and he knew it. His silver eyes narrowed and that familiar, mocking smile turned up his thin upper lip. "Prove it."

"Maybe Miss Marston doesn't want a bookkeeper."

"She does," he returned.

She hesitated. "She might not like me."

"She will."

She let out an exasperated sigh. "I can't make a decision that important in a few seconds," she told him. "I have to think about it."

"Take your time," he replied. "Nobody's rushing you."

"It would be lovely if you came back, though," Abby said with a smile. "No matter how many friends we have, we can always use one more."

"Exactly," Corrigan told her. His eyes narrowed. "Of course, you needn't consider me in your decision. I'm not trying to get you to come back for my sake. But I'm sure there are plenty of other bachelors left around here who'd be delighted to give you a whirl, if you needed an incentive."

His lean face was so hard and closed that not one flicker of emotion got away from it.

Abby was eyeing him curiously, but she didn't say a word, not even when her gaze fell to his hand on the silver knob of the cane and saw it go white from the pressure.

He eased up on the handle, just the same. "Well?"

"I'd like to," Dorie said quietly. She didn't look at him. Odd, how his statement had hurt, after all those years. She looked back on the past with desperation these days, wondering how her life would have been if she hadn't resisted him that night he'd tried to carry her to bed.

She hadn't wanted an affair, but he was an honorable man, in his fashion. Perhaps he would have followed up with a proposal, despite his obvious distaste for the married state. Or perhaps he wouldn't have. There might have been a child...

She grimaced and lifted the cup of chocolate to her lips. It was tepid and vaguely distasteful.

"Go see Clarisse, why don't you?" he added. "You've

nothing to lose, and a lot to gain. She's a sweet woman. You'll like her."

Did he? She didn't dare wonder about that, or voice her curiosity. "I might do that," she replied.

The tap of the cane seemed unusually loud as he turned back to the door. "Give the brothers my best," Corrigan told Abby. He nodded and was gone.

Only then did Dorie look up, her eyes on his tall, muscular body as he walked carefully back to the big double-cabbed black ranch pickup truck he drove.

"What happened to him?" Dorie asked.

Abby sipped her own hot chocolate before she answered. "It happened the week after you left town. He went on a hunting trip in Montana with some other men. During a heavy, late-spring snow, Corrigan and another man went off on their own in a four-wheel-drive utility vehicle to scout another section of the hunting range."

"And?" Dorie prompted.

"The truck went over a steep incline and overturned. The other man was killed outright. Corrigan was pinned and couldn't get free. He lay there most of the night and into the next day before the party came looking for them and found him. By that time, he was unconscious. The impact broke his leg in two places, and he had frostbite, as well. He almost died."

Dorie caught her breath. "How horrible!"

"They wanted to amputate the leg, but..." she shrugged. "He refused them permission to operate, so they did the best they could. The leg is usable, just, but it will always be stiff. They said later that it was a miracle he didn't lose any toes. He had just enough sense left to wrap himself in one of those thin thermal sheets the men had carried on the trip. It saved him from a dangerous frostbite."

"Poor man."

"Oh, don't make that mistake," Abby mused. "Nobody is allowed to pity Corrigan Hart. Just ask his brothers."

"All the same, he never seemed the sort of man to lose control of anything, not even a truck."

"He wasn't himself but he didn't lose control, either."

"I beg your pardon?"

Abby grimaced. "He and the other man, the one who was driving, had been drinking. He blamed himself not only for the wreck, but for the other man's death. He knew the man wasn't fit to drive but he didn't try to stop him. They say he's been punishing himself ever since. That's why he never comes into town, or has any social life. He's withdrawn into himself and nobody can drag him back out. He's become a hermit."

"But, why?"

"Why was he drinking, you mean?" Abby said, and Dorie nodded. Still, Abby hesitated to put it into words.

"Tell me," came the persistent nudge from Dorie.

Abby's eyes were apologetic. "Nobody knows, really. But the gossip was that he was trying to get over losing you."

CHAPTER TWO

"BUT HE WANTED to lose me," Dorie exclaimed, shocked. "He couldn't get out of my house fast enough when I refused…refused him," she blurted. She clasped her hands together. "He accused me of being frigid and a tease…"

"Corrigan was a rounder, Dorie," Abby said gently. "In this modern age, even in Jacobsville, a lot of girls are pretty sophisticated at eighteen. He wouldn't have known about your father being a minister, because he'd retired from the church before the Harts came to take over their grandfather's ranch. He was probably surprised to find you less accommodating than other girls."

"*Surprised* wasn't the word," Dorie said miserably. "He was furious."

"He did go to the bus depot when you left."

"How did you know that?"

"Everybody talked about it," Abby admitted. "It was generally thought that he went there to stop you."

"He didn't say a word," came the quiet reply. "Not one word."

"Maybe he didn't know what to say. He was probably embarrassed and upset about the way he'd treated you. A man like that might not know what to do with an innocent girl."

Dorie laughed bitterly. "Sure he did. You see her off

and hope she won't come back. He told me that he had no intention of marrying."

"He could have changed his mind."

Dorie shook her head. "Not a chance. He never talked about us being a couple. He kept reminding me that I was young and that he liked variety. He said that we shouldn't think of each other in any serious way, but just enjoy each other while it lasted."

"That sounds like a Hart, all right," Abby had to admit. "They're all like Corrigan. Apparently they have a collective bad attitude toward women and think of them as minor amusements."

"He picked on the wrong girl," Dorie said. She finished her hot chocolate. "I'd never even had a real boyfriend when he came along. He was so forceful and demanding and inflexible, so devoid of tenderness when he was with me." She huddled closer into her sweater. "He came at me like a rocket. I couldn't run, I couldn't hide, he just kept coming." Her eyes closed on a long sigh. "Oh, Abby, he scared me to death. I'd been raised in a such a way that I couldn't have an affair, and I knew that was all he wanted. I ran, and kept running. Now I can't stop."

"You could, if you wanted to."

"The only way I'd come back is with a written guarantee that he wanted nothing more to do with me," she said with a cold laugh. "Otherwise, I'd never feel safe here."

"He just told you himself that he had no designs on you," Abby reminded her. "He has other interests."

"Does he? Other…women interests?"

Abby clasped her fingers together on the table. "He goes out with a rich divorcée when he's in need of company," she said. "That's been going on for a long time now. He probably was telling the truth when he said that

he wouldn't bother you. After all, it's been eight years."
She studied the other woman. "You want to come home,
don't you?"

Caught off guard, Dorie nodded. "I'm so alone," she
confessed. "I have bolts and chains on my door and I
live like a prisoner when I'm not at work. I rarely ever
go outside. I miss trees and green grass."

"There's always Central Park."

"You can't plant flowers there," she said, "or have a
dog or cat in a tiny apartment like mine. I want to sit out
in the rain and watch the stars at night. I've dreamed of
coming home."

"Why haven't you?"

"Because of the way I left," she confessed. "I didn't
want any more trouble than I'd already had. It was bad
enough that Dad had to come and see me, that I couldn't
come home."

"Because of Corrigan?"

"What?" For an instant, Dorie's eyes were frightened.
Then they seemed to calm. "No, it was for another reason
altogether, those first few years. I couldn't risk coming
here, where it's so easy to find people…" She closed up
when she realized what she was saying. "It was a problem I had, in New York. That's all I can tell you. And
it's over now. There's no more danger from that direction. I'm safe."

"I don't understand."

"You don't need to know," Dorie said gently. "It
wouldn't help matters to talk about it now. But I would
like to come back home. I seem to have spent most of
my life on the run."

What an odd turn of phrase, Abby thought, but she
didn't question it. She just smiled. "Well, if you decide

to come back, I'll introduce you to Clarisse. Just let me know."

Dorie brightened. "All right. Let me think about it for a day or two, and I'll be in touch with you."

"Good. I'll hold you to that."

FOR THE NEXT two days, Dorie thought about nothing else except coming back to her hometown. While she thought, she wandered around the small yard, looking at the empty bird feeders and the squirrel feeder nearby. She saw the discarded watering pot, the weed-bound flower beds. Her father's long absence had made its mark on the little property. It needed a loving hand to restore it.

She stood very still as an idea formed in her mind. She didn't have to sell the property. She could keep it. She could live here. With her math skills, and the book-keeping training she'd had in business school, she could open a small bookkeeping service of her own. Clarisse could be a client. She could have others. She could support herself. She could leave New York.

The idea took wing. She was so excited about it that she called Abby the next morning when she was sure that the boys would be in school.

She outlined the idea to her friend. "Well, what do you think?" she asked enthusiastically.

"I think it's a great idea!" Abby exclaimed. "And the perfect solution. When are you going to start?"

"Next week," she said with absolute certainty. "I'll use the Christmas vacation I would have had as my notice. It will only take a couple of days to pack up the few things I have. I'll have to pay the rent, because I signed a lease, but if things work out as I hope they will, that won't be a problem. Oh, Abby, it's like a dream!"

"Now you sound more like the Dorothy I used to know," Abby told her. "I'm so glad you're coming home."

"So am I," Dorie replied, and even as she said it, she tried not to think of the complications that could arise. Corrigan was still around. But he'd made her a promise of sorts, and perhaps he'd keep it. Anyway, she'd worry about that situation later.

A WEEK LATER, Dorie was settled into her father's house, with all her bittersweet memories of him to keep her company. She'd shipped her few big things, like her piano, home by a moving service. Boxes still cluttered the den, but she was beginning to get her house into some sort of order.

It needed a new roof, and some paint, as well as some plumbing work on the leaky bathtub faucet. But those were minor inconveniences. She had a good little nest egg in her savings account and it would tide her over, if she was careful, until she could be self-supporting in her business again.

She had some cards and stationery printed and put an ad in the Jacobsville weekly newspaper. Then she settled in and began to work in the yard, despite the cold weather. She was finding that grief had to be worked through. It didn't end at the funeral. And the house was a constant reminder of the old days when she and her father had been happy.

So it was a shock to find Corrigan Hart on her doorstep the first Saturday she was in residence.

She just stared at him at first, as if she'd been stunned. In fact, she was. He was the last person she'd have expected to find on her doorstep.

He had a bouquet of flowers in the hand that wasn't holding the cane and his hat. He proffered them brusquely.

"Housewarming present," he said.

She took the pretty bouquet and belatedly stood aside. "Would you like to come in? I could make coffee."

He accepted the invitation, placing his hat on the rack by the door. He kept the cane and she noticed that he leaned on it heavily as he made his way to the nearest easy chair and sat down in it.

"They say damp weather is hard on injured joints," she remarked.

His pale eyes speared into her face, with an equal mixture of curiosity and irritation. "They're right," he drawled. "Walking hurts. Does it help to have me admit it?"

"I wasn't trying to score points," she replied quietly. "I didn't get to say so in the café, but I'm sorry you got hurt."

His own eyes were pointed on the scar that ran the length of her cheek. "I'm sorry you did," he said gruffly. "You mentioned coffee?"

There it was again, that bluntness that had frightened her so much at eighteen. Despite the eight years in between, he still intimidated her.

She moved into the small kitchen, visible from the living room, and filled the pot with water and a premeasured coffee packet. After she'd started it dripping, and had laid a tray with cups, saucers and the condiments, she rejoined him.

"Are you settling in?" he asked a minute after she'd dropped down onto the sofa.

"Yes," she said. "It's strange, after being away for so many years. And I miss Dad. But I always loved this house. Eventually it will be comforting to live here. Once I get over the worst of the grieving."

He nodded. "We lost both our parents at once, in a flood," he said tersely. "I remember how we felt."

He looked around at the high ceilings and marked walls, and the open fireplace. He nodded toward it. "That isn't efficient. You need a stove in here."

"I need a lot of things in here, but I have to eat, too," she said with a faint smile. She pushed back her short, wavy platinum hair and curled up on the sofa in her jeans and gray sweatshirt and socks. Her shoes were under the sofa. Even in cold weather, she hated wearing shoes around the house.

He seemed to notice that and found it amusing, judging by the twinkle in his pale eyes.

"I hate shoes," she said.

"I remember."

That was surprising. She hardly remembered the girl she'd been eight years ago. It seemed like a lifetime.

"You had a dog, that damned little spaniel, and you were out in the front yard washing him one day when I drove by," he recalled. "He didn't like a bath, and you were soaked, bare feet, cutoffs, tank top and all." His eyes darkened as he looked at her. "I told you to go in the house, do you remember?"

"Yes." The short command had always puzzled her, because he'd seemed angry, not amused as he did now.

"I never said why," he continued. His face tautened as he looked at her. "You weren't wearing anything under that tank top and it was plastered to you," he added quietly. "You can't imagine what it did to me... And there was that damned Bobby Harris standing on the sidewalk gawking at you."

Bobby had asked her out later that day, and she'd refused, because she didn't like him. He was an older boy; her father never had liked him.

"I didn't realize," she said, amazed that the memory should be so tame now, when his odd behavior had actually hurt in the past. She actually flushed at the thought that he'd seen her that way so early in their relationship.

"I know that, now, eight years too late," he said abruptly.

She cocked her head, studying him curiously.

He saw her gaze and lifted his eyes. "I thought you were displaying your charms brazenly for my benefit, and maybe even for Bobby's," he said with a mocking smile. "That's why I acted the way I did that last night we dated."

Her face thinned with distress. "Oh, no!"

"Oh, yes," he said, his voice deep with bitterness. "I thought you were playing me for a sucker, Dorie. That you were pretending to be innocent because I was rich and you wanted a wedding ring instead of an affair."

The horror she felt showed in her wan face.

"Yes, I know," he said when she started to protest. "I only saw what I wanted to see. But the joke was on me. By the time I realized what a hell of a mistake I'd made about you, you were halfway on a bus out of town. I went after you. But I couldn't manage the right words to stop you. My pride cut my throat. I was never that wrong about anyone before."

She averted her gaze. "It was a long time ago. I was just a kid."

"Yes. Just a kid. And I mistook you for a woman." He studied her through narrow lids. "You don't look much older even now. How did you get that scar?"

Her fingers went to it. The memories poured over her, hot and hurting. She got to her feet. "I'll see about the coffee."

She heard a rough sound behind her, but apparently it wasn't something he wanted to put words to. She escaped into the kitchen, found some cookies to put in a bowl and carried the coffee back to the coffee table on a silver tray.

"Fancy stuff," he mused.

She knew that he had equally fancy stuff at his place. She'd never been there, but she'd certainly heard about the Hart heirlooms that the four brothers displayed with such pride. Old Spanish silver, five generations old, dating all the way back to Spain graced their side table. There was crystal as well, and dozens of other heirlooms that would probably never be handed down. None of the Harts, it was rumored, had any ambitions of marrying.

"This was my grandmother's," she said. "It's all I had of her. She brought this service over from England, they said."

"Ours came from Spain." He waited for her to pour the coffee. He picked up his cup, waving away cream and sugar. He took a sip, nodded and took another. "You make good coffee. Amazing how many people can't."

"I'm sure it's bad for us. Most things are."

He agreed. He put the cup back into the saucer and studied her over its rim. "Are you planning to stay for good?"

"I guess so," she faltered. "I've had stationery and cards printed, and I've already had two offers of work."

"I'm bringing you a third—our household accounts. We've been sharing them since our mother died. Consequently each of us insists that it's not our turn to do them, so they don't get done."

"You'd bring them to me?" she asked hesitantly.

He studied her broodingly. "Why shouldn't I? Are you afraid to come out to the ranch and do them?"

"Of course not."

"Of course not," he muttered, glaring at her. He sat forward, watching her uneasy movement. "Eight years, and I still frighten you."

She curled up even more. "Don't be absurd. I'm twenty-six."

"You don't look or act it."

"Go ahead," she invited. "Be as blunt as you like."

"Thanks, I will. You're still a virgin."

Coffee went everywhere. She cursed roundly, amusing him, as she searched for napkins to mop up the spill, which was mostly on her.

"Why are you?" he persisted, baiting her. "Were you waiting for me?"

She stood up, slamming the coffee cup to the floor. It shattered with a pleasantly loud crash, and she thanked goodness that it was an old one. "You son of a...!"

He stood up, too, chuckling. "That's better," he mused, watching her eyes flash, her face burn with color.

She kicked at a pottery shard. "Damn you, Corrigan Hart!"

He moved closer, watching her eyelids flutter. She tried to back up, but she couldn't go far. Her legs were against the sofa. There was no place to run.

He paused a step away from her, close enough that she could actually feel the heat of his body through her clothing and his. He looked down into her eyes without speaking for several long seconds.

"You're not the child you used to be," he said, his voice as smooth as velvet. "You can stand up for yourself, even with me. And everything's going to be all right. You're home. You're safe."

It was almost as if he knew what she'd been through. His eyes were quiet and full of secrets, but he smiled. His hand reached out and touched her short hair.

"You still wear it like a boy's," he murmured. "But it's silky. Just the way I remember it."

He was much too close. He made her nervous. Her hands went out and pressed into his shirtfront, but instead of moving back, he moved forward. She shivered at the feel of his chest under her hands, even with the shirt covering it.

"I don't want a lover," she said, almost choking on the words.

"Neither do I," he replied heavily. "So we'll be friends. That's all."

She nibbled on her lower lip. He smelled of spice and leather. She used to dream about him when she first left home. Over the years, he'd assumed the image of a protector in her mind. Strange, when he'd once frightened her so much.

Impulsively she laid her cheek against his chest with a little sigh and closed her eyes.

He shivered for an instant, before his lean hands pressed her gently to him, in a nonthreatening way. He stared over her head with eyes that blazed, eyes that he was thankful she couldn't see.

"We've lost years," he said half under his breath. "But Christmas brings miracles. Maybe we'll have one of our own."

"A miracle?" she mused, smiling. She felt ever so safe in his arms. "What sort?"

"I don't know," he murmured, absently stroking her

hair. "We'll have to wait and see. You aren't going to sleep, are you?"

"Not quite." She lifted her head and looked up at him, a little puzzled at the familiarity she felt with him. "I didn't expect that you'd ever be comfortable to be around."

"How so?"

She shrugged. "I wasn't afraid."

"Why should you be?" he replied. "We're different people now."

"I guess."

He brushed a stray hair from her eyebrow with a lean, sure hand. "I want you to know something," he said quietly. "What happened that night... I wouldn't have forced you. Things got a little out of hand, and I said some things, a lot of things, that I regret. I guess you realize now that I had a different picture of you than the one that was real. But even so, I wouldn't have harmed you."

"I think I knew that," she said. "But thank you for telling me."

His hand lay alongside her soft cheek and his metallic eyes went dark and sad. "I mourned you," he said huskily. "Nothing was the same after you'd gone."

She lowered her eyes to his throat. "I didn't have much fun in New York at first, either."

"Modeling wasn't all it was cracked up to be?"

She hesitated. Then she shook her head. "I did better as a stenographer."

"And you'll do even better as a financial expert, right here," he told her. He smiled, tilting up her chin. "Are you going to take the job I've offered you?"

"Yes," she said at once. Her gaze drew slowly over his face. "Are your brothers like you?"

"Wait and see."

"That sounds ominous."

He chuckled, moving slowly away from her to retrieve his cane from the chair. "They're no worse, at least."

"Are they as outspoken as you?"

"Definitely." He saw her apprehension. "Think of the positive side. At least you'll always know exactly where you stand with us."

"That must be a plus."

"Around here, it is. We're hard cases. We don't make friends easily."

"And you don't marry. I remember."

His face went hard. "You have plenty of reason to remember that I said that. But I'm eight years older, and a lot wiser. I don't have such concrete ideas anymore."

"You mean, you're not still a confirmed bachelor?" She laughed nervously. "They say you're taken with the gay divorcée, just the same."

"How did you hear about her?" he asked curtly.

His level, challenging gaze made her uneasy. "People talk," she said.

"Well, the gay divorcée," he emphasized, his expression becoming even more remote, "is a special case. And we're not a couple. Despite what you may have heard. We're friends."

She turned away. "That's no concern of mine. I'll do your bookkeeping on those household accounts, and thank you for the work. But I have no interest in your private life."

He didn't return the compliment. He reached for his hat and perched it on his black hair. There were threads of gray at his temples now, and new lines in his dark, lean face.

"I'm sorry about your accident," she said abruptly, watching him lean heavily on the cane.

"I'll get by," he said. "My leg is stiff, but I'm not crippled. It hurts right now because I took a toss off a horse, and I need the cane. As a rule, I walk well enough without one."

"I remember the way you used to ride," she recalled. "I thought I'd never seen anything in my life as beautiful as you astride a horse at a fast gallop."

His posture went even more rigid. "You never said so."

She smiled. "You intimidated me. I was afraid of you. And not only because you wanted me." She averted her eyes. "I wanted you, too. But I hadn't been raised to believe in a promiscuous lifestyle. Which," she added, looking up at his shocked face, "was all you were offering me. You said so."

"God help me, I never knew that your father was a minister and your mother a missionary," he said heavily. "Not until it was far too late to do me any good. I expected that all young women were free with their favors in this age of no-consequences intimacy."

"It wouldn't be of no consequence to me," she said firmly. "I was never one to go with the crowd. I'm still not."

"Yes, I know," he murmured drily, giving her a long, meaningful glance. "It's obvious."

"And it's none of your business."

"I wouldn't go that far." He tilted his hat over his eyes. "I haven't changed completely, you know. I still go after the things I want, even if I don't go as fast as I used to."

"I expect you do," she said. "Does the divorcée know?"

"Know what? That I'm persistent? Sure she does."

"Good for her."

"She's a beauty," he added, propping on his stick. "Of an age to be sophisticated and good fun."

Her heart hurt. "I'm sure you enjoy her company."

"I enjoy yours as much," he replied surprisingly. "Thanks for the coffee."

"Don't you like cookies?" she asked, noting that he hadn't touched them.

"No," he said. "I don't care for sweets at all."

"Really?"

He shrugged. "We never had them at home. Our mother wasn't the homey sort."

"What was she like?" she had to ask.

"She couldn't cook, hated housework and spouted contempt for any woman who could sew and knit and crochet," he replied.

She felt cold. "And your father?"

"He was a good man, but he couldn't cope with us alone." His eyes grew dark. "When she took off and deserted him, part of him died. She'd just come back, out of money and all alone, from her latest lover. They were talking about a reconciliation when the flood took the house where she was living right out from under them." His face changed, hardened. He leaned heavily on the cane. "Simon and Cag and I were grown by then. We took care of the other two."

"No wonder you don't like women," she murmured quietly.

He gave her a long, level look and then dropped his gaze. She missed the calculation in his tone when he added, "Marriage is old-fashioned, anyway. I have a dog, a good horse and a houseful of modern appliances. I even have a housekeeper who can cook. A wife would be redundant."

"Well, I never," she exclaimed, breathless.

"I know," he replied, and there was suddenly a wicked glint in his eyes. "You can't blame that on me," he added. "God knows, I did my best to bring you into the age of enlightenment."

While she was absorbing that dry remark, he tipped his hat, turned and walked out the door.

She darted onto the porch after him. "When?" she called after him. "You didn't say when you wanted me to start."

"I'll phone you." He didn't look back. He got into his truck laboriously and drove away without even a wave of his hand.

At least she had the promise of a job, she told herself. She shouldn't read hidden messages into what he said. But the past he'd shared with her, about his mother, left her chilled. How could a woman have five sons and leave them?

And what was the secret about the fifth brother, Simon, the one nobody had ever seen? She wondered if he'd done something unspeakable, or if he was in trouble with the law. There had to be a reason why the brothers never spoke of him much. Perhaps she'd find out one day.

CHAPTER THREE

IT WAS THE next day before she realized she hadn't thanked Corrigan for the flowers he'd brought. She sent a note out to the ranch on Monday, and got one back that read, simply, "You're welcome." So much for olive branches, if one had been needed.

She found plenty to keep her busy in the days that followed. It seemed that all her father's friends and the people she'd gone to school with wanted her to come home. Everyone seemed to know a potential client. It wasn't long before she was up to her ears in work.

The biggest surprise came Thursday morning when she heard the sound of many heavy footsteps and looked up from her desk to find three huge, intimidating men standing on her porch just beyond the glass-fronted door. They'd come in that big double-cabbed pickup that Corrigan usually drove, and she wondered if these were his brothers.

She went to open the door and felt like a midget when they came tromping inside her house, their spurs jingling pleasantly on boots that looked as if they'd been kept in a swamp.

"We're the Harts," one of them said. "Corrigan's brothers."

As she'd guessed. She studied them curiously. Corrigan was tall, but these men were giants. Two were dark-haired like Corrigan, and one had blond-streaked brown hair. All were dark-eyed, unlike him. None of them would have made any lists of handsome bachelors. They were rugged-looking, lean and tanned, and they made her nervous. The Hart boys made most people nervous. The only other local family that had come close to their reputations for fiery tempers were the Tremayne boys, who were all married and just a little tamer now. The Harts were relative newcomers in Jacobsville, having only been around eight years or so. But they kept to themselves and seemed to have ties to San Antonio that were hard to break. What little socializing they did was all done there, in the city. They didn't mix much in Jacobsville.

Not only were they too rugged for words, but they also had the most unusual first names Dorie could remember hearing. They introduced themselves abruptly, without even being asked first.

Reynard was the youngest. They called him Rey. He had deep-set black eyes and a thin mouth and, gossip said, the worst temper of the four.

The second youngest was Leopold. He was broader than the other three, although not fat, and the tallest. He never seemed to shave. He had blond-streaked brown hair and brown eyes, and a mischievous streak that the others apparently lacked.

Callaghan was the eldest, two years older than Corrigan. He had black eyes like a cobra. He didn't blink. He was taller than all his brothers, with the exception of Leopold, and he did most of the bronc-breaking at the ranch. He looked Spanish, more than the others, and he had the bearing and arrogance of royalty, as if he belonged in another century. They said he had the old-fashioned attitudes of the past, as well.

He gave the broader of the three a push toward Dorie. He glared over his shoulder, but took off his hat and forced a smile as he stood in front of Dorie.

"You must be Dorothy Wayne," Leopold said with a grin. "You work for us."

"Y…yes, I guess I do," she stammered. She felt surrounded. She moved back behind the desk and just stared at them, feeling nervous and inadequate.

"Will you two stop glaring?" Leopold shot at his taciturn brothers. "You're scaring her!"

They seemed to make an effort to relax, although it didn't quite work out.

"Never mind," Leopold muttered. He clutched his hat in his hand. "We'd like you to come out to the ranch," he said. "The household accounts are about to do us in. We can't keep Corrigan still long enough to get him to bring them to you."

"He came over Saturday," she said.

"Yeah, we heard," Leo mused. "Roses, wasn't it?"

The other two almost smiled.

"Roses," she agreed. Her gray eyes were wide and they darted from one giant to another.

"He forgot to bring you the books. The office is in a hel…heck of a mess," Leo continued. "We can't make heads nor tails of it. Corrigan scribbles, and we've volunteered him to do it mostly, but we can't read his writing. He escaped to a herd sale in Montana, so we're stuck." He shrugged and managed to look helpless. "We can't see if we've got enough money in the account to buy groceries." He looked hungry. He sighed loudly. "We'd sure appreciate it if you could come out, maybe in the morning, about nine? If that's not too early."

"Oh, no," she said. "I'm up and making breakfast by six."

"Making breakfast? You can cook, then?" Leopold asked.

"Well, yes." She hesitated, but he looked really interested. "I make biscuits and bacon and eggs."

"Pig meat," the one called Reynard muttered.

"Steak's better," Callaghan agreed.

"If she can make biscuits, the other stuff doesn't matter," Reynard retorted.

"Will you two shut up?" Leopold asked sharply. He turned back to Dorie and gave her a thorough appraisal, although not in the least sexual. "You don't look like a bookkeeper."

"Nice hair," Reynard remarked.

"Bad scar on that cheek," Callaghan remarked. "How did it happen?"

Heavens, he was blunt! She was almost startled enough to tell him. She blurted that it had been in an accident.

"Tough," he said. "But if you can cook, scars don't matter much."

Her mouth was open, and Leopold stomped on his big brother's foot, hard.

Callaghan popped him one on the arm with a fist the size of a ham. "Cut it out!"

"Don't insult her, she won't come!"

"I didn't!"

Reynard moved forward, elbowing the other two out of the way. He had his own hat in his hand. He tried to smile. It looked as if he hadn't had much practice at it.

"We'd like you to come tomorrow. Will you?"

She hesitated.

"Now see what you've done!" Leopold shot at Callaghan. "She's scared of us!"

"We wouldn't hurt you," Reynard said gently. He gave

up trying to smile; it was unnatural, anyway. "We have old Mrs. Culbertson keeping house for us. She carries a broomstick around with her. You'll be safe."

She bit back a laugh. But her eyes began to twinkle.

"She carries the broomstick because of him," Reynard added, indicating Leopold. "He likes to…"

"Never mind!" Leopold said icily.

"I was only going to say that you…"

"Shut up!"

"If you two don't stop, I'm going to lay you both out right here," Callaghan said, and looked very much as if he meant it. "Apologize."

They both murmured reluctant apologies.

"All right, that's that." He put his hat back on. "If you can come at nine, we'll send one of the boys for you."

"Thank you, I'd rather drive my own car."

"I've seen your car. That's why I'm sending one of the boys for you," Callaghan continued doggedly.

Her mouth fell open again. "It's a…a nice old car! And it runs fine!"

"Everybody knows Turkey Sanders sold it to you," Callaghan said with a disgusted look. "He's a pirate. You'll be lucky if the wheels don't fall off the first time you go around a curve."

"That's right," Rey agreed.

"We'll stop by on our way out of town and talk to him," Leopold said. "He'll bring your car back in and make sure it's perfectly safe to drive. He'll do it first thing tomorrow."

"But…"

They put their hats back on, gave her polite nods and stomped back out the way they'd come.

Callaghan paused at the front door, with the screen

open. "He may talk and act tough, but he's hurt pretty bad, inside where it doesn't show. Don't hurt him again."

"Him?"

"Corrigan."

She moved forward, just a step. "It wasn't like that," she said gently. "He didn't feel anything for me."

"And you didn't, for him?"

She averted her gaze to the floor. "It was a long time ago."

"You shouldn't have left."

She looked back up, her eyes wide and wounded. "I was afraid of him!"

He let out a long breath. "You were just a kid. We tried to tell him. Even though we hadn't seen you, we knew about you from other people. We were pretty sure you weren't the sort of girl to play around. He wouldn't listen." He shrugged. "Maybe we corrupted him. You might ask him sometimes about our parents," he added coldly. "Kids don't grow up hating marriage without reason."

There was a lot of pain in his lean face. He was telling her things she'd never have dared ask Corrigan. She moved forward another step, aware of the other two talking out on the porch in hushed whispers.

"Is he still…like that?"

His eyes were cold, but as they looked into hers, they seemed to soften just a little. "He's not the same man he was. You'll have to find out the rest for yourself. We don't interfere in each other's lives, as a rule." His gaze went over her wan face. "You've been to hell and back, too."

He was as perceptive as his brother. She smiled. "I suppose it's part of becoming an adult. Losing illusions and dreams and hope, I mean." She locked her fingers together and looked up at him quietly. "Growing up is painful."

"Don't let go," he said suddenly. "No matter what he says, what he does, don't let go."

Her surprise widened her eyes. "Why?"

He pulled his hat lower over his forehead. "They don't make women like you anymore."

"Like me?" She frowned.

His dark eyes glittered. He smiled in a way that, if she hadn't been half-crazy about Corrigan, would have curled her toes. "I wish we'd met you before," he said. "You'd never have gotten on that bus." He tilted the hat. "We'll send Joey for you in the morning."

"But…"

The door closed behind him. He motioned to the other two and they followed him down the steps to the four-door pickup truck. It had a big cab. It was streamlined and black, and it had a menacing look not—unlike Corrigan Hart's brothers!

She wondered why they'd all come together to ask her to go out to the ranch, and why they'd done it when Corrigan was gone. She supposed she'd find out. She did wonder again about the fifth brother, the mysterious one that Corrigan had mentioned. None of these men were named Simon.

LATER, THE TELEPHONE RANG, and it was Turkey Sanders. "I just wanted you to know that I'm going to have that car I sold you picked up in the morning and put to rights," he said at once. "I guarantee, it's going to be the best used car you've ever driven! If you would, just leave the keys in it, and I'll have it picked up first thing. And if there's anything else I can do for you, little lady, you just ask!"

He sounded much more enthusiastic than he had when he'd sold her the rusty little car. "Why, thank you," she said.

"No problem. None at all. Have a nice day, now."

He hung up and she stared blankly at the receiver. Well, nobody could say that living in Jacobsville wasn't interesting, she told herself. Apparently the brothers had a way with other businessmen, too. She'd never have admitted that the car had worried her from the time Turkey had talked her into buying it, for what seemed like a high price for such a wreck. She had a driver's license, which she had to have renewed. But never having owned a car in New York, it was unique to have one of her own, even if it did look like ten miles of bad road.

It was a cold, blustery morning when a polite young man drove up in a black Mercedes and held the door open for her.

"I'm Joey," he told her. "The brothers sent me to fetch you. I sure am glad you took on this job," he added. "They won't give me any money for gas until that checkbook's balanced. I've been having to syphon it out of their trucks with a hose." He shook his head ruefully as he waited for her to move her long denim skirt completely out of the doorframe so that he could close the door. "I hate the taste of gasoline."

He closed the door, got in under the wheel and took off in a cloud of dust.

She smiled to herself. The brothers were strange people.

The ranch was immaculate, from its white wood fences to the ranch house itself, a long elegant brick home with a sprawling manicured lawn and a swimming pool and tennis court. The bunkhouse was brick, too, and the barn was so big that she imagined it could hold an entire herd of horses.

"Big, huh?" Joey grinned at her. "The brothers do things on a big scale, but they're meticulous—especially Cag. He runs the place, mostly."

"Cag?"

"Callaghan. Nobody calls him that in the family." He glanced in her direction, amused. "They said you're the reason Corrigan never married."

Her heart jumped. "No kidding?"

"Oh, yeah. He doesn't even look at women these days. But when he heard that you were coming back, he shaved and bought new clothes." He shook his head. "Shocked us all, seeing him without a beard."

"I can't imagine him with one," she said with some confusion.

"Pity about his leg, but he's elegant on a horse, just the same."

"I think he gets around very well."

"Better than he used to." He pulled up in front of the house, turned off the engine and went around to help her out.

"It's right in here."

He led her in through the front door and down a carpeted hall to a pine-paneled office. "Mrs. Culbertson will be along any minute to get you some coffee or tea or a soft drink. The brothers had to get to work or they'd have been here to meet you. No worry, though, Corrigan's home. He'll be here shortly and show you the books. He's trying to doctor a colt, down in the barn."

"Thank you, Joey."

He tipped his hat. "My pleasure, ma'am." He gave her a cursory appraisal, nodded and went back out again.

He'd no sooner gone than a short, plump little woman with twinkling blue eyes and gray hair came in, rubbing her hands dry on her apron. "You'd be Miss Wayne. I'm Betty Culbertson," she introduced herself. "Can I get you a cup of coffee?"

"Oh, yes, please."

"Cream, sugar?"

"I like it black," she said.

The older woman grinned. "So do the boys. They don't like sweets, either. Hard to get fat around here, except on gravy and biscuits. They'd have those every meal if I'd cook them."

The questions the brothers had asked about her cooking came back to haunt her.

"None of them believe in marriage, do they?" she asked.

Mrs. Culbertson shook her head. "They've been bachelors too long now. They're set in their ways and none of them have much to do with women. Not that they aren't targeted by local belles," she added with a chuckle. "But nobody has much luck. Corrigan, now, he's mellowed. I hear it's because of you."

While Dorie flushed and tried to find the right words to answer her, a deep voice did it for her.

"Yes, it is," Corrigan said from the doorway. "But she isn't supposed to know it."

"Oops," Mrs. Culbertson said with a wicked chuckle. "Sorry."

He shrugged. "No harm done. I'll have coffee. So will she. And if you see Leopold..."

"I'll smash his skull for him, if I do," the elderly

woman said abruptly, and her whole demeanor changed. Her blue eyes let off sparks. "That devil!"

"He did it again, I guess?"

She made an angry noise through her nose. "I've told him and told him…"

"You'd think he'd get tired of having that broomstick thrown at him, wouldn't you?" Corrigan asked pleasantly.

"One of these days he won't be quick enough," Mrs. Culbertson said with an evil smile.

"I'll talk to him."

"Everybody's already talked to him. It does no good."

"What does he do?" Dorie asked curiously.

Mrs. Culbertson looked at Corrigan, who'd started to answer, with eyes that promised culinary retribution.

"Sorry," he said abruptly. "I can't say."

Mrs. Culbertson nodded curtly and smiled at Dorie. "I'll just get that coffee. Be back in a jiffy."

She left and Corrigan's dark eyes slid over Dorie's pretty figure.

"You look very nice," he said. His eyes lifted to her wavy hair and he smiled appreciatively. "I always loved your hair. That was a first for me. Usually I like a woman's hair long. Yours suits you just as it is."

Her slender hand went to the platinum waves self-consciously. "It's easy to keep like this." She shifted to the other foot. "Your brothers came to the house yesterday and asked me to come out here and look at the household accounts. They say they're starving."

"They look like it, too, don't they?" he asked disgustedly. "Good God, starving!"

"They were very nice," she continued. "They talked to Turkey Sanders and he's repairing my car."

"His mechanic's repairing your car," he told her. "Turkey's having a tooth fixed."

She knew she shouldn't ask. But she had to. "Why?"

"He made a remark that Cag didn't like."

"Cag. Oh, yes, he's the eldest."

He brightened when he realized that she remembered that. "He's thirty-eight, if you call that old." Anticipating her next question, he added blithely, "Leo's thirty-four. I'm thirty-six. Rey's thirty-two."

"So Cag hit Turkey Sanders?"

He shook his head.

"Then who broke his tooth?"

"Leo."

"Cag got mad, but Leo hit Turkey Sanders?" she asked, fascinated.

He nodded. "He did that to save him from Cag."

"I don't understand."

"Cag was in the Special Forces," he explained. "He was a captain when they sent him to the Middle East some years back." He shrugged. "He knows too much about hand-to-hand combat to be let loose in a temper. So we try to shield people from him." He grinned. "Leo figured that if he hit Turkey first, Cag wouldn't. And he didn't."

She just shook her head. "Your brothers are…unique," she said finally, having failed to find a good word to describe them.

He chuckled. "You don't know the half of it."

"Do they really hate women?"

"Sometimes," he said.

"I'll bet they're sought after," she mentioned, "especially when people get a good look at this ranch."

"The ranch is only a part of the properties we own,"

he replied. "Our people are fourth-generation Texans, and we inherited thousands of acres of land and five ranches. They were almost bankrupt when the old man died, though," he mused. "He didn't really have a head for figures. Broke Grandad's heart. He saw the end of his empire. But we pulled it out of the fire."

"So I see," she agreed.

"The only problem is, none of us are married. So if we don't have descendants, who's going to keep the empire going?"

She thought of the most terrible answer to that question, and then got the giggles.

He raised an eyebrow.

She put a hand over her mouth until she got herself back under control. "Sorry. I was only thinking of that movie about the man who got pregnant…!"

He gave her a level look, unsmiling.

She cleared her throat. "Where are the accounts?"

He hesitated for a minute, and then opened the desk drawer and took out a set of ledgers, placing them on the spotless cherrywood desk.

"This is beautiful," she remarked, stroking the silky, high-polished surface.

"It was our grandfather's," he told her. "We didn't want to change things around too much. The old gentleman was fond of the office just the way it is."

She looked around, puzzled by the plain wood paneling. There were no deer heads or weapons anywhere. She said so.

"He didn't like trophies," he told her. "Neither do we. If we hunt, we use every part of the deer, but we don't have the heads mounted. It doesn't seem quite sporting."

She turned as she pulled out the desk chair, and looked at him with open curiosity.

"None of your brothers are like I pictured them."

"In what way?"

She smiled. "You're very handsome," she said, averting her eyes when his began to glitter. "They aren't. And they all have very dark eyes. Yours are gray, like mine."

"They favor our mother," he said. "I favor him." He nodded toward the one portrait, on the wall behind the desk. It looked early twentieth century and featured a man very like Corrigan, except with silver hair.

"So that's what you'll look like," she remarked absently.

"Eventually. Not for a few years, I hope."

She glanced at him, because he'd come to stand beside her. "You're going gray, just at the temples."

He looked down into her soft face. His eyes narrowed as he searched every inch of her above the neck. "Gray won't show in that beautiful mop on your head," he said quietly. "It'll blend in and make it even prettier."

The comment was softly spoken, and so poetic that it embarrassed her. She smiled self-consciously and her gaze fell to his shirt. It was open at the collar, because it was warm in the house. Thick black hair peered over the button, and unwanted memories of that last night they'd been together came flooding back. He'd taken his shirt off, to give her hands total access to his broad, hair-roughened chest. He liked her lips on it…

She cleared her throat and looked away, her color high. "I'd better get to work."

His lean hand caught her arm, very gently, and he pulled her back around. His free hand went to the snaps that held the shirt together. He looked into her startled eyes and slowly, one by one, he flicked the snaps apart.

"What…are you…doing?" she faltered. She couldn't breathe. He was weaving spells around her. She felt weak-kneed already, and the sight of that broad chest completely bare drew a faint gasp from her lips.

He had her by the elbows. He drew her to him, so that her lips were on a level with his collarbone. She could hear his heartbeat, actually hear it.

"It was like this," he said in a raw, ragged tone. "But I had your blouse off, your breasts bare. I drew you to me, like this," he whispered unsteadily, drawing her against the length of him, "and I bent, and took your open mouth under my own…like this…"

It was happening all over again. She was eight years older, but apparently not one day less vulnerable. He put her cold hands into the thick hair on his chest and moved them while his hard mouth took slow, sweet possession of her lips.

He nudged her lips apart and hesitated for just a second, long enough to look into her eyes and see the submission and faint hunger in them. There was just the hint of a smile on his lips before he parted them against her soft mouth.

CHAPTER FOUR

SHE HAD NO pride at all, she decided in the hectic seconds that followed the first touch of his hard mouth. She was a total washout as a liberated woman.

His hands had gone to her waist and then moved up to her rib cage, to the soft undersides of her breasts. He stroked just under them until she shivered and moaned, and then his hands lifted and took possession; blatant possession.

He felt her mouth open. His own answered it while he touched her, searched over her breasts and found the hard nipples that pushed against his palms.

His mouth grew rougher. She felt his hands move around her, felt the catch give. Her blouse was pushed up with a shivering urgency, and seconds later, her bare breasts were buried in the thick hair that covered his chest and abdomen.

She cried out, dragging her mouth from his.

He looked into her eyes, but he wouldn't let her go. His hard face was expressionless. Only his eyes were alive, glittering like gray fires. He deliberately moved her from side to side and watched her face as he did it, enjoying, with a completely masculine delight, the pleasure she couldn't hide.

"Your nipples are like rocks against me." He bit off the words, holding her even closer. "I took your breasts inside my mouth the night we made love, and you arched up right off the bed to give them to me. Do you remember what you did next?"

She couldn't speak. She looked at him with mingled desire and fear.

"You slid your hands inside my jeans," he whispered roughly. "And you touched me. That's when I lost control."

Her moan was one of shame, not pleasure. She found his chest with her cheek and pressed close to him, shivering. "I'm sorry," she whispered brokenly. "I'm so sorry...!"

His mouth found her eyes and kissed them shut. "Don't," he whispered roughly. "I'm not saying it to shame you. I only want you to remember why it ended the way it did. You were grass green and I didn't know it. I encouraged you to be uninhibited, but I'd never have done it if I'd known what an innocent you were." His mouth slid over her forehead with breathless tenderness while his hands slid to her lower back and pulled her even closer. "I was going to take you," he whispered. His hands contracted and his body went rigid with a surge of arousal that she could feel. His legs trembled. "I still want to, God help me," he breathed at her temple. "I've never had the sort of arousal I feel with you. I don't even have to undress you first." His hands began to tremble as he moved her sensually against his hips. His mouth slid down to hers and softly covered it, lifting and touching and probing until she shivered again with pleasure.

"I thought you knew," she whimpered.

"I didn't." His hands moved to the very base of her spine and lifted her gently into the hard thrust of his body.

He caught his breath at the wave of pleasure that washed over him immediately. "Dorie," he breathed.

She couldn't think at all. When he took one of her hands and pressed it to his lower body, she didn't even have the will to protest. Her hand opened and she let him move it gently against him, on fire with the need to touch him.

"Eight years," she said shakily.

"And we're still starving for each other," he whispered at her mouth. His hand became insistent. "Harder," he said and his breath caught.

"This…isn't wise," she said against his chest.

"No, but it's sweet. Dorie…!" He cried out hoarsely, his whole body shuddering.

Her hand stilled at once. "I'm sorry," she whispered frantically. "Did I hurt you?"

He wasn't breathing normally at all. His face was buried in her throat and he was shaking like a leaf. She brushed her mouth over his cheek, his chin, his lips, his nose, whispering his name as she clung to him.

His hand gripped her upper thigh, and it was so bruising that she was afraid she was going to have to protest. He fought for sanity, embarrassed by his weakness.

She was still kissing him. He felt her breasts moving against his chest, intensifying the throbbing, hellish ache below his belt.

He held her firmly in place with hands that shook.

She subsided and stood quietly against him. She knew now, as she hadn't eight years ago, what was wrong with him. She felt guilty and ashamed for pushing him so far out of control.

Her fingers touched his thick, cool hair lovingly. Her lips found his eyelids and brushed softly against them.

He was vulnerable and she wanted to protect him, cherish him.

The tenderness was doing strange things to him. He still wanted her to the point of madness, but those comforting little kisses made his heart warm. He'd never been touched in such a way by a woman; he'd never felt so cherished.

She drew back, and he pulled her close again.

"Don't stop," he whispered, calmer now. His hands had moved up to the silken skin of her back, and he smiled under the whisper of her lips on his skin.

"I'm so sorry," she whispered.

His fingers slid under the blouse again and up to explore the softness of her breasts. "Why?" he asked.

"You were hurting," she said. "I shouldn't have touched you…"

He chuckled wickedly. "I made you."

"I still can't go to bed with you," she said miserably. "I don't care if the whole world does it, I just can't!"

His hands opened and enfolded her breasts tenderly. "You want to," he murmured as he caressed them.

"Of course I want to!" Her eyes closed and she swayed closer to his hands. "Oh, glory," she managed to say tightly, shivering.

"Your breasts are very sensitive," he said at her lips. "And soft like warm silk under my hands. I'd like to lay you down on my grandfather's desk and take your blouse off and put my lips on you there. But Mrs. Culbertson is making coffee." He lifted his head and looked into her dazed, soft gray eyes. "Thank God," he whispered absently as he searched them.

"Thank God for what?" she asked huskily.

"Miracles, maybe," he replied. He smoothed the blouse

up again and his eyes sketched her pretty pink breasts with their hard dark pink crowns. "I could eat you like taffy right now," he said in a rough tone.

The office was so quiet that not a sound could be heard above the shiver of her breath as she looked up at him.

His pale eyes were almost apologetic. "I think I have a death wish," he began huskily as he bent.

She watched his mouth hover over her breast with a sense of shocked wonder. Her eyes wide, her breath stopped in her throat, she waited, trembling.

He looked up then, and saw her eyes. He made a sound in the back of his throat and his mouth opened as he propelled her closer, so that he had her almost completely in that warm, moist recess.

She wept. The pleasure grew to unbearable heights. Her fingers tangled in his hair and she pulled him closer. She growled sharply at the sensations she felt. Her hips moved involuntarily, searching for his body.

The suction became so sweet that she suddenly arched backward, and would have fallen if it hadn't been for his supporting arm. She caught her breath and convulsed, her body frozen in an arc of pure ecstasy.

He felt the deep contractions of her body under his mouth with raging pride. His mouth grew a little rough, and the convulsions deepened.

Only when he felt her begin to relax did he lift his head and bring her back into a standing position, so that he could look at her face.

She couldn't breathe. She sobbed as she looked up into his pale eyes. The tears came, hot and quick, when she realized what had happened. And he'd seen it!

"Don't," he chided tenderly. He reached for a handkerchief and dried her red eyes and wiped her nose. "Don't be embarrassed."

"I could die of shame," she wept.

"For what?" he asked softly. "For letting me watch you?"

Her face went red. "I never, never...!"

He put a long forefinger against her lips. "I've never seen a woman like that," he whispered. "I've never known one who could be satisfied by a man's mouth suckling at her breast. It was the most beautiful experience I've ever had."

She wasn't crying now. She was staring at him, her eyes wide and soft and curious.

He brushed back her wild hair. "It was worth what I felt earlier," he murmured drily.

She colored even more. "I can't stay here," she told him wildly. "I have to go away..."

"Hell, no, you don't," he said tersely. "You're not getting away from me a second time. Don't even think about running."

"But," she began urgently.

"But what?" he asked curtly. "But you can't give yourself to me outside marriage? I know that. I'm not asking you to sleep with me."

"It's like torture for you."

"Yes," he said simply. "But the alternative is to never touch you." His hand slid over her blouse and he smiled gently at the immediate response of her body. "I love this," he said gruffly. "And so do you."

She grimaced. "Of course I do," she muttered. "I've never let anyone else touch me like that. It's been eight years since I've even been kissed!"

"Same here," he said bluntly.

"Ha! You've been going around with a divorcée!" she flung at him out of frustration and embarrassment.

"I don't have sex with her," he said.

"They say she's very pretty."

He smiled. "She is. Pretty and elegant and kind. But I don't feel desire for her, any more than she feels it for me. I told you we were friends. We are. And that's all we are."

"But…but…"

"But what, Dorie?"

"Men don't stop kissing women just because they get turned down once."

"It was much worse than just getting turned down," he told her. "I ran you out of town. It was rough living with that, especially when your father took a few strips off me and told me all about your past. I felt two inches high." His eyes darkened with the pain of the memory. "I hated having made an enemy of him. He was a good man. But I'd never had much interest in marriage or let anyone get as close to me as you did. If you were afraid, so was I."

"Cag said your parents weren't a happy couple."

His eyebrow lifted. "He never talks about them. That's a first."

"He told me to ask you about them."

"I see." He sighed. "Well, I told you a little about that, but we're going to have to talk more about them sooner or later, and about some other things." He lifted his head and listened and then looked down at her with a wicked grin. "But for the present, you'd better fasten your bra and tuck your blouse back in and try to look as if you haven't just made love with me."

"Why?"

"Mrs. Culbertson's coming down the hall."

"Oh, my gosh!"

She fumbled with catches and buttons, her face red, her hair wild as she raced to put herself back together. He snapped his shirt up lazily, his silvery eyes full of mischief as he watched her frantic efforts to improve her appearance.

"Lucky I didn't lay you down on the desk, isn't it?" he said, chuckling.

There was a tap on the half-closed door and Mrs. Culbertson came in with a tray. She was so intent on getting it to the desk intact that she didn't even look at Dorie.

"Here it is. Sorry I took so long, but I couldn't find the cream pitcher."

"Who drinks cream?" Corrigan asked curiously.

"It was the only excuse I could think of," she told him seriously.

He looked uneasy. "Thanks."

She grinned at him and then looked at Dorie. Her eyes were twinkling as she went back out. And this time she closed the door.

Dorie's face was still flushed. Her gray eyes were wide and turbulent. Her mouth was swollen and when she folded her arms over her chest, she flinched.

His eyes went to her blouse and back up again. "When I felt you going over the edge, it excited me, and I got a little rough. Did I hurt you?"

The question was matter-of-fact, and strangely tender.

She shook her head, averting her eyes. It was embarrassing to remember what had happened.

He caught her hand and led her to the chairs in front of the desk. "Sit down and I'll pour you a cup of coffee."

She looked up at him a little uneasily. "Is something wrong with me, do you think?" she asked with honest concern. "I mean, it's unnatural…isn't it?"

His fingers touched her soft cheek. He shook his head. "People can't be pigeonholed. You might not be that responsive to any other man. Maybe it's waiting so long. Maybe it's that you're perfectly attuned to me. I might be able to accomplish the same thing by kissing your thighs, or your belly."

She flushed. "You wouldn't!"

"Why not?"

The thought of it made her vibrate all over. She knew that men kissed women in intimate places, but she hadn't quite connected it until then.

"The inside of your thighs is very vulnerable to being caressed," he said simply. "Not to mention your back, your hips, your feet," he added with a gentle smile. "Lovemaking is an art. There are no set rules."

She watched him turn and pour coffee into a ceramic cup. He handed it to her and watched the way her fingers deliberately touched his as he drew them away.

He wanted her so much that he could barely stand up straight, but it was early days yet. He had to go slowly this time and not push her too hard. She had a fear not only of him, but of real intimacy. He couldn't afford to let things go too far.

"What sort of things are we going to talk about later?" she asked after she'd finished half her coffee.

"Cabbages and kings," he mused. He sat across from her, his long legs crossed, his eyes possessive and caressing on her face.

"I don't like cabbage and I don't know any kings."

"Then suppose we lie down together on the sofa?"

Her eyes flashed up to see the amusement in his and back down to her cup. "Don't tease. I'm not sophisticated enough for it."

"I'm not teasing."

She sighed and took another sip of coffee. "There's no future in it. You know that."

He didn't know it. She was living in the past, convinced that he had nothing more than an affair in mind for them. He smiled secretively to himself as he thought about the future. Fate had given him a second chance; he wasn't going to waste it.

"About these books," he said in a businesslike tone. "I've made an effort with them, but although I can do math, my penmanship isn't what it should be. If you can't read any of the numbers, circle them and I'll tell you what they are. I have to meet a prospective buyer down at the barn in a few minutes, but I'll be somewhere close by all day."

"All right."

He finished his coffee and put the cup back on the tray, checking his watch. "I'd better go." He looked down at her with covetous eyes and leaned against the arms of her chair to study her. "Let's go dancing tomorrow night."

Her heart jumped. She was remembering how it was when they were close together and her face flushed.

His eyebrow lifted and he grinned. "Don't look so apprehensive. The time to worry is when nothing happens when I hold you."

"It always did," she replied.

He nodded. "Every time," he agreed. "I only had to touch you." He smiled softly. "And vice versa," he added with a wicked glance.

"I was green," she reminded him.

"You still are," he reminded her.

"Not so much," she ventured shyly.

"We both learned something today," he said quietly.

"Dorie, if you can be satisfied by so small a caress, try to imagine how it would feel if we went all the way."

Her eyelids flickered. Her breath came like rustling leaves.

He bent and drew his mouth with exquisite tenderness over her parted lips. "Or is that the real problem?" he asked at her mouth. "Are you afraid of the actual penetration?"

Her heart stopped dead and then ran away. "Corrigan!" She ground out his name.

He drew back a breath so that he could see her eyes. He wasn't smiling. It was no joke.

"You'd better tell me," he said quietly.

She drew her lower lip in with her teeth, looking worried.

"I won't tell anyone."

"I know that." She took a long breath. "When my cousin Mary was married, she came to visit us after the honeymoon was over. She'd been so happy and excited." She grimaced. "She said that it hurt awfully bad, that she bled and bled, and he made fun of her because she cried. She said that he didn't even kiss her. He just… pushed into her…!"

He cursed under his breath. "Didn't you talk to anyone else about sex?"

"It wasn't something I could discuss with my father, and Mary was the only friend I had," she told him. "She said that all the things they write about are just fiction, and that the reality is just like her mother once said—a woman deals with it for the pleasure of children."

He leaned forward on his hands, shaking his head. "I wish you'd told me this eight years ago."

"You'd have laughed," she replied. "You didn't believe I was innocent, anyway."

He looked up into her eyes. "I'm sorry," he said heavily. "Life teaches hard lessons."

She thought about her own experience with modeling. "Yes, it does."

He got to his feet and looked down at her with a worried scowl. "Don't you watch hot movies?"

"Those women aren't virgins," she returned.

"No. I don't guess they are." His eyes narrowed as he searched her face. "And I don't know what to tell you. I'd never touched an innocent woman until you came along. Maybe it does hurt. But I promise you, it would only be one time. I know enough to make it good for you. And I would."

"It isn't going to be that way," she reminded him tersely, denying herself the dreams of marriage and children that she'd always connected with him. "We're going to be friends."

He didn't speak. His gaze didn't falter. "I'll check back with you later about the books," he said quietly.

"Okay."

He started to turn, thought better of it and leaned down again with his weight balanced on the chair arms. "Do you remember what happened when I started to suckle you?"

She went scarlet. "Please…"

"It will be like that," he said evenly. "Just like that. You won't think about pain. You may not even notice any. You go in headfirst when I touch you. And I wasn't even taking my time with you today. Think about that. It might help."

He pushed away from her again and went to the desk to pick up his hat. He placed it on his head and smiled at her without mockery.

"Don't let my brothers walk over you," he said. "If one of them gives you any trouble, lay into him with the first hard object you can get your hands on."

"They seem very nice," she said.

"They like you," he replied. "But they have plans."

"Plans?"

"Not to hurt you," he assured her. "You should never have told them you could cook."

"I don't understand."

"Mrs. Culbertson wants to quit. They can't make biscuits. It's what they live for, a plateful of homemade buttered biscuits with half a dozen jars of jam and jelly."

"How does that concern me?"

"Don't you know?" He perched himself against the desk. "They've decided that we should marry you."

"We?"

"We're a family. Mostly we share things. Not women, but we do share cooks." He cocked his head and grinned at her shocked face. "If I marry you, they don't have to worry about where their next fresh biscuit is coming from."

"You don't want to marry me."

"Well, they'll probably find some way around that," he said pointedly.

"They can't force you to marry me."

"I wouldn't make any bets on that," he said. "You don't know them yet."

"You're their brother. They'd want you to be happy."

"They think you'll make me happy."

She lowered her eyes. "You should talk to them."

"And say what? That I don't want you? I don't think they'd believe me."

"I meant, you should tell them that you don't want to get married."

"They've already had a meeting and decided that I do. They've picked out a minister and a dress that they think you'll look lovely in. They've done a rough draft of a wedding invitation…"

"You're out of your mind!"

"No, I'm not." He went to the middle desk drawer, fumbled through it, pulled it farther out and reached for something pushed to the very back of the desk. He produced it, scanned it, nodded and handed it to her. "Read that."

It was a wedding invitation. Her middle name was misspelled. "It's Ellen, not Ellis."

He reached behind him for a pen, took the invitation back, made the change and handed it back to her.

"Why did you do that?" she asked curiously.

"Oh, they like everything neat and correct."

"Don't correct it! Tear it up!"

"They'll just do another one. The papers will print what's on there, too. You don't want your middle name misspelled several thousand times, do you?"

She was all but gasping for breath. "I don't understand."

"I know. Don't worry about it right now. There's plenty of time. They haven't decided on a definite date yet, anyway."

She stood up, wild-eyed. "You can't let your brothers decide when and who you're going to marry!"

"Well, you go stop them, then," he said easily. "But don't say I didn't tell you so."

He pulled his hat over his eyes and walked out the door, whistling softly to himself.

CHAPTER FIVE

FIRST SHE DID the accounts. Her mind was still reeling from Corrigan's ardor, and she had to be collected when she spoke to his brothers. She deciphered his scribbled numbers, balanced the books, checked her figures and put down a total.

They certainly weren't broke, and there was enough money in the account to feed Patton's Third Army. She left them a note saying so, amused at the pathetic picture they'd painted of their finances. Probably, the reason for that was part of their master plan.

She went outside to look for them after she'd done the books. They were all four in the barn, standing close together. They stopped talking the minute she came into view, and she knew for certain that they'd been talking about her.

"I'm not marrying him," she told them clearly, and pointed at Corrigan.

"Okay," Leo said easily.

"The thought never crossed my mind," Rey remarked.

Cag just shrugged.

Corrigan grinned.

"I'm through with the books," she said uneasily. "I want to go home now."

"You haven't eaten lunch," Rey said.

"It's only eleven o'clock," she said pointedly.

"We have an early lunch, because we work until dark," Cag volunteered.

"Mrs. Culbertson just left," Rey said. He sighed. "She put some beef and gravy in the oven to warm. But she didn't make us any biscuits."

"We don't have anything to put gravy on," Leo agreed.

"Can't work all afternoon without a biscuit," Cag said, nodding.

Corrigan grinned.

Dorie had thought that Corrigan was making up that story about the brothers' mania for biscuits. Apparently it was the gospel truth.

"Just one pan full," Leo coaxed. "It wouldn't take five minutes." He eyed her warily. "If you can really make them. Maybe you can't. Maybe you were just saying you could, to impress us."

"That's right," Rey added.

"I can make biscuits," she said, needled. "You just point me to the kitchen and I'll show you."

Leo grinned. "Right this way!"

HALF AN HOUR LATER, the pan of biscuits were gone so fast that they might have disintegrated. Leo and Corrigan were actually fighting over the last one, pulled it apart in their rush, and ended up splitting it while the other two sat there gloating. They'd had more than their share because they had faster hands.

"Next time, you've got to make two pans," Corrigan told her. "One doesn't fill Leo's hollow tooth."

"I noticed," she said, surprisingly touched by the way they'd eaten her biscuits with such enjoyment. "I'll make you a pan of rolls to go with them next time."

"Rolls?" Leo looked faint. "You can make homemade rolls?"

"I'll see about the wedding rings right now," Rey said, wiping his mouth and pushing away from the table.

"I've got the corrected invitation in my pocket," Cag murmured as he got up, too.

Leo joined the other two at the door. "They said they can get the dress here from Paris in two weeks," Leo said.

Dorie gaped at them. But before she could say a word, all three of them had rushed out the door and closed it, talking animatedly among themselves.

"But, I didn't say...!" she exclaimed.

"There, there," Corrigan said, deftly adding another spoonful of gravy to his own remaining half of a biscuit. "It's all right. They forgot to call the minister and book him."

Just at that moment, the door opened and Leo stuck his head in. "Are you Methodist, Baptist or Presbyterian?" he asked her.

"I'm...Presbyterian," she faltered.

He scowled. "Nearest Presbyterian minister is in Victoria," he murmured thoughtfully, "but don't worry, I'll get him here." He closed the door.

"Just a minute!" she called.

The doors of the pickup closed three times. The engine roared. "Too late," Corrigan said imperturbably.

"But didn't you hear him?" she burst out. "For heaven's sake, they're going to get a minister!"

"Hard to get married in church without one," he insisted. He gestured toward her plate with a fork to the remaining chunk of beef. "Don't waste that. It's one of our own steers. Corn fed, no hormones, no antibiotics, no insecticides. We run a clean, environmentally safe operation here."

She was diverted. "Really?"

"We're renegades," he told her. "They groan when they see us coming at cattle conventions. Usually we go with Donavan. He's just like us about cattle. He and the Ballenger brothers have gone several rounds over cattle prods and feed additives. He's mellowed a bit since his nephew came to live with him and he got married. But he likes the way we do things."

"I guess so." She savored the last of the beef. "It's really good."

"Beats eating pigs," he remarked, and grinned.

She burst out laughing. "Your brother Cag had plenty to say on that subject."

"He only eats beef or fish. He won't touch anything that comes from a pig. He says it's because he doesn't like the taste." He leaned forward conspiratorially. "But I say it's because of that movie he went to see. He used to love a nice ham."

"What movie?"

"The one with the talking pig."

"Cag went to see that?"

"He likes cartoons and sentimental movies." He shrugged. "Odd, isn't it? He's the most staid of us. To look at him, you'd never know he had a sense of humor or that he was sentimental. He's like the others in his lack of conventional good looks, though. Most women can't get past that big nose and those eyes."

"A cobra with a rabbit," she said without thinking.

He chuckled. "Exactly."

"Does he hate women as much as the rest of you?"

"Hard to tell. You haven't seen him in a tuxedo at a social bash. Women, really beautiful women, followed him around all night dropping their room keys at his feet."

"What did he do?"

"Kept walking."

She put down her fork. "What do you do?"

He smiled mockingly. "They don't drop room keys at my feet anymore. The limp puts them off."

"Baloney," she said. "You're the handsomest of the four, and it isn't just looks."

He leaned back in his chair to look at her. His eyes narrowed thoughtfully. "Does the limp bother you?"

"Don't be ridiculous," she said, lifting her gaze. "Why should it?"

"I can't dance very well anymore."

She smiled. "I don't ever go to dances."

"Why not?"

She sipped coffee. "I don't like men touching me."

His eyes changed. "You like me touching you."

"You aren't a stranger," she said simply.

"Maybe I am," he murmured quietly. "What do you know about me?"

She stared at him. "Well, you're thirty-six, you're a rancher, you've never married, you come from San Antonio."

"And?"

"I don't know any more than that," she said slowly.

"We were a couple for several weeks before you left town. Is that all you learned?"

"You were always such a private person," she reminded him. "You never talked about yourself or your brothers. And we never really talked that much when we were together."

"We spent more time kissing," he recalled. "I was too

wrapped up in trying to get you into bed to care how well we knew each other," he said with self-contempt. "I wasted a lot of time."

"You said that we shouldn't look back."

"I'm trying not to. It's hard, sometimes." He moved forward to take her hands under his on the table. "I like classical music, but I'm just as happy with country or pop. I like a good chess game. I enjoy science fiction movies and old Westerns, the silent kind. I'm an early riser, I work hard and I don't cheat on my tax returns. I went to college to learn animal husbandry, but I never graduated."

She smiled. "Do you like fried liver?"

He made a horrible face. "Do you?"

She made the same face. "But I don't like sweets very much, either," she said, remembering that he didn't.

"Good thing. Nobody around here eats them."

"I remember." She looked around at the comfortably big kitchen. There was a new electric stove and a huge refrigerator, flanked by an upright freezer. The sink was a double stainless-steel one, with a window above it overlooking the pasture where the colts were kept. Next to that was a dishwasher. There was plenty of cabinet space, too.

"Like it?" he asked.

She smiled. "It's a dream of a kitchen. I'll bet Mrs. Culbertson loves working in here."

"Would you?"

She met his eyes and felt her own flickering at the intensity of his stare.

"If you can make homemade bread, you have to be an accomplished cook," he continued. "There's a high-tech mixer in the cabinet, and every gourmet tool known to man. Or woman."

"It's very modern."

"It's going to be very deserted in about three weeks," he informed.

"Why is Mrs. Culbertson quitting?"

"Her husband has cancer, and she wants to retire and stay at home with him, for as long as he's got," he said abruptly. He toyed with his coffee cup. "They've been married for fifty years." He took a sharp breath, and his eyes were very dark as they met hers. "I've believed all my life that no marriage could possibly last longer than a few years. People change. Situations change. Jobs conflict." He shrugged. "Then Mrs. Culbertson came here to work, with her husband. And I had to eat my words." He lowered his eyes back to the cup. "They were forever holding hands, helping each other, walking in the early morning together and talking. She smiled at him, and she was beautiful. He smiled back. Nobody had to say that they loved each other. It was obvious."

"My parents were like that," she recalled. "Dad and Mom loved each other terribly. When she died, I almost lost him, too. He lived for me. But the last thing he said on his deathbed—" she swallowed, fighting tears "—was her name."

He got up from the table abruptly and went to the window over the sink. He leaned against it, breathing heavily, as if what she'd said had affected him powerfully. And, in fact, it had.

She watched him through tears. "You don't like hearing about happy marriages. Why?"

"Because I had that same chance once," he said in a low, dull tone. "And I threw it away."

She wondered who the woman had been. Nobody had said that any of the Hart brothers had ever been engaged.

But there could have been someone she hadn't heard about.

"You're the one who keeps saying we can't look back," she remarked, dabbing her eyes with her napkin.

"It's impossible not to. The past makes us the people we are." He sighed wearily. "My parents had five of us in ten years. My mother hadn't wanted the first child. She didn't have a choice. He took away her checkbook and kept her pregnant. She hated him and us in equal measure. When she left it was almost a relief." He turned and looked across the room at her. "I've never been held with tenderness. None of us have. It's why we're the way we are, it's why we don't have women around. The only thing we know about women is that they're treacherous and cold and cruel."

"Oh, Corrigan," she said softly, wincing.

His eyes narrowed. "Desire is a hot and unmanageable thing. Sex can be pleasant enough. But I'd gladly be impotent to have a woman hold me the way you did in my office and kiss my eyes." His face went as hard as stone. "You can't imagine how it felt."

"But I can," she replied. She smiled. "You kissed my eyes."

"Yes."

He looked so lost, so lonely. She got up from the table and went to him, paused in front of him. Her hands pressed gently against his broad chest as she looked up into his eyes.

"You know more about me than I've ever told anyone else," he said quietly. "Now don't you think it's time you told me what happened to you in New York?"

She sighed worriedly. She'd been ashamed to tell him how stupid she'd been. But now there was a bigger reason. It was going to hurt him. She didn't understand how she knew it, but she did. He was going to blame himself all over again for the way they'd separated.

"Not now," she said.

"You're holding back. Don't let's have secrets between us," he said solemnly.

"It will hurt," she said.

"Most everything does, these days," he murmured, and rubbed his thigh.

She took his hand and held it warmly. "Come and sit down."

"Not in here."

He drew her into the living room. It was warm and dim and quiet. He led her to his big armchair, dropped into it and pulled her down into his arms.

"Now, tell me," he said, when her cheek was pillowed on his hard chest.

"It's not a nice story."

"Tell me."

She rubbed her hand against his shirt and closed her eyes. "I found an ad in the paper. It was one of those big ads that promise the stars, just the thing to appeal to a naive country girl who thinks she can just walk into a modeling career. I cut out the ad and called the number."

"And?"

She grimaced. "It was a scam, but I didn't know it at first. The man seemed very nice, and he had a studio in a good part of town. Belinda had gone to Europe for the week on an assignment for the magazine where she worked, and I didn't know anyone else to ask about it. I assumed that it was legitimate." Her eyes closed and she pressed closer, feeling his arm come around her tightly, as if he knew she was seeking comfort.

"Go ahead," he coaxed gently.

"He gave me a few things to try on and he took pictures of me wearing them. But then I was sitting there, just in a two-piece bathing suit, and he told me to take it off." His breathing stilled under her ear. "I couldn't," she snapped. "I just couldn't let him look at me like that, no matter how good a job I could get, and I said so. Then he got ugly. He told me that he was in the business of producing nude calendars and that if I didn't do the assignment, he'd take me to court and sue me for not fulfilling the contract I'd signed. No, I didn't read it," she said when he asked. "The fine print did say that I agreed to pose in any manner the photographer said for me to. I knew that I couldn't afford a lawsuit."

"And?" He sounded as cold as ice.

She bit her lower lip. "While I was thinking about alternatives, he laughed and came toward me. I could forget the contract, he said, if I was that prudish. But he'd have a return for the time he'd wasted on me. He said that he was going to make me sleep with him."

"Good God!"

She smoothed his shirt, trying to calm him. Tears stung her eyes. "I fought him, but I wasn't strong enough. He had me undressed before I knew it. We struggled there on the floor and he started hitting me." Her voice broke and she felt Corrigan stiffen against her. "He had a diamond ring on his right hand. That's how he cut my cheek. I didn't even feel it until much later. He wore me down to the point that I couldn't kick or bite or scream. I would never have been able to get away. But one of his girls, one of the ones who didn't mind posing nude, came into the studio. She was his lover and she was furious when she saw him with me…like that. She started screaming and throwing things at him. I grabbed my clothes and ran."

She shivered even then with the remembered humiliation, the fear that he was going to come after her. "I managed to get enough on to look halfway decent, and I walked all the way back to Belinda's apartment." She swallowed. "When I was rational enough to talk, I called the police. They arrested him and charged him with attempted rape. But he said that I'd signed a contract and I wasn't happy with the money he offered me, and that I'd only yelled rape because I wanted to back out of the deal."

He bit off a curse. "And then what?"

"He won," she said in a flat, defeated tone. "He had friends and influence. But the story was a big deal locally for two or three days, and he was furious. His brother had a nasty temper and he started making obscene phone calls to me and making threats, as well. I didn't want to put Belinda in any danger, so I moved out while she was still in Europe and never told her a thing about what had happened. I got a job in New Jersey and worked there for two years. Then Belinda moved out to Long Island and asked me to come back. There was a good job going with a law firm that had an office pretty close to her house. I had good typing skills by then, so I took it."

"What about the brother?" he asked.

"He didn't know where to find me. I learned later that he and the photographer were having trouble with the police about some pornography ring they were involved in. Ironically they both went to prison soon after I left Manhattan. But for a long time, I was even afraid to come home, in case they had anyone watching me. I was afraid for my father."

"You poor kid," he said heavily. "Good God! And after

what had happened here…" His teeth ground together as he remembered what he'd done to her.

"Don't," she said gently, smoothing out the frown between his heavy eyebrows. "I never blamed you. Never!"

He caught her hand and brought it to his mouth. "I wanted to come after you," he said. "Your father stopped me. He said that you hated the very mention of my name."

"I did, at first, but only because I was so hurt by the way things had worked out." She looked at his firm chin. "But I would have been glad to see you, just the same."

"I wasn't sure of that." He traced her mouth. "I thought that it might be as well to leave things the way they were. You were so young, and I was wary of complications in my life just then." He sighed softly. "There's one other thing you don't know about me."

"Can't you tell me?"

He smiled softly. "We're sharing our deepest secrets. I suppose I might as well. We have a fifth brother. His name is Simon."

"You mentioned him the first time you came over, with that bouquet."

He nodded. "He's in San Antonio. Just after you left town, he was in a wreck and afterward, in a coma. We couldn't all go back, and leave the ranch to itself. So I went. It was several weeks before I could leave him. By the time I got back, you weren't living with Belinda anymore and I couldn't make her tell me where you were. Soon after that, your father came down on my head like a brick and I lost heart."

"You called Belinda?"

"Yes."

"You wanted to find me?"

He searched her eyes quietly. "I wanted to know that

you were safe, that I hadn't hurt you too badly. At least I found that much out. I didn't hope for more."

She traced his eyebrows, lost in the sudden intimacy. "I dreamed about you," she said. "But every time, you'd come toward me and I'd wake up."

He traced the artery in her throat down to her collarbone. "My dreams were a bit more erotic." His eyes darkened. "I had you in ways and places you can't imagine, each more heated than the one before. I couldn't wait to go to bed, so that I could have you again."

She blushed. "At first, you mean, just after I left."

His hand smoothed onto her throat. "For eight years. Every night of my life."

She caught her breath. She could hardly get it at all. His eyes were glittering with feeling. "All that time?"

He nodded. He looked at her soft throat where the blouse had parted, and his face hardened. His fingers trailed lightly down onto her bodice, onto her breast. "I haven't touched a woman since you left Jacobsville," he said huskily. "I haven't been a man since then."

Her wide eyes filled with tears. She had a good idea of what it would be like for a man like Corrigan to be incapable with a woman. "Was it because we fought, at the last?"

"It was because we made love," he whispered. "Have you forgotten what we did?"

She averted her eyes, hiding them in embarrassment.

"You left a virgin," he said quietly, "but only technically. We had each other in your bed," he reminded her, "naked in each other's arms. We did everything except go those last few aching inches. Your body was almost open to me, I was against you, we were moving together...and you cried out when you felt me there. You squirmed out from under me and ran."

"I was so afraid," she whispered shamefully. "It hurt, and I kept remembering what I'd been told…"

"It wouldn't have hurt for long," he said gently. "And it wouldn't have been traumatic, not for you. But you didn't know that, and I was too excited to coax you. I lost my temper instead of reassuring you. And we spent so many years apart, suffering for it."

She laid her hot cheek against his chest and closed her eyes. "I didn't want to remember how far we went," she said through a mist. "I hurt you terribly when I drew back…"

"Not that much," he said. "We'd made love in so many ways already that I wasn't that hungry." He smoothed her soft hair. "I wanted an excuse to make you leave."

"Why?"

His lips touched her hair. "Because I wanted to make you pregnant," he whispered, feeling her body jump as he said it. "And it scared me to death. You see, modern women don't want babies, because they're a trap. My mother taught me that."

CHAPTER SIX

"THAT'S NOT TRUE!" She pressed closer. "I would have loved having a baby, and I'd never have felt trapped!" she said, her voice husky with feeling. Especially your baby, she added silently. "I didn't know any of your background, especially anything about your mother. You never told me."

His chest rose and fell abruptly. "I couldn't. You scared me to death. Maybe I deliberately upset you, to make you run. But when I got what I thought I wanted, I didn't want it. It hurt when you wouldn't even look at me, at the bus stop. I guess I'd shamed you so badly that you couldn't." He sighed. "I thought you were modern, that we'd enjoy each other and that would be the end of it. I got the shock of my life that last night. I couldn't even deal with it. I lost my head."

She lifted her face and looked into his eyes. "You were honest about it. You'd already said that you wanted no part of marriage or a family, that all you could offer me was a night in your arms with no strings attached. But I couldn't manage to stop, or stop you, until the very last. I was raised to think of sleeping around as a sin."

His face contorted. He averted his eyes to keep her from seeing the pain in them. "I didn't know that until it was much too late. Sometimes, you don't realize how much things mean to you until you lose them."

His fingers moved gently in her hair while she stood quietly, breathing uneasily. "It wasn't just our mother who soured us on women. Simon was married," he said after a minute. "He was the only one of us who ever was. His wife got pregnant the first time they were together, but she didn't want a child. She didn't really want Simon, she just wanted to be rich. He was crazy about her." He sighed painfully. "She had an abortion and he found out later, accidentally. They had a fight on the way home from one of her incessant parties. He wrecked the car, she died and he lost an arm. That's why he doesn't live on the ranch. He can't do the things he used to do. He's embittered and he's withdrawn from the rest of us." He laughed a little. "You think the four of us hate women. You should see Simon."

She stirred in his arms. "Poor man. He must have loved her very much."

"Too much. That's another common problem we seem to have. We love irrationally and obsessively."

"And reluctantly," she guessed.

He laughed. "And that."

He let her go with a long sigh and stared down at her warmly. "I suppose I'd better take you home. If you're still here when the boys get back, they'll tie you to the stove."

She smiled. "I like your brothers." She hesitated. "Corrigan, they aren't really going to try to force you to marry me, are they?"

"Of course not," he scoffed. "They're only teasing."

"Okay."

It was a good thing, he thought, that she couldn't see his fingers crossed behind his back.

He took her home, pausing to kiss her gently at the front door.

"I'll be along tomorrow night," he said softly. "We'll go to a movie. There's a new one every Saturday night at the Roxy downtown."

She searched his eyes and tried to decide if he was doing this because he wanted to or because his brothers were pestering him.

He smiled. "Don't worry so much. You're home, it's going to be Christmas, you have a job and plenty of friends. It's going to be the best Christmas you've ever had."

She smiled back. "Maybe it will be," she said, catching some of his own excitement. Her gaze caressed his face. They were much more like friends, with all the dark secrets out in the open. But his kisses had made her too hungry for him. She needed time to get her emotions under control. Perhaps a day would do it. He was throwing out broad hints of some sort, but he hadn't spoken one word of love. In that respect, nothing had changed.

"Good night, then," he said.

"Good night."

She closed the door and turned on the lights. It had been a strange and wonderful day. Somehow, the future looked unusually bright, despite all her worries.

THE NEXT MORNING, Dorie had to go into town to Clarisse's shop to help her with the bookkeeping. It was unfortunate that when she walked in, a beautiful woman in designer clothes should be standing at the counter, discussing Corrigan.

"It's going to be the most glorious Christmas ever!" she was telling the other woman, pushing back her red-gold hair and laughing. "Corrigan is taking me to the Christmas party at the Coltrains' house, and afterward we're going to Christmas Eve services at the Methodist Church." She sighed. "I'm glad to be home. You know, there's been some talk about Corrigan and a woman from his past who just came back recently. I asked him about it, if he was serious about her." She laughed gaily. "He said that he was just buttering her up so that she'd do some bookkeeping for him and the brothers, that she'd run out on him once and he didn't have any intention of letting her get close enough to do it again. I told him that I could find it in my heart to feel sorry for her, and he said that he didn't feel sorry for her at all, that he had plans for her..."

Clarisse spotted Dorie and caught her breath. "Why, Dorothy, I wasn't expecting you...quite so soon!"

"I thought I'd say hello," Dorie said, frozen in the doorway. She managed a pasty smile. "I'll come back Monday. Have a nice weekend."

"Who was that?" she heard the other woman say as she went quickly back out the door and down the street to where she'd parked the car Turkey Sanders had returned early in the morning, very nicely fixed.

She got behind the wheel, her fingers turning white as she gripped it. She could barely see for the tears. She started the engine with shaking fingers and backed out into the street. She heard someone call to her and saw the redhead standing on the sidewalk, with an odd expression on her face, trying to get Dorie's attention.

She didn't look again. She put the car into gear and sped out of town.

She didn't go straight home. She went to a small park inside the city and sat down among the gay lights and decorations with a crowd that had gathered for a Christmas concert performed by the local high-school band and chorus. There were so many people that one more didn't matter, and her tears weren't as noticeable in the crush of voices.

The lovely, familiar carols were oddly soothing. But her Christmas spirit was absent. How could she have trusted Corrigan? She was falling in love all over again, and he was setting her up for a fall. She'd never believe a word he said, ever again. And now that she'd had a look at his beautiful divorcée, she knew she wouldn't have a chance with him. That woman was exquisite, from her creamy skin to her perfect figure and face. The only surprising thing was that he hadn't married her years ago. Surely a woman like that wouldn't hang around waiting, when she could have any man she wanted.

Someone offered her a cup of hot apple cider, and she managed a smile and thanked the child who held it out to her. It was spicy and sweet and tasted good against the chill. She sipped it, thinking how horrible it was going to be from now on, living in Jacobsville with Corrigan only a few miles away and that woman hanging on his arm. He hadn't mentioned anything about Christmas to Dorie, but apparently he had his plans all mapped out if he was taking the merry divorcée to a party. When had he been going to tell her the truth? Or had he been going to let her find it out all for herself?

She couldn't remember ever feeling quite so bad. She finished the cider, listened to one more song and then got up and walked through the crowd, down the long sidewalk to where she'd parked her car. She sat in it for a moment, trying to decide what to do. It was Saturday and she had nothing planned for today. She wasn't going to go home. She couldn't bear the thought of going home.

She turned the car and headed up to the interstate, on the road to Victoria.

CORRIGAN PACED UP and down Dorie's front porch for an hour until he realized that she wasn't coming home. He drove back to town and pulled up in front of Tira Beck's brick house.

She came out onto the porch, in jeans and a sweatshirt, her glorious hair around her shoulders. Her arms were folded and she looked concerned. Her frantic phone call had sent him flying over to Dorie's house hours before he was due to pick her up for the movie. Now it looked as if the movie, and anything else, was off.

"Well?" she asked.

He shook his head, with his hands deep in his jacket pockets. "She wasn't there. I waited for an hour. There's no note on the door, no nothing."

Tira sighed miserably. "It's all my fault. Me and my big mouth. I had no idea who she was, and I didn't know that what I was telling Clarisse was just a bunch of bull that you'd handed me to keep me from seeing how much you cared for the woman." She looked up accusingly. "See what happens when you lie to your friends?"

"You didn't have to tell her that!"

"I didn't know she was there! And we had agreed to go to the Coltrains' party together, you and me and Charles Percy."

"You didn't mention that you had a date for it, I guess?" he asked irritably.

"No. I didn't realize anyone except Clarisse was listening, and she already knew I was going with Charles."

He tilted his hat farther over his tired eyes. "God, the webs we weave," he said heavily. "She's gone and I don't know where to look for her. She might have gone back to New York for all I know, especially after yesterday. She had every reason to think I was dead serious about her until this morning."

Tira folded her arms closer against the cold look he shot her. "I said I'm sorry," she muttered. "I tried to stop her and tell her that she'd misunderstood me about the party, that I wasn't your date. But she wouldn't even look at me. I'm not sure she saw me. She was crying."

He groaned aloud.

"Oh, Corrigan, I'm sorry," she said gently. "Simon always says you do everything the hard way. I guess he knows you better than the others."

He glanced at her curiously. "When have you seen Simon?"

"At the cattle convention in San Antonio last week. I sold a lot of my Montana herd there."

"And he actually spoke to you?"

She smiled wistfully. "He always speaks to me," she said. "I don't treat him like an invalid. He feels comfortable with me."

He gave her an intent look. "He wouldn't if he knew how you felt about him."

Her eyes narrowed angrily. "I'm not telling him. And neither are you! If he wants me to be just a friend, I can settle for that. It isn't as if I'm shopping for a new husband. One was enough," she added curtly.

"Simon was always protective about you," he recalled. "Even before you married."

"He pushed me at John," she reminded him.

"Simon was married when he met you."

Her expression closed. She didn't say a word, but it was there, in her face. She'd hated Simon's wife, and the feeling had been mutual. Simon had hated her husband, too. But despite all the turbulence between Tira and Simon, there had never been a hint of infidelity while they were both married. Now, it was as if they couldn't get past their respective bad marriages to really look at each other romantically. Tira loved Simon, although no one except Corrigan knew it. But Simon kept secrets. No one was privy to them anymore, not even his own brothers. He kept to himself in San Antonio. Too much, sometimes.

Tira was watching him brood. "Why don't you file a missing persons report?" she suggested suddenly.

"I have to wait twenty-four hours. She could be in Alaska by then." He muttered under his breath. "I guess I could hire a private detective to look for her."

She gave him a thoughtful look and her eyes twinkled. "I've got a better idea. Why not tell your brothers she's gone missing?"

His eyebrows lifted, and hope returned. "Now that's a constructive suggestion," he agreed, nodding, and he began to grin. "They were already looking forward to homemade biscuits every morning. They'll be horrified!"

AND THEY WERE. It was amazing, the looks that he got from his own kinfolk when he mentioned that their prized biscuit maker had gone missing.

"It's your fault," Rey said angrily. "You should have proposed to her."

"I thought you guys had all that taken care of," Corrigan said reasonably. "The rings, the minister, the gown, the invitations…"

"Everything except the most important part," Cag told him coldly.

"Oh, that. Did we forget to tell her that he loved her?" Leo asked sharply. "Good Lord, we did! No wonder she left!" He glared at his brother. "You could have told her yourself if you hadn't been chewing on your hurt pride. And speaking of pride, why didn't you tell Tira the truth instead of hedging your bets with a bunch of lies?"

"Because Tira has a big mouth and I didn't want the whole town to know I was dying of unrequited love for Dorie!" he raged. "She doesn't want to marry me. She said so! A man has to have a little pride to cling to!"

"Pride and those sort of biscuits don't mix," Rey stressed. "We've got to get her back. Okay, boys, who do we know in the highway patrol? Better yet, don't we know at least one Texas Ranger? Those boys can track anybody! Let's pool resources here…"

Watching them work, Corrigan felt relieved for himself and just a little sorry for Dorie. She wouldn't stand a chance.

She didn't, either. A tall, good-looking man with black hair wearing a white Stetson and a Texas Ranger's star on his uniform knocked at the door of her motel room in Victoria. When she answered it, he tipped his hat politely, smiled and put her in handcuffs.

They were halfway back to Jacobsville, her hastily packed suitcase and her purse beside her, before she got enough breath back to protest.

"But why have you arrested me?" she demanded.

"Why?" He thought for a minute and she saw him scowl in the rearview mirror. "Oh, I remember. Cattle rustling." He nodded. "Yep, that's it. Cattle rustling." He glanced at her in the rearview mirror. "You see, rustling is a crime that cuts across county lines, which gave me the authority to arrest you."

"Whose cattle have I rustled?" she demanded impertinently.

"The Hart Brothers filed the charges."

"Hart... Corrigan Hart?" She made a furious sound under her breath. "No. Not Corrigan. Them. It was them! Them and their damned biscuits! It's a put-up job," she exclaimed. "They've falsely accused me so that they can get me back into their kitchen!"

He chuckled at the way she phrased it. The Hart brothers and their mania for biscuits was known far and wide. "No, ma'am, I can swear to that," he told her. His twinkling black eyes shone out of a lean, darkly tanned face. His hair was black, too, straight and thick under that wide-brimmed white hat. "They showed me where it was."

"It?"

"The bull you rustled. His stall was empty, all right."

Her eyes bulged. "Didn't you look for him on the ranch?"

"Yes, ma'am," he assured her with a wide smile. "I looked. But the stall was empty, and they said he'd be in it if he hadn't been rustled. That was a million-dollar bull, ma'am." He shook his head. "They could shoot you for that. This is Texas, you know. Cattle rustling is a very serious charge."

"How could I rustle a bull? Do you have any idea how much a bull weighs?" She was sounding hysterical. She calmed down. "All right. If I took that bull, where was he?"

"Probably hidden in your room, ma'am. I plan to phone

back when we get to the Hart place and have the manager search it," he assured her. His rakish grin widened. "Of course, if he doesn't find a bull in your room, that will probably mean that I can drop the charges."

"Drop them, the devil!" she flared, blowing a wisp of platinum hair out of her eyes. "I'll sue the whole damned state for false arrest!"

He chuckled at her fury. "Sorry. You can't. I had probable cause."

"What probable cause?"

He glanced at her in the rearview mirror with a rakish grin. "You had a hamburger for lunch, didn't you, ma'am?"

She was openly gasping by now. The man was a lunatic. He must be a friend of the brothers, that was the only possible explanation. She gave up arguing, because she couldn't win. But she was going to do some serious damage to four ugly men when she got back to Jacobsville.

THE RANGER PULLED UP in front of the Harts' ranch house and all four of them came tumbling out of the living room and down to the driveway. Every one of them was smiling except Corrigan.

"Thanks, Colton," Leo said, shaking the ranger's hand. "I don't know what we'd have done without you."

The man called Colton got out and opened the back seat to extricate a fuming, muttering Dorie. She glared at the brothers with eyes that promised retribution as her handcuffs were removed and her suitcase and purse handed to her.

"We found the bull," Cag told the ranger. "He'd strayed just out behind the barn. Sorry to have put you to this trouble. We'll make our own apologies to Miss Wayne, here."

Colton stared at the fuming ex-prisoner with pursed lips. "Good luck," he told them.

Dorie didn't know where to start. She looked up at Colton and wondered how many years she could get for kicking a Texas Ranger's shin.

Reading that intent in her eyes, he chuckled and climbed back into his car. "Tell Simon I said hello," he called to them. "We miss seeing him around the state capital now that he's given up public office."

"I'll tell him," Cag promised.

That barely registered as he drove away with a wave of his hand, leaving Dorie alone with the men.

"Nice to see you again, Miss Wayne," Cag said, tipping his hat. "Excuse me. Cows to feed."

"Fences to mend," Leo added, grinning as he followed Cag's example.

"Right. Me, too." Rey tipped his own hat and lit out after his brothers.

Which left Corrigan to face the music, and it was all furious discord and bass.

She folded her arms over her breasts and glared at him.

"It was their idea," he said pointedly.

"Arrested for rustling. Me! He... That man... That Texas Ranger tried to infer that I had a bull hidden in my motel room, for God's sake! He handcuffed me!" She held up her wrists to show them to him.

"He probably felt safer that way," he remarked, observing her high color and furious face.

"I want to go home! Right now!"

He could see that it would be useless to try to talk to her. He only made one small effort. "Tira's sorry," he said quietly. "She wanted to tell you that she's going to the Coltrains' party with Charles Percy. I was going to drive, that's all. I'd planned to take you with me."

"I heard all about your 'plan.'"

The pain in her eyes was hard to bear. He averted his gaze. "You'd said repeatedly that you wanted no part of me," he said curtly. "I wasn't about to let people think I was dying of love for you."

"Wouldn't that be one for the record books?" she said furiously.

His gaze met hers evenly. "I'll get Joey to drive you home."

He turned and walked away, favoring his leg a little. She watched him with tears in her eyes. It was just too much for one weekend.

JOEY DROVE HER home and she stayed away from the ranch. Corrigan was back to doing the books himself, because she wouldn't. Her pride was raw, and so was his. It looked like a complete stalemate.

"We've got to do something," Cag said on Christmas Eve, as Corrigan sat in the study all by himself in the dark. "It's killing him. He won't even talk about going to the Coltrains' party."

"I'm not missing it," Leo said. "They've got five sets of Lionel electric trains up and running on one of the most impressive layouts in Texas."

"Your brother is more important than trains," Rey said grimly. "What are we going to do?"

Cag's dark eyes began to twinkle. "I think we should bring him a Christmas present."

"What sort of present?" Rey asked.

"A biscuit maker," Cag said.

Leo chuckled. "I'll get a bow."

"I'll get out the truck," Rey said, shooting out the front door.

"Shhh!" Cag called to them. "It wouldn't do to let him know what we're up to. We've already made one monumental mistake."

They nodded and moved more stealthily.

CORRIGAN WAS NURSING a glass of whiskey. He heard the truck leave and come back about an hour later, but he wasn't really interested in what his brothers were doing. They'd probably gone to the Christmas party over at Coltrain's ranch.

He was still sitting in the dark when he heard curious muffled sounds and a door closing.

He got up and went out into the hall. His brothers looked flushed and flustered and a little mussed. They looked at him, wide-eyed. Leo was breathing hard, leaning against the living-room door.

"What are you three up to now?" he demanded.

"We put your Christmas present in there," Leo said, indicating the living room. "We're going to let you open it early."

"It's something nice," Cag told him.

"And very useful," Leo agreed.

Rey heard muffled noises getting louder. "Better let him get in there. I don't want to have to run it down again."

"Run it down?" Corrigan cocked his head. "What the hell have you got in there? Not another rattler...!"

"Oh, it's not that dangerous," Cag assured him. He frowned. "Well, not quite that dangerous." He moved forward, extricated Leo from the door and opened it, pushing Corrigan inside. "Merry Christmas," he added, and locked the door.

Corrigan noticed two things at once—that the door was locked, and that a gunnysack tied with a ribbon was sitting in a chair struggling like crazy.

Outside the door, there were muffled voices.

"Oh, God," he said apprehensively.

He untied the red ribbon that had the top securely tied, and out popped a raging mad Dorothy Wayne.

"I'll kill them!" she yelled.

Big booted feet ran for safety out in the hall.

Corrigan started laughing and couldn't stop. Honest to God, his well-meaning brothers were going to be the death of him.

"I hate them, I hate this ranch, I hate Jacobsville, I hate you…mmmfff!"

He stopped the furious tirade with his mouth. Amazing how quickly she calmed down when his arms went around her and he eased her gently out of the chair and down onto the long leather couch.

She couldn't get enough breath to continue. His mouth was open and hungry on her lips and his body was as hard as hers was soft as it moved restlessly against her.

She felt his hands on her hips and, an instant later, he was lying between her thighs, moving in a tender, achingly soft rhythm that made her moan.

"I love you," he whispered before she could get a word out.

And then she didn't want to get a word out.

His hands were inside her blouse and he was fighting his way under her skirt when they dimly heard a key turn in the lock.

The door opened and three pairs of shocked, delighted eyes peered in.

"You monsters!" she said with the last breath she had. She was in such a state of disarray that she couldn't manage anything else. Their position was so blatant that there was little use in pretending that they were just talking.

"That's no way to talk to your brothers-in-law," Leo stated. "The wedding's next Saturday, by the way." He smiled apologetically. "We couldn't get the San Antonio symphony orchestra to come, because they have engagements, but we did get the governor to give you away. He'll be along just before the ceremony." He waved a hand at them and grinned. "Carry on, don't mind us."

Corrigan fumbled for a cushion and flung it with all his might at the door. It closed. Outside, deep chuckles could be heard.

Dorie looked up into Corrigan's steely-gray eyes with wonder. "Did he say the governor's going to give me away? Our governor? The governor of Texas?"

"The very one."

"But, how?"

"The governor's a friend of ours. Simon worked with him until the wreck, when he retired from public office. Don't you ever read a newspaper?"

"I guess not."

"Never mind. Just forget about all the details." He bent to her mouth. "Now, where were we…?"

THE WEDDING WAS the social event of the year. The governor did give her away; along with all four brothers, including the tall, darkly distinguished Simon, who wore an artificial arm just for the occasion. Dorie was exquisite in a Paris gown designed especially for her by a well-known couturier. Newspapers sent representatives. The whole world seemed to form outside the little Presbyterian church in Victoria.

"I can't believe this," she whispered to Corrigan as they were leaving on their Jamaica honeymoon. "Corrigan, that's the vice president over there, standing beside the governor and Simon!"

"Well, they sort of want Simon for a cabinet position. He doesn't want to leave Texas. They're coaxing him."

She just shook her head. The Hart family was just too much altogether!

That night, lying in her new husband's arms with the sound of the ocean right outside the window, she gazed up at him with wonder as he made the softest, sweetest love to her in the dimly lit room.

His body rose and fell like the tide, and he smiled at her, watching her excited eyes with sparks in his own as her body hesitated only briefly and then accepted him completely on a gasp of shocked pleasure.

"And you were afraid that it was going to hurt," he chided as he moved tenderly against her.

"Yes." She was gasping for air, clinging, lifting to him in shivering arcs of involuntary rigor. "It's…killing me…!"

"Already?" he chided, bending to brush his lips over her swollen mouth. "Darlin', we've barely started!"

"Barely…? Oh!"

He was laughing. She could hear him as she washed up and down on waves of ecstasy that brought unbelievable noises out of her. She died half a dozen times, almost lost consciousness, and still he laughed, deep in his throat, as he went from one side of the bed to the other with her in a tangle of glorious abandon that never seemed to end. Eventually they ended up on the carpet with the sheet trailing behind them as she cried out, sobbing, one last time and heard him groan as he finally shuddered to completion.

They were both covered with sweat. Her hair was wet. She was trembling and couldn't stop. Beside her, he lay on his back with one leg bent at the knee. Incredibly, he was still as aroused as he'd been when they started. She sat up gingerly and stared at him, awed.

He chuckled up at her. "Come down here," he dared her.

"I can't!" She was gasping. "And you can't... You couldn't...!"

"If you weren't the walking wounded, I sure as hell could," he said. "I've saved it all up for eight years, and I'm still starving for you."

She just looked at him, fascinated. "I read a book."

"I'm not in it," he assured her. He tugged her down on top of him and brushed her breasts with his lips. "I guess you're sore."

She blushed. "You guess?"

He chuckled. "All right. Come here, my new best friend, and we'll go to sleep, since we can't do anything else."

"We're on the floor," she noted.

"At least we won't fall off next time."

She laughed because he was outrageous. She'd never thought that intimacy would be fun as well as pleasurable. She traced his nose and bent to kiss his lips. "Where are we going to live?"

"At the ranch."

"Only if your brothers live in the barn," she said. "I'm not having them outside the door every night listening to us."

"They won't have to stand outside the door. Judging from what I just heard, they could hear you with the windows closed if they stood on the town squa… Ouch!"

"Let that be a lesson to you," she told him drily, watching him rub the nip she'd given his thigh. "Naked men are vulnerable."

"And you aren't?"

"Now, Corrigan…!"

She screeched and he laughed and they fell down again in a tangle, close together, and the laughter gave way to soft conversation. Eventually they even slept.

When they got back to the ranch, the three brothers were gone and there was a hastily scrawled note on the door.

"We're sleeping in the bunkhouse until we can build you a house of your own. Congratulations. Champagne is in the fridge." It was signed with love, all three brothers— and the name of the fourth was penciled in.

"On second thought," she said, with her arm around her husband, "maybe those boys aren't so bad after all!"

He tried to stop her from opening the door, but it was too late. The bucket of water left her wavy hair straight and her navy blue coat dripping. She looked at Corrigan with eyes the size of plates, her arms outstretched, her mouth open.

Corrigan looked around her. On the floor of the hall were two towels and two new bathrobes, and an assortment of unmentionable items.

He knew that if he laughed, he'd be sleeping in the barn for the next month. But he couldn't help it. And after a glance at the floor—neither could she.

* * * * *

An unlikely attraction brings comfort, joy and unforgettable romance this holiday season in this sparkling tale by *New York Times* bestselling author

RaeAnne Thayne

Librarian Julia Winston is ready to ditch the quiet existence she's been living. She's made a list of new things to experience, but falling for Jamie Caine, her sexy military pilot neighbor, isn't one of them. Julia's looking to conquer life, not become the heartbreaker's latest conquest. But when two young brothers wind up in Julia's care for the holidays, she'll take any help she can get—even Jamie's.

Happy to step in, Jamie reveals a side of himself that's much harder to resist. Not only is he fantastic with kids, he provides the strength Julia needs to tackle her list. She knows their temporary family can't last beyond the holidays, but the closer she gets to Jamie, the more she wonders if things could be this merry and bright forever...

Available September 26

Order your copy today!

HQN™

Get 2 Free Books,
Plus 2 Free Gifts -
just for trying the Reader Service!

STRS17R2

Get 2 Free Books,
Plus 2 Free Gifts—
just for trying the Reader Service!

HARLEQUIN Romance

HRLP17R2